of

Anarwyn

——+·+——

Book 2

UNDEAD

J.W. ELLIOT

Bent Bow
Publishing, LLC

Copyright © 2022
J.W. Elliot

Bent Bow Publishing, LLC
82 Wendell Ave., STE 100
Pittsfield, MA 01201
USA

ISBN 978-1-953010-19-3

Cover Art by T Studio and Lukiyanova Natalia Frenta

Cover Design by Brandi Doane McCann

If you enjoy this book, please consider leaving an honest review on Amazon and sharing on your social media sites.

Please sign up for my newsletter where you can get a free short story and more free content at: www.jwelliot.com

For my son, Mark, who grew up with the tales of the marks.

Book Two

UNDEAD

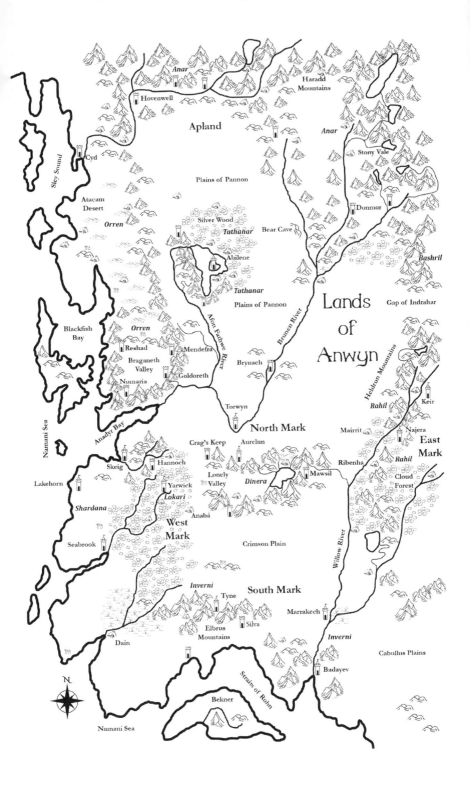

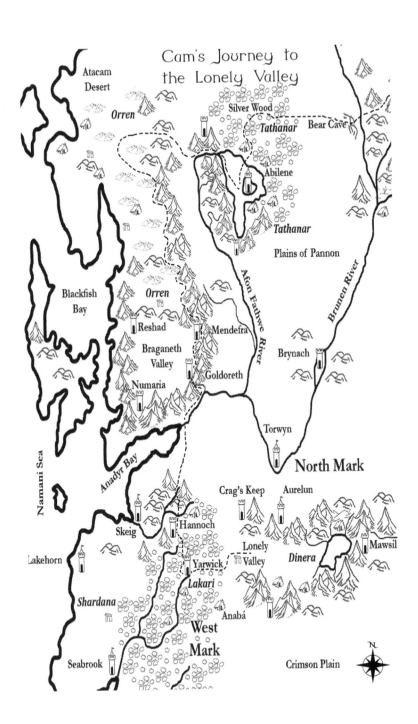

Cam's Journey to the Lonely Valley

Prologue
Flesb and Stone

LORNA RACED AGAINST DEATH, knowing she would probably lose. She leaned over the mare's neck and hissed in her ear. The wind whipped at her hair and the prairie grasses stung her legs as the horse's hooves pounded the earth. The sick knot in her stomach tightened. Bardon had not been satisfied with murdering their father and riding through the gates of Torwyn with his head on a pike. Now, he was after their brother, Maelorn. She *had* to stop him.

The sun sank into the western horizon as the aroma of parched grass mingled with the sharp tang of earth and horse musk. Sweat matted her hair and slid down her neck. The rolling prairie stretched on forever. Its vast emptiness filled her with a peculiar dread. What if she didn't reach them in time? What if she found them both dead? No, that couldn't happen. She wouldn't let it. Kicking her horse to greater speed, she gave her more rein.

Her whole life converged on this one moment—this last desperate ride to save what was left of her family. The horse broke the crest of the hill and sped up as she dropped over the rise. Maelorn and Tara strode toward each other under the shadow of the lone tree with their servants and guards waiting at a respectful distance, holding the reins of their horses.

Lorna stood in the stirrups. "No!" she shouted, but the wind swallowed her cry. Her horse's hooves thundered on the earth.

Undead

"Wait!" she called again. "Don't! Please!" her voice broke as Maelorn and Tara embraced.

A wave of energy burst over the prairie, flattening the grasses. Their attendants tumbled to the earth, and their horses shied and galloped away. A translucent black bubble enveloped Maelorn and Tara, pulsing with the strange, perverted energy of the Bragamahr. A sob tore from Lorna's throat. What had Bardon done? Had he betrayed everything he once loved?

She had to do something—anything. Mentally forging a dyad with the sapphire and the malachite in the pendant she wore around her neck, she raised her hand. The crystal green column of energy leaped across the hundred paces between her and the expanding black sphere. A crack louder than any known thunder snapped through the air. A flood of energy rippled through the earth, followed by a blast of hot wind, tearing branches and leaves from the lone tree and kicking up dust and debris into a boiling cloud. Lorna clung to her horse as the wind rushed back, and the earth buckled beneath the mare's feet.

The horse stumbled. Lorna reeled in the saddle as her horse tripped, throwing her onto the broken ground. She lay there trembling, too weak and scared to move until the wind subsided and the dust settled. An eerie, otherworldly silence settled over the little valley. No birds sang. No crickets chirped. Nothing. She lifted her head with enormous effort, terrified she might find Maelorn and Tara's bodies broken and bleeding on the dry prairie. What she saw sent a pang of horror burning through her chest.

"No," Lorna choked. Tears sprang to her eyes as she struggled to her knees. A perfect circle of bare earth had been scoured of every living thing within twenty paces of the tree. In the center now loomed a marble statue of the loveliest clear crystal and black obsidian. Maelorn and Tara had enfolded each other in an eternal embrace of solid stone—expressions of pain frozen onto their faces.

Lorna rose and staggered to them, ignoring the cries of the servants and guards. What had she done? She hadn't saved them. Laying a hand on the stone, she reached out with the power of the Anarwyn. An angry surge of energy shoved her back, and she understood. In that fleeting moment of contact, she sensed that Maelorn and Tara were alive, trapped within the stone.

Flesh and Stone

A sob escaped her. In desperation, she drew on the healing power of the agate and sent its energy into the stone. It was thrown back in her face. Growing despondent, she tried every dyad ever used by the Varaná—and even some deemed so dangerous she could barely control them.

Nothing worked.

The cold, silent stone repelled every attempt to undo what she had done. Exhausted and heartbroken, Lorna fell at her brother's feet and wept. In her attempt to save them from being killed by Bardon, she had done something infinitely worse. She had sealed them eternally in tombs of solid stone.

Chapter One
The Sting of Death

CAM LEARNED TO EMBRACE the pain by the time his Inverni captors drew rein on the edge of a muddy wallow somewhere on the Plains of Pannon. That he could feel pain meant he was still alive—for now. Why his captors hadn't killed him outright he did not know. It could only mean they planned some fate for him that was worse than death.

A few deer and wild cattle scattered as they approached, only to pause and look back curiously. Cam, Rebecca, and the three Inverni who captured them at the great bend of the Afon Fathwe River had been riding west across the Plains of Pannon since early morning. The sun hovered directly overhead. Sweat trickled into Cam's eyes, making him blink at the sting.

The three Inverni, with their mottled cloaks and strange, loose-fitting trousers, swung down from their saddles and led their horses to the water. They untied Cam and Rebecca and dragged them from their horses' backs, letting them fall to the trampled, muddy earth.

Cam winced at the jarring thump that made his ribs ache again. His hands were still tied behind his back, and the ropes gnawed painfully at his flesh. Warm blood slipped over his fingers. His tongue was tacky, and he harbored a savage thirst. The tall, sharp prairie grass scraped against his bare feet, leaving them raw and bleeding.

The Sting of Death

The musky stink of cattle and deer mingled with the aroma of wet earth and crushed grass. He struggled to adjust his position so he could see if Rebecca was all right.

The muscles in his legs complained, but he forced himself to stretch them. He hadn't ridden a horse in a long while, and the past weeks of running and canoeing hadn't prepared his backside for the saddle or the bruising trot they had maintained all morning. With his feet tied underneath the horse's belly, he couldn't use the stirrups to post and rise with the trot. Instead, he sat heavy in the saddle and endured the teeth-rattling pounding as the miles had disappeared behind them.

Rebecca rolled onto her side to peer at him. She looked terrible. Her face was bright red from the sun and heat, and her ankles where the ropes secured her to the horse were caked with dried blood and dirt. Her blonde hair clung to her sweating face and neck. Despite all that, she gave him a brave smile.

He nodded encouragement to her and struggled to sit up. The baby-faced Inverni, who was the apparent leader, knelt beside him and pressed a wooden cup filled with muddy water from the wallow to his lips. Cam jerked his head away, and the Inverni grabbed his hair, yanking his head around.

"This is the only water you're gonna get, boy," he said.

"Give it to Rebecca first," Cam stammered.

Baby Face jammed the cup to Cam's lips. "Drink it now or you'll get nothing."

When the water spilled into Cam's mouth, the burning thirst overpowered his will to resist, and he drank. The water was gritty and tasted of mud. It would probably make him sick. Still, his thirst was so terrible he downed two cups of the stuff before the Inverni jerked the cup away and stalked to Rebecca. The water gurgled through Cam's stomach, and he waited for the rush of nausea. It didn't come.

"Took 'im long enough," one of the other Inverni said, motioning with his head to someone behind Cam.

Cam wriggled around to follow the direction of their gaze. A slender man, wearing almost nothing, strode toward them.

The other two Inverni shuffled about in agitation. They were twins, sharing the same round face, needle-sharp nose, and black, scraggly beards. One of them sported a long scar across his forehead, and the other had different colored eyes—one blue and one brown. The way the wild-eyed Inverni examined them made Cam's skin crawl. There was something crafty about the set of his jaw and the intensity of his gaze as his eyes roamed over Rebecca's body.

The scar-faced twin turned from peering to the west with one hand on the long knife he wore in his belt. "I don't like this."

Baby Face grunted and climbed the little incline to stand beside him. "You don't have to like it."

A tall, slender man wearing nothing but a leather loincloth and close-fitting leather shoes stopped before Baby Face and extended his hand. Baby Face shook it and gestured for him to join them at the wallow.

The newcomer's jet-black hair was greased so that it shone in the sunlight. He wore it in one thick braid down his back. His eyes were dark, and his bare skin was tanned a deep russet brown. Squatting at the edge of the wallow, the man studied them without saying a word. Cam eyed him curiously. He had never seen or heard of anyone like him.

A blue tattoo resembling a bird colored the man's cheek. His face was angular, and he possessed a quiet dignity about him that Cam found immediately appealing.

"Let's kill 'em and be done with it," the wild-eyed twin said, ignoring the stranger.

"Our orders are to carry them to the ship," Baby Face said.

Wild Eyes snorted in annoyance. "Across a burning desert where the only water is found in rancid little holes—when there's any water at all." He gestured to the stranger. "And all he can give us is this ignorant savage as a guide. It's a death sentence, not an order. I say we finish 'em and go back south where the action is."

Scar Face rubbed his hands together. "We never agreed to tend a couple of children."

Baby Face sneered at them. "Afraid of a little desert? I thought you were men."

Wild Eyes balled his fists and stepped toward Baby Face. Cam tensed. Maybe they'd kill each other and be done with it. Then he could convince the man in the loincloth to untie them and set them free.

Wild Eyes lunged at Baby Face, swinging a big fist. Baby Face ducked the blow and punched his fist into his attacker's groin. He reached behind to cup his hand on Wild Eyes's heel, braced the man's knee with the other, and swept the foot out so Wild Eyes crashed to the ground. His head cracked against a rock.

Baby Face glanced at Scar Face who had drawn his knife. "Don't try it. You two agreed to carry them to the ship. Once you've done that, you can do what you want."

"Bardon wants 'im dead anyway," Scar Face said. "Why not do it now?"

"Because Jathneel wants them alive, and he's the one who's paying us. Bardon demands much and gives little in return."

Wild Eyes crawled to his feet and spat. "So long as we get half."

"That's what we agreed," Baby Face said.

They staggered away and fed their horses a bit of grain in their muzzle bags. The set of their shoulders and their mumbling curses proved they had only been temporarily subdued. The fight had not gone out of them.

While they worked, Baby Face sidled over and squatted in front of Cam. He held up the opal Life Stone that Hebron had given Cam when he presented him with the sword of King Hewel of the West Mark all those weeks ago. The opal was simply beautiful with a gentle, iridescent blue and swirling clouds of white.

"That's mine," Cam said and struggled to loosen his bands. The stone was connected to the sword and belonged to the legitimate kings of the West Mark. Lorna explained that one of her ancestors had infused it with the right to rule the West Mark and only someone who possessed it freely could use it. The stone had already accepted him and even helped him. The sight of it in the hands of this scoundrel sent Cam's blood racing. "Get your filthy hands off that."

Baby Face smiled maliciously and flipped the opal around in his fingers.

"Is this what you used to create that fire, boy?" Baby Face spoke low so the others wouldn't hear. "You teach me how to use it, and I can make sure you escape before we reach the ship."

"It belongs to me," Cam insisted. He wasn't about to explain to this Inverni how the stone worked. The more this man knew, the more dangerous their situation.

Baby Face raised his eyebrows and cocked his head in contemplation. "Why are Jathneel and Bardon fighting over you, I wonder? Eh?"

Undead

Cam pinched his lips tight, and the Inverni clicked his tongue in annoyance. He held up the dyad Lorna had given Cam back in Abilene.

"Or maybe it was this," Baby Face said. "I've heard of these stones."

The dyad was made from an orange-brown agate and a green malachite connected by a little band of silver. It was a pretty trinket, though its purpose was far more important—to free Maelorn and Tara from their stone prison in the Lonely Valley. Lorna insisted Cam was the only one who could do it, but that wouldn't matter if he couldn't retrieve it, or worse, ended up dead.

When Cam refused to speak, Baby Face grunted.

"Have it your way. You should know, however, that once we reach the ship, Jathneel will kill you anyway. Maybe he'll let my two friends here have your girl. They would enjoy that. She might too." He barked a nasty laugh.

The muscles in Cam's jaw tightened as he ground his teeth, struggling not to let his emotions show.

"Think about it," Baby Face said. "You've only got a few days, and you're not likely to find any friends out here."

Baby Face sneered as he slipped the Life Stone and the dyad into his pocket and strode away to tend to his horse.

Cam glanced at the stranger crouching silently beside the wallow. The man carried a short bow and half a dozen arrows in his hand. He also wore a long knife at his hip. A gourd and a satchel dangled over one of his shoulders. The man studied Cam and Rebecca. The slight downturn of his brow indicated he didn't like what he saw.

He rose. "We should go," he said with a thick accent. "The sun goes down while we sit."

The twins scowled in his direction, but Baby Face gestured for them to mount. They secured Cam and Rebecca to their saddles again by tying the rope to one ankle, stringing it through the stirrups and underneath the horse's belly, before securing it to the other ankle. The rope burned in the already inflamed sores. Rebecca sucked in her breath as they cinched the rope tight. Cam glanced at her, wishing he could get her out of the clutches of these fools.

In minutes, they were trotting out of the depression with the nearly naked guide jogging along in front. Cam's backside smarted as the pounding trot commenced again, and he thought how ironic it was that he had complained when Alaric ran him all night. He'd wanted a horse then. Now, he wished he could be on foot wearing a pair of soft leather shoes, like their guide. His and Rebecca's boots had been tucked into the men's saddlebags. What he wouldn't give to be free of the burning ropes and able to ride like a man, rather than strapped down like a sack of grain.

The prairie grass thinned and became shorter as the miles slipped behind them. Strange plants with long, meaty leaves erupted from the soil. Tall rods budding with yellow flowers shot up from the leafy clusters. Here and there, prickly pears clung tenaciously to the sparse soil amidst the rocks. These were much larger than the ones that bore white flowers he had known in the mountains. Occasionally, a band of antelope or deer bolted away with their tails raised high. Distant hills on the western horizon possessed a strange, red hue. It was a wild, lonely country. There was no sign of human habitation or any evidence that people had ever wandered this land.

They paused occasionally at little watering holes, where they refreshed the horses, and Baby Face gave them more dirty water to drink. The nasty stuff made Cam's bowels churn and cramp. He was afraid he might soil his trousers.

The stranger in the loincloth led them on hour after hour, deeper and deeper into an increasingly forbidding landscape. Prairie grasses gave way to an immense variety of cacti and prickly bushes. Soft prairie earth transitioned to hard-packed clay and stone and then to sparkling sand. They wound their way among the bushes and cacti that clawed and snatched at them like bad-tempered cats. At long last, the sun drooped behind the red hills in the distance, and their guide led them through a gap in the rock he called Arakaná, which he translated as the Pass of Judgment.

A deep sadness seeped into Cam as they penetrated this desolate, hostile landscape along with a sense of loss he didn't understand. It was as if the land itself were in mourning or preparing for some great cataclysm. He craned his head around to see if Rebecca had noticed it. She made no sign that she did. She rode with her head held high, far more suited to the saddle than he was. He supposed as a lady of the king's court, she had been given the best training available, while he learned through hard experience and rarely enjoyed the chance to ride far.

Undead

He closed his eyes against the glare of the sun and tried to let his mind extend into the landscape the way it did when he used the Life Stone. The jarring pain of every step of his horse made it difficult, but he persisted until the throbbing soreness receded to a dull ache. He reached out to that sense of sadness.

It lived in the rocks themselves, infused the plants and animals, coiled around every grain of sand. This land was ancient, scoured by millions of years of wind and water. It belonged to neither the Anarwyn nor the Bragamahr, and it wanted neither.

Far off in the distance, something familiar stirred. The Bragamahr sent tendrils of thought in his direction, enticing him with the promise of power. Trussed up and aching like he was, the temptation to yield proved beguiling. If he accepted the Bragamahr, he could save Rebecca from whatever terrible fate awaited them.

The Anarwyn was of no use to him now. He had lost the stones and was separated from all his friends except Rebecca. The black sand in the scars on his knuckles and at his temple itched. He had already accepted the Anarwyn to save his friends. Would it be so bad to accept the Bragamahr to save Rebecca?

Even as the desire boiled up and he considered the prospect, the earth trembled, and his horse staggered. Cam snapped out of the trance-like state.

"Run!" the twins shouted.

Cam looked up. Stones tumbled down from the rocks above in a roar and a cloud of dust. The horses bolted and fled as stones rumbled into the narrow pass, bouncing among them. A stone struck a glancing blow off the side of Cam's head. If he hadn't been tied to the horse, it would have torn him from the saddle.

The twins whipped their horses as if the rockslide had been their fault. Cam knew better. The land did not want them here. They brought with them the potential of the Bragamahr. This land would not accept them, and in his desperation to save Rebecca, Cam had endangered them all. The guide had been right. This was the Pass of Judgment, and it had rejected them.

The horses clattered over the broken stone into a dry wash beyond the pass.

"What just happened?" Baby Face demanded of their guide. "Did you plan that?"

The Sting of Death

The guide scowled. "The land of the Orren knows who is friend and who is foe."

Cam had guessed right. There was something in this land that was older than either the Anarwyn or the Bragamahr. He checked to make sure Rebecca was uninjured. She was white-faced and tight-lipped but seemed to be unhurt. Her horse bled from a wound on its shoulder, and it was trembling. Blood dribbled down Cam's cheek. He ignored it.

After casting a knowing glance at Cam, the guide started out again, following the wash for another mile until he called them to a halt. Baby Face untied Cam and Rebecca's hands one at a time so they could eat a sparse meal of jerked meat and some rock-like cake that tasted like wheat and rye with a bit of honey and herbs. The taste was pleasing, but Cam's throat was so dry he could barely swallow.

Baby Face only allowed each of them three sips of water before he tore the waterskin away and replaced the stopper. When they finished, he retied their hands and feet, made them lie down beside each other, and threw a single blanket over them before retreating to the fire and rolling into his own blanket.

Cam wriggled around until he was facing Rebecca. They had been kept apart all day. Now, he lay beside her, touching her, feeling her body against his. A shiver swept through him, and he shook himself. This was not the time for such thoughts.

Rebecca watched him with her gentle, gray eyes. Bits of twigs and clumps of sand matted her blonde hair. Her face was scratched and streaked with dirt and small trails of blood. And yet, she was so beautiful.

"You all right?" Cam whispered.

"A little sore," she said. "But I'll manage. How about you?"

Cam was far more than a little sore, but he wasn't going to admit that to Rebecca. "Same. I'm gonna get us out of this."

Rebecca smiled. "You have a plan?"

Cam glanced around. Tied up like he was and lost in a vast de-vouring desert, there weren't many options. "Not yet," he admitted.

"We'll think of something," Rebecca said.

"How did they capture you?"

Her eyes narrowed, and she frowned. "I strolled upstream for a bit of privacy, and Briallen followed me."

Cam stiffened and regretted it immediately. Everything hurt from his head down to the soles of his feet.

"He tried to convince me to run off with him," she said.

Cam scowled. "Where to?"

"To Badayev."

The implications stunned Cam. "You mean he wanted you to marry him?"

Rebecca gave a little non-committal bob of her head. "I suppose." She briefly described her encounter with Briallen, how he understood that she was restless and hankering for adventure anywhere but in Abilene, how he promised to make her wealthy and powerful.

Cam found himself temporarily choked with an irrational, jealous rage that made speaking impossible. When he mastered himself, he said, "That underhanded, son of a—"

"That's not the worst of it," Rebecca interrupted.

Cam steeled himself. He didn't want to think about what could be worse than losing Rebecca to a man like Briallen.

"While we were talking, I saw Zenek in the bushes speaking to an Inverni on a horse."

"What?" Zenek had been Cam's paddling companion from Abilene and all the way down the Afon Fathwe River.

"Somehow," Rebecca continued, "he told Bardon's riders where to find us. That's how they knew to wait for us at the great bend in the river."

"No." Cam didn't want to believe it. He remembered how the Mahrowaith attacked him at the Afon Darodel, and he suspected that Zenek had been using the paddle to hold him under the water. He had convinced himself he imagined it. Now, it all made sense.

"By the breath of the Bragamahr," Cam cursed. "I can't believe it." He recalled Ewan's words before the last rapids. "Ewan guessed there was a traitor among us. He said something was wrong."

"What about the rest of the men?" Rebecca's voice was unusually thick, and Cam realized she was on the verge of tears. "Drakeman?"

"He was alive when I was captured," Cam said. "They were retreating into the river in the canoes."

"Then how did they capture *you*?"

"Draig." Cam struggled to keep the knot from forming in his

throat. "Draig saved my life from the Mahrowaith, and the Inverni shot him down."

"I'm sorry," Rebecca whispered and gave a little sniffle. "He saved my life, too." She shivered and pressed her body closer to Cam. "It's cold."

The temperature dropped surprisingly fast for a place that had scorched them all day. Cam shifted, trying to find a comfortable position. With his hands and feet tied, he couldn't do much. He didn't want to tell Rebecca how much he had longed to be this close to her, though he'd imagined it under different circumstances.

"So, we could be all that is left of the company?" Rebecca asked.

Cam hadn't let himself think this. But now that she said it, he had to admit that it was possible. If the riders had cut them off from the canoes or chased them downriver, they might have killed everyone. After all their effort, how could things have gone so wrong?

He opened his mouth to reply when Scar Face plodded up to take the first watch on a big boulder not ten paces from them. He grunted as he found his seat and stretched his legs.

"One peep out of either of you and I'll slit your throats," he snarled.

"Where are you taking us?" Cam demanded.

Scar Face sneered and drew his knife. "You don't listen, do you, boy?"

"Not to cowards who run from battle and kidnap innocent people."

Scar Face rose to his feet. "I'll slit her throat first then, shall I?"

"All right, all right," Cam said, afraid his bravado was placing Rebecca in danger. "I'll be quiet." The thought of anything like that happening to Rebecca sent cold dread coursing through him.

"Yes, you will." Scar face sank back down and leaned against the rock with a sigh.

Cam watched Rebecca until she closed her eyes. The weariness of the journey swept over him, and he allowed himself to drift off into a fitful sleep filled with wild dreams and the faces of his friends swimming in a river of blood. His nightmare lingered and shifted to no apparent purpose until he jerked violently awake as a strong hand smelling of woodsmoke and deer fat clamped over his mouth. His eyes popped open and he struggled, desperate to get free. Rebecca started awake beside him. At any moment, Cam expected to see the flash of a knife and feel the bite of its blade.

"Say that again," Bardon growled.

He glowered at the messenger dripping rainwater over his expensive blue woolen carpet of the finest Anar weave. The man's mottled cloak was ragged and charred at the edges. Even his beard, of which the Inverni were so proud, was singed. He stank like an old funeral pyre. A ray of afternoon sunlight cut through the gap in the tent flap to slice a golden blade across the carpet. The messenger rotated his steel skull cap round and round in his hands and kept his gaze on the carpet.

Bardon traced a finger along the black scar on the back of his hand to calm himself. The raised scar had a rough texture from the fine grains of obsidian glass he had rubbed into it. The pattern was a six-sided hexagon—the shape of a quartz crystal. Candles in the lanterns set on poles wavered as a gust of wind shook the felt tent. Yellow light flickered on the man's face, showing the streaks of red in his beard.

"Speak!" Bardon shouted.

The messenger jumped and snapped his head up, his eyes wild with fright. "The fortress at Brynach is gone, My Lord."

"You mean destroyed," Bardon corrected.

"No, My Lord." The man swallowed. "We were repulsed, and our boats destroyed."

"Repulsed by whom?" Bardon snapped.

This was impossible. No one lived at Brynach. The nearest army was more than a week away in Abilene, and they were in no condition to mount a major expedition to save an old castle. Lorna had set magical barriers to prevent *him* from entering, though that shouldn't have affected his men. Taking an unoccupied castle with several thousand men ought to have been a simple matter. If they couldn't open the gates or scale the walls, the trebuchets should have beaten the walls down.

"The Tathanar, My Lord," the man said. "They murdered the men we sent in to open the gate and set fire to the city surrounding the castle. Then they poured fire on the water. We withdrew to let the city burn. Then there was a horrible explosion of red light and a rushing wind that flattened our camp. When we recovered, the castle was…" he paused, fiddling with his cap, "…gone."

Bardon clenched his jaw and willed himself to remain calm. Surely the man was mistaken, confused. He was nothing but a common peasant, after all. His last report of Lorna was that she was traveling with some new whelp she hoped could free their imbecilic brother, who should have been dead already. No one else could have done this. He had made sure of it.

Decades of careful searching and targeted assassinations had rid the land of any true heirs of the Anarwyn. The reawakening of the Mahrowaiths had simplified the task considerably. They could sniff out those who possessed even a small sensitivity to the Anarwyn. It was an easy matter to send bands of Inverni to follow them and ensure the task was completed.

He had tried twice before to enter Brynach on his own, but his sister's spells had outwitted him. Only in recent years did he realize how important that quartz crystal would be and that he must have it. Now that he'd rebuilt his army, he'd sent an entire brigade to seize what he could not. And this sniveling messenger brought word of their failure. Fury burned through Bardon's chest.

"You saw this with your own eyes?" he asked, struggling to keep his voice even.

"Yes, My Lord."

Bardon toyed with the delicate pink gem on one of his rings. It was the Carreg Agorial, or the Opening Stone. The Tathanar called it morganite and had no idea what it could do. Bardon wore twelve rings—one for each of his fingers with two on each middle finger. Each ring was set with a gemstone that harnessed the power of the Bragamahr. He kept them in close contact with his person, which was required for any use of the magic.

Bardon breathed deeply to focus his mind. "Look at me," he snarled.

The messenger raised his terrified gaze to meet Bardon's, and Bardon used the Opening Stone to enter the man's mind—to expand it to the presence of the Bragamahr and so perceive what the man had seen. The man screamed in agony and crumpled to the ground, his skull cap thumping hollowly against the carpet. Bardon tensed against the shock of contact. He had tried to make the process less painful for himself but in this, too, he failed. The messenger writhed in anguish. Bardon persisted until the shadowy images formed in his own mind's eye, and he stepped into them as if through a fog.

Confused scenes of a great red pyramid of light burst over the towers of Brynach. The pulsing light infused the walls, coursed through the edifice, and exploded in a burst of power. There was a moment of darkness where the man was picking himself up off the ground before casting his gaze back to the island where Brynach had sprawled only moments before. The high rocky bluffs of the island were empty of all signs of human presence. The ancient keep of the Varaná had vanished.

Bardon cursed. "By the fires of the Bragamahr, I will destroy her."

Somehow, his sister had deprived him of the storehouse of gems kept at Brynach—in particular, the giant quartz crystal he so desperately needed. Perhaps what this man saw was only an illusion. He would have to go there himself to be sure. Lorna might be using the Anarwyn to conceal Brynach, to make it appear as if she'd destroyed it.

He released the man, who curled into a ball, clutching his head. Blood poured from his nose. Such an invasion could be a devastating thing. Bardon had accidentally killed the first few people he experimented on.

"Get up," Bardon snapped.

The messenger groaned. "Please, My Lord."

"I said get up!" Bardon dragged the man to his feet. The man nearly fell, but Bardon held him and slapped him across the face. "Get a hold of yourself man."

"My Lord," the man mumbled. Blood dripped from his chin. His eyes rolled as he wavered and fell again.

A small black and gold stone the size and shape of a pearl dangled from the man's neck. Bardon narrowed his eyes. This man had failed him. They had all failed him. Someone would have to pay. He would need to make an example.

Bardon glowered at the man. "What of the army? You said you were repulsed."

The man struggled to his feet, leaving his skull cap on the blue woolen carpet.

The Sting of Death

"We lost more than eight hundred and a thousand were wounded."

"Half my army!" Bardon whirled and paced, feeling the soft wool carpet give under his feet. "Lorna," he sneered.

He should have dealt with her long ago, but he had not been powerful enough. It took time to discover the ways of the Bragamahr on his own. Not even Jathneel had probed it so deeply. Now, he was ready. Finally ready. He spun, channeling the power through the topaz ring, the Carreg Crynodial, or the Concentration Stone.

A beam of delicate blue light leaped from the stone and burned through the cowering man before him, bursting from his back and sending up a reeking smoke. The messenger screamed in agony and stumbled toward the flap of the tent.

Bardon sneered and reached out mentally to the obsidian and pyrite stone the man wore around his neck. Let the rest of his army understand what happened to those who failed him. He activated the obsidian as he followed the man through the opening into the warm sunlight in the center of his camp. He hadn't yet used the obsidian in this way, and he wanted to see how well it would work.

The man collapsed to his knees and scrambled around to stare up at Bardon with a stricken face.

"My Lord," he said, "please, have mercy."

The obsidian in the necklace melted and clung to the man's skin, crawling out along the man's neck until it encircled his throat. The golden pyrite fell away. The man clawed at the creeping black death as smoke curled up from where it bored into his skin, cinching itself ever tighter, cutting inward. The man's cries gurgled in his throat until they were cut off entirely as the obsidian passed through his windpipe. A fountain of blood erupted from his neck, and the man's head rolled from his shoulders and fell to the earth with a hollow thump.

"Interesting," Bardon said and smiled in grim satisfaction. He had been looking for an excuse to try this new use of the Bragamahr. Let the rest of his men beware. He would set it to trigger anytime one of them betrayed him.

"General!" he called.

A wizened Inverni jogged up to him and fell to one knee, careful to avoid the bloodstained grass. "Yes, My Lord?"

"Prepare a company of one hundred men to accompany me to Brynach."

Undead

"Yes, My Lord."

He would see for himself what Lorna had done and maybe pick up her trail. Though she had employed the power of the Anarwyn to hide from him all these years, she had come out into the open at last. Now was his chance.

"Please," the man's voice croaked as Zenek peered down at him, dripping river water from his soaked clothing and hair.

Morning light slanted across the man's face. He was a Tathanar warrior Zenek hadn't met until this expedition. Zenek searched for his name but couldn't recall it. An arrow had punched through the man's side and a vicious saber cut opened his skull where it leaked gray matter. How the man was still alive Zenek couldn't guess.

"Water," the man whispered through cracked lips.

Zenek drew his sword. He had dragged himself from the waters of the Brunen River moments before and was shivering with an unearthly chill. That Rebecca and Briallen had seen him conversing to the Inverni changed everything. The hour he had spent hiding in the rushes had done nothing to soothe his temper. Even if it had, Zenek couldn't let this man live. Not now that the man had seen Zenek.

Zenek raised the sword without a word, and the man's eyes widened. Lifting a feeble hand, the Tathanar attempted to ward off the blow. Zenek struck. One swift slash and the man's throat lay open. The blood gurgled out onto the muddy earth, and the life faded from the man's eyes. Regrettable but necessary.

He gave a quiet curse and inspected the other bodies. He killed three Inverni and another Tathanar to ensure that no one remained to reveal that he had returned to the battlefield.

His plan had come unraveled at the moment of victory, and he had escaped into the river where he watched the battle rage and despaired as Hebron and Cam destroyed another one of the magnificent beasts of the Bragamahr. Drakeman and the survivors fled in the canoes, with Bardon's riders galloping after them. Cam had been dragged away and should even now be lying dead, entangled in the prairie grasses.

Zenek stomped his feet to get the blood flowing again. It had been a simple matter to betray Cam to Bardon. At least that part of his plan had been successful. The Inverni rid him of Cam, but now he needed a new plan. To return to the Tathanar would mean certain death. If not now, then eventually. Deeds like the ones he just committed had a way of being revealed. Rebecca had been silenced, but Briallen might have seen him. If he had, then he certainly would have informed Drakeman of Zenek's treachery already. Perhaps it was time to move on.

He searched for his equipment in the piles of discarded baggage. By some good fortune, his pack was still there, trampled in the mud, but otherwise undamaged. His long-planned surprise would have been complete if Rebecca hadn't seen him and given the alarm. Why Rebecca had been off alone with Briallen when she and Cam were supposed to be so close, he couldn't guess. That was none of his concern.

Zenek undid the leather ties that closed his pack and removed the little pouch. He wiggled the laces loose and withdrew the bloodred, twelve-faced garnet. A tiny rune had been carved into the twelve facets—one for each of the stones of power. A sigh of relief escaped his lips.

The facets caught the morning light in a dazzling array. It had been his mother's and her mother's before her in an unbroken chain all the way back to the daughter of Sameel, one of the few to survive the slaughter of the Tamil after the Fall of Goldereth. There had been several others, but they forgot their heritage and merged with the Tathanar. Three or four families still lived in the village of his youth who spoke of the days when they had ruled all of Anwyn. But now, they were gone. He alone survived to avenge the wrongs done to his people. He lived among the Tathanar, biding his time, waiting to see what Bardon would do, waiting for his chance.

It came when the Mahrowaiths returned, and the boy, Cam, arrived at Abilene. Zenek came so close to killing Cam at Afon Darodel, but Drakeman's arrival had forced him to save the boy. That Lakari, Ewan, kept a watchful eye on Zenek after that, and the wolf had never left Cam's side. No other opportunity presented itself before they arrived at the great bend. With Cam now dead at the hands of the Inverni, Zenek needed to make new plans. The time had come to do what he promised his mother he would do. The

Undead

valley of the Braganeth wasn't far. If he proved receptive, he could join Bardon—or perhaps replace him.

Zenek slipped the garnet back into its pouch and checked his gear. He scrounged enough food from among the scattered supplies to last him several weeks and dragged a canoe into the shallows. He couldn't descend the river in the daylight, or he would be seen. If Drakeman didn't know already, he would soon guess what Zenek had done.

The Tathanar would not let him live if they suspected him of treachery. It was best to remain unseen. He waded upstream for nearly a mile to a fallen oak whose branches sifted the waters of the Brunen. Debris piled on the upstream side, creating a deep hollow where he could wait unseen until dark. Zenek snapped the few remaining branches on the downstream side to make room and maneuvered the canoe into the shadows. He wedged it in place and climbed inside. His soft green trousers woven from the bark of the Silver Trees dripped water to pool in the bottom. After eating a slow, thoughtful breakfast of penemel and pilchard washed down with cool water from the Brunen, he settled in to sleep. Tonight, he would begin the journey he'd been waiting for all his life.

Chapter Two
Waterless Wasteland

A SPIRAL OF BLACK SMOKE twisted into the pale blue sky. Bardon chewed his lip in frustration as he sat his horse staring out over the churning waters of the Brunen River to the great island of rock upon which Brynach had been built. The westering sun cast a slanting light across the island, filtering through the tendrils of smoke rising from the underbrush alongside the river. Somehow, he never expected to find this. The absence of the jagged battlements and high towers of the once-proud castle of Brynach left a nagging impression that something was missing, like the hole left after pulling a tooth.

All around lay the refuse of battle. Undergrowth along the river smoked. Charred bodies bobbed in the water amid the wreckage of dozens of boats. Trebuchets towered over piles of stinking corpses, their ropes swaying in the wind, and an acrid, oily reek hung over the plain and its charred prairie grass. Bardon ground his teeth in annoyance as a hundred men around him shifted in their saddles with much creaking of leather. Their horses shuffled their feet and bobbed their heads, obviously disturbed by the smells of death. His army had been savagely mauled. This would delay his plans by some weeks.

Still, with the magical defenses gone, Bardon might find a way into wherever Lorna had hidden the treasury of the Varaná. She must have hidden it. To destroy Brynach with all its books and stores of gemstones would never have occurred to her. It would be an act of madness. He needed to find a way in. If he was to destroy the Anarwyn once and for all, he would have to acquire that giant quartz crystal held in Brynach's vault. The other gemstones would also be useful, but it was the quartz he needed.

Bardon had entered the castle only once before, and it had been a bloody affair. A grim smile spread over his face at the memory. He had come to kill his sister and as many of the Varaná as he could. His sister escaped, but the Varaná turned on one another, doing much of the work of destruction for him. They were so easily manipulated, accepting the lies and half-truths he spread. It was almost effortless to get people to believe the worst of each other, especially in a competitive system like the one the Varaná created.

The fools had no idea what they were doing. In their mania to conceal all knowledge of the Bragamahr and how it functioned, they ensured that when someone like him did unravel the mystery of that power, they would be completely incapable of doing anything to stop him.

Bardon touched the pale pink gemstone. He closed his eyes to settle his mind and channeled the Bragamahr through the stone. He examined the island, trying to discover what Lorna had done, to find another way in. The current of the Bragamahr sweeping beneath the castle stirred at his presence.

The Anarwyn was there, as well, but it recoiled from him, refusing to let him read it. This was why he needed that crystal. As his mind roamed over the island, probing, searching, he could sense the skeletal remains of the great structure, but it appeared to be truly gone. He scowled. Had Lorna destroyed the archive and the treasury of the Varaná? Was she truly that desperate?

His probing brought him to a flat outcrop of stone near the middle of the island where he sensed a lingering power. Magic left a residue, especially when so much had been used. He reached out to probe it when a burst of power flashed through his mind like a strike of lightning. He cried out and tumbled from his horse.

Lorna's voice reverberated inside his skull. "You cannot enter here."

Bardon curled into a ball, clasping at the agony in his head, struggling against the nausea that threatened to twist his stomach inside out. He reached out to the emerald ring, the Carreg Deruid, and summoned its aid. The power of the Bragamahr infused his body and slowly the agony receded. He struggled to a sitting position. His men watched him, wary and frightened, yet unconcerned for his well-being. No one dared dismount to offer him a hand. Bardon snarled and scrambled to his feet, wiping the black ash from his clothes. Did his sister really think he could be overcome so easily?

She *had* been here, and she *had* sealed the castle, not destroyed it. That meant the seal could be broken. If not, he would find another way.

Lorna gasped at the sudden ripple of fear that reverberated through the Anarwyn. She reined her horse to a stop and swiveled in the saddle to gaze north toward Brynach. Geirrod and the three hundred men trailing behind him paused with her, looking around in confusion.

"What is it, My Lady?" Geirrod said.

"I don't know. Give me a moment."

Though they had ridden hard all day following the Brunen River south toward the fords above Torwyn, they were still a good day's ride from the crossing. Their saddlebags were packed with a quantity of penemel, the special cake the Tathanar made from powdered meat, stenel berries, the grain called prin, and honey. They also carried salted pilchard, an oily fish from the Silver Lake prized by the Tathanar. This Tathanar army would not want for supplies on their journey to the Lonely Valley in search of Cam, though she would not be going with them.

Evening was now upon them, making it too dark to discern much of the rolling hills that stretched in every direction. The threat resonated through the Anarwyn. Lorna drew on the opal, called the Carreg Golug, or the Vision Stone, one of the many stones of power set in the golden pendant she wore about her neck. With this stone she let her mind flow into the Anarwyn, reaching out toward Brynach, terrified that somehow Bardon had broken through her defenses. She found his presence immediately and retreated in case he was also searching for her. She didn't have time for a confrontation, nor was she ready. He would know what she had done at Brynach, and he would be hunting for her. It was best to remain unseen.

Undead

"Bardon is at Brynach," she said. "But we're safe for now."

Creating a dyad of malachite, the Carreg Puer, and turquoise, or Carreg Doethineb, she cloaked her presence and that of the army from all magical inspection, before urging her horse into a trot.

"He knows I was there," she called back over her shoulder as Geirrod galloped to catch her. "We need to hurry."

She needed to reach King Trahern of the East Mark and his son, Gareth, before Bardon could recover from this setback. The Tathanar warriors fell in behind her, and they continued their mile-eating canter.

As she rode, Lorna's mind wandered to Cam and the party she had sent the long way around to the Lonely Valley. Jathneel's declaration that she had sent Cam to his death worried her, especially when she considered the story of Alys and Galad in which the young Varaná saved her love by transferring her life force to him.

She was more convinced than ever that she had made a dreadful mistake. Hopefully, the men she sent to search for Drakeman would find them in time. Geirrod and his three hundred men would ride for the Lonely Valley, while she raced to reach King Trahern and secure his aid. If she failed, all her other efforts would be for naught. Then she would rush for the Lonely Valley and intercept Cam before anything could happen to him. Perhaps her messengers would find them before they crossed the Brunen where Bardon's men might be waiting to intercept them. It was a slender hope, but she clung to it and rode on because she had no other choice.

Cam fought against the powerful hand clamped over his mouth. However, with his hands and feet tied, there was little he could do. A knee pressed on his ribs to hold him still, and a man bent low over him. The light of the newly risen moon washed the face of their long-haired guide who placed a finger to his lips.

"I will not harm you," he whispered. "Do not wake the guard." His speech was thick with a lilting cadence that was pleasant to hear.

Cam stopped struggling, and the man lifted his hand from his mouth. Rebecca lay there, wide awake and staring.

"My name is Peylog. Why do these men wish to kill you?"

Waterless Wasteland

Cam glanced at the twin who slouched against the boulder breathing deeply, and decided to tell the truth—or at least part of it.

"Because we're fighting against Bardon," he whispered.

Peylog nodded. "Then you fight against the Bragamahr also."

The way he said this made Cam pause. He couldn't decide if Peylog approved of the Bragamahr or not. This strange man narrowed his eyes to study Cam as if he were deciding something.

"I will help you," he said, "but it will take time, and you will suffer much. His face assumed a hard expression. "Tomorrow night, I will leave you, but I will follow and bring you water at night while these fools sleep. When they are weakened, I will kill them."

Cam was so surprised by this declaration that he stared for a long moment. "Why?" he finally said. "Why would you place yourself in so much danger for us?"

A smile curved Peylog's lips. "Danger comes whether we seek it or not. But this is my country, and the danger is greater to them."

Peylog lifted Rebecca to a sitting position and let her drink from the gourd he carried around his neck. When she finished, she whispered, "Thank you."

He also helped Cam up so he could drink. The liquid was surprisingly refreshing and coursed through his veins. He drank until his burning thirst was quenched. Peylog helped them lie back down and replaced the blanket over them. He patted Rebecca on the shoulder.

"You are a strong and brave woman," Peylog said. "You must keep your courage for what you will face." He rose and simply melted into the night.

"Do you think he'll do it?" Rebecca whispered.

"I hope so." If Peylog didn't help them, Cam couldn't see how they would escape, and if they did manage it, they had little chance of surviving in this barren land. Scar Face snorted and rubbed at his face, and Cam and Rebecca fell silent.

Come to me, the words floated through Zenek's brain. They were alluring and terrifying with their sense of power. He shifted, and his mother's face smiled at him with that wicked sense of knowing secrets no one else knew.

Undead

Zenek jerked awake to a stinging on his neck. Slapping at the painful bite, he crushed the fly between his fingers. He rubbed the bite as he studied his surroundings. Evening was creeping over the land. The river smelled of fish and wet earth. It was nearly time to be on his way.

The power of the words lingered in his mind the way the aftertaste of a sour apple dawdled in the mouth. It told him he had made the right decision. A sense of excitement gushed through him, and he was ready to begin.

He grabbed a few moments to relieve himself and to eat a small meal before dragging the canoe from his hideaway and jumping into the middle. He knelt on the bottom, resting his backside against the thwart, and deftly maneuvered the canoe into the current. The rush of speed gave him a thrill. Canoeing was second nature to him, the paddle and canoe mere extensions of his body, and today he was paddling toward his destiny.

The canoe skimmed along with the current, rounding the bend where several canoes stretched out on the beach. The crumpled remains of the Mahrowaith sprawled in the grass, but something was different. Zenek paused in mid-stroke to study the green hillside more carefully. Crows and vultures flapped about competing for the putrefying flesh of men and horses, though none of them approached the Mahrowaith. What was it that disturbed him? Then he saw it. The great wolf was gone, and another Mahrowaith lay there sliced in two.

Zenek surveyed both banks. Only one man could have done this to a Mahrowaith. Hebron must have returned, searching for Cam. For days, Zenek had watched Hebron carry that accursed blade. The bane of Sameel. The hammer of the Mahrowaiths. The blade of Galad had been found at the moment the Anarwyn was weaker than it had ever been. And it had slain not one, but two Mahrowaiths this day.

Returning his attention to his paddle, Zenek stroked with more urgency. He needed to be free of this place before he was discovered. He possessed no power to resist that sword—at least, not yet.

"The scouts haven't returned, My Lady."

Waterless Wasteland

Geirrod adjusted the girth strap on his horse. His face was streaked with sweat and grime. He seemed older than he had when they began this venture. Perhaps it was the loss of his only son, Hamlen, at Brynach. A pang of guilt punched into Lorna's gut, and she winced. It was her fault. She had sacrificed four good men to seal Brynach from Bardon's grasp. She hoped they hadn't died in vain.

They were less than half a mile from the ford. Having ridden all day, they shivered at the cold chill of evening settling over the hill country north of the old city of Torwyn. The sun had slipped behind the western mountains. They paused to give the horses a break while the scouts checked the ford to ensure it was safe to approach. The delay gnawed at her. Every moment allowed Bardon to draw his net tighter.

Sighing to calm herself, she let her gaze roam over the shadowed hills. She had spent much of her youth riding the undulating folds of land rising from the river to merge with the wide Plains of Pannon to the north. Torwyn, the city of her childhood, now abandoned and fallen to ruin, lay only a few miles farther south beyond the ford. What she wouldn't give to go back to those sweet days of innocence when Bardon was her companion in childish mischief and her father's boisterous laugh echoed in the halls of the palace.

"We can't wait much longer," Lorna said.

"I'll send two more to check on them," Geirrod said.

Lorna patted her horse's muzzle and used the agate to send the mare a flood of healing warmth. The mare whinnied and bobbed her head. A horn rang out bright and shrill in the still morning air. Geirrod spun around to peer at their back trail. The call cut off abruptly.

"Mount!" Geirrod shouted. "Jacob, form a rear guard. To the ford in battle order."

The Tathanar horsemen responded without question, and Lorna joined them in a coordinated gallop to the ford. The men were strung out on either side of her and Geirrod in three ranks. The archers filled the first rank and the lancers formed the next two, their lances barely visible in the pale twilight. Shouts erupted behind them, and Lorna twisted in the saddle. The rear guard engaged a company of horsemen. They had clearly been stealing up on them while they rested.

Undead

Lorna swiveled in her saddle as her horse crested the rise. At least two hundred riders in mottled cloaks sat on their prancing mounts this side of the river. The bodies of the four scouts Geirrod had sent sprawled at their feet. The ford was held against them.

"Volley!" Geirrod shouted, and the men with bows drew arrows to their ears and loosed. Arrows zipped through the air, hissing as they passed, and punched into the Inverni riders. Dozens fell, but they held their ground. This would not do. Lorna had no time for an all-out battle, and they could not spare the men. Forming a dyad of jasper and pearl, she sent a pulse of energy into the earth under the feet of the Inverni horses.

The ground exploded in a fountain of stone a hundred paces long. Horses screamed and reared. Warriors tumbled from their saddles, broken and bleeding. She let the dyad collapse and formed a new one with sapphire and jade. The river paused in its flow and curled back on itself as a rushing wind whipped up the channel. A wave grew into a giant tsunami that she sent toward the struggling Inverni. It crashed into the shore, sweeping it clean of men and horses. By the time Lorna and the Tathanar splashed into the receding flood, the water was up to the horses' bellies.

They charged across and whirled to see how their rear guard fared. They were giving ground, having formed a tight circle with the lancers in front and the archers in the middle. Geirrod gestured to a soldier with a long battle horn, and he gave three short blasts. The Tathanar loosed a volley and whirled as one, racing toward the ford.

"Volley!" Geirrod shouted again as his rear guard broke away from the surprised Inverni. Strings slapped, and arrows buzzed. There was a long silence, and then the arrows found their marks in Inverni bodies, disrupting their pursuit. The rear guard reached the ford and pounded across.

"Ride!" Geirrod shouted, and they galloped up the bank only to find a hundred more horsemen barring their way.

Geirrod cursed and spun to face Lorna.

"Ride, My Lady. I will hold them."

"But—" she protested.

"You must reach Najera!" Geirrod shouted. "Go!"

He was right, of course. The best way to help these men was to bring them the aid of the East Mark. She paused long enough to send a bolt of lightning into the ranks of the Inverni, scattering them as Geirrod's men slammed into them. She whirled her horse due east, away from the river and the men who risked so much to help her.

The night seethed with tension as Zenek maneuvered the canoe to the far western shore, listening to the ominous hiss of the black waters of the Brunen as they swept him along. The moon had risen, casting the churning water of the river in a sparkling light. Still, a snag of deadwood or an errant stone could spell disaster. He avoided the extreme edges of the river where fallen trees strained the water and would have caught him in their clutches. Without the moonlight, such a journey would have been suicide.

He had to endure the dangers of night travel on the rushing river because the Tathanar with whom he had lived for so long would be alert to any danger of the Inverni returning for another attack. They may have escaped complete annihilation, but they now knew the enemy was about and would be on their guard for any noise that did not belong to the darkness.

Hushed voices drifted over the water, and Zenek stiffened. There in the center of the river, a light flickered, and the scent of burning wood and cooking food floated to him. The murmur of voices grew louder, and Zenek quit paddling. He kept his paddle in the water and applied pressure here and there to keep the bow pointed down river as he let the current sweep him downstream. He barely dared to breathe.

Even in the dark, Drakeman could hit a noise with that powerful longbow of his. Zenek had seen him do it before. More lights flickered until a dozen campfires were clearly visible in the darkness. The Brunen flowed swift and deep here. Still, anything could be bobbing in the water. He just needed to survive until he reached the shallows northeast of Goldereth.

The thought of the shallows and what lay beyond the ragged mountains to the west sent a thrill surging through him. He was returning to the lands of his forefathers, the homeland of Dengra, the great hunter, the first to wield the power of the Bragamahr. This was the native land of the Tamil. Governed by the Black Council, the Tamil spread from the Namani Sea to the banks of the Brunen, building great cities and dominating every tribe they encountered. It was a sacred land.

A ripple of water alerted him to some obstruction in the channel. He snapped out of his reveries and dragged the paddle to slow the canoe until he saw the flash of moonlight on a wet rock. Zenek swung the paddle out for a powerful sidestroke. He was too late. The canoe bumped into the rock with a hollow thump and leaned dangerously to the side. Water slipped over the gunnel as Zenek braced off the paddle and snapped his hips to stabilize the canoe before it took on too much water. The canoe righted itself and slipped past the stone. Zenek's skill with the paddle saved the canoe from capsizing, though he had no time to enjoy his success.

Someone shouted, and Zenek ducked low in the canoe so his head and shoulders would not be silhouetted in the darkness. If the night watch saw the black shape drifting on the waters, maybe they would think it was a log. The hiss of an arrow sped overhead to slap into the water. Another slammed into the side of the canoe not five inches from Zenek's head with a hollow thump. Zenek tensed, ready to paddle. Drakeman wouldn't have missed that shot. Where was he? Why wasn't he with his men?

Zenek waited, listening for the sound of pursuing canoes until he was sure he had passed the islands and no one was following. Raising his head, he found the flicker of firelight far behind him. It disappeared when he rounded a bend, and he resumed his paddling with powerful rhythmic strokes, anxious to place as much distance as possible between him and the Tathanar before daylight. Then he would have to leave the river again to avoid being spotted and travel west to the land of his forefathers. A little while now, and he would claim his birthright or die trying.

The Inverni grabbed Cam and Rebecca by the hair and yanked them to a sitting position, startling them from sleep. The sun had not yet risen, and the gray netherworld of light was punctuated by the shadows of the Inverni saddling their horses.

Waterless Wasteland

Baby Face spared them a swallow of water, a bite of jerked meat, and some of the honey cake before they started again with the half-naked guide leading the way. The rising sun revealed a wild, unfamiliar landscape on this western side of the ragged hills. Cam did not recognize any of the plants. The terrain was awash with color. Streaks of reds, browns, yellows, and whites in all their shades flowed through everything. Great piles of stones and hulking outcrops broke the landscape with brilliantly colored layers stacked one on top of the other in disordered beauty.

Cam's head ached from the blow he'd received in the rockslide, and the Inverni showed no inclination to treat the injury. At first, he thought he might be hallucinating as they met stones twisted into bizarre shapes, curving in weird contortions. Even the wild chaos of color and the echoing passes between the outcrops left him feeling confused and disoriented. He allowed himself to succumb to the strange, contradictory sense of enchantment. The scenery was harsh and beautiful. Oppressive and inspiring. Engaging and repulsive. And it would likely be his grave.

But he was determined to save Rebecca no matter what it cost him. He worked at the knots binding his wrists as they rode. It might be a waste of time, but it gave him something to do. And if he could get loose, maybe he could seize a weapon and cut them both free before the Inverni could respond.

He fumbled with the knot for hours until his hands and wrists ached from the effort. By mid-morning, the pain in his head subsided to a dull ache, and the guide stopped them in a wash filled with glistening white sand. Peylog dropped to his knees and scooped a hole in the sand. The Inverni dismounted to seek out what shade they could find among the thin, spindly plants and clumps of prickly pear while they waited. They left Cam and Rebecca baking in the heat of the sun. Cam caught Rebecca's gaze and mouthed to her, "Are you all right?"

She nodded, though her face was bright red and her lips cracked. Cam didn't know how much more of this they could stand. Still, he had to trust Peylog. He didn't have a choice.

"Where are the watering holes you promised?" Wild Eyes spat at their guide.

Peylog ignored him and kept digging. The sand became moist,

and soon he had a small puddle of water. The sight and smell of water made Cam's savage thirst rage all the more. Peylog rose and gestured to the water. "This is a watering hole," he said.

The Inverni shoved him aside, issuing a string of curses.

"Is this all you can find?" Scar Face groused. "There's not enough here for a single man."

Despite their complaints, they accepted the water. The hole refilled every time they emptied it, and soon they had watered their horses and filled their waterskins before they let Cam and Rebecca have a few swallows. The water was bitter, muddy tasting, and smelled of sulfur, but it was better than nothing.

The wild-eyed Inverni, with his one blue eye and one brown eye, scowled at Peylog. "You promised plentiful water."

Peylog gestured to the muddy hole in the sand. "There is plenty for all."

Wild Eyes raised his hand to strike Peylog. "That's not a watering hole. It's a rancid seep. You find us a nice clean spring next time."

Peylog didn't flinch, the tattoo on his cheek quivered as he flexed his jaw muscles. He looked at Scar Face without emotion before spinning away.

All that day as the sun rose into the pale blue sky and beat down upon them with a fury, the two brothers unleashed their frustration on Peylog.

"We should be heading due west," Scar Face growled.

"Not if you want water," Peylog replied.

"You've been giving us nothing but mud," Wild Eyes said.

"You're alive," Peylog said.

Cam was amazed at Peylog's self-control. He would have given in to the temptation to stuff their mouths full of sand long ago. These Inverni were idiots if they didn't realize their lives were in Peylog's hands.

By dusk, they had descended into a rock-strewn valley filled with a vicious cactus with springy segments that leaped out and embedded its spines painfully into both man and beast. Cam's legs and feet were so covered in spines they looked like shriveled porcupines. And yet, he barely noticed the pain. It was like a background annoyance to the raging thirst that had transformed his tongue into a block of wood.

Peylog stopped them by a large boulder and counted some

stones that had been lined up by it.

"What's he doing now?" Scar Face snapped.

Peylog ignored him and stepped to the head of the line stones and paced off a short distance. Finding another large stone, he spun and strode in a different direction until he came to a wide flat rock twenty paces from where they waited. He flipped the stone over, revealing a small pool of water. He knelt to sniff the water and dipped a finger in to taste it. He spat it out and wiped his mouth on the back of his hand, shaking his head.

"The water is bad," he said.

"Bad?" cried the twins at once.

Wild Eyes shoved Peylog aside and tested it himself. He spat it out with a grimace. "Our waterskins are empty, and you can only find bad water."

"Patience," Peylog said.

Wild Eyes bellowed in rage and slapped Peylog across the face.

Peylog received the blow with dignity. A red handprint covered the blue tattoo on his cheek. He spoke to Baby Face. "I am paid to lead you to the sea, not to be abused. If you can do better, then go." He gestured with his hand.

"No," Baby Face pleaded. "I will punish them, but you must go on leading us."

Peylog glared at the two brothers with contempt and climbed out of the little vale. Cam worked on the knots again, afraid that Peylog would get killed or maybe even decide not to come back. They traveled the rest of that day without finding any water and bedded down for the night under the shadow of a colorful rock overhang.

Baby Face untied Cam and Rebecca for a few minutes so they could pluck the spines from their legs and feet. He gave them some of the honey cake to eat, but neither of them could swallow it.

Rebecca looked pitiful with her sunburned face streaked with dirt and her cracked and swollen lips. If Cam hadn't been so dehydrated, he would have cried at seeing her suffering. He tried to speak to her but found that no sound would come out of his dry throat. Rebecca simply gazed at him with a quiet determination. What else could either of them do?

That night Peylog came as promised and unbound their wrists and ankles. Cam glanced around to see if one of the twins was guarding them, but the three Inverni had apparently decided there was nowhere for their captives to go and were determined to get as much rest as they could.

Cam insisted that Peylog give Rebecca the water first and struggled not to fidget while he waited his turn. His thirst was so overpowering that he thought he might go mad. He fought the urge to leap upon Peylog and tear the waterskin from his grasp.

Peylog whispered to Rebecca and massaged her throat until she was able to drink. He didn't let her drink too much before he did the same for Cam. At first, Cam couldn't swallow. His tongue had become so swollen and his throat so raw and dry that when he tried to swallow it felt like someone had poured sand down his throat. Peylog gently massaged his throat with his rough, calloused hands and eventually, Cam was able to drink.

Peylog returned to Rebecca and gave her more water. He crawled back and forth between them until their thirst was sufficiently quenched and enough moisture returned to their bodies to allow them to consume a soft, white cake Peylog gave them.

"This is more nourishing than what they give you," he said.

The cake was remarkably filling and renewed Cam's energy. While they ate, Peylog washed their wounds before applying a translucent balm that helped dull the pain. He also extracted the rest of the cactus spines from their feet and legs and applied the same salve to their feet. While rubbing the salve into the rope burns on Cam's wrist, Peylog paused to peer at Cam's knuckles where the sand of the Bragamahr had left black scars.

Peylog glanced up at Cam with a scowl, and Cam hurried to distract his attention.

"How far are we from the sea?" Cam croaked.

"Two more days," Peylog replied, "but you will not make it."

The breath caught in Cam's throat, and he exchanged a nervous glance with Rebecca.

"Someone follows us," Peylog whispered.

Had the other Inverni tracked them? What would happen if Cam and Rebecca got caught in a tug of war between the servants of the Bragamahr?

Waterless Wasteland

Lorna drooped in the saddle as her horse plodded to a stop. She flinched awake and nearly toppled to the ground. Clutching the pommel of the saddle, she gazed around, searching for that vague sense of threat lingering on the edge of her conscious mind. It came from all around her.

Maybe in her weariness, she was imagining things. The moon had already passed its zenith and was sinking toward the western horizon, casting a pale light over the rolling plains. No clouds marred the sparkling beauty of the heavens, and Lorna welcomed the coolness of the breeze against her cheek.

Her horse's head sagged, and Lorna patted the mare's neck and dismounted, groaning at the stiffness and pain in her legs and backside. She hadn't ridden this hard or this long in many decades, and though she looked younger than she really was, the long years were beginning to tell.

She had fled the fords of Torwyn and ridden through the night and the next day without stopping, save only to water and feed the horse for an hour or so. Now, she was well out on the plains at the brink of exhaustion. Her horse was near its breaking point, and despite her urgency, she would have to let the animal rest.

The horse paused in a narrow valley with a few scraggly trees encircling a water-filled depression. After dismounting, Lorna slipped off the saddle and bridle and led her horse to the water. Using the agate healing stone set into her pendant, she laid a hand on the horse's neck and did what she could to heal its pain and weariness. The power of the Anarwyn would help, but the horse needed rest, and so did she.

While the animal grazed, Lorna brushed the mare's coat, enjoying the silky smoothness. The powerful aroma of horse musk filled her nostrils, reminding her of better days in her father's stables at Torwyn where she first learned to ride as a child. She gave the horse a little grain in a nose bag to give her a bit more energy for the long ride ahead before hobbling her so she wouldn't wander off.

Having finished tending to the horse, Lorna settled back against her saddle, took a swallow from her waterskin, and nibbled some penemel. A few hours ago, she had crossed the tracks of the army Bardon sent against Brynach. The wagon wheels cut deep ruts into the land. There were a few stragglers scurrying south as if driven by their master's whip. She had carefully avoided them.

Once again, she questioned the wisdom of leaving Cam and racing to the East Mark, though she couldn't see any other way to do what was needed. Perhaps she should try contacting him herself in case her riders didn't find him. There hadn't been time until now, and though she was fatigued, she determined to make an attempt.

Mentally forging a dyad with the opal and the sapphire in her pendant, Lorna closed her eyes and relaxed. Having all the stones of power set in the pendant made them readily available should she need them. Creating a dyad was simply a matter of extending her consciousness into the stones, seeking the gentle musical harmony they produced, and then welding them together. This process could happen in an instant and took very little strength. Using the power once it had been summoned, however, required concentration and force of will.

As Lorna's mind centered and her awareness expanded, she reached north and west searching for Cam. By this time, he must have made it through the gorge of the Afon Fathwe and should be well on his way to the Brunen. Long moments passed as her perception stretched across the distance—seeking, searching. There was only silence.

She sensed Spider's presence at one point, though the connection was muffled and filled with fear. At the extreme edge of her perception, she sensed the featherlight brush of Cam's mind. She struggled to focus, only to recoil at the flash of pain and despair that washed over her. What had happened to him? Why wasn't he on the Afon Fathwe?

The tenuous connection almost snapped. Lorna clung to it through her weariness. In desperation, she sent him a message that he was in danger. "Bardon knows you are coming." The connection wavered and collapsed. Lorna drew in a deep, steadying breath. She was too spent to do more.

After taking one last bite of the penemel, she wrapped it and replaced it in her saddlebag, when she sensed again the threat of the odd stone Geirrod had given her after she sealed Brynach. It had exerted power over the mind of the Tathanar warrior who placed it around his neck, and it was now the source of that perpetual feeling of dread which had been troubling her. Perhaps she should deal with it now.

She lifted it out of the bag by the string that bound it, taking care not to touch it. The obsidian and pyrite glinted in the light of the waning moon. It was shaped into a perfect sphere resembling a pearl—half-obsidian and half-pyrite. The Shardana merchants of the coast called this strange metal *Anar gold* in a sarcastic reference to the supposed lack of commercial sense among the Anar who couldn't distinguish between real gold and the glittering golden pyrite.

Though nothing of how the power of the Bragamahr worked survived the purging of the records by the ancient Varaná, it obviously used gems and crystals in much the same way as the Anarwyn. The obsidian and topaz circle she destroyed in Abilene was proof of that. Spider told her the blood of the Mahrowaiths dried to form a type of obsidian rock with red streaks and could attack anything that touched it. Perhaps this trinket worn by Bardon's men was meant to do the same thing.

The descriptions of the valley of the Braganeth, where the Bragamahr resides, all mentioned a black stone that was as sharp as glass when broken. And Cam had bits of black sand in the scars on his knuckles and forehead. Clearly, obsidian was the central stone of the Bragamahr's hierarchy of gemstones in the same way the sapphire served as the most important and powerful stone of the Anarwyn. She held up the pendant. This little pearl, combining obsidian and pyrite, was some sort of dyad that harnessed the power of the Bragamahr.

Gingerly, she reached out with the power of the Anarwyn to probe the beautiful little stone. She reeled with the contact as the compulsion to kill raged through her. The stone grew heavy in her hand. *You are the enemy. You must die.* Her arm grew rigid, and the stone swung toward her, drawn to her by some terrible hunger. Lorna tried to jerk her hand away, but she couldn't move. She knew with a sudden and frightening certainty that if that stone touched her skin, it would destroy her.

In desperation, Lorna summoned the power of the blue turquoise in her pendant and created a dyad with the green malachite in an attempt to ward off the stone. The stone paused, repelled by the powerful shield, and she seized the chance to create a second dyad with the sapphire and the white pearl. For one fleeting instant, she perceived her brother's mind. He was intent on burning the life from her, and he knew about Cam's expedition. The contact broke, and she invoked the lightning from the little pearl. It flashed with a crackle into the obsidian and pyrite stone. The stone exploded in a burst of white light, its fragments scattering over the ground, igniting the grass.

Released from her paralysis, Lorna jumped up and stamped out the flames. Her breath came in ragged gasps as her panic subsided. She had been so foolish. Her brother had always been crafty. It was like him to create an object of beauty whose sole purpose was to control and destroy.

Once she was certain the grass would not reignite and burn her while she slept, she settled down to try to grab a few hours' rest. Slumber came slowly to her exhausted mind, though the persistent dread of the stone had disappeared. She used the agate to help herself relax and slipped into the comforting darkness of sleep.

Lorna only dozed for a few hours before she awoke to her horse whinnying and stomping about. The faint gray of the coming dawn colored the low horizon. Lorna rolled from her blankets to saddle and bridle the horse when an eerie, keening wail broke the stillness. She froze as the creeping terror washed over her. It was different from the unease the little stone had caused. This was a mind-numbing, crippling terror that stole her breath away. She sprang to her feet and bounded to the horse's side. Fumbling with the hobbles, she yanked them loose and swung the blanket and saddle onto the mare's back.

"Sorry, old girl," she said, "but we have to run."

After slipping the bridle onto the horse and cinching the girth strap tight, Lorna vaulted into the saddle and urged the horse into a gallop. Another heart-stopping wail rolled through the darkness, followed by an answering cry behind her. Lorna leaned low over the horse's neck.

"Run, girl," she said, "because your life and mine depend on it."

Waterless Wasteland

"Who's following us?" Cam whispered. Using his voice was still painful, but the last thing they needed was some group of Inverni chasing them down. Things were already bad enough. The way Baby Face and Wild Eyes had been arguing, it was clear that Baby Face was not following orders from Bardon. Maybe the other Inverni had figured out what was going on and had come after them.

Peylog finished dressing their injuries and retied the ropes more loosely.

"It is a war-like party being led by an Inverni on horseback."

Cam's insides constricted. He had guessed right.

"But," Peylog continued, "he has with him a red-bearded man of the Lakari, two of the Anar, and a Tathanar." He paused. "They bring a large prairie wolf with them into the desert." He shook his head in wonder, like this was the most astonishing thing he'd ever seen.

The release of tension almost made Cam cry. He didn't know who the Inverni might be, but the others were obvious. He grinned and suppressed the urge to give a whoop of joy. He glanced at Rebecca and found her smiling.

"They're our friends," Rebecca whispered.

Peylog's brow furrowed. "You have strange friends." He patted Rebecca's arm thoughtfully before rising and disappearing into the darkness.

Refreshed with new hope filling his heart, Cam rolled onto his side so he could peer at Rebecca.

"It'll be all right," he said, scooting close to her.

"As long as they get here before those twins go mad and kill us." She frowned. "I really am sorry for what I did to Spider." Shivering from the cold, she nestled against his chest for warmth.

"I know," Cam whispered in her ear. There wasn't anything he could do about it, and he couldn't explain how much her stoic endurance of their deprivations had given him strength. Still, he wondered if Spider was with them. Peylog had said *two* Anar. One must be Slone. Could the other be Spider?

He and Spider had exchanged harsh words the night before the company left Abilene. Maybe Spider had remained in the city and hadn't tried to follow Cam at all. Or maybe he gave up and returned home to Stony Vale. Cam didn't want to tell Rebecca about the fight between him and Spider. Now was not the time to make her feel guilty.

"I'm sure Spider's eating like a king in Abilene and chasing all the palace girls," he joked.

"I'm glad you're with me," Rebecca said. "I don't know what I would have done on my own."

"Me neither," he said. "I'll get you out of this."

"Not trussed up like a pig ready for roasting, you won't." Her voice was muffled and tired.

"Roasting is right," Cam said. "I never knew it could get so hot during the day and so cold at night."

Rebecca grunted, and he shifted so he could look down on her face. The lines of worry smoothed out as her eyes closed, and her breathing deepened before he let sleep overcome him.

Somewhere in that realm between sleep and wakefulness, he sensed a presence. It was far away and very weak, but it was urgent. A sense of peace and comfort reached for him, followed by the words, *Bardon knows you are coming.*

His eyes popped open to search the darkness, and his heart thudded against his ribs. He recognized that voice. It was Lorna's. What did she mean? Did she know somehow that they were being carried away and Bardon was waiting for them? Or did she mean that Bardon knew of their mission to the Lonely Valley?

The impression cut away, and he was left with the sinking feeling that if his friends did not catch up with them soon, he and Rebecca would not live to see the ocean toward which they were being carried.

Chapter Three
Pursued

GRIPPING TERROR CLUTCHED at Lorna's throat as her horse pounded up and over the rise, fleeing the growing chorus of undulating cries. The mare broke into a wild gallop, the tall prairie grass whipping at Lorna's booted feet. Horrible, piercing wails rang again. Where were they coming from?

The horse shied, lunging to the right, and a strangling stench wafted over Lorna. She instinctively produced a green shimmering shield with the power of the malachite around her and her horse. As the shield snapped into place, a grasping, clawed hand materialized inside her shield, severed from the beast to which it belonged. Lorna leaned back with a curse to avoid it. The hideous creature slammed into the shield and fell away with a shriek as its severed arm flopped to the ground, spewing black blood. The stench filling the air made it difficult to breathe.

That beast came out of nowhere, perfectly invisible in the pale morning light, and had nearly caught her. Lorna glanced back. The injured monster loped after her on two legs, which slowed its progress. She reached for the pearl in her pendant and sent a flash of white lightning into the beast. It exploded with a crackle of blue-white light and a dying shriek. She whirled to face the direction of their wild flight. Because it was too dark to see clearly, she relied on the horse to find the best path over the uneven prairie. Still, the terror persisted.

"Sweet waters of Anarwyn," she swore.

These must be Mahrowaiths, the ancient beasts of the Brag-amahr. Though she had never encountered one, she could not be mistaken. The hideous flat faces, burning eyes, wretched stink, and ability to blend in with their background could not belong to any other creature.

Another unseen beast slammed into her shield and fell away with a crackle of power. Her horse snorted and shied again. Anoth-er Mahrowaith jumped at them. Then another. The horse leaped a creek and bounded up a rocky hillside. Lorna leaned into the rise, trying to help the mare as much as she could.

They reached the crest and found yet another Mahrowaith hur-tling at them. Veering to the left, the horse nearly threw Lorna from the saddle. She clung to the mare's mane as they raced down the hill at an angle until they reached the bottom. The horse stumbled, righted herself, and then fell, hurling Lorna to the earth. Her pro-tective shield collapsed as she lost her concentration and tumbled among the sharp rocks and tall grass. The horse neighed in terror and thrashed, struggling to get to her feet.

Lorna crawled to her hands and knees, ignoring the pain in her arm and leg and the blood trickling into her eye. She clutched her pendant and called up the power of the amber Fire Stone. Extending her other hand, she sent a yellow ball of crackling fire to envelop five Mahrowaiths bounding toward her. They shrieked but kept coming. One burst from the fire and leaped onto the horse's back as the mare found her feet. She bucked, and Lorna formed a dyad with the pearl and the sapphire and sent a bolt of crackling lightning into the Mahrowaith. It exploded in a shower of blood and stone.

Two more broke through her wall of fire, trailing smoke. Their eyes burned red. She sent the lightning flashing over the prairie, de-stroying them in mid-air. The remaining two turned tail and scam-pered away, trailing yellow flame that ignited the prairie grass.

Lorna sprang to her feet and raced to her horse before the ani-mal could bolt in terror. She needed to make sure none of the black, acidic blood had fallen on the mare. The blood would eat the horse's flesh, and once it took hold, there was nothing she could do to stop it. The mare balked and shied away from her. She caught the reins and called up the power of the agate healing stone—soothing the animal's terror enough to lead her back to the creek where Lorna tore up handfuls of grass. She used them and the water from the creek to wipe the horse down just in case.

Lorna healed the horse's wounds as best she could and continued calming her.

"Steady girl," she whispered. "They're gone now. Steady."

The prairie grass before her was alight with an orange-yellow fire that consumed the dry grass. The only open path was back the way they had come, but Lorna couldn't afford to go that way. There were sure to be more Mahrowaiths following her.

Calling up the power of the sapphire water stone, she summoned water from the creek to splash over her and her horse before sending it rolling into the wall of flames. The water sputtered and hissed as it cut through the fire, casting up clouds of steam.

"Come on, girl," she said, and grabbing the reins, she led the horse toward the gap her spout of water created through the wall of fire. The horse bobbed her head and tugged at the reins before lunging forward, yanking Lorna off her feet and tearing the reins from her grasp.

Lorna clambered to her feet and staggered after her fleeing horse into the steaming, smoking gap, limping along as fast as she could. She never should have meddled with the little obsidian and pyrite stone. It had alerted Bardon and his demons to her presence—a mistake she would not make twice. Maybe she wouldn't get the chance. She was on foot, encircled by boiling flames, and her horse had galloped off with her waterskins and food packets. Under such circumstances, anyone could be justified in believing the world had turned against them. Perhaps it had.

Cam awoke to shouts of anger. Rebecca lay next to him, exuding warmth. The commotion grew louder, and he struggled to free himself from the entangling blanket as terror gripped his throat. He wriggled around, expecting to see the twins descending on him with their swords. The gray of dawn was filtering through the rocky outcrops and spindly trees. His wrists and ankles burned from the ropes, but he kept at it until the blanket slipped free to fall beside him onto the white, sandy ground.

"He's abandoned us!" Wild Eyes cried. "That filthy savage has led us out here to die of thirst."

"That does it," Scar Face growled. "Let's finish 'em and go back the way we came before it's too late."

He drew his sword and stalked toward Cam and Rebecca. His lips were cracked and bleeding, and his scar gleamed white on his sunburned face. "I'll not waste another drop of water on you," he snarled.

"No," Rebecca gasped and squirmed around in an attempt to kick out at Scar Face.

He raised the sword, but before he could bring it crashing down on Cam's head, Baby Face leaped in and deflected the blow. The tip of Scar Face's sword plunged into the sand beside Cam. Baby Face stomped on it, snapping the blade near the hilt.

Cam experienced a sudden burst of hope. Maybe these Inverni would kill each other and save Peylog the trouble of doing it.

"I'll do you first, then," Scar Face bellowed at his comrade.

He jerked a long knife from the sheath on his belt and lunged at the leader. Baby Face sidestepped, bringing his blade down with a crunch on Scar Face's arm. Scar Face howled in pain, grabbing at his arm, where blood spurted from the vicious wound.

Wild Eyes jumped to his brother's aid. Before he had charged two steps, Baby Face whirled and threw his own long knife in an underhand toss that buried the blade to its hilt in Wild Eyes's belly. The twin gasped, and his eyes opened wide. He stumbled to his knees, clutching at the blade.

"No!" Scar Face screamed, and snatching up his fallen knife in his good hand, he attacked Baby Face. The big Inverni leader backed up, deflecting the blows with his sword until he stumbled over a boulder and dropped onto his backside.

Scar Face roared in triumph. Instead of rushing Baby Face and finishing him like Cam expected, he whirled and raced toward Cam and Rebecca. He raised the knife and stabbed it toward Rebecca's chest. Cam swung his legs around in horrified desperation, trying to do anything he could to save Rebecca. She twisted out of the way at the last moment, and Cam's feet caught the Inverni at the knees,

Pursued

snapping them back and bringing him to a sudden stop. Rebecca rolled away as the Inverni cursed and dove at Cam. Cam twisted to the side, and the blade grazed his cheek, slicing a long gash. A sickening crunch sounded, followed by the spray of blood.

For one horrible moment, Cam thought Scar Face had killed him or Rebecca. But Baby Face loomed over them, panting, covered in gore. Scar Face swayed and fell with a quiet thump. His blood soaked into the white sand. He had been nearly cloven in two from his collar bone to his belly. The sight and smell brought the bile into Cam's throat.

"I think we're done here," Baby Face said. "Get up."

Cam didn't bother telling him that with his hands and feet bound he couldn't get up on his own. Baby Face growled something and used his sword to cut the ropes that bound their feet and hauled them into the saddles. The stink of him was overpowering. He scavenged the waterskins and food from the twins' saddlebags, rummaged in their pockets, and then mounted his horse.

"Don't think I won't do the same to you if you give me trouble," Baby Face growled. "If I have to kill you to survive, I will."

Lorna patted her horse's neck. "I'm sorry, girl. You can rest now."

The poor horse couldn't go on. She slowed to a walk and then stopped altogether beside a sluggish little creek. The mare's sides heaved, and white foam lathered her flanks and chest where the breast strap rubbed. The early morning sun cut through the pall of gray smoke on the eastern horizon.

Lorna shivered at the memory of the horrible beasts and understood the devastation they could cause in a city, such as Goldereth, whose inhabitants had never encountered them before. Her eyes burned from lack of sleep. Her throat was raw from the smoke. It had taken Lorna several hours to catch the horse after she fled through the tunnel of flame and then another to convince the frightened beast to let her ride again. The unfortunate animal had endured so much.

Lorna dismounted, unsaddled the horse, and let the mare graze and drink from the creek. She couldn't keep riding her like this, or she would kill her. Still, the urgency to get off the open plains and reach the safety of Najera gnawed at her. She brushed down the horse before seeing to her own burns and cuts. None of her injuries were serious, but she couldn't afford to get an infection. After washing and cleansing them, she closed her eyes for a few minutes' rest. Using so much power left a hollow feeling inside, which meant she was overreaching. Much more of this and she might not get any farther.

The Anarwyn maintained a mutually beneficial, symbiotic relationship with humans—which allowed the Anarwyn to thrive and spread throughout the land while the Anarwyn enhanced human skills, completing them in a way that made them more successful as a group. There were limits, however. The Anarwyn was not contained by the human mind or body, and if the wielder of the magic were not careful, they could draw in too much power and kill themselves.

Despite her desperate urgency, Lorna forced herself to conserve her strength and that of her horse. To do otherwise would be foolish and counterproductive.

When she awoke, the sun was near its zenith. Little balls of white clouds skittered before the wind. She stretched and found that the horse had wandered far down the swampy little creek. Lorna ate a little and collected the horse, saddled her, and rode away from the gray haze where the fires continued to burn. The rolling prairie rose as the Heldrun Mountains of the East Mark drew near. In between, something dark spotted the pale blue sky. It was twisting and whirling, like a cloud with a mind of its own.

Lorna straightened in the saddle and kicked her horse into a trot. Carrion birds often followed scouting patrols or warbands, and it was possible that she might be able to contact the Rahil of the East Mark. They could provide her with a fresh horse and an escort into Najera.

She drew closer to the swirling black dots as she rode. When she caught the sickly sweet scent drifting on the breeze, her heart sank. She topped the rise and gazed down into a beautiful valley with a wide, slow creek, a tumble of boulders, and a line of willows with long, waving branches. Beneath the sweeping willows lay at least a hundred corpses dressed in the royal blue tunics of the king of the East Mark—their bodies horribly mutilated with throats slashed and bellies ripped open. Lorna covered her mouth with her hand as her horse shuffled her feet and whinnied. An answering whinny came from within the trees.

Lorna dismounted and wandered among the corpses to see if any yet lived. They were all dead, apparently caught off guard as some were still tangled in their sleeping blankets. Cooking fires smoldered where pots of overturned stew spilled onto the trampled earth. The huge wolf-like prints of the Mahrowaiths marred the ground. They must have come across this scouting patrol on their way to reach her. Lorna lifted a torn and bloody standard of the East Mark from the soil. It contained a black rearing horse set against a blue background in honor of the Rahil's origins. The Rahil began as riders from the far eastern lands who settled on the edge of the vast prairie and colonized the mountains and woodlands of the Heldrun. Few Varaná ever came from the Rahil. They were a different people without much Anar or Tathanar blood.

The sight of so many good men brutally mauled by the beasts of Bardon turned her stomach and steeled her resolve. This had to be stopped no matter the cost. She collected two horses, unsaddled her mare, and patted her neck.

"Thanks, old girl," she said.

She placed her saddle and saddlebags on a fresh mount and found a second saddle for a spare horse. After stuffing the bloody standard into her saddlebags, she surveyed the scene one last time before trotting out of the valley southeast toward Najera with the spare horse in tow. She wouldn't stop again until she reached it.

"Move, you lazy beast," Baby Face croaked and lashed his horse cruelly. The horse's legs trembled as it shuffled two faltering steps before it stumbled and fell, throwing Baby Face onto the sparkling white sand.

Baby Face had led Cam and Rebecca due west after the battle with the twins. As the sun rose, the horses slowed. Their water ran out before midday, but Baby Face drove them on until they entered a narrow wash where all three horses stopped as one. Their heads sagged low, and their bellies heaved. That's when Baby Face's mount collapsed.

Undead

Cam remained in his saddle, though a burning thirst tortured him. His body no longer sweat. There was nothing left to do but die, and right now, he thought maybe they should just get on with it.

Baby Face crawled to his feet and beat the helpless animal. It was no use. The horse was dying. Baby Face fell to his knees and tore at the sand with his long knife until he'd excavated a hole two feet deep. No water seeped into the hole. Baby Face sat back on his haunches and stared at Cam. The man was covered in grime. His face was bright red and withered like a desiccated corpse. His cracked lips trailed blood into his beard.

At length, Baby Face rose and, slipping the Life Stone and the silver dyad from his pocket, he dragged Cam and Rebecca from their saddles before falling to his knees beside Cam. The man had a sour, rancid stink about him.

"All right, boy," he rasped. "Use this magic to bring us some water, or I'll run you through."

Cam shook his head. "The magic doesn't work that way." His mouth and throat were so dry, his voice came out in a whisper.

Baby Face snarled. "You *make* it work!"

He cut the binding on Cam's wrists and placed the Life Stone and the dyad in his hands. Cam's fingers were so numb he fumbled and dropped the stone and dyad. Scooping up the Life Stone, he glanced at Rebecca. He had no idea if the stone could do anything, especially without the sword to which it was attuned. Still, maybe he could do something to save Rebecca. The opal let off a delicate, iridescent light. The touch of it brought a sharp stab of relief. He needed this stone in a way he didn't understand. After it had accepted him as the heir of King Hewel of the West Mark, he had been tied to it by a thread of mutual necessity. Without it, he was diminished. With it, he was complete.

"Do it now," Baby Face growled.

Slowly, cautiously, Cam tried to concentrate as Lorna had taught him back in Abilene. He reached out to the aqua blue opal. The power of the Anarwyn swept through him. Instead of showing him water, the stone opened a vision before his eyes.

Spider hovered over Draig on a bloody battlefield with a stranger standing beside him. It was an Inverni with a long mustache. The blue fire shifted, and he saw Hebron balancing precariously on a narrow, iron footbridge spanning a churning river. Blood trickled down his face, and he held Galad's sword before him as a Mahrowaith advanced toward him. A red flame tore into the footbridge, causing it to waver and buckle. Hebron toppled over the side.

Cam recoiled from the awful scene and gaped at Baby Face's angry scowl, his heart racing. This was like the time the Life Stone warned of danger in Afon Darodel—only it was much more explicit. Hebron was going to die on a footbridge somewhere in the mountains.

Cam couldn't continue this suicidal quest. He wasn't strong enough to watch his friends die. Let the Anarwyn and Lorna find someone else. His hand trembled as he lowered the stone that still let off a gentle glow.

"Well, boy? Where is it?"

Cam shook his head.

Baby Face slammed a fist into Cam's jaw, snapping his head back. Cam's vision blurred, and he barely clung to consciousness.

"I'm through playing games, boy. Where's the water?"

Cam spat blood from his mouth. "It didn't tell me where any water is. I told you, it doesn't work that way."

Baby Face's jaw flexed. He retied Cam's hands behind his back before he rose and drew his sword. "Then I'll drink your blood."

He raised the sword for the kill. Sunlight glinted off the polished metal. Baby Face's lips lifted in a snarl. Cam glanced at Rebecca. How could he save her? The shock and horror constricted her face, and she wrestled against her bonds.

"No," she croaked.

Cam kicked at Baby Face's knees and used the leverage to vault himself sideways. The sword rang against the rock as Baby Face cursed and whirled to chase Cam, who struggled to wrench away from the deadly blade.

Baby Face stomped on Cam's ankle, grinding it into the earth. "Hold still," he growled.

Cam peered back over his shoulder, grimacing in pain. With his hands tied behind his back, there was nothing he could do. Death had come for him at last, and he wasn't ready. He needed to save Rebecca first. The sword rested against the side of Cam's neck, and he tensed, waiting for the burst of pain.

A feathered shaft materialized in Baby Face's chest with a hollow thud and a puff of dust that rose from his dirty tunic. He stumbled backward with the impact. Baby Face gaped down in confusion at the arrow shaft. The sword slipped from his fingers and fell to the stones with a clang. Something smashed into his head with a sickening crack, and he folded in on himself like a limp rag and crumpled to the ground without a sound.

Cam swung around to find Spider bounding over the broken stone. Draig beat him there, licking Cam's face with a rough, dry tongue. Joy swelled in Cam's chest, and a sob of relief burst from his throat as Spider knelt beside him and gathered him into a brotherly embrace.

"She must be heading for Najera," Bardon said. He sensed his sister's presence far out on the plains south of Brynach, which surprised him. She should be traveling with the boy she had sent to the Lonely Valley. Instead, she had gone to Brynach to thwart him. Now, she was fleeing to Najera. Why? He pondered it all the way back from Brynach to Mawsil. There could be only one solution now and it would include his sister's death

Bardon spun to face the little man slouching at the entrance to his tent. "You have her description?"

"Yes, My Lord."

"I want it done in public."

"I understand, My Lord." The man had a scraggly beard that most Inverni would have found shameful for a man his age. He was said to be the most accomplished archer in all the South Mark. Bardon's little obsidian and pyrite jewel hung around his neck. It had proven its value of late, and now he insisted that everyone serving him wear one. Their minds became more malleable to suggestions this way. And he was able to punish them more effectively when they failed him. He didn't want a mindless army, just a biddable one.

"And I want no mistakes. She must not leave Najera alive."

"It shall be done, My Lord." The man bowed and backed out of the tent.

Bardon fingered his rings thoughtfully. What was Lorna planning? How had she known he needed to get into the vault at Brynach?

Pursued

More than fifty years had passed since he'd seen his older sister. His memories of her were clouded and distorted. She must be an old crone by now. He had loved her once, though he couldn't remember why. He still retained a few fleeting impressions of moments of tenderness between them. But he no longer felt anything but burning hatred for the woman who had so often foiled his plans and denied him his right to rule.

She hadn't been like the other arrogant nobles at first, but after she accepted the Anarwyn, she escaped to that breeding ground of pomposity at Brynach and came back thinking she was more important than he was. She had even dared to pity him when the Anarwyn rejected him and betrayed him to their father, so he sought refuge with the only man alive who could help him acquire the power he needed. Jathneel had been easy to persuade because he wanted revenge against the Varaná, who had scorned him and cast him out.

When Bardon returned with the power of the Bragamahr coursing through his veins, she had the impudence to call *him* a traitor. A mirthless smile twisted his lips. He had shown them how weak and ill-prepared they were to confront the awesome power of the Bragamahr.

His father's fat nobles who lived off the labor of better men and women, pursuing their vapid squabbles regardless of the interests of the poor, had to be stopped. And, like any good farmer knew, the only way to eradicate a pest from his fields was to burn it out. That is what he proposed, and the Anarwyn was too weak to understand this or to stop him.

Yet, even Jathneel was too timid, too dependent on the Anarwyn. Only Bardon dared to delve more deeply into the power of the Bragamahr than anyone since the ancient days before the construction of Goldereth. In his wanderings and experimentations with the Bragamahr, he discovered something that Lorna could never guess. There was a way to end the relentless battle between the Bragamahr and the Anarwyn. He alone possessed the courage and understanding to do it. First, however, he needed to prevent the complication of his brother returning from the living death to which Lorna had condemned him. That meant stopping the boy.

He had yet to receive word from his men searching the upper reaches of the Afon Fathwe. It was time to send another band to watch its confluence with the Brunen. If the boy escaped, he would have to flee south along the river. While his men searched, he would turn his attention to the quest for a new quartz crystal large enough to channel the power he would force through it.

"Eric!" he bellowed. His white-haired general poked his head through the flap. "Send a company of one hundred men to the juncture of the Brunen and the Afon Fathwe with orders to kill anyone who attempts to cross to the southern shore. Leave none alive."

Chapter Four
A Sentient Land

REBECCA STRUGGLED AGAINST her bonds to sit up. The relief burning in her chest competed with the terror of having to face Spider after so many weeks and admit what she had done to him. Her body trembled. She was too dehydrated to shed tears. Peylog smiled down on her as Drakeman knelt beside her and cut the ropes before lifting her into his arms. She clung to Drakeman's neck and sobbed, ignoring the pain surging through her body. It was such a relief to let go of all the fear.

"It's all right," he whispered. "I've got you."

"I'm sorry," she mumbled. His soft green tunic smelled of smoke and sweat.

She had admired Drakeman her entire life—and she had been jealous of him. He was so good, so confident. His men loved him to a fault. He had escaped the confines of Abilene for weeks and months at a time and came back with stories and experiences she would never have. She had wanted to hate him for all he could do, for all he was. And yet, he had always been so tender toward her, like an older brother might have been.

Drakeman set her down away from Baby Face's dead body in the paltry shade of a spindly little tree. Slone knelt beside her and draped an arm around her shoulders to give her a squeeze.

"I've missed you," he said. "You're my guardian spirit."

Undead

His bushy brown beard tickled her face. He wore a light blue tunic over his big barrel chest. It was now torn and stained with blood.

Rebecca smiled, making her chapped lips crack. "Dragging you from the river doesn't count since I was the one who pushed you in."

"It counts," Slone said, "at least to me."

Alaric gathered the horses, while Hebron, with his flaming red hair, Spider, and a strange Inverni sporting a bullhorn mustache either tended to Cam or checked through the pockets and saddlebags of their dead captors. Drakeman let her drink from his waterskin and tore off a piece of penemel for her to eat. It tasted so sweet after the poor fare they had been given. Better still was the sight of her friends alive and huddled around them.

While she ate, Drakeman examined her injuries and washed them with clean water. "Your feet are pretty swollen," he said. "But that should subside now that they're untied. How do you feel?"

"It was Zenek," Rebecca blurted.

Drakeman paused and stared at her. "What?"

"I saw him speaking with an Inverni before the attack. Briallen should have seen them. Didn't he tell you?"

"Briallen is dead."

Rebecca scowled and cast a glance at Cam who craned his head to look at them.

"You killed him?" Rebecca asked, trying to decide how she felt about this news. She had been flattered by Briallen's interest, even though he tried to get her to abandon people who trusted her.

"No," Drakeman answered, "he was seriously injured trying to rescue you, and he fought alongside us until an arrow found its mark."

"And Zenek?"

"I didn't see him after the battle. I assumed he'd fallen."

"I don't understand," Rebecca said around a mouthful of penemel. "Why would Zenek betray us?"

Drakeman's scowl deepened as he gently massaged her legs and arms to help get the blood flowing again. "People are seldom driven by a single motive, Rebecca. Perhaps he was paid, or maybe he has some grievance against me."

Rebecca sucked in her breath as Drakeman rubbed a salve into the wounds on her wrists and ankles. "Do you think you can ride?"

"If you tie me to the saddle," Rebecca said.

A Sentient Land

"There's been enough of that," he replied. "I'll carry you. Peylog says there's a pleasant little waterhole a few hours from here where we can rest tonight."

"Thank you," Rebecca said, "for coming for me."

Drakeman smiled. "You're as dear to me as any sister could be." He patted her leg before leaning in to kiss her on the cheek. "Now, let's get away from this ghastly scene and give you and Cam a chance to rest."

Rebecca gazed past Drakeman to where the baby-faced Inverni lay in a crumpled heap and nodded. She winced as Drakeman slipped socks over her feet and helped her wiggle into her boots he retrieved from the saddlebags. He supported her as she rose to her feet. Her knees trembled like reeds in the wind, and her boots pinched her prickling feet. With Drakeman's help, she managed to hobble over to where the others gathered. Hebron, Alaric, Slone, and Spider crouched beside Cam, debating energetically. Spider glanced at her. She avoided his gaze.

"It is good to see you on your feet, My Lady," Alaric said. He extended a gloved hand to help her sit, and she took it. Alaric possessed a quiet confidence that belied his slender build. He hailed from the North Mark, though he had been among the men sent to protect Cam when he was carried north by Queen Elisedel of the West Mark. The long scar curving along the side of Alaric's face gave the impression that he was always squinting with one eye.

"Thank you," she said. "Just call me Rebecca."

Alaric cast Drakeman a sardonic smile. "You've rubbed off on her, Drakeman. Soon, King Chullain won't let anyone use *his* title."

"I doubt that," Drakeman said.

Rebecca noted the strange man with the bullhorn mustache and gave Drakeman a puzzled glance. This Inverni wore a tanned leather jerkin, hunting boots, and a leather cap on his head. Had Drakeman captured him? If so, why was he wearing weapons?

Drakeman saw her expression and shook his head as if he read her mind.

"This is Laird. Spider brought him along."

Rebecca nodded to him, and she forced herself to look at Spider. He sat beside Cam with his long legs drawn up to his barrel-shaped chest. He gave her a surly glare, and she almost spun away but instead forced herself to admit her shame.

"I'm sorry," she said. "I meant no harm."

Spider's scowl deepened, and he raised a hand to rub the back of his head. "That hurt, you know, and you left me there alone."

"I'm sorry," Rebecca repeated.

Laird slapped Spider on the back. "Relax. A little knock on the head was a small price to pay to have me as your guide."

Spider snorted. "A guide who never lets me sleep, throws me off cliffs, and tries to feed me to bears."

Everyone chuckled at Spider's sense of injustice—except Rebecca. It stung knowing she'd betrayed his trust.

"I really am sorry, Spider," she said.

Spider wavered, glanced around at all the smiling faces, and shrugged. "I suppose it could have been worse."

"Yes," Slone interjected. "You could have been hit by an ugly street urchin."

Rebecca smiled then. Her cracked lips pulled and started to bleed again. Draig padded up to her, and she rested a hand on his head, scratching him behind the ears. She caught Cam's gaze and gave him a more subdued smile that didn't stretch her lips so much. Would he ever know how much she had relied on his strength over the last few days?

Slone stepped up to her and held out his arms. "May I, lass?"

She embraced him. All this show of affection made her cheeks burn. "I've missed your smile," he whispered.

Then he bent and picked up her sword. "I found this in their baggage, and I thought you might like it back."

"Thank you," she said and buckled it on. This was the sword Chullain had specially made for her. She treasured it. Tears brimmed in her eyes, and Slone hugged her again. "It's all right, lass. We've got you now."

The horses she and Cam had ridden were near collapse. Laird gave them some water from a hat and rubbed them down, whispering to them as he worked. In a few moments, the animals were able to follow them, though they were too weak to be ridden. Drakeman hefted Rebecca up into the saddle of one of the horses they brought and climbed up behind her. These horses were in bad shape, though not as miserable as the ones they had been riding.

A Sentient Land

Apparently, these horses enjoyed more success finding watering holes and not being deliberately led away from them as her and Cam's had been. Hebron helped Cam onto the other horse, and the rest set out on foot. For the first time in days, Rebecca believed they might survive. And she was determined to make a difference this time, instead of being a burden.

After the reunion at the dry wash, Peylog led them back the way they had come through the scorching desert until they reentered the western foothills of the ragged little mountains. He turned south, and at last, they halted at the base of a huge pile of boulders rising abruptly from the rolling hills of sand and cactus. Halfway up, several twisted trees struggled to exist in the barren wasteland. Peylog led them through a narrow cleft in the rock, barely wide enough for the horses, and brought them out in front of a huge natural cistern of water. Lush grass flourished in the soil captured in the gaps and depressions in the rock. The horses trotted to the water.

"There is water in the desert for those who know where to find it," Peylog said.

Spider and Cam settled down beside the glittering little pool of water in the shade cast by the boulders above them.

"I'm sorry," Spider said. "I didn't mean what I said about you being afraid of competition."

Cam grinned at him. He'd forgiven Spider long ago and only felt guilt for the way he treated his dearest friend.

"I'll let you go raise the dead by yourself, if you want."

Spider smirked. "They couldn't stink any worse than you do."

They laughed together just like old times.

"I'm sorry too," Cam said as their mirth died down. "I wish I hadn't gotten you mixed up in all this."

"We were mixed up in it before we were born," Spider said.

Cam grunted. He couldn't argue with that. Spider rose to help tend to the horse, and when Cam tried to join him, he pushed him back down.

"I'll get it," Spider said. "I haven't been tied to a horse for four days."

Undead

Cam eased back down gratefully and leaned against the red and white sandstone boulder. The shadows cast by the overhang were surprisingly refreshing. Peylog had already kindled a crackling fire and was preparing to roast several long, slender lizards over the flames.

The desert heat dissipated as the shadows lengthened, and an evening breeze blew down from the peaks of the jagged mountains, whisking away the smoke and casting up the mouth-watering aroma of roasting meat. Cam had never eaten a lizard before, but he was so hungry he'd give anything a try.

Drakeman deposited Rebecca beside Cam, and Laird strolled over to tend to their injuries while Spider joined the others who were arranging the camp. Cam suppressed a smile at the sight of Laird's enormous mustache rippling in the wind. Didn't that thing get in the way? It was comical, even for an Inverni, who were so proud of their facial hair.

"Spider says you healed Draig," Cam said.

Laird nodded but kept his focus on his work.

"But how? That arrow must have pierced his heart."

"Not quite," Laird said. He glanced around at the others who were occupied in caring for their equipment or cooking the meal. "Now, close your eyes for a moment and relax."

Cam considered whether he should trust this Inverni after what he and Rebecca had been through. Everyone else in the group seemed completely unconcerned by him, so Cam laid his head back against the warm stone as Laird gently massaged his feet.

"You're a healer, then?" Rebecca asked.

"Of sorts. Close your eyes. Both of you."

Cam opened one eye. Rebecca lay her head back, breathing deeply. He would miss lying close to her at night, and he wondered if *she* would miss it, too. And why was Laird being so mysterious about what he planned? Cam was too exhausted to do anything else. He closed his eye, thinking how good it would be to sleep without his hands and feet being bound.

Laird rested one hand lightly on Cam's swollen foot. A gentle, comforting warmth spread through the foot, up his ankle, and into his leg. As the warmth spread, the pain and stiffness abated until Cam was filled with a glow that lulled him to sleep.

A Sentient Land

When he awoke, it was dark, and everyone had gathered around the glowing fire, speaking in hushed voices. Cam raised up on one elbow. All his pain was gone, simply washed away. He felt his cheek, but his wound was no longer there. Tossing the blanket from his feet, he found the swelling had diminished, leaving nothing but a thin line where the ropes had cut his ankles and dozens of little red dots where the cactus spines had pierced his skin.

He checked his wrists and found the same thing. When he gave Laird a questioning look, he found Laird studying him. Laird gave him a subtle shake of the head, and Cam scowled. He glanced at Rebecca who was also awake. She shrugged and raised her eyebrows.

Cam studied Laird with renewed interest. Had this man used the power of the Anarwyn to heal them? He had never seen Dara do anything quite like this, though she was a skilled healer.

"Are you two done napping while we do all the work?" Hebron asked. The fire made his red beard glow.

Cam scooted over to join them where Peylog was dividing up the steaming lizard meat. "Just letting you all feel useful," he said.

Hebron grunted.

"How are you feeling?" Alaric asked.

Cam glanced at Laird. "Better than I've been in days."

He accepted the meat Peylog offered him and slipped it into his mouth. It had little fat and was a bit stringy. Yet, it tasted better than many a chicken Cam had eaten. "Mmm, that's good."

Peylog smiled and stabbed a blackened prickly pear pad from the fire and offered it to him.

"Go ahead," Spider said. "We all tried it."

"Does it taste good?"

No one answered.

"I'll take that as a *no*."

"Just try it," Hebron said.

Cam broke off a piece and bit into it. It had the mild taste of asparagus, though it was a little slimy. Not altogether unpleasant—just odd. "Interesting. But I think I prefer the lizard."

Peylog clicked his tongue. "You must learn to savor what the land has to offer."

Cam swallowed. "I am savoring."

"Where are we?" Rebecca asked before slipping a piece of

roasted lizard into her mouth.

"You are in the Atacam Desert," Alaric answered. "Homeland of the Orren."

"Who?" Spider asked.

"My people," Peylog said with a frown. The blue tattoo on his cheek pinched, making it look like the bird had fluttered its wings.

"Oh, sorry," Spider said. "I meant no offense."

"You do not offend me. We are forgotten by everyone, but we lived here long before the marks, since the days of the breaking of the Black Council. Those who fight the Bragamahr are my friends."

"I don't think I've heard of this Black Council," Spider said.

"Yes, you have," Drakeman answered. "Lorna mentioned it in Abilene." He leaned back against a red sandstone boulder. "Long before the Anarwyn was known to humans, the Bragamahr had been active. The Black Council was like the Varaná. They governed the use of the power, and they controlled the people of Braganeth."

"What happened to them?" Cam asked. He figured he ought to find out everything he could about the magics that threatened to tear the land apart.

"Our knowledge of those early days is dim," Drakeman said.

Peylog shifted and scowled. "*My* people remember." They focused on him, and he continued. "The Black Council ruled with an iron fist until the High Priestess of the Bragamahr rebelled and fled with her daughter and a small band of followers. The Council fought among themselves, causing great devastation. My people fled the wars into the desert, and we remain here still, safe from both the power of the Bragamahr and the Anarwyn."

Cam studied Peylog with renewed interest. "Do you mean that both magics are dangerous?"

Peylog sniffed. "All power is dangerous. We simply refuse to be governed by magics which care more about their own survival than they do about us."

That thought gave Cam pause. In some ways, it reflected his own reluctance to accept the Anarwyn. He had accepted it in the end to save his friends from the Mahrowaith. And he had been sorely tempted to accept the Bragamahr. In fact, the constant lure of the dark magic haunted him. Deep down, he knew the Anarwyn would eventually lead him to his death, but he would have accepted it all

A Sentient Land

over again if it meant he could lounge here around the popping fire with all the people he cared for most. Still, he didn't want to become a mere tool of either magic. To use them meant to succumb to them, and he was going to resist that as long as he could.

"That's a laudable sentiment," Slone said, "one I think most Anar would agree with. But now we ought to consider our next move." He drew his small axe from the loop at his belt and fiddled with it like it was a toy. "We can't go to the coast where Bardon's men will be waiting for us. Nor can we go back the way we came without adding a week to our journey."

"They weren't Bardon's men," Cam said. He glanced at Rebecca who nodded her agreement. "They were paid by Jathneel."

Alaric considered. "That amounts to the same thing."

"I don't think so," Cam said. "That man you killed was their leader. He saved us a couple of times from the twins, and he said Jathneel wanted us alive."

"Have the master and the student fallen out?" Hebron asked, raising an eyebrow.

"The real question," Drakeman said, "is which one is now the master and which the student?"

"That doesn't alter the fact that we have no clear road," Slone said.

Laird poked a stick into the fire. "There is another way," he said as if reluctant to mention it. "We can go where Bardon will never expect us to go."

"No," Drakeman snapped. "I would not venture anywhere near the Braganeth."

"You mean the valley where the Bragamahr is supposed to live?" Spider said.

"The very one."

A chill swept through Cam, and he instinctively knew which direction that land lay. It had been calling to him ever since he entered the lands of the Orren.

"I thought it was a myth," Spider said with fear in his voice.

Alaric sniffed. "You and Cam seem to think every story you hear is a myth. Don't be so quick to discount the knowledge that comes to us from the past."

"Is there a safe way through?" Slone tested the sharpness of his axe on a blade of grass, which it slit cleanly down the center.

Undead

"There is no safe way through that accursed valley," Peylog said. "No traveler has passed the gates of Goldereth in over twelve hundred years and lived to tell the tale."

"I have," Alaric said.

The light of the fire flickered and danced in the deepening gloom as everyone gaped at him.

"Whatever for?" Slone slipped the little axe into its sheath.

Alaric rubbed the back of his neck. "I was searching for Cam and Hebron, but that is of no importance now. There is a way to skirt the valley, though I agree with Drakeman. We shouldn't go there unless we have no safer road."

"One other path exists." Peylog snatched up an errant twig and sketched a rough map into the dirt. "But it will lead you back to the other side of the mountains to the plain where the river you call the Afon Fathwe flows." He traced a squiggly line in the dirt.

"That will put us squarely in the path of Bardon's riders," Hebron said.

"We could avoid the river." Slone pointed to the eastern side of the mountains Peylog had drawn. "And skirt the eastern flank of the mountains."

"How far is this pass?" Alaric gestured to the gap Peylog had drawn in the mountains.

"We will reach it by midday—if the young ones don't sleep too late." Peylog smiled at Cam and Rebecca.

"Every road is dangerous," Drakeman said as he leaned back against the boulder, "but this is a much safer road than the Braganeth."

"Cam," Hebron said, "what do you think?"

The thought of going anywhere near the Bragamahr turned his blood cold. Even now, he could feel the pull of it, drawing him south. For one desperate moment, he considered riding back across the Plains of Pannon all the way to Stony Vale. What had he accomplished anyway in all these weeks of running and fighting? Still, he couldn't do it. Too many people were counting on him.

"Let's take the safer route," he said.

"I vote for the pass," Spider said, "as long as there are no tunnels. Thanks for asking."

"Tunnels?" Peylog gave him a quizzical look.

"Never mind," Hebron said. "Spider is afraid of the dark."

A Sentient Land

"I am not."

Peylog studied Spider. "Why would the dark frighten you? Darkness can do no harm. It is the creatures that inhabit the night that one should fear."

"Exactly my point," Spider said. "That nasty tunnel Alaric sent us into was filled with nasty monsters."

"You exaggerate," Hebron said, "but anyway, Rebecca, what do you think?"

Rebecca gave Hebron a startled look. "Me?"

"You're part of our company," he said. "Everyone has the right to speak, except maybe Spider, who speaks too much already." He grinned at Spider's snort of disgust.

Rebecca's face flushed. "I think we should try the safest route first if we can."

"Then it's settled," Drakeman said.

"Does everything in this desert want to make us bleed?" Spider mumbled as they trudged through the forbidding landscape.

He yanked a long spine from his leg where he had brushed a cactus. He jogged to catch up with the rear of the company as they filed over the narrow trail that wound its tortuous way amid the jagged rocks and spindly bushes. This was a wild, forlorn land with no sign of human occupation. It was rugged, and the ground lay exposed with no covering of leaves or deep rich soil. Scrubby plants and cacti sprung up from the hard-packed earth.

Deep down, this land possessed a lurking hostility. All the plants sprouted thorns of some kind. The rocks were rough and jagged. The white, pink, and dull hues of soil threw the sun right back into his face. The heat of it sucked the moisture from his body.

Even the animals were strange. Huge lizards with bright yellow or red and black stripes skittered about. He had never seen so many rattlesnakes in one place in his life. It was as if the land itself rebelled against humanity and would much prefer to kill them than to have them scuffling about on its back. The sooner they escaped this land the better. How Peylog and his people lived here, he couldn't guess.

What Peylog called a pass was nothing more than a narrow cleft in the rock, barely wide enough for the horses to squeeze through. They all had to dismount or risk having their legs become wedged between rock and horse.

"This does come out the other side, doesn't it?" Spider called out to Peylog from the rear of the line.

Peylog paused to let him catch up. "It does, but the way is steep. You will have to lead the horses."

Spider peered up the sheer rock face at the pale blue sky visible through the crack. The sun would soon reach its zenith, making the day grow miserably hot. Sweat dripped from his hair. The rock was smooth, meaning there would be no way to climb out if things went bad. Nervous anticipation tickled the back of Spider's brain. He shrugged it off. This wild land was unnerving him.

"Spider's a little sensitive about tight places," Hebron teased as Peylog led out again and Spider tugged on his horse's reins.

"Or places that want to cook me alive," Spider mumbled.

They spread out as the incline steepened so the horses would have room to lunge their way up the slippery, loose stone. Spider's little chestnut mare gave him a baleful look as if to ask why he was making her do this. Her ribs were starting to show from the hard riding and lack of proper nourishment in this wasteland.

"Sorry," Spider said and patted her on the muzzle. "I don't like it either."

Stones clattered down from above, and Spider jerked his head up. A shadow passed over them. The now-familiar creeping terror gripped his heart, and he cursed as the party paused. That peculiar sulfuric stink wafted into the narrow canyon. Draig's hackles raised, and he let out a quiet snarl.

"Not again," Spider moaned.

"Quiet," Alaric ordered. "Hebron, Peylog, come with me."

The three of them hefted their weapons and slinked off up the trail, disappearing around an outcrop. Spider caught Cam's eye, and Cam raised his eyebrows and shook his head. Cam also slipped his hand into the pouch about his neck and withdrew the amber Fire Stone Spider had returned to him. They waited in breathless silence as the horses rolled their eyes and yanked on the reins. Spider patted his mare's neck.

"Easy girl," he whispered.

A Sentient Land

Rebecca edged closer to him. "Is that a Mahrowaith?" she breathed.

"Real friendly feeling, isn't it?"

"What should I do to fight it?" she asked in a low voice.

Spider gave her grudging respect. Rebecca may have clubbed him over the head from behind, but she was no coward.

"Avoid it, if you can," Spider said. "If you can't, strike for the neck. For some reason, the armor isn't as strong there. And whatever you do, don't let any of that blood get on you."

Rebecca pinched her lips tight and nodded before peering up at the narrow gap of light above them. "This is a lonely place to die."

Spider sniffed. "We're *not* dying here—not if I have anything to say about it."

Laird gestured for them to be quiet, and Rebecca returned to her horse. Draig prowled around them moving back and forth between Cam and Rebecca. Spider's mouth had gone dry, but he couldn't risk it. He didn't want to be caught unprepared if one of those monsters decided to drop on top of them.

Scraping came from up the trail, and Slone, who was in the front, slipped his axe from its sheath. Laird drew his sword, and they stood ready. Tortuous minutes passed before Peylog appeared and gestured for them to come. Spider let out a long breath and led his horse around the outcrop to a spot where the trail widened and flattened enough for the horses to turn around.

They found Alaric and Hebron there, crouching behind some boulders.

"The pass is guarded," Peylog whispered.

"Why would anyone guard this pass?" Spider asked.

Slone clicked his tongue. "You have to ask?"

"How could they know we might come this way? No one even knows we're here, do they?"

"Lorna said the Mahrowaiths are drawn to the power of the Anarwyn," Rebecca said.

Hebron rose and stepped over to them. "We have not one, but six Mahrowaiths to deal with here, maybe more."

"We should go back then," Slone said.

Drakeman sheathed his sword and shifted his feet. "I don't like venturing into Braganeth. It's too dangerous."

Undead

"More dangerous than half a dozen Mahrowaiths?" Alaric asked.

"It might be," Drakeman said, his brow crinkling.

"I don't think we have a choice now," Slone interjected. "If there are a bunch of Mahrowaiths here, there are probably Inverni at the entrance to the pass."

"We should move before they find us," Laird said.

"Then we go back and follow the path through Goldereth?" Drakeman rubbed his chin in thought.

Everyone watched Cam, who shifted his feet before answering.

"Are we sure there is a way through?"

Apprehension churned in his friend's eyes. Cam's fear of going to this place only heightened Spider's. What greater evil could there be than the murderous Mahrowaiths? He didn't really want to find out.

Cam clutched the Fire Stone until it made his palm ache. This talk of going through Goldereth sent a shiver of cold dread rippling up his spine. Somehow he knew the Bragamahr wanted him to take that path. It had been trying to lure him that way since he had been captured.

"If we can pass Braganeth," Alaric said, "a narrow footbridge crosses the gorge on the other side of Goldereth, allowing access to the valley beyond."

Cam stiffened and realized that he was grinding his teeth. "I don't like the idea of the footbridge."

"Why?" Drakeman asked.

Scowling, Cam shook his head. "The Life Stone showed me that it wasn't safe. We could die there."

"We'll die *here* if we attempt to pass that many Mahrowaiths," Slone said.

Cam's heart sank. Slone was right. Still, the image of Hebron falling over the side of a footbridge made him sick. He had no idea where that bridge was. For all he knew, it had been in this pass, and they would escape it by turning back. What proof did he have that the one Alaric mentioned was the one the Life Stone had shone him? He was guessing.

"We need to move," Laird said more insistently, glancing up at the rocks above them.

"Are you sure there is no other path?" Cam asked Peylog.

"I know these lands," Peylog said. 'There is no other path."

"You've got three choices," Hebron said, ticking them off on his fingers as he named them. "You can go back and try to avoid Bardon's riders, delaying us another week or more. You can try to force this pass, or you can take the road through Goldereth. No path is safe for us now."

Cam vacillated. He might not be interpreting the vision from the Life Stone correctly. And he had escaped the Mahrowaith at Afon Darodel. Maybe the path through Goldereth would be the safest.

"All right," Cam said, though he fiddled with his sword belt and glowered. "I guess we go back and make for Goldereth."

A sulfuric stench wafted down the crevice. Creeping horror crawled up his legs into his gut, followed by the gripping terror. His chest constricted. He couldn't breathe.

Alaric whirled and released an arrow at a shadow on the rocks. The earth buckled under their feet. Their Horses reared. A roar of broken, tumbling stone filled the chasm above them, followed by the gut-rending shriek of a Mahrowaith. Its black shape joined the rock fall, its arms, and legs flailing. The beast landed with a sickening crunch as the boulders rumbled down to bury it in a pile of jagged rocks.

Cam struggled to control his rearing horse as stones and debris bounced down the trail toward them.

"What in the black sands just happened?" Spider shouted before coughing on the cloud of dust that filled the crevice.

No one spoke for a long moment. Cam shared a knowing glance with Rebecca. This had happened when they first entered this land.

"I guess that settles it," Slone said, covering his mouth with his sleeve as he peered at the pile of stone blocking the path they had been following.

"It did it again," Rebecca said. She spun to stare at Peylog. "The mountains did it again."

Peylog gave her a knowing smile. "I told you that the lands of the Orren know friend from foe."

"I'm not sure I'm following," Laird said while attempting to soothe his jittery horse.

"We Orren do not belong to either of the magics, and our land will not be subjected to them, least of all the Bragamahr."

Cam shivered at the sudden sense of uncleanliness that swept through him.

"Uh," Spider said, "the land couldn't possibly…." He paused and threw up his hands in surrender. "Oh, what do I know, anyway?"

"Precisely," Hebron said. "I suggest we leave—now."

They wheeled their horses around and began the tortuous descent. The creeping terror followed them, though it diminished and finally disappeared as Peylog led them south to skirt the cliffs and crags of the mountains. Cam glanced back. Why hadn't the Mahrowaiths attacked them? One clearly meant to, but the mountain had stopped it. Still, if they were close enough for them to feel their terror, more Mahrowaiths must have sensed their presence. Were they being herded like sheep toward the valley of the Braganeth?

Chapter Five
Black Sand

ZENEK PAUSED TO WIPE the sweat from his brow. He squinted up at the piercing light of the westering sun as it plunged beneath the crest of the mountain. The pines had fallen away hours ago. The mountain top was nothing but bare, black rock with the occasional stubby shrub, a splash of yellow lichen, or bit of stiff grass. A warm wind whipped up the sulfuric stink of the valley beyond. Far below to his right on the wide plateau sprawled the ruins of the Tathanar city of Mendefra.

Built on the foundations of the great Tamil city of Jandal, Mendefra stood as one more witness of the brutality and arrogance of the Tathanar and their Anar allies. In their panic to wipe the earth clean of the memory of the Bragamahr, they slaughtered eight thousand men, women, and children on that high plateau for the crime of being Tamil. Then they dismantled the city and erected the monstrosity slouching on the sacred landscape, empty and silent, finally cleansed of their contamination.

Zenek spat in the dust. His mother had recounted the tale on long winter nights in their hut on the far northern borders of the Silver Wood. She had shown him the beautiful garnet jewel, handed down from parent to child for more than twelve hundred years. She caused the stone to glow, lighting their hut with a crimson light that sparkled in her eyes as she whispered the forbidden knowledge. She taught him to quiet his mind and reach out to the latent power of the stone.

"You are a child of the Bragamahr," she had said. "The last prince of the Tamil. Our people have been driven into hiding, and still, we keep the memory alive for the day when we might return to the sacred valley and awaken the Bragamahr once again."

When he asked her about Bardon, she had said, "He is a meddler. But he may be the key that allows us to step into the light and assume our place as the rulers of the land that our fathers governed. We will need to watch and wait. When the servants of the Bragamahr return, we will know that it is time."

The Mahrowaiths *had* returned, but he had not been able to save them from Hebron's sword. All the way down the river, he pondered what to do about that weapon. He had succeeded in using Bardon's riders to get Cam killed and so eliminate one of the threats to the resurgence of the Bragamahr.

Still, he couldn't live long in the valley of the Braganeth. The land was too harsh and forbidding. He didn't know what he would find beyond the jagged hills or even if the Bragamahr would recognize him and accept him. Perhaps, he should flee south and join Bardon.

Zenek hesitated with indecision. Fear of being rejected by the Bragamahr almost caused him to retreat down the mountainside—until he remembered his mother's face with the red light of the garnet flashing in her eyes.

She and the rest of the Tamil died not long after she showed him the jewel during the bitter intervillage warfare that sometimes flared on the northernmost reaches of the Tathanar kingdom. Zenek had traveled to Abilene and become a Tathanar warrior, biding his time. He never forgot his roots, nor his destiny. Now that the servants of the Bragamahr stalked the land again, his time had come.

Zenek wiped at the sweat. He would risk it all in this valley. If the Bragamahr rejected him, it didn't matter where he went or what he did. He would have failed his mother and all those who came before him.

Taking a deep breath, Zenek continued the long, tortuous climb over the sharp, porous rock. Beyond that jagged peak, glistening black in the waning light, lay his destiny. He would seize it or die trying.

Black Sand

Lorna sagged in the saddle as her weary horse plodded through the gates of Najera under the glare of the midday sun. The exhaustion penetrated so deep not even the use of the agate could dispel it. She left the other horses behind on the plain, lame or dying, having run without ceasing for days. Her tunic and trousers were covered in soot and dust, and she could only imagine what her face and hair looked like. Now was not the time to worry about appearances. Too much was at stake. She wound her way through the crowded streets, earning the occasional glare of annoyance or stare of curiosity.

Najera was a comfortable city with a clear stream flowing through the town, tumbling down from the snowy peaks of the Heldrun Mountains. The stream wriggled its way under the city walls and across the fertile plain that was crisscrossed with low stone walls and rolling fields all the way to the wide slow waters of the Willow River. The Rahil of the East Mark had not suffered as much in the civil wars following Bardon's betrayal. Bardon took little interest in them because the blood of the descendants of the Anarwyn flowed weakly in their veins.

The Rahil migrated off the vast eastern plains that stretched beyond the knowledge of any living in Anwyn during the prosperity of the Third Age when Goldereth was at the height of its power. They were a people apart—and, by choice, kept apart—from the other kingdoms, except to trade their fine silks.

Lorna stilled the upwelling of anger as she remembered how King Wilahi of the Rahil had arrogantly refused to send aid to her father, his liege lord. Instead, he had withdrawn across the Willow River and let the North Mark rip itself apart. King Trahern was his grandson who maintained his own grudge against Lorna, so she entertained no expectations of a welcome reception. Still, she had to try. If they would listen to anyone, it would be her.

Najera enjoyed a happy location, nestled between the spurs of two high mountains above the plain with solid walls of rock protecting its flanks and a rugged pass behind it. The road wound upward through a series of guarded towers. Noisy, jostling people hawking their wares filled the lower levels. Though a fresh breeze whispered down from the mountains, the streets still exuded that peculiar, spicy smell from the blood sausage and blood pudding so prized among the Rahil.

Round, buxom women, sporting brightly colored silk blouses and trousers or ankle-length skirts, elbowed their way through the streets. More than one cast her a wary glance with their clear blue, gray, or hazel eyes. The men tended toward stoutness with short, scruffy beards that would make an Inverni blush with shame. Most of them had red or blonde hair with a few sandy-brown heads added to the mix.

Lorna paused before the narrow gate that led into the palace complex near the center of the city. A guard stepped out from his position in the shadow of the portcullis to peer up at her. He wore a purple cloak with a silver clasp over his leather brigandine but was otherwise unremarkable.

"I must speak with King Trahern urgently," she said.

The guard studied her, taking in her grimy, disheveled appearance. "And who are you to demand such an audience?"

"I am Lorna Carnawyth, Crown Princess of the North Mark, and Grand Mistress of the Varaná. Please escort me to the King immediately."

The man's eyes widened, and he glanced behind her as if expecting to find an escort. When he perceived that she was alone, he said, "Just a moment," and spun away with a creak of his leather armor. He returned with an officer who wore a bright red cloak over his right shoulder clasped with a golden broach of a galloping horse. Lorna considered using the Anarwyn to encourage them to hurry but decided against it. The King wouldn't like it if he found out she used the power of the Anarwyn in his realm, and she was too tired in any case.

"Greetings, My Lady," the officer said with a bow of his head. "May I inform the King of the nature of your business?"

Lorna unbuckled her saddlebag and withdrew the bloodied and torn pennant with the black rearing horse on a blue field and held it up for them to see. "The King's patrol has been massacred. I must speak with him at once."

"Yes, My Lady," the officer said without showing any visible reaction to the bloody pennant. He nodded to the guards who had followed him. "I'll take you to him."

The guards formed a circle around her, their spears glinting in the afternoon sun. They were there to protect the King from her, and she couldn't blame them for being cautious. They had even less experience with the Anarwyn than most people and were deeply suspicious of it.

The palace garden and buildings were less sophisticated than Abilene's. The architecture possessed a wild, free aspect with its flowing script carved into the walls for decoration, high arches, and plaster facades depicting scenes of great hunts on the plains.

When they entered a square courtyard with a gurgling fountain spewing from a horse's mouth, Lorna dismounted and handed the reins to a stable hand. "Please brush the horse well and give it an extra helping of grain," she said as she retrieved her saddlebags and flung them over her shoulder. "The poor animal has earned it."

Lorna followed the guard into the cool shadows of a hallway and waited outside the door while the guard introduced her. She slapped at the dust on her tunic and tugged at the muddy wrinkles. She must be a sight. Threading her fingers through her hair, she plucked at the snarls and errant twigs. The guard reappeared and waved her in.

The chamber was comfortably furnished with silk-lined chairs and couches and a game table off to the side. Despite the warm spring day, a fire crackled in the marble fireplace. King Trahern reclined on a long red couch, propped up on purple cushions. He had been a vigorous, handsome man in his early forties when she had last seen him. Now, he was old and feeble, with long, white hair as fine as silk draped over a gaunt cheek. He was wrapped in a purple robe and wore purple slippers.

The King rose up on an elbow with a cry of surprise. His eyes widened, and a snarl curled on his lips. Before he could say anything, his son, Gareth, jumped to his feet, took her hand in his, and kissed it. "You are most welcome, My Lady."

The young woman in her started at his commanding presence. He must be in his thirties now, and he possessed a physique that would have sent many a woman into a twitter. The gray eyes, framed by a shock of light brown hair, seemed to see her very soul.

"Don't get ahead of yourself, son," King Trahern mumbled from his couch.

Lorna glanced around Gareth's shoulder to see the King's eyes narrowed in dislike. Gareth's face flushed, and he gave her a little shrug of apology before backing away so Lorna could approach the King.

Undead

She bowed low. "Your Majesty, I apologize for coming to you in this state. I have a most urgent message."

Gareth gestured to a vacant chair at the table. "May we get you some refreshment, My Lady?"

"Yes, thank you," Lorna replied. Anything would be better than the old penemel and pilchard she had been eating for days.

Gareth waved to a servant, and Lorna settled into the chair. King Trahern kept his watery gaze on her.

"I swore never to let one of you Varaná sully my hall again," Trahern said. His voice was still strong and deep despite his age. He eyed her warily. "You haven't aged a day. Are you using that villainous magic to seduce us?"

"No," Lorna said. There was no point arguing with the man.

"Speak quickly before I have you thrown out."

"Father," Gareth protested, "she is our guest."

"I see she's turned your head already."

Gareth scowled. "Please, Father."

Lorna held up the bloody pennant, deciding to get straight to the point. "Your patrol was destroyed by Bardon's beasts, which are called Mahrowaiths. Bardon has attacked the keep at Brynach and is preparing for war on your borders. I come to warn you and to beg your assistance."

"Beg?" Trahern snapped. His wrinkled face contorted in rage, and one lip lifted in a sneer. "Beg? I seem to remember a young King begging you for help, and what did I get?"

Lorna knew exactly what the King was referring to. She had visited Najera a few decades ago in search of a renegade Varaná when the Queen entered a difficult labor with her second child. By the time Lorna arrived, the Queen and her baby were dying. There was nothing she could have done, but the grieving King could not accept that.

"I gave the Queen all the aid I could," Lorna said. "Even the Anarwyn cannot reverse death when it has claimed its victims."

The servant arrived with a goblet of wine and a tray of cheese and bread. Gratefully, Lorna ate and drank while King Trahern glowered at her.

"Has Bardon attacked the Dinera?" Gareth asked when she had finished.

"Not yet. He was more intent on Brynach." Lorna set the goblet on the tray.

"Why?"

Lorna dusted the crumbs from her lap. "The archive and treasury of Brynach contain objects of power and knowledge that Bardon wanted desperately."

"Did Brynach fall, then?" Gareth asked.

"No. It has been sealed from Bardon's reach until it is safe to restore it."

"Sealed?" Gareth gave a confused scowl.

Lorna waved an impatient hand at him. They didn't need to understand this. Time was too pressing to explain Bardon's motives, which she only partly understood anyway. "You must summon your vassals and go to the aid of the other marks, or all is lost."

Trahern snorted. "The other marks have no desire to receive my aid, and I have no desire to give it. Let them fend for themselves."

The old fool is just like his grandfather, Lorna thought, keeping her hands carefully folded in her lap.

"Father," Gareth interjected, "this is the third patrol we have lost to these beasts. We must do something."

"Your forests and mountains will not protect you forever," Lorna said. "Your day of reckoning will come, sooner or later."

After a moment's silence, Trahern spoke in a hushed, yet determined, voice.

"I will do what I must to protect *my* people. But I will not help the other marks, nor will I serve the Varaná who have betrayed me."

"How long do you think—" Lorna began to protest.

Trahern cut her off. "I have spoken my mind, and nothing you can say will change it." He gave a dismissive flip of his hand. "Gareth, see to her comfort. I suppose even a lying Varaná deserves the honor of my hospitality." He pointed a crooked finger at Lorna and added, "But I expect you to be gone from my city before I awaken."

With that, he closed his eyes and instantly started snoring.

Gareth and Lorna exchanged glances. The King had clearly dismissed her. She rose with Gareth, who was blushing furiously, and followed him out of the room.

"I apologize for his behavior," he said, closing the door behind them. "I've been trying to convince him ever since these monsters came slinking around to send messengers to Abilene and the other marks, but he will not hear of it."

"There really was nothing I could do for your mother," Lorna said. She wanted someone in the royal family to understand.

"I know. He's so used to being obeyed that he couldn't forgive you."

Lorna nodded, grateful for his understanding. "Is there nothing you can do to help the other marks?"

Gareth gave a sidelong glance. "Perhaps," he said, "but you should rest first." He led her into her rooms, where a maidservant scurried about, readying a bath. "I will call you if anything changes."

"Thank you," Lorna said. She considered roaming about the palace a bit to see if she could learn anything useful. However, after she had bathed and wrapped herself in a clean, silk evening dress, she was far too exhausted. She collapsed onto the bed strewn with herbs and snuggled into the down-filled mattress, breathing in the fragrance of lavender.

A pounding on her door awakened her as the gray light of the coming dawn slipped in through the open window. Her momentary disorientation gave way to the realization that she had slept the afternoon and night away.

She dressed in her freshly laundered tunic and trousers that some servant must have brought in mere moments before and said, "Come."

A soldier of the King's personal guard wearing the blue surcoat with the golden crown in the center stepped in and bowed. "Please come with me at once, My Lady. King Trahern commands your presence."

Lorna raised an eyebrow, wondering what was afoot. She picked up the bloodied pennant and followed the guard, still arranging her attire and combing her fingers through her hair. The King's Privy Council had been hastily summoned. Nobles filed into the throne room in various stages of undress. The old King occupied the head of a long wooden table with Gareth seated on his right. A great number of lords were there. Perhaps she could find the opportunity to redirect the discussion to the question of supporting the other marks against Bardon.

When they were seated, the King's chamberlain called the Council to order by pounding his wooden staff against the marble floor.

Black Sand

"Gentlemen," King Trahern said, "I apologize for disturbing you so early, but we have a pressing matter that requires immediate attention." He paused. "William, will you kindly tell them what you told me?" The King gestured to a smallish man with a soiled bandage on his head and black soot on his sweat-streaked face.

The man's chubby hands lay on the wooden table, and he clasped and unclasped them with nervous energy. His eyes were wide, and his voice shook as he spoke.

"They came out of nowhere," he began. "Yesterday morning, a horde of Inverni swooped down on the villages along the edge of the Crimson Plain. Then they sacked Mairrit and burned it to the ground."

An angry mumble circled the table. It quieted as William continued.

"They left no one alive. They even slaughtered the women and children." An involuntary sob escaped his lips. "Oh, I can still see it. They burned everything. Killed everyone. It's gone. They're gone. It was horrible, just horrible." With that, he covered his face with his hands and sobbed.

Voices erupted in fury and would not be quieted until Gareth pounded the table.

"Gentlemen," the King said, "you do not know everything yet. Please hold your discussion until you do."

He motioned for Lorna to come forward.

Trahern sneered. "I believe most of you remember Lorna Carnawyth, the Varaná. She arrived with news yesterday."

All heads turned toward her, and she noted the guarded interest in some, the open anger and fear in others, while yet others gave her the calculated wanton inspection she used to get when she was younger. A momentary temptation to cow them all with the power of the Anarwyn swept through her, but she mastered it. She needed friends, not enemies.

Lorna related the attack on Brynach, the Mahrowaiths, their pursuit of the heirs of Anarwyn, and their destruction of the King's patrol. She held out the bloody pennant and dropped it on the table. "This is what Bardon brings you," she said. "Bloodshed and destruction."

"He is not so strong nor the Inverni so numerous," one of the lords said.

Undead

Lorna shook her head wearily. "You are sorely misinformed on both accounts. The only chance you have against Bardon is to unite with the other marks under the leadership of the Undead King."

Laughter erupted in the hall, echoing off the walls.

"You expect us to believe in Varaná fables?" someone shouted. "Are we to follow a statue?"

Lorna stood rigid until the jeering subsided. "I have sent an embassy to release him."

Stunned silence greeted her words. She continued, "You would do well to heed my warning. Your mountains will provide no refuge once Bardon has seized the other marks. He will come for you and he will use the power of the Bragamahr to beat down your walls and blast your towers to rubble."

Now the room exploded into a cacophony of voices that reverberated amid the vaulted ceiling, making it impossible to distinguish a single word.

"Enough!" King Trahern shouted while his crier pounded the floor with his staff. When they had quieted Trahern leaned forward, resting one hand on the arm of his throne. "We're not here to discuss the other marks, you slippery-tongued Varaná," he snapped. "Sit down, and don't speak again until I give you leave."

Lorna remained standing, her jaw working as she struggled to control the fury boiling in her chest. This man was more than an old fool. He was a *dangerous* old fool. Slowly, she settled into a chair.

"Gentlemen," the King continued, "the question is what do *we* do?"

One nobleman with graying temples rose to his feet. He radiated the confident bearing of a seasoned warrior, and his clothes and hair were immaculate.

"Roderick," the King said in acknowledgment.

"Your Majesty," Roderick said, "if what her Ladyship tells us is true, we are not simply dealing with another band of Bardon's raiders. They must be part of the army he sent to destroy Brynach—an army that has come from an embarrassing defeat and is now bent on plunder. My Lord, it is my opinion that anything less than a general mobilization would be unwise and perhaps suicidal."

Several men called out, "Here, here," and slapped the table.

"Your Majesty," another man rose, giving a condescending smirk to the one who had finished speaking. He wore long gray robes and tied his hair back with a piece of leather. His hooked nose drew one's gaze to his narrow-set eyes.

"Yes, Sarruge."

"What evidence do we have of this supposed threat save the word of this Varaná who has already once betrayed us?" Sarruge gestured to William. "How do we know she hasn't bewitched this man to weave this sad tale? A general mobilization would be expensive and to no purpose."

Nearly half of the men present grunted their assent and slapped the table with their hands. The rest held either decidedly neutral faces or were clearly in opposition to the honey-voiced man.

"You weren't there," William sobbed. "You didn't see it. Your wife and children yet live."

William's words left a palpable silence in the room. There were obviously two factions in the King's Council, each led by these two men.

"Escort him out," King Trahern ordered the guard and waited while they helped the sobbing William from his chair and half dragged him from the hall.

"My Liege," Roderick said, "as captain-general of Your Majesty's armies, I beg you to carefully consider your response to this question. We cannot allow a large and belligerent army to roam our borders, slaughtering our people at will. And if the Undead King magically arises, we should be ready to support him."

"There is no Undead King," the Sarruge growled.

"Says the man who secretly corresponds with Bardon," Roderick snapped.

A deadly hush settled over the chamber as the men glowered at each other.

"Enough," King Trahern said. He swiveled his gaze between them. "I care nothing for this Undead King or for the North Mark."

Lorna stiffened at the King's words, and Sarruge sneered at Roderick.

"However," the King continued, "we do not have time for a general mobilization if there is an army raiding our borders." He glanced at Sarruge. "Perhaps we can compromise. I will send the home guard to check on the situation and ascertain the facts. In the meantime, we will warn my vassals to prepare for a possible campaign and call up the reserve levies, should they be needed. In this way, we may meet any immediate threat and still prepare if the danger is greater than we anticipate."

After the orders were issued and sealed, the meeting was adjourned. The men left, carrying on whispered conversations. As Lorna rose to return to her quarters, Gareth came to her side and seized her elbow, guiding her toward the opposite door.

"Walk with me," he whispered and released her elbow as she strode beside him into one of the corridors.

"That went better than I feared," Gareth said quietly. "But you can see that we have an uphill battle to fight."

"Indeed," Lorna replied. "Who is this Sarruge?" She indicated with her chin to the man who had spoken against the general mobilization.

"The Earl of Keir. He is one of the most powerful men in the kingdom and one to be feared."

"I gathered that." They stepped through the door and angled down a narrow hallway. "Where are we going?"

"To another meeting. This one is private."

Gareth led Lorna along the gray stone corridors, up several flights of stairs to an upper level of the palace, and escorted her into a small sitting room. Several men were already present, including, Roderick, the King's captain-general. Most of them had attended the Privy Council.

They waited in silence for some time until a young knight arrived, closed the door, and stood in front of it with his arms folded across his chest.

Gareth began without any ceremony. "What are we to do, my friends? The moment we have long feared has arrived."

Roderick spoke first. "I'll command the home guard. The reserve levies should be ready within a week. That would give us six or seven thousand men. Once we have secured our borders, if the Undead King has arisen, I can march to his aid."

Several of the men shifted their feet and averted their gazes.

"That would mean direct disobedience to the King's orders, Roderick," one of them objected. "Do you think the men would follow you?"

"I'm aware of the risk," Roderick replied coldly. "And yes, the home guard will follow me. I can't speak for the reserves."

Black Sand

"Is there nothing that will convince the King to change his mind?" another young man asked.

"Nothing short of bringing my father's first wife back to life," Gareth muttered.

"What's that?" the young man asked.

"No, nothing," Gareth said.

The others looked at one another and shook their heads.

"We've tried every argument and artifice we know," Gareth said. "Aside from treason, there seems to be little we can do."

"What would happen if an . . . uh . . . accident occurred to Sarruge?" a burly brown-headed man with intense gray eyes asked.

The men shifted nervously.

"You're speaking of murder, Prian," one of them said.

"No," Prian said, gaining fervor as he spoke, "I'm speaking of the execution of a traitor."

A young man with an uncanny resemblance to Roderick spoke. The firelight twinkled in his brown eyes and glinted dully off his long brown hair. "We know that Sarruge carries on a secret correspondence with Bardon. But the King refuses to see it."

"Exactly, Connac," the gray-eyed man retorted. "So why not seize the opportunity and get rid of him while we still have time before he springs whatever trap he's been preparing?"

The others remained silent until Gareth spoke.

"Prian," he said, "until Sarruge has openly defied the laws, any move we make against him would be perceived as treason on our part."

Prian grunted his disapproval.

Gareth continued. "I'll not permit Roderick to shoulder all the responsibility. I will take the field with him. When the time is right, we may have to defy my father and go to the aid of the North and West Marks."

The others glanced at each other uncomfortably.

"I will personally ask the lords we can trust to prepare their vassals," Gareth continued. "That will provide a few thousand more men that could be ready at a moment's notice." He turned to Lorna. "You said you've sent an embassy to release Maelorn. How will this be accomplished after all these years?"

Lorna extended her hand in a gesture of surrender. "I cannot give you details, but you must prepare."

Undead

"You see what we are risking," one of the men said. "Surely you can—"

"I can't," she interrupted. "Lives other than yours are at stake. You will have to trust me."

The silent, sullen glowers she received proved that trust was one thing these men did not give freely. She would have to earn it.

Peylog roused the company long before dawn. The stars sparkled in the inky-black sky. "Better to travel while it is cool and sleep while it is hot," he said.

Cam rubbed the sleep from his eyes and stretched. Peylog had a point, but he would have liked a few more hours.

When Cam stepped to saddle the horses, Peylog gestured for him to leave them. "They cannot survive where we are going."

"That makes me feel real comfortable," Spider said, jamming his blanket into his pack.

"So, we're just going to leave them?" Cam asked.

"They know how to find their way back to the prairie," Peylog said.

Cam patted his horse and ran a hand over her muzzle. "Thanks," he said. "Try to stay alive."

They packed what they could carry and set out winding southward through the scrub and rock, hugging the edges of the mountains. Everything in this wasteland was armed to kill or to at least cause pain. The rocks were sharp, and every shrub or scraggly tree bristled with thorns. Red and orange dust kicked up as they traveled, parching Cam's throat. Colored lizards and snakes scurried or slithered away from them. Draig had a fit when an obstinate rattlesnake attempted to hold the narrow game trail against them.

Peylog let Draig distract the rattlesnake while he slipped behind it and tossed a rock onto its head. The rattling ceased, and the snake curled and writhed around the stone that pinned it to the ground. Draig attempted to approach the snake, but Peylog jumped in front of him and, with one deft slice of his knife, cut off the head before tossing it far up into the rocks.

"A dead rattler can kill as easily as a live one." He slung the snake's headless body over his shoulder, letting the blood drip down his back. He continued as if nothing unusual had happened.

Spider stepped up to Cam. "Why does he scare me?"

Cam slipped his thumbs under the straps of his pack to ease their pinching of his armpits. "Because without him we'd be dead." And it was true. Peylog had saved Cam's life several times now.

"Do you think there are many of the Orren?" Spider asked.

"No idea, but if they're all as tough as Peylog, I wouldn't mind having an army of them at my back."

Cam tried to ignore the constant lure of the two magics. The farther south they traveled, the more he became aware of the Bragamahr and the more he wrestled with the hostility of this land. It would have been nice to forget for a little while that he was struggling toward his own death.

When the sun was burning down upon them with a special vengeance, Peylog led them up into the tumble of boulders where another wide pool of water settled into a natural cavity in the rock.

Draig wandered off to hunt while they settled down into the shade and shared around the strips of rattlesnake flesh that Peylog cooked for them. Rebecca nibbled at it.

"Don't you like it?" Slone asked.

"I've had better," Rebecca said with a guilty glance at Peylog.

"It will keep you alive," Peylog said.

Wrinkling his nose, Spider said, "I get that, but I feel like I'm eating a starved whitefish. It's all sinewy and full of tiny bones." He picked a bone out of his mouth. "I say we try for a lizard next time."

Cam had to agree. The meat itself was bland, and the texture was not pleasing.

Peylog cast an annoyed glance at the older men. "You have pampered them."

Hebron guffawed, and Alaric and Slone chuckled. Laird held up his hands in surrender. "Don't blame me. They were already like this when I met them."

Drakeman slipped a piece of steaming snake meat into his mouth. "It's nothing a little Galentyne sauce couldn't cure."

"Some what?" Cam asked. He swallowed his last piece of rattlesnake flesh and followed it up with some salt pilchard to help it go down.

"It's a wine and vinegar sauce with cinnamon and ginger that we use on fish," Drakeman explained.

Peylog clicked his tongue and set about roasting some long roots amid the coals of the fire. "You can keep your nasty sauces. I eat what food the Mother provides and do not complain."

They all stopped laughing, and an awkward silence settled over them. They had offended Peylog.

"We're sorry," Hebron said. "You're right. We are grateful."

Cam opened his mouth to apologize when Draig clambered over the rocks to sit beside him. His snout was covered in blood and rabbit fur.

Peylog glanced at him. "The wolf knows how to eat."

Rebecca gave Peylog a sad frown. Cam knew that she cared for Peylog as much as he did and didn't like the idea that they had hurt his feelings. "I remember Master Gari teaching me a story about a snake," Rebecca said. Peylog was still scowling, and Rebecca rushed on with her tale. "In a village outside of Reshad, a child was sleeping in a basket on the edge of the field when a huge rattlesnake climbed onto the child's belly and dropped a stone."

Peylog shifted to study her with interest as he chewed another mouthful of the rattlesnake.

"The child grabbed the stone and wouldn't let go. Her face started glowing with a bright clear light. The stone was a huge transparent sapphire the size of a robin's egg. At first, the parents were terrified, but they saw the snake had revealed their child as an heir of Ilsie. So, they kept the snake and fed it in gratitude for the gift."

"Sounds like a stupid idea," Spider mumbled.

Rebecca waved him away and continued. "When the child was fifteen years old, the beasts of the Bragamahr destroyed the four cities of the Tathanar, but the girl saved her family and the snake by using the sapphire. When Galad heard of her, he sought her out and found her hiding on an island in the Brunen River. Together, they founded the Order of the Varaná and destroyed the Mahrowaiths. The girl collected all the talismans of the Bragamahr, carried them to the Braganeth to destroy them, but she never returned. When the other Varaná searched for her, all they found was a glittering sapphire clamped in the jaws of a dead rattlesnake."

Peylog wiped the grease from his mouth. "We know this tale. It was the Orren who led them to the snake and the stone." He slipped a root from the coals and peeled it open. He handed it around and everyone tried it, but without any more jokes.

"I've seen a sapphire that size," Cam said. "In Lorna's pendant."

Rebecca's eyes widened. "I didn't think of that." She gaped at Drakeman. "Do you think it's the same one?"

Drakeman shrugged. "Could be. Lorna taught me the pendant belonged to the head of the Order."

"The island must have been Brynach, then," Alaric said.

"I believe it was." Drakeman tried the root and smiled. "It's sweet."

"Peylog," Laird said, "do you know where the Orren found the sapphire?"

"My people speak of a great eruption in the valley that shook the hills. Fearing some new power of the Bragamahr, two hunters searched until they found a great chasm. On the lip, they found a rattlesnake four paces long coiled up with the sapphire clamped in its jaws. Its eyes had burned away, and it was dead. When the Varaná came searching for their mistress, they led them to the place."

Drakeman studied Peylog with renewed interest. "Peylog," he said, "I invite you to come to Abilene so you can teach the lore masters the knowledge the Orren have preserved."

Peylog scratched his arm. "We are a lonely people with long memories."

Cam glanced at Rebecca and smiled in gratitude. He understood what she had done. By telling her story, she deflected Peylog's attention away from his hurt feelings, and now Drakeman had complimented him. It was skillfully done.

She grinned back at him, and the company settled in to catch what sleep they could before starting their nighttime march. Cam curled up in the shade of a boulder and closed his eyes, but he couldn't sleep. The closer they came to the Braganeth, the more the black scabs on his knuckles and forehead burned and itched. He wriggled and flopped, trying to force away the growing sense of doom until he gave up and rose to a sitting position. Spider was reclining against a boulder nibbling some penemel and watching him. He crawled over to plop down beside Cam.

"What's got your tail in a knot?" Spider said.

Cam smirked and reached out to scratch Draig behind the ear, seeking some comfort in the wolf's strength and confidence.

Undead

"I can feel them," Cam said.

"The magics?"

Cam nodded. "It's like there's a war going on inside me, and I don't know how to stop it."

"We could cut that black sand out," Spider suggested.

Cam raised his hand and traced a finger over the scars on his knuckles. The idea was tempting, though he knew he couldn't. "I would, but Lorna said I have to be able to use both powers if I'm going to break the spell." He frowned. "I have to keep them."

Spider took another bite. "It's in *your* body," he mumbled around a mouth of penemel.

"It knows I'm coming," Cam said. "Whatever is in that valley knows."

Spider scowled. "I think you should tell Hebron and Alaric."

Cam glanced at the sleeping men. "They know."

"If it's any consolation," Spider said, leaning in close to whisper, "I think Laird can also use the Anarwyn."

"Agreed," Cam said.

Spider drew back in surprise that his statement didn't elicit more of a response.

"He healed Rebecca and me," Cam said, "but he didn't want us to say anything."

"There's more," Spider whispered. "When we were attacked by the Mahrowaith at the great bend of the river, I swear I saw some kind of greenish light surrounding him and Draig. The Mahrowaith galloped right past them as if they weren't there."

"You think he's more than a healer?"

Spider shrugged. "I don't know. I've seen him stuffing a stone into one of his pouches, and I know he healed Draig. That wolf was as good as dead."

"Why do you think he doesn't want anyone to know?"

"He said Bardon came after him," Spider scratched behind his ear, "and I think he meant he was trying to kill him. I'm sure his family died in an attack, and he has never gone back to the South Mark."

Cam studied Laird's sleeping form. What could this mean? How many more heirs were out there hiding?

Spider adjusted his seat. "One thing I know for sure is that I'm not eating any more snakes." He rose and dusted himself off. "I'm gonna set some snares."

Cam considered joining him, but he was so tired. The constant wrestling with the hostile land and the two magics demanding his attention had worn him down. How long could he live split between two competing powers before one or the other devoured him?

Zenek paused at the crest of the hill as the valley of Braganeth expanded before him. He paused to survey the scene in awe. The tortured landscape possessed a rugged, wild beauty. The encircling teeth of mountains glittered in the slanting evening light. Glistening sand stretched from the base of the mountains into the dense mist that hugged the center of the valley.

Rolling crags of black basalt peeked through the mist. Zenek sucked in his breath in wonder at the beautiful sight, and the sudden impression that the eyes of some great power rested upon him.

"I have returned," he whispered to the warm wind that did nothing to cool the sweat on his brow.

Come. A deep resonant voice echoed in his head, and a thrill of anticipation swept through him. Was this the voice of the Bragamahr? Had his master deigned to speak to him already?

Scrambling in nervous anticipation, Zenek slipped and skidded down the slope through the broken stone. His heart pounded in his ears, and he nearly fell in his haste. Forcing himself to calm down, he descended more slowly, more deliberately. There was no rush. A few more hours were nothing to the years he had waited for this moment.

Nightfall found him encamped in a cleft of the rock where he enjoyed a clear view of the rolling mist that churned with an orange-yellow glow. The black sand glistened in the light of his feeble fire. Checking to make sure his tools were ready, he positioned himself so the light shone brightly on his left forearm, which he had bared to the elbow. His knife lay beside him and next to that lay a pile of fine black sand he had collected from the valley. Using a piece of charcoal, he traced the shape of a twelve-pointed star on his flesh. When he was satisfied that it looked right, he unsheathed his knife and held it poised above the design.

This was the moment of real decision. There could be no turning back. He either gave himself wholly to the Bragamahr or he did not. Pinching his lips against the stab of pain, he plunged the tip into his arm.

Blood welled up around the silver blade as he carved the pattern into his flesh. The first sting of the blade was the worst. He forced himself to continue as the upwelling of blood spread over his arm to drip onto the solid, black basalt.

He worked until he had a bloody twelve-pointed star cut into his forearm. Then he grabbed a handful of sand and rubbed it into the wound. The sharp edges of the sand burned and abraded the cut, but he refused to cry out. He worked the sand in, careful to make sure the shape of the star was completely black. A groan escaped him, and he lay back and whispered the words his mother taught him. "Dewder ereem. Ewllys edominud." Then he repeated them in the common tongue. "Courage to power. Will to dominate."

A wave of energy slammed into him, followed by a rushing wind that cast up a cloud of black sand, billowing and churning, bringing with it a sulfuric stink. The sand coiled and condensed, taking the form of a man with high cheekbones and broad shoulders. He was a man with a commanding presence and stern face. Zenek's limbs trembled.

What will you sacrifice for this gift? the Bragamahr demanded.

"All that I am and have," Zenek whispered, overcome by the Bragamahr's dreadful presence.

Would that you were more, the Bragamahr said, and Zenek experienced a sinking feeling. Perhaps he had been too rash in seeking out the Bragamahr. Would the magic deem him unworthy even after all he had suffered and sacrificed to come here?

I will take these, the Bragamahr continued, and Zenek shuddered at his touch. Several of the precious memories of his mother faded to mere shadows hovering just beyond his ability to recall.

Now, I accept you, heir of Dengra, child of the Tamil. The last of a noble line.

"And I you," Zenek murmured.

The rush of elation brought a surge of tears to his eyes. He had fulfilled his mother's dying wish at last. Now, he was the true prince of the Tamil. And yet, to become such, he had sold his freedom to a creature of magic that might never be satisfied—that deemed him unworthy.

Black Sand

"How may I serve?" he whispered. He would prove that he was more capable and dangerous than the Bragamahr believed him to be.

A broad grin spread over the face of the Bragamahr. "One approaches who bears the black sand. He must be forced to accept us or perish."

"I understand," Zenek said. His voice was thick with awe. "I will not fail you."

Chapter Six
Poisoned Touch

"I TELL YOU," Lorna said to King Trahern, "you are wasting time."

"I'll remind you that you do not rule in this kingdom," King Trahern spat.

She shuffled along beside the old King through his enclosed gardens. Gareth held his elbow to support him as they wandered. This was her last chance. There had to be something she could say to convince him to act.

The garden stretched between two towers and was flanked by colonnaded walkways. It was too early in the season for flowers, but the garden enjoyed that rich fragrance of life that comes from tilled earth and a manicured garden. Balconies overlooked the maze of exotic trees and shrubs, many of which were carried in from the wide plains to the east in remembrance of the Rahil's homeland.

"You must go to their aid," Lorna insisted. "Don't let your anger with me cause you to make an error in judgment."

Trahern rounded on Lorna, his face red and his eyes flashing. "Do not lecture me."

Lorna clasped her hands, trying to keep her frustration from showing. She peered up into King Trahern's scowling face. How could she convince him that the only wise course of action was to raise his armies and march out onto the plain?

"The North Mark is no more," Trahern snarled. "Our alliance

ended long ago. Get out and leave me to govern as I see fit without your fairy tales and interference."

Lorna opened her mouth to reply when an overwhelming sense of danger swept over her. She instinctively stepped back from him, thinking he might attack her in his madness. Something buzzed past her face, and she ducked. A hollow thwack sounded, and Gareth reeled with a cry. He fell backward clutching at his shoulder where a dark-feathered shaft protruded. Another arrow zipped past Lorna's head as she whirled to grab the King. She dragged him down behind a shrub. He grunted as a third arrow pierced his thigh.

Reaching for the ruby, Lorna cast up a shimmering red shield just as a fourth arrow would have punched into the King's chest. Instead, it slammed into the shield and erupted into flames. She swung around, maintaining the protective shield, searching for the assassin or assassins. That first arrow had been intended for her. She was sure of it.

"Guards!" Gareth shouted. He staggered to his feet, clutching the feathered shaft, blood dripping from between his fingers. "Guards!"

The slap of booted feet approached, followed by cries of dismay, and shouts of "Assassins! Assassins!" raised throughout the palace.

"There," Gareth pointed with a bloody hand to an upper balcony. The slap of booted feet smacked against stone as guards raced to catch the assassins.

Lorna activated the agate and bent to assist the King, whose face had gone as white as chalk. The shaft had buried itself deep into Trahern's right thigh, and his trousers were soaked with blood. Lorna sought the pressure points to try to stop the flow and sent the healing power of the agate into the wound, suppressing the momentary twinge of guilt at touching a sovereign King without his express permission. The arrow would have to be extracted, but she had to save his life before he bled to death.

Gareth knelt beside them. "Father," he said through a grimace, "Father, are you all right?"

The old man opened his eyes and peered into his son's face.

"I've had worse," he managed. "But I was younger then."

Roderick raced up to them, shoving his way through the crowd with Sarruge and the surgeon fast on his heels. He paused with wide, frightened eyes at the sight of the shimmering red shield, and Lorna let it fall. Roderick dropped to his knees beside the King. "My Liege," he said, his face taut with concern, "I've brought your surgeon."

Lorna shifted to let the battle surgeon examine the wound. He glanced up at her.

"Can you heal?" he asked.

"A bit. But I am not skilled."

The surgeon probed the wound with a finger and cursed. The King cried out and grabbed Gareth's arm in a white-knuckled grip.

"It's barbed," the surgeon said. "If they used poison, it may be too late."

"Poison!" Gareth gasped.

The surgeon didn't answer. After giving the King a draft of something from a glass vial, he drew two flexible tubes from his bag. He inserted them into the wound while probing with his finger as before. The King jerked and sucked in his breath.

When the two tubes were set on the barbs, the surgeon glanced at Lorna. "I will extract it and cleanse it. You must stop the bleeding."

Lorna rested her hand on the King's thigh.

"No!" he snarled. "Don't let her touch me."

She didn't bother to tell him she had already used the power of the Anarwyn to ease his pain and bleeding. She drew her hand back. The fool would rather die than accept her help.

"Father, please," Gareth said, but the surgeon gestured to the guards.

"Hold him," he said. They hesitated until Gareth ordered them to obey. "Do it!"

The surgeon yanked the arrow free, and bright red blood boiled up behind it. He poured whiskey over the wound. The King screamed in agony and thrashed about.

Gareth clung to him. "Father," he whispered, "everything is going to be fine." Tears slipped down his cheeks.

The surgeon scraped rust from an old nail into the wound before nodding to Lorna. The rust was supposed to stop infections, but Lorna was dubious of its effectiveness. She closed her eyes and settled her breathing. Reaching deep for the healing power of the agate, she staunched the flow of blood, weaving the torn flesh back together as best she could. Something was wrong. There was something already in the blood that was flowing toward the King's heart. She tried to isolate it, but it was too late.

She opened her eyes and sat back in alarm.

"Is there poison?" the surgeon asked.

"Yes."

Gareth swore, and the surgeon drew a glass vial with a clear liquid from his satchel and shoved it into Roderick's hand. "Give this to the king."

The surgeon shifted his attention to Gareth and performed the same operation to extract the arrow from his shoulder. Lorna assisted and found the same poison coursing through Gareth's veins. She used all of her skill to isolate the poison and slow it down while the surgeon made him drink the clear liquid before examining the two arrows.

A black substance darkened the shaft behind the broadheads. This was an old Inverni practice that allowed them to handle the arrows without fear of accidental poisoning from the sharp blades. To place the poison directly on the point would have meant the slightest scratch could bring death. This way, the arrow delivered the poison only to its intended target, and the warmth of the blood softened the paste, letting the poison spread more rapidly.

A cold dread infused Lorna's chest. If both Trahern and Gareth died, the kingdom would erupt into civil war. Maybe that had been the point, after all.

The surgeon sniffed at the black paste on the shaft and raised his gaze to Lorna's. "Smells putrid. Might be snake venom mixed with rotten flesh. I can't be sure." He shook his head. "I've done all I can."

Roderick bowed his head and grasped the King's hand, his face stricken. Gareth raised his pleading gaze to Lorna. Once again, she was in a position where there was nothing she could do, but because she possessed the power of the Anarwyn, people expected miracles.

"Can you do anything else?" Gareth asked.

"I've tried to slow it," she said.

Gareth glanced around at the faces peering down at him until his gaze fell upon Sarruge. His eyes narrowed. "What do you know of this?"

Undead

Sarruge scowled over his hooked nose. "I beg your pardon?" His close-set eyes gave him a wily, shifty appearance.

"Did you have anything to do with this?" Gareth said.

"My prince, I am deeply hurt by your insinuation." Sarruge's creased brow made him appear more annoyed than hurt.

"I will find out," Gareth said.

The surgeon interrupted. "We'll know if you've escaped the poison in a few hours. Bring litters and carry them to the King's chambers."

Lorna watched as her hopes for the support of the East Mark faded. The North and West Marks would have to stand alone. Her journey here had wasted time and may have ensured this attack. The assassin *had* shot his first arrow at her. This could only be Bardon's doing, which meant he knew where she was and what she had planned.

"Do you get the feeling this land wants to kill us?" Cam asked Rebecca and Spider as they paused for a break. They crouched in the shadow of a dwarfish tree with green bark. It didn't provide much relief from the late afternoon sun, but it was better than nothing. Peylog had been in a rush and started them traveling before the sun had fully set.

The colorful sandstone of the mountains varied from bright red to pink to orange. In some places, wonderfully twisted formations lined the trail, giving the rock the appearance of rippled sand on the bottom of a creek.

"I mean," Cam continued, "it's like it wants to make us bleed."

"I think it just wants to be left alone," Rebecca said. She raised her gaze to follow the path of a yellow-striped lizard as it made its way to the upper branches of the tree. She adjusted her seat, so she wasn't beneath it.

"It's not a soft land, I'll give you that," Spider said. "But look at it. It's kind of enchanting."

Cam snorted, then checked to make sure Peylog hadn't heard him. "I wouldn't call it enchanting. Cursed maybe, but not enchanting."

"Do you think the Bragamahr did something to it after Peylog's people escaped here?" Spider asked.

"I've never heard anything like that," Rebecca said.

Cam swallowed a mouthful of water. "I'm not sure we made the right choice." He couldn't escape that nagging feeling that something wasn't right. That they should have gone some other way.

Spider and Rebecca studied him, waiting for him to continue.

"Something is going to happen. I can feel it—like I did a few days before the Mahrowaith attacked me at the Afon Darodel."

"Has the opal shown you anything new?" Rebecca asked.

"No." He hadn't liked what it had shown him last time Baby Face made him look, and he had no desire to let it draw him in again. "But if the Bragamahr does live in that valley, it isn't going to let me pass. It knows I'm coming."

Spider and Rebecca exchanged glances.

"Is there something we can do?" Rebecca asked.

Cam fixed them with a steady gaze, his pulse throbbing at his neck. "Don't let me hurt anyone."

"What?" Rebecca scowled in confusion.

Spider only nodded. He clearly understood what Cam meant.

"Look," Cam said, "if it seems like I can't control the power and I endanger any of you, you *have* to kill me."

Rebecca gasped, and Spider glared at him.

"I'm not joking," Cam said.

His throat tightened. How could he get them to understand? "I won't be able to live with myself if this magic makes me hurt the people I love."

He paused as Rebecca's eyes widened and Spider gave him a sad frown. Cam's face burned. He had just admitted without intending to that he loved Rebecca, and she had been quick to guess his meaning. Spider maintained his dejected frown, as if Cam had finally gone someplace he could not follow. How did he fix this?

"Like it did my mother," he said, but it sounded lame.

Spider came to his rescue. "You used the magic on the Mahrowaith, and it didn't hurt you."

Cam glanced at Rebecca. A pink color flushed her cheeks and unshed tears glistened in her eyes. Had he offended her?

"It almost didn't work," Cam countered. "There's something wrong inside me. Something that tries to block the Anarwyn."

Undead

"Come," Peylog called, and they rose and dusted themselves off. Slone, Laird, Drakeman, Alaric, and Hebron were already moving up the trail carrying their packs with their swords swinging from their sheaths or their weapons in hand.

"Don't forget what I said," Cam insisted as they followed the rest of the group south into the narrow canyons of twisted rock. He needed them to understand. Some things were worse than death.

One day bled into two, then three as they settled into the pattern of rising early, resting during the hottest part of the day until late afternoon, before starting again and traveling through the night. Spider's snares added fresh rabbit to their diet. Peylog took delight in Spider's method of constructing snares, and the two of them spent hours sharing devious methods for trapping animals. Draig brought down a peccary he allowed them to share after he devoured the internal organs.

By the evening of the third day, they were footsore, covered in grime and sweat, and their clothing was torn from the many thorny bushes and cacti. The setting sun found them trudging through a landscape modified by human hands. Crumbling ruins of buildings littered the wide plain. Dry canals and raised fields created a patchwork where vegetation clustered in the more fertile soil in an impenetrable tangle of thorns and vines. The refuse of humanity poked from the soil—bits of metal or cracked leather, broken pottery and the ever-present bleached bones and wide-eyed skulls. High above, the ragged teeth of a deserted city cut the sky.

Cam shivered and drew closer to Spider and Rebecca, casting a nervous glance at the lengthening shadows. A haunting presence filled this wide valley. It sent a tremor of terror and loss surging in his chest to grip his throat. Had the thousands who died here ever truly left?

Spider stepped around a skeleton, whose bones had been scattered in a wide circle, and paused. Cam and Rebecca stopped with him.

"A child," Spider murmured.

Rebecca gasped and covered her mouth with her hand. Draig sniffed at the bones but took no interest in them.

"Get used to it," Alaric said with a coldness that annoyed Cam.

He glanced up to see that Alaric and the others had turned to watch them.

Poisoned Touch

Alaric gave a broad sweep with his hand. "The whole land from here to the Brunen is covered in bones."

"Mahrowaiths did it?" Rebecca asked. Her face grew pale, and her eyes widened.

Alaric nodded.

"Those that survived fled to Abilene or farther south," Drakeman said. He surveyed the bones. "These are my kin. Tathanar cut down by the Bragamahr's beasts."

"This is a cursed land," Peylog said. "My people do not come here."

"It sure likes to make a body bleed," Slone said as he yanked a thorn from his arm.

"Have you been here before, Laird?" Spider asked.

Laird twisted one end of his mustache thoughtfully. "No, I keep to more hospitable lands." He glanced at Peylog. "No offense, my friend, but your land is difficult for those not accustomed to it."

"This is the point," Peylog said. "We have no wish to be dragged into wars that bring nothing but sorrow. Kings and lords start wars and the poor fight and die in them."

Cam could not fault his logic. He glanced up at the ruined city perched in the cleft of the mountains above them. "Is that Goldereth?"

"No," Drakeman said. "It's Mendefra—one of the four great cities guarding the entrances to Braganeth Valley."

"Can we go through there to the other side of the mountains and the Afon Fathwe River?" Spider asked.

"No," Alaric and Drakeman said at the same time. Alaric gestured for Drakeman to explain.

"There used to be a broad road that carried trade from Mendefra to Abilene, but an earthquake in the days of my grandfather caused a landslide that blocked the passage."

"So, we have to go into the valley?" Cam asked. A prickling sensation filled him as he remembered the vision the Life Stone had shown him.

"There's a raised causeway," Alaric explained, "that should let us skirt the edge of the valley. I didn't follow it when I was here, but I could see it from Goldereth."

"Then we should continue," Peylog said. "We have some miles to go yet."

Undead

"I'd rather be in the mountains," Slone said and hefted his pack higher up onto his shoulders. Sweat cascaded from his brow.

They continued their weary march over the sand-covered streets chased by the ghosts of those who died such cruel deaths. The light faded, and they had to take care not to tread upon the bones of the dead.

"I had no idea there were so many people," Spider said to Cam and Rebecca.

"It's awful," Rebecca said.

Cam remained silent. The dread of what they would find in the valley beyond turned his blood cold. Rebecca glanced at him and reached for his hand. The boldness of it surprised him. He clasped her hand in his, grateful for the comfort she offered.

Peylog called them to a halt in a wide courtyard beside a pool set in a basin of chiseled stone. The glitter of stars splashed across the placid surface. Rising above the water, the statue of a woman loomed. She wore a flowing dress and one hand extended, holding a smooth round stone.

Cam recognized her immediately. "Ilsie," he whispered.

Rebecca glanced at him. Starlight flickered in her eyes.

Cam squeezed her hand. "That's what the Anarwyn looked like when she appeared to me."

"Then why did you say Ilsie?" Spider asked.

Cam shrugged. "The Anarwyn is a magic without a body, but it manifests as a young woman."

"If you say so."

"And Ilsie was the first to accept and be accepted by the Anarwyn."

"Is there a point to this?" Spider asked.

Cam snorted in disgust, and Rebecca smiled. "The Bragamahr came to us in the form of a strong man," he explained, "and the Anarwyn in the form of a young woman. I think they assume the form of the first person to wield their power."

"It's true," Drakeman said from the other side of the basin. "At least that's what Lorna taught me when I was a boy."

"That's what they say in the South Mark, as well," Laird added.

They slipped off their packs and settled in around the pool. Draig lapped from its mirrored waters, and Slone built a cooking fire over which they roasted one of Spider's rabbits.

"What are they?" Spider asked.

Poisoned Touch

Hebron glanced at the rabbit flesh he was lifting to his mouth and scowled at Spider as if he had lost his mind.

"No," Spider said, "I mean the magics."

"He stays on task, this one," Alaric said.

"Mind like one of his snares," Laird chuckled.

"I'm serious," Spider said. "I mean I know they are different kinds of magic, but *what* are they? Are they like spirits or some kind of living thing we can't see?"

"They are power," Peylog said. "Energy."

"I'm not sure that helps," Spider said. Cam understood his confusion. He'd wondered the same thing.

"The legends say they were born in the creation," Peylog said, "the offspring of the tumult and convulsions that lifted the dry land from the oceans and carved the mountains and valleys." He shifted and dropped a few more sticks onto the fire. His face was long and sad. "For ages, my people served the Bragamahr and those who wielded the power. When we saw that no creation of the Bragamahr endured and we understood that everything it touched diminished until it was wholly evil, we fled our servitude. The desert gave us refuge, for neither the Bragamahr nor the Anarwyn ever penetrated this land. Then came the breaking of the Black Council, and we hid in our desert fastness as the world crumbled and kings came and went. Always, we remained the Orren, the free people of Atacam."

A knot rose in Cam's throat, and he blinked at the sting of tears. Peylog was rightly proud of what his people had achieved. If only the Anar and the Tathanar had been able to find such peace. Perhaps peace could be achieved only if everyone refused to wield either magic.

"You make me want to visit your villages and listen to your tales," Slone said.

"You would be welcome," Peylog answered.

Alaric stretched out on the hot earth. "We had better rest. I want to leave at first light. We don't dare brave the city and the valley after dark."

"Why?" Rebecca said. "What lives in there?"

"That's the point," Hebron said. "We don't know."

"Right."

They quieted, and Cam laid back and stared up at the great band of stars that swept from horizon to horizon. What were they—the stars? Huge gemstones casting the sun's light back to earth?

Undead

Tomorrow. Tomorrow we enter the lair of the magic that wants me dead.
Cam offered a silent prayer to the Anarwyn that he would be strong
enough to resist and survive whatever the Bragamahr had prepared
for him.

Three days after the assassination attempt, Lorna fidgeted at
the window of her room. A gentle breeze lifted the scents of the
city to her—cooking fires, horses, human waste. The westering sun
slumped on the horizon, casting long shadows over the tiled roofs
and towers of Najera.

She had lost so much time. Cam and the others were striding
into danger, and she had no idea if her messengers had found them.
She needed to be there in the Lonely Valley when he attempted to
use the dyad in case it did something she had not anticipated. She
needed to be there to beg Maelorn's forgiveness and to help him
gather his forces to resist Bardon's army.

Toying with the golden pendant at her neck, she watched the
home guard file through the gates of the city below her. Their
spears and helmets glinted in the slanting rays of the morning light.
The Privy Council had decided that Bardon's raiders needed to be
stopped, but Roderick would not leave his King. Instead, he sent his
son, Connac, to lead the home guard. She wished she was riding with
them. This delay was taking too long. She had tried and failed last
night to find Cam. Where was he? Was he even still alive?

A knock thumped against her door. "Come," she called.

A young page in tight hose and bright blue tunic bowed to her.
"The Lord King commands your presence."

"The King?" Lorna breathed and scurried after the page. Could
he mean Gareth? Had Trahern succumbed to the poison?

She found Roderick hovering over King Trahern, who lay
stretched on a narrow couch. His eyes were closed, and he looked
dead. Gareth sat beside him, holding his hand, also pale and sweating. A sickly stench filled the room, and Lorna scowled at the withered form of the King.

King Trahern's eyes popped open. "I hear your tread." His eyes
were sunken and dark circles settled below them. His flesh clung to

his bones, giving him a skeletal appearance.

Lorna bowed. "I am glad to see you awake, Your Majesty."

"I grow tired and am not long for this good world." A pink tongue wet his lips.

"An old warrior like yourself will not die so easily," Gareth said.

The King shook his head. "An old warrior like myself knows when death can no longer be cheated." He gazed at Lorna before turning to Gareth. "The assassin was slain before he could be questioned?"

"Yes, Father."

"He was Inverni?"

"Yes."

He swiveled his gaze to Roderick. "Call my Privy Council."

Most of the members of the Council were already waiting for news in the sitting room and so within a few minutes, the whole Privy Council was huddled around the King's bed.

"I give you my son, Gareth, as your king," he said. "Let there be no disputations among you. You must act as one. Mobilize for war and do so immediately. Once you have secured our borders, you must send an army to support the Undead King if he arises. The time has come to act or perish."

Lorna experienced a surge of hope. Trahern had finally seen sense, but at a tremendous cost.

The King coughed and tried to wet his lips again. His gaze rested on Sarruge.

"Set your differences aside. This is your dying King's last wish and command. Now, leave me."

The men filed out. Lorna considered joining them, but the King had not dismissed her. Roderick remained and knelt by the King's side. Tears flowed freely down his face.

"My Liege," he whispered.

The King opened his watery, bloodshot eyes to look at him. "My faithful friend and companion."

Roderick swallowed hard. "I am your man of life and limb even in death, My Lord," he said, bending to kiss the King's ring.

"Do me this one last favor then," Trahern whispered.

"You have only to ask."

"Protect my son and my people. Save this kingdom for him."

Undead

"That has always been my only desire."

The King nodded feebly. "I know. I should have listened to you years ago."

He reached out and seized Roderick and Gareth by the hand. "I only hope it is not too late."

He closed his eyes, and his breathing grew more and more shallow until it ceased completely. Lorna waited while Gareth wept for his father, wrestling against the urgent need to fly in search of Cam.

Gareth raised a tearstained face to her. "We will come—as soon as we are able."

Lorna studied him, wondering if he would recover or die as his father had and if the East Mark would descend into civil war as the nobles fought over the throne. She bowed. "I'm sorry, but I must leave at once."

"Take what horses you need from the stable," Gareth said, "and any supplies you deem necessary."

"Thank you, My Lord."

Gareth's lip lifted in a snarl. "Bardon will regret what he has done to my father."

Lorna excused herself and rushed to her room. She had been packed and ready for two days. Grabbing up her saddlebags, she raced to the stables, selected two sturdy horses, saddled them, and galloped through the palace gates to clatter down the streets of the waking city. She would ride day and night until she reached the Lonely Valley. If Cam wasn't there, she would go in search of him.

Chapter Seven
Eternal Tomb

REBECCA ROSE BEFORE the others stirred and strode over to join Slone, who was sitting the last watch. They would be leaving soon in the hopes of passing through the city and the valley beyond in the light of day when they could see what might threaten them. The idea of knowingly striding into a place filled with creatures who wanted them dead had kept her awake most of the night.

She had only taken a few steps when she narrowly missed impaling herself on a plant with meaty leaves that were armed with long, stiff spines.

"Gotta watch out for those," Slone said from the shadow of a ruined building.

"We could use one of these as a spear," Rebecca replied. Slone had selected his spot well. Even though she knew where he was, his shape was obscured by the shadows so that he looked like a part of the rock itself.

He smiled up at her as she approached, showing white teeth. "Sleep well, My Lady?"

"You don't have to call me that," Rebecca said, and she sank down beside him. "I'm no high-born Lady."

"Perhaps, but you are still a lady."

This wasn't what Rebecca wanted to talk about. She shifted

to settle onto the hard earth. "Do you know what we're going to find in that valley?"

"I've only heard rumors. It is said to be an evil place."

Rebecca plucked a rock from underneath her and tossed it away. "What I don't understand is why the Mahrowaiths haven't followed us here."

"Maybe they want us to take this path."

"Exactly," Rebecca said, "which is a strong argument against going this way, don't you think?"

"It has already been decided," Slone said, shifting his axe where it lay across his knees.

"I don't want to go in there."

"Neither do I. But we do what we must."

Rebecca rubbed at the sleep in her eyes. "What if Briallen was right and this is all a waste of time?"

Slone snorted and peered at her. "Do you really think that pampered peacock understood what is happening here?"

"Well, I…" she trailed off, feeling her face grow hot.

Slone grasped her hand in his and patted it. His fingers were as thick as tree roots and calloused. He was a strong man for all his tenderness toward her. "You have to trust the goodness and honesty of people like Drakeman and Lorna."

"Even if they're wrong?"

"To live is to take risks," Slone said, "and to fail. If we fail, we will know we fought on the side of goodness and right."

"Will we?" Rebecca whispered. Cam was always saying that the Anarwyn wasn't what everyone thought it was. He had seen a dark side to it, and she was worried he might be right.

She blinked against the sting of tears in her eyes. It was at times like these that she most missed her parents. And yet, at all the crucial moments in her life, there had been someone like Chullain or Drakeman or Lorna or Slone to fill the void—however incompletely.

"Thanks," she said and coughed to conceal the strangled sob that escaped.

"Never be ashamed of fear." Slone patted her hand again. "Fear is the constant companion of those who resist evil."

On an impulse, Rebecca leaned over and hugged Slone. "Thank you," she whispered.

Eternal Tomb

By now, the pearly blush of dawn stained the ridges of the mountains to the east, and the others were extracting themselves from their blankets. She drew away from Slone and rose. He gave her a smile that sent a surge of warmth through her. Whatever she had done wrong, no matter what other stupid things she might do today, she would always be able to rely on Slone.

She wanted to say something, to tell him how much his kindness meant to her, but her throat tightened, and she found that she had no voice. Pinching her lips tight, she whirled away so Slone wouldn't see the tear trickle down her cheek.

Peylog was already coaxing the glowing coals from the last night's fire to life, and she joined him. He paused to study her face. "The Orren have a saying," he said. "To know oneself is to confront what you should really fear."

Rebecca pondered what that meant while Peylog filled a pot with water and set it on a stone beside the flames. From his pouch, he drew some herbs that he sprinkled into the water. He stirred the contents with a stick and sat back to study her.

"You will rise to face whatever wind blows your way," he said. "You were not meant to die in the valley of the Braganeth."

Rebecca started. "Die?"

"Is that not what you fear?"

What was it that gnawed at her? "I'm afraid for all of us." She glanced to where Cam was tying his pack shut.

"I understand. Now eat. You will need your strength."

Something about Peylog was off this morning. There was a finality to his calculated movements that left Rebecca wondering what she was failing to understand.

When everyone had eaten and they were rising to prepare for the march, Peylog summoned them to the fire.

"Come, my friends," he said, "I would speak with you."

They gathered round, exchanging questioning glances.

"Today I leave you."

A rock landed in Rebecca's gut. "Leave us?" she breathed.

"What?" Cam said in a voice that was almost a shout.

Rebecca understood how he felt. She had grown so used to leaning on Peylog's quiet confidence that she wasn't sure she could do without it—not in this wild, forbidding landscape.

Undead

Peylog raised a hand to silence their questions.

"I can go no farther. Already, I have passed the boundary of my lands. But I wish to bid you farewell with a cup, as is my people's custom."

He withdrew a tiny, intricately carved horn cup from his satchel and poured the steaming liquid into it. The cup was carved with the same peculiar shape of the bird that Peylog had tattooed on his cheek. A sweet aroma filled the air. He held the cup on his palm and turned it three times before lifting it to his lips. Then he handed it to Cam and gestured for him to do the same. Each of them repeated the ritual until Hebron handed the cup back to Peylog.

"We have sealed our friendship with the cup of healing," Peylog said. "We are now brothers and sisters." He circled the group, giving each of them a brief hug.

"Thank you." Rebecca choked on the last word as he embraced her. The rich fragrance of woodsmoke, sweat, and the herbs he carried about him filled her nostrils. "I can never repay you."

Peylog held her at arm's length and wiped away her tear. "Do not cry, my child. You are braver than you know."

When Cam embraced Peylog, Cam swallowed and blinked rapidly. They separated and shifted awkwardly.

"I owe you my life," Cam said in a husky voice. "We all do."

"If you succeed, you will have paid the debt," Peylog said in his thick accent. Then he lifted Cam's hands to study the black scars on his knuckles. "You will soon face the choice of what kind of man you will become. Choose well."

Cam scowled, and Rebecca wondered what Peylog meant. Hadn't Cam already chosen?

"Will you not come with us?" Cam asked.

Peylog shook his head. "It is forbidden." He shouldered his satchel and waterskin and picked up his bow and arrows. After tossing his thick braid over one shoulder, he smiled at them. "I will sing for your safety and that we may meet again." He turned and strode off into the morning light.

They shuffled about awkwardly, watching him go until the wasteland that was his home swallowed him in a shifting mirage.

Rebecca sniffled.

"I'll miss that sly old fox," Slone said.

Eternal Tomb

Rebecca wiped her eyes and raised her chin. She would be brave because Peylog thought she was. Whatever awaited them in the valley would have to be faced and overcome.

Cam stared up the road that curved away from the fountain where they had camped. It passed between two square towers and onward up the rippled stone toward the ragged battlements of the city of Mendefra, now visible in the ethereal light of the coming dawn. His throat burned from his parting with Peylog, and his stomach churned at the realization that by the time the sun fell, he might be in the valley of the Braganeth. What new terrors awaited them there he could only guess.

"Well," Alaric said as he hefted his pack onto his back, "staring at the road doesn't make the climb any easier."

Cam shrugged his pack higher on his back and hooked his thumbs under the shoulder straps. "Lead the way."

Alaric strode out, and one by one, they fell into line behind him. All morning they toiled up the broken road strewn with corpses of men and beasts. Flowering cacti sprouted from the cracks in the cobbled street. Brambles clogged the gutters. Buildings sagged with blank, unshuttered windows glowering balefully down at them. Stubby, green-barked trees stabbed through roofs or poked through windows, looking like javelins thrust through eyes or heads. Cam shook his head at the morbid thoughts.

It was impossible to keep one's heart from sinking at the sight of so much destruction. Underneath it all surged that penetrating sense of great age and great suffering. It felt as though the pain of the people whose lives were cut short had seeped into the very stones and was calling to Cam for vengeance. They marched on in silence until Alaric came to a dead stop before a huge pile of cut stones. A round tower that had once overlooked the road had collapsed onto it in some distant age.

Spider let out a dramatic sigh. "If you tell me I have to scramble over that, I'm going to chuck a rock at you."

Alaric grunted and placed his hands on his hips when Drakeman called to them from farther down the road. "This way."

Undead

They trudged over to where he pointed to a stairway cut into the living rock.

"Spider might prefer the stairs," he said.

"Yep," Spider said and started climbing.

"Shouldn't he be spinning a web for us or something?" Slone asked.

"I heard that," Spider shouted but kept climbing.

Cam shared a smile with Rebecca and then followed Spider up the long, winding staircase. It was made treacherous by years of exposure to the weather. Bits had broken off or the stones had been so weathered by the blasting sand that they were rounded and smoothed. In some places, half a step had cracked and slid a few inches to the side. Cam slipped more than once. By the time the stairs disgorged them onto the high plateau upon which the city had been built, his hands were raw, and his legs were burning from exertion.

Spider paused, staring up at the towering walls. Cam joined him, wiping the sweat from his eyes, and trying to catch his breath.

Walls of stone soared above them. The jagged teeth of crumbling towers and buildings climbed even higher.

"It's..." Spider panted, "even...bigger than...Abilene."

Alaric joined them. "Which is why we need to hurry. Follow me."

Spider lolled his head back and groaned. "If you ever tell me we're going to take a trip with Hebron and Alaric again, I'm just going to hide until you all go away."

Hebron slapped him on the back as he passed. "No time to rest."

They circled to the front of the city, passing the remains of shops and houses to where the gates sagged on rusted hinges. Slipping through, Alaric led them around the inner walls. Blackened beams stabbed up from ruined buildings. Majestic arches carved with flowers and vines soared over the crumbling walls and lichen-crusted stone to bear mute witness to the grandeur of the past.

Bleached skeletons with shreds of fabric still clinging to their bones littered the streets or draped out of windows. Glittering jewel-encrusted belts and necklaces made the moldering corruption seem even more horrible. Thousands had perished. Draig sniffed at the corpses but left them alone.

"Blood and ashes," Cam cursed. "It's even worse up here."

"Why didn't they bury the dead?" Rebecca asked.

"There were too few when the battles ceased," Drakeman said.

Eternal Tomb

"Those who remained agreed to let the cities become tombs."

And it *was* a tomb. No animal stirred or called. Not even the wind dared to make a noise as it blustered down the streets, kicking up little cyclones of dust. Everything was silent. Brooding. Expectant.

Spider stopped and reached to pick up a golden belt, when a hiss from Drakeman brought him up short.

"Touch nothing," Drakeman warned.

Spider jerked in surprise and scowled. "Why? They won't need it."

"Would you rob a grave?" Drakeman snapped. He seemed to grow in size, and his eyes flashed with menace.

Spider cowered and stepped away from the corpse and its glittering golden belt. Cam wondered if the jewels would channel the power of the Anarwyn, like the lump of amber did for him. Still, he wasn't about to touch anything in this forsaken city of the dead.

He stared at a skull that had long brown hair attached to it. A glittering gem on a chain lay directly in the center of the forehead. Cam imagined this must have been a rich and beautiful woman.

"They wore them for luck," Rebecca said to him.

Cam yanked his gaze away from the skull. "What?"

"The Tathanar used to wear gemstones as talismans against the power of the Bragamahr. They wore some against their foreheads or temples to give them wisdom."

"I didn't see anyone in Abilene doing that," Cam said.

Rebecca shook her head. "After the Mahrowaiths drove them from their cities, they quit believing in the power of their amulets."

"Do not linger," Alaric called and increased his pace.

Cam, Spider, and Rebecca scurried to catch up. In an hour, the company passed to the other side where an arched gateway yawned wide. Braganeth Valley stretched from horizon to horizon. It was a broken, black land of pocked stone that crumpled and curled into tortured shapes. Green cedars found purchase in the cracks and seams along the hillsides. Low-lying bushes and bunches of stubbly grass clung to the thin soils.

At the base of the hill stretched a wide field of black sand, merging with a tumble of boulders and a gray fog that floated wraithlike above the tangle of brush and undergrowth. A brackish pond was visible beneath the haze. The valley lay as still as death.

"I didn't expect fog," Spider said.

Undead

"Water collects in the valley," Drakeman said, "and there are foul vapors that spew out of the earth."

"*That* I can smell," Spider said, wrinkling his nose.

So could Cam. It was a pungent, sulfuric stench that burned in his nostrils. It reminded him of the stink of the Mahrowaiths.

Soaring above the thick fog rose the serrated spine of the mountains that ringed the valley. On the valley's southern end, ignited with the fire of the afternoon sun, slouched a fortress that was imposing even at this distance. Its towers and ramparts stabbed defiantly above the mist far to the south.

"Is that Goldereth?" Cam asked.

"Yes," Alaric said, "and we should try to get as many miles behind us as we can. I don't relish spending the night in the valley."

They set out without stopping to eat as Alaric sped into that loping jog he had used that nearly killed Cam the first day they met.

Laird and Spider scowled at Alaric and back at Cam.

"Is he serious?" Laird asked.

"Prepare for pain," Cam answered and quickened his pace to follow. Draig trotted at his side.

The raised causeway wound its way down the hillside into the valley and skirted the edge of the black sand as if the builders wanted to avoid getting closer to the valley floor than necessary. Alaric didn't keep his bone-jarring pace for long. Once out on the flat, they slowed to navigate the maze of rotting wagons and carts that sprawled over the causeway, mingling with the bones of those who had tried to flee the destruction.

Still, they were making good time until they rounded a tumbled heap of the black-pitted stone near the middle of the valley. Alaric lurched to an abrupt halt. The causeway was simply gone. A great hole yawned in the ground, dropping into the blackness. Foul-smelling vapors belched from the belly of the earth. Alaric picked up a stone and tossed it into the crevice. No sound of it striking bottom reached their ears.

"Blood and ashes," Spider cursed. "It doesn't have a bottom."

Cam gazed at the rocks surrounding them, thinking they were going to have to climb up to get around the crevice. There was no path up. Though the stone was pitted, it provided no handholds he could see.

"Do we go back?" Laird asked.

Alaric scowled at them. "I don't know any other way."

Spider stepped to the edge of the road to peer down into the valley. "The way down looks easy enough."

"For a spider," Hebron grumbled.

"That crack doesn't extend far down into the valley," Slone said. "If we can get down the embankment here, we can circle around the crack and climb back up to the causeway."

"We should avoid the valley floor, if possible," Drakeman said. He cast a nervous glance to the center of the valley where the haze roiled, agitated by some wind they couldn't feel.

"It knows we're here," Cam said. The haunting feeling had grown stronger as they descended into the valley. No one asked what he was referring to, but he could see in their faces that they all knew. It was impossible not to feel it.

"Unless Spider can sprout wings and fly us over," Laird said, "you've only got one choice. We can't go back because there is no way through the mountains that isn't guarded, and we can't climb up and around this. That only leaves going down to the valley floor. If we hurry, we should be around the crevice and back on the road by nightfall."

All eyes focused on Cam, and he shrank under their gaze. Why did he have to be the one to choose? His gut told him that to descend into the valley was worse than foolish, yet Laird was right. They had no other options.

"Let's do it quickly," he said. "I don't want to be on the valley floor when it gets dark."

The slope was steep, but gentle enough for Draig to clamber down without trouble. Slone and Hebron came last, sending a shower of stone and debris cascading onto the rest of the party.

They hastened out onto the black sand, skirting wide around the crevice in case the ground wasn't stable. A narrow trail showed where animals had likewise circled around the gaping hole in the earth, and they followed it. Though Cam hadn't seen any animals, some must occasionally venture into the valley. Noxious fumes wafted up from the crevice. Black sand crunched under his feet.

Cam let Rebecca go first, and she jogged beside Slone. A burst of steam spewed from the crevice. Rebecca leaped aside to avoid

Undead

it when the sand under her feet shifted. She shrieked in surprise and fought to keep her footing, swimming in a downward cascade of glistening black sand. Cam jumped to catch her but missed and barely avoided going down with her.

Cursing, Slone dropped to his belly, extending the handle of his axe to her.

"Grab it," he shouted.

Cam joined him, but Rebecca was sliding farther down into the hole. At any moment, Cam expected the ground to give way completely and open into a bottomless pit like the crevice, but something far worse emerged from the sand.

The snapping jaws of some horrible creature burst upward, reaching for Rebecca's feet. The beast had a furry, flat head and dark, bug-like eyes. The sand turned into an inverted cone that sloped right toward its vicious jaws. Draig snarled.

"Sweet waters of the Anarwyn," Slone cursed.

Chapter Eight
Phantom in the Mist

CONNAC RAISED HIS HAND to bring the home guard to a stop. From the top of the knoll overlooking the valley of the Willow River, the scale of the destruction Bardon's raiders had inflicted on the Rahil of the East Mark became apparent. They'd been encountering refugees fleeing toward the mountains for days. Still, nothing they said prepared him for this. The town of Ribenha burned. Great columns of black smoke lifted into the sky like the coils of a writhing snake. Everywhere, hamlets and villages were in flames. The bitter taste of smoke and ash settled on his tongue.

King Trahern's refusal to confront reality now seemed much more than petulant. It had been downright negligent, a betrayal of his duty to protect his people.

"Fan out," Connac called.

The Rahil were bred to the saddle from a young age. They had lost some of the finesse their ancestors had once possessed, but they were still the finest horsemen in all the marks.

A thousand lancers formed a line two riders deep behind him, and the archers occupied the wings in a company of five hundred each. If there were marauders about, he didn't want to be caught strung out in a line and vulnerable to attack. A scout galloped up the knoll.

"Sir," he said, "a party of the enemy a few hundred strong are working their way up the river from Ribenha."

"Where?"

The scout pointed to a thin line of trees set between two wide fields. A tumble of stones separated them from the woods.

"We'll swing north to come around the hill and catch them in the open," Connac said. "Keep an eye on them, and let me know if they change direction."

"Yes, sir."

Connac snapped out his orders and the home guard rode down the north side of the knoll into the scattered forest of beech and oak. He needed to lay the ambush perfectly or his advantage in horsemanship would be lost. Woods and rocky ravines were no place for the kind of elegant horsemanship the Rahil were capable of executing.

They worked through to the edge of the wood, where they lined up in battle formation under the cover of trees. The rocky knoll to his left concealed the enemy's disposition from view, so he relied on the scouts to give him warning.

His horse shuffled its feet and bobbed its head. Connac laid a hand on his neck to calm it. "It's all right."

The first of the Inverni horsemen galloped around the knoll, and Connac raised his hand in preparation to give the signal. Another Inverni followed, his mottled cloak flapping as he rode. Connac spied a boy struggling through a ditch, carrying a child in his arms. The Inverni saw him too and hooted with glee. Connac hissed and his horse leaped into a gallop. He would not stand by and let them murder two innocent children. Nor could he have the child caught between two armies.

At the same instant, a cry came from behind, and his men were enveloped in a horde of Inverni horsemen and foot soldiers swooping down from the hillside. Arrows flew thick. Horses reared. Chaos swept through the ranks of his army. Connac had to abandon the boy to save his command.

Panic gripped Cam's throat as Spider's sling snapped, and a stone punched into one of the bulbous eyes of the beast waiting to catch Rebecca. Its head was square and flat with jagged, three foot-long, sickle-like jaws yawning wide. Three pairs of spindly legs ending in hooked claws sprouted from its segmented thorax. A thick tuft of fur covered its head and back. It was as large as a black bear, and far more terrifying.

Cam's mind whirled. What could he do? How could he save Rebecca? Despite her efforts to reach Slone's extended axe, she was sliding down the funnel of black sand. Drakeman's bow sang, and a feathered shaft plunged into the beast's neck. At least this thing wasn't armored like the Mahrowaiths.

A dry, rattling snarl sounded, and the monster snapped its jaws, heaving its bulk out of the sand toward Rebecca, who scrambled in the downward cascade of sand. Draig growled again and made a tentative effort to climb down inside the cone but backed up as the ground gave way beneath him. Rebecca's desperate scrabbling slowed her downward slide, but it wouldn't be enough. Stones and arrows also had little effect on the beast. There was only one thing left to do.

Cam lunged to his feet and drew his sword. Shouting in defiance, he leaped into the pit. He landed astride the monster's neck behind the square head and plunged his sword into the uninjured eye up to its hilt. The monster roared and thrashed about. Cam held on as the sand cascaded around him. He dragged the sword free and plunged it into the monster again and again. His blade severed two of its six long, spider-like legs as it screamed and writhed at the bottom of the cone, snapping its jaws and nearly burying Cam with sand.

A hideous reek of the beast filled Cam's nostrils. He made one last desperate sweep of the blade that sliced into the beast's neck. A fountain of greenish liquid spewed from the wound, and Cam rolled away, trying to gain his footing in the shifting sand.

Rebecca slid down beside him, with her back to the sand. She stopped herself with one foot on the monster's back. Her sword flashed, and she drove it into the beast's side. The monster screeched an unearthly, bone-chilling, gurgling cry that lingered in the air. It jerked, quivered, and then went limp. Its gigantic, furry body lay covered in black sand and caked in greenish gore. Cam drove his sword into its heart for good measure and stepped on its body to keep from being dragged down by the sand. Rebecca lay on her back in the cone with one boot braced against the beast, her sword still buried in its side. She stared at Cam with wide eyes. Her chest heaved.

Cam glanced down at the beast and back at her. "You have a way of picking dangerous friends."

Her eyes filled with tears, and he sheathed his sword and stepped over the beast to gather her into his arms.

"I'm sorry," he said. "Are you okay?"

She sniffled into his shoulder and nodded.

"Let's get you two out of there," Hebron called from above.

Cam started. In all the horror of the encounter, he had forgotten the others were there. The heat rose in his face as he gave Drakeman an apologetic look. Drakeman shook his head and extended his bow to them, which they could barely reach. Once they had both scrambled out in a shower of sand, they collapsed at the top of the cone, gazing down at the beast. Cam's knees wouldn't stop shaking.

"What was that thing?" Spider asked.

Slone curled his lip in disgust. "Some creature twisted by the power of the Bragamahr, no doubt."

"Let's hope he doesn't have any relatives nearby," Spider said.

At the word *Bragamahr*, a shiver swept through Cam, and he remembered what Lorna told him about the sand. He grabbed Rebecca in sudden desperation. "Are you cut or scraped anywhere?" he demanded.

Rebecca scowled at him.

Cam shook her and repeated, "Are you cut anywhere?"

She jerked away and raised her bleeding fingers to stare at them. Cam grabbed his waterskin and poured the water over her hands, carefully brushing away any flecks of black sand. He was heedless of wasting the precious water. Nothing mattered but getting every bit of black sand from Rebecca's injuries.

"Ouch," Rebecca said, shaking her hand in the air. "What is wrong with you?" She tried to pull away, but Spider grabbed her from behind.

"Hold still," he whispered.

The fear in Spider's voice gave Cam added urgency. Spider had been there when Lorna explained what the black sand would do. Cam had to get every tiny grain out.

"What's wrong?" Rebecca demanded.

"Cam?" Hebron asked, stepping up to him as if deciding whether he should restrain him or not.

Phantom in the Mist

Cam ignored him as he scrubbed and searched, probing each cut, and then scrubbed again until he could find no more bits of black sand. He held Rebecca's bleeding hands. "Are you cut or scraped anywhere else?"

"I don't think so."

"You must be certain," Cam insisted. The terror twisted his insides into a knot. He couldn't let the Bragamahr have Rebecca. He had no idea if she was even sensitive to the magic, but it was a risk he couldn't take.

Spider released her.

Rebecca paused and shook her head. "It was just my hands. The sand cut them."

Cam sighed and stepped back.

"What?" Rebecca demanded. "Why did you grab me like that?" She shifted her gaze between Cam and Spider.

Cam glanced around at the company. They were studying him with varying degrees of concern. Slone fingered his axe and surveyed Cam as if deciding whether to use it on him. Draig sat on his haunches with his head canted to the side. Hebron and Alaric exchanged knowing glances while Laird studied him, twisting his mustache thoughtfully.

Cam couldn't tell them what he and Spider knew. Lorna had sworn them to secrecy. Still, they deserved some explanation. He shifted his feet and glanced at Spider.

"This is the valley of the Bragamahr," he said. "We can't take *anything* from this valley with us. Especially not its sand."

Hebron, Alaric, and Drakeman nodded as if they understood more than he said. Slone kept scowling.

Laird picked up his pack and said, "Daylight is wasting."

His words galvanized the rest of them, and soon they were striding away from the pit where the furry beast sprawled in death, being careful to keep their feet on the thin game trail.

Laird fell back to plod along beside Rebecca and Cam.

"If I understand you correctly," he said to Cam in a quiet voice that would not carry, "we can't afford to have any open wounds down here."

"Yes," Cam said.

"May I?" Laird said, turning to Rebecca.

"Yes." Rebecca extended her hands toward him.

Laird grasped a hand in one of his and reached his other hand into one of his pockets. He kept walking but his breathing slowed. Cam watched in awe as the blood stopped flowing from Rebecca's fingers and the raw flesh closed. A gentle glow of light seeped from Laird's pocket. Laird released her hand and repeated this, healing her other.

Rebecca stared at him with wide eyes. "Thank you," she whispered.

"A useful talent," he said, "but one I would prefer to keep secret, for now."

"I understand," she said.

The terror of the encounter with the beast coursed through Cam, and he gazed out at the fog-filled valley. The thing he feared the most in the world was out there, watching him, waiting for him to make a mistake.

Connac drew his sword and charged into the cluster of Inverni who were trying to encircle his men and pen them up in the woods where their horses and lances would be of little use. He hacked and slashed, scattering the Inverni.

"To me, men of Rahil!" he shouted, and his men whirled as one and charged out onto the open field, leaping the ditch, until they had space to swing about and reform ranks. A thousand Inverni pressed them close, trying to keep them disorganized, but the Rahil home guard was supremely disciplined. They were the best warriors in the East Mark, carefully selected and trained. The archers swung wide and swept the flanks of the Inverni with arrows before wheeling away and circling back. Lancers charged into the disorganized ranks. The Inverni gave way, seeking the shelter of the woods.

"Fall back!" Connac shouted, and the man with the horn blew two sharp blasts. The Rahil wheeled and reformed in the muddy field.

Connac rode down the ditch, searching for the boy and the child. He found them cowering in the rushes.

"Caleb," he called. A man rode up to him. "Take care of them," Connac said, gesturing to the children, and rode back to the center of his line.

A few Inverni straggled on the edge of the woods, though they didn't venture out again. They clearly had not expected such disciplined and deadly resistance.

Connac gestured to the commander of the archers. "Flush them out. I want every one of them dead before the sun sets."

Cam couldn't sleep. The whispering in his head and the desperate fear of what might lay concealed in that fog made him fidget and toss around until he was helplessly entangled in his blanket. About midnight he gave up, extricated himself from the tangle, and rose to relieve Spider at the watch. The moon was slipping over the ragged hills, casting long shadows. Spider leaned against the stone at the base of a column of black rock. The causeway curved around an outcropping away from where they camped, making it impossible for them to reach it before nightfall. They were still far out on the shifting sands. Spider faced the center of the valley, where a dim, orange glow infused the roiling fog with an eerie, ghostly light.

"Do you think it's watching us?" Spider asked as Cam settled in beside him.

"Probably," Cam said. "It knows I'm here. It's waiting for something."

Spider clicked his tongue. "You have a way of instilling confidence."

"No point in lying about it," Cam replied. "Thanks, by the way."

"For what?"

"For helping with Rebecca."

"I don't want to see her turned into a Mahrowaith," Spider said. "She's dangerous enough without the claws."

Cam drew up his knees. "I doubt that's what would happen." He paused. "You still sore about her knocking you on the head?"

"You would be too," Spider said, rubbing his head as if the mere mention of it made it hurt again.

Cam grunted. "I suppose."

"This place makes me want to scream and run."

"You can scamper to your bedroll if you want," Cam said. "I'll take the watch. Can't sleep anyway."

Spider stretched and rose. "All right. Hebron's next. Don't let him sleep too long. Now's your chance to get even for all those times he forced us out of bed before the sun was up."

Cam drew his sword from its sheath and rested it across his knees. It gave him a bit of comfort in this dreary land. He peered up at the band of stars winking through the sky. So much had happened since he fled Stony Vale. It seemed like a lifetime ago, and yet, it had only been a few weeks. The Anarwyn stirred inside him, responding to the nervous dread that churned in his gut. He had accepted it, which meant he'd also accepted that he would die. However, he still wanted to protect his friends as long as he could.

The power of the Fire Stone had struck the Mahrowaith back at the great bend of the Afon Fathwe River, but Cam hadn't been able to kill it. Hebron had with Galad's sword. Some barrier lurked inside him, resisting the Anarwyn. Was it his own fear?

His mind wandered to his mother and the painful memory of her death. Why hadn't the Anarwyn allowed her to protect herself? Cam raised his knuckles absently to rub at them and scratched the rough scar on his forehead before he realized what he was doing. The bits of black sand under his skin itched. His gaze focused on the eerie cloud with the orange light, when a woman's face materialized in the mist, silvery and translucent. He would have recognized her anywhere.

"Mother?" Cam whispered and scrambled to his feet, letting his sword fall to the sand. It nicked his hand, and he raised his hand to his mouth to suck his cut for a moment. He snatched up his sword and continued to stare at the apparition.

The face assumed the full-bodied form of a beautiful woman in a flowing dress. Her face and shape were exactly the way he remembered—high cheekbones, wide, caring eyes, with a pretty smile haunting the edges of her mouth. She beckoned to him.

Cam hesitated. This might be some trick of the Bragamahr to lure him away from his friends and leave them vulnerable. His mother beckoned to him again, and he found his feet moving. The desperate longing to know, to understand overwhelmed every other thought. Cam strode to greet her, the sand grinding under his feet. He had so yearned for this moment—this chance to tell her that he was sorry she had died protecting him.

As if she read his mind, her voice whispered in his ear. "I will show you what happened. You need to know before it is too late."

Cam kept walking. Perhaps he would receive an answer to the burning question that had tortured him for weeks. He lengthened his stride to keep up with her as she withdrew. "Come, my son, and I will show you."

The clouds boiled, and the scene reformed with his mother poised protectively in front of a tree with a gemstone in one hand as a man, whose face remained hidden in the shadow of a hood, drew a sword and crouched, ready to spring. His mother extended her hand.

"You cannot have him," she said.

"It isn't the brat I seek," the man said.

His mother raised her hand, and a pearly white glow burned from between her fingers. A bolt of lightning shot out from her fist. Instead of striking the assassin, it curved around him and slammed into her own chest. The explosion knocked the assassin off his feet. His mother's body fell with a thud to stare at the boy she had tried to save. Her fingers were blackened, and a beautiful, white pearl rolled in her palm.

Horror pinched Cam's throat. The Anarwyn had killed her on purpose. It refused to protect her and murdered her when she most needed its power."

The scars on his knuckles and head burned. His mother's image rotated to peer at him.

"The Anarwyn will do this to you, too," she said. "The Anarwyn only promises and uses. It never allows its playthings to benefit from the power. In the end, it will betray you, just as it did me."

"Cam!" The voice floated through the rush of fury. Hands grabbed him and shook him. Hebron's face slid in and out of focus.

"Cam!" Hebron's voice was stronger now. "Don't listen to her."

Cam tried to push past him and was aware of the water splashing around his feet.

"It's all lies and deceit," Hebron shouted. "Whatever she's been telling you isn't true." He shook Cam violently and slapped him across the face.

Cam blinked at him. "Are you calling my mother a liar?" If he accepted the Bragamahr, he could make Hebron pay for that slap. Make the Anarwyn pay for taking his mother. Make certain the Anarwyn never betrayed anyone else ever again.

Undead

Come to us, a man's voice said in his mind. *You belong to us. We can protect you.*

"Cam!" Hebron yelled, "that's not your mother. She was never that beautiful, and she wouldn't lure you away from camp."

Something punched from out of the fog, flinging Hebron aside like he was nothing more than an annoying fly. The sight of Hebron sprawling headlong into the sand roused Cam's desperate need to protect his friends. In that instant, his vision cleared.

He stood knee-deep in brackish, fetid water. Wind rushed past him, filled with malice and sulfuric stink. The earth shook and heaved. Shouts rang out. He recognized their voices. They were his friends.

The Bragamahr materialized in front of him—the strong hunter with the condescending expression. *You need us*, he sneered. *The Anarwyn will betray you.*

"No!" Cam screamed and plunged his hand into his pouch to clutch the Fire Stone. He yanked it free and begged the Anarwyn to help him. The magic was slow to respond as if fighting against some restraint. Maybe here in the valley of the Braganeth, the Anarwyn wouldn't work for him.

"Please," Cam begged and strained with his entire being. A sound like the roar of a thousand waterfalls filled the valley. A great ball of yellow flame sprang from the amber stone to surround Cam. With it came the rushing sense of safety and purpose. He concentrated, focusing all his thoughts on the stone and the safety of his friends. The wall of fire burned away the mist, and the Bragamahr drew back, its face contorted in rage.

If you do not accept us, you and your friends will perish.

The mist sizzled and hissed as the fire expanded until it formed a barrier between the Bragamahr and Cam's friends. They rushed toward him with their weapons drawn, though Cam knew such toys could never harm the Bragamahr.

"I will never accept you," Cam snarled. "You are weak. I will be controlled by no one."

He spun and splashed back through the water to where Hebron was climbing to his feet. He helped him rise, and they raced to join the others. The wall of fire cast a sparkling light off the black sand, flinging an eerie light around them, but it kept the Bragamahr at bay.

Phantom in the Mist

"It's time to go," Cam shouted. He snatched his backpack and sheathed his sword.

Blood dripped from the cut on his hand to splash onto the sand. He clamped a hand over the cut to keep the black sand from getting in. He didn't want any more of it inside him.

Blood of your body. Fragment of my soul, the Bragamahr's voice burst into his mind.

A geyser of steam erupted from the spot where the blood spattered, casting up a whirling, grinding, cloud of black sand. Pain surged through Cam's mind, and he reeled away from the churning sand as he shouldered his pack. He sucked on the hand to keep more blood from falling to the sand. A tearing sensation rippled through his body, and he staggered after the others as they dashed toward the causeway. What was happening?

Cam glanced back as he ran. The Bragamahr rose into the air, hovering close to the yellow wall of fire that followed them. A swirling column of sand churned the air in front of the Bragamahr as a grinding, screeching sound filled the air.

You have chosen death, the Bragamahr said. This time his voice was audible and rang over the desolate land.

"And that is why I will live," Cam shouted.

"Blood and ashes," Spider cursed.

"Keep running," Laird shouted.

Rebecca cast a nervous glance at Cam and raced ahead to catch up with Spider and Draig.

Slone and Hebron grabbed Cam's arms to help him as he lurched along, fighting the agony bursting inside him. His memory of his mother's face dimmed. Was the Bragamahr tearing him apart one piece at a time? The screeching sound behind them grew louder.

"No," Cam breathed. He would not succumb to this new attack by the Bragamahr.

"What did it do to you?" Hebron panted.

"I don't know. It tried to use my own mother against me."

Maybe the Anarwyn did betray his mother, but the Bragamahr was no better. He would choose his own path. Not even the Anarwyn would tell him what to do. He staggered as fast as he could, desperate to escape the accursed valley and the power that wanted to consume him.

Chapter Nine
Blood of Your Body

ZENEK CROUCHED IN THE SHADOW of a giant obsidian boulder, its surface pitted and worn by the blast of thousands of years of black sand. Great flashing lights lit the valley with orange and yellow flame. Tiny figures scuttled about in front of the ominous yellow glow of a wall of light that traveled across the empty valley.

Kill him, the voice of the Bragamahr burst painfully into Zenek's mind, and he curled up in a ball, clutching at his head. Why did it hurt so much?

Forcing himself to rise against the pain, he stumbled his way through the maze of sharp, black rocks until he reached the causeway. He had been watching for several days. The yellow flame disappeared, but he could hear the slap of running feet and heavy breathing. Reaching into his pocket, he withdrew the red garnet, careful to shield its light from unwelcome eyes.

He drew himself up to his full height in the shadow of a column of basalt. This was his first task. He would not fail. He stilled his breathing as his mother had taught him and whispered, "Courage to power. Will to dominate."

The garnet flared, and the startled faces of a snarling wolf, Alaric, Hebron, Drakeman, Slone, Rebecca, two others he did not know—and Cam flashed in the bloodred light. It couldn't be. Cam was supposed to be dead. How did they come to be here?

Blood of Your Body

Surprise paralyzed Zenek for a moment before he released the power of the Bragamahr to attack them. A burst of energy rushed down his arm and exploded from the stone. The earth heaved and rolled, and he staggered. Something wrenched inside him in a torrent of pain that brought a cry of dismay from his lips. The memory of his mother's face faded, becoming increasingly transparent. He struggled against the agony, fighting to control the rushing energy until he managed to concentrate it into a bolt of red lightning that flashed toward Cam. Hebron jumped to intercept the light with Dorandel.

The dark blade caught the lightning, drawing it into itself. The magic of the Bragamahr recoiled from the blade, and Zenek struggled in confusion. The power wrestled to be set free, expanding inside him relentlessly like ice in the crack of a rock—slowly, patiently rending it asunder. Panic surged into his gut. What should he do?

A furry body bowled him over. Teeth slashed at his neck. The red flame flared, throwing the wolf off him. The earth trembled, and a cascade of stone tumbled down around him, burying him in debris. A stone slammed into his head, and the red fire died. Voices shouted, but then he was left alone with the pain and confusion.

Zenek groaned and shoved against the weight of the stones. Their sharp edges cut his fingers as he dug himself from the pile. Once he was free, he rolled to his hands and knees. He still clutched the red garnet in his hand. Why had he failed? Was he truly not worthy to bear such a gift? A terrible, irresistible weariness swept over him, and he flopped onto his belly and closed his eyes, surrendering to the exhaustion.

When he awoke, the mist clung to him, enfolding him in a chilly blanket. He rolled to his back and sat up, wincing at the throbbing headache. A rush of wind stirred his hair and cast up a small cyclone of fine, black dust. The personification of the Bragamahr swirled and shifted before him.

You have failed us, the deep voice growled.

Zenek fell on his face. "I am sorry, Master."

I will give you servants of your body.

Zenek raised his head to peer at the frowning apparition. What could it mean?

Take the blade, the Bragamahr commanded.

Undead

Glancing at the shard of obsidian resting by his knee, Zenek picked it up, careful not to cut himself.

Blood of your body. Fragment of my soul, the Bragamahr chanted.

Zenek stared at the Bragamahr in astonishment.

Give me of your blood, the Bragamahr insisted.

As understanding dawned on him, Zenek scrambled to his knees and raised the sharp piece of obsidian. He sliced a gash in his palm. He cupped his hand to let the blood pool until it flowed through his fingers and then tossed it out over the black sand. Everywhere a drop of blood landed, a hissing geyser of steam burst from the sand, casting up a cloud of black dust. The clouds whirled and churned, creating a grinding, cracking noise that echoed off the rocks.

As the screeching cyclones of sand revolved before him, an unbearable agony swept through Zenek as if the marrow of his bones were being sucked out. Anguish exploded in his mind and bits of his being ripped free. Zenek collapsed to his knees, groaning. He writhed as the pain was intensified by the rushing of the wind. What was happening? Had he finally given his body and soul to the Bragamahr? Would he die here without achieving the revenge for which he longed?

A cry of torment escaped his lips as he groveled in the sand. Memories of his childhood flowed out of him. His identity wavered and was lost in the burning soul of the Bragamahr. It was a being of intense emotion, fragmented, divided, longing to be whole. And it was stripping his identity from him with a devouring hunger.

"No," Zenek gasped, struggling to hang onto himself.

First, one churning column stopped, then another, and the grinding screech subsided. Zenek's pain receded to a dull ache, and he crawled to his hands and knees. Sweat dripped from his hair, and his body trembled like a leaf in the wind. The sand settled, revealing a dozen sets of bright red eyes gleaming at him through the darkness.

Zenek struggled to rise, but his head swam, and he fell into the black oblivion of the Bragamahr. When the burning fire diminished and he opened his eyes, daylight thrust through the concealing fog of the Braganeth. He had lain senseless all night.

He sat up to find twelve pairs of bright red eyes staring at him, watching, waiting like faithful hounds for their master's command. He knew each of them. Sensed their presence. They were a part of

Blood of Your Body

him. A grin spread over Zenek's face. These weren't mindless beasts. They were magnificent creatures, bred to the chase and to battle.

"Blood of my body," he whispered. "Fragment of your soul." He rose, wincing at the ache in his torso and the weakness in his limbs. "Come," he said. "We hunt together."

He staggered into the wall, fell, and then righted himself. He slowed to a limping walk, clutching at the ache in his chest. The Bragamahr had almost killed him, but it had given him a dozen Mahrowaiths who followed along behind him, shadows of death in a dead land.

Bardon started and lurched awake. A rush of satisfaction, mingled with fury, rippled through the Bragamahr. He had never felt anything like it. The Bragamahr had always been slow and ponderous, deliberate and deadly, as enduring as the stony hills from which it sprang.

This energy felt like a child, petulant yet ecstatic. Something had happened. Something the Bragamahr believed was in its favor. Bardon threw off his sleeping furs and scrambled to his feet, facing northwest. The upwelling of energy came from that direction, the direction of Braganeth Valley.

He pondered the possibilities. It could only mean that someone had accepted the Bragamahr. The boy Lorna had sent to the Lonely Valley should be dead by now, and Lorna was in Najera—if she was still alive. Who else could it be? Bardon scowled. There were only two possible explanations. Either Cam hadn't been killed and he had somehow found his way to the Braganeth, or there was someone he didn't know about. Someone who had escaped the Mahrowaiths.

Would this person become a new threat, capable of wielding both the power of the Bragamahr and the Anarwyn? No. The Anarwyn would kill that person rather than permit it. Only *he* knew how to force a union between the two powers. Not even Jathneel dared to conceive of such a thing.

Bardon threw off his blankets and lunged toward the entrance of his tent to call for his horse before he stopped himself. He couldn't run off, not when Lorna was in the East Mark. If she survived his assassins, she might head to the Lonely Valley in the hope of assisting the boy. As Lorna was the greatest threat to his plans, he needed to know what she was doing before he did anything rash.

Slowing his breathing to focus his mind, Bardon eased back onto his sofa and drew the power through the pale pink morganite stone, the Carreg Agorial, set into a golden ring on his finger. A sudden rush of space and time expanded all around him, and his perception sharpened. There was a disturbance in the Bragamahr somewhere on the Crimson Plain west of Najera. It felt like Lorna, which would mean she had escaped his assassins. He couldn't have that. Bardon called to the Mahrowaiths scattered far and wide over the lands south of the Brunen. A thrill of power flowed through him, extending his conscious thought, stretching out to touch the minds of the Mahrowaiths.

"Come," he said. "Come to the Lonely Valley."

A hundred minds responded to his summons. These minds were childlike, uncomplicated. They hungered after raw flesh and the scent of blood. Their hatred of the Anarwyn was instinctive. They could sense the presence of the heirs to the magic from hundreds of miles and smell them from more than twenty miles' distance. He needed them to form a barrier of tooth and claw between anyone who sought to release Maelorn and Tara.

"Come my friends. Your master calls."

The bestial minds of the Mahrowaiths heard and answered his summons. If his scouts did not catch Lorna before she reached Mawsil, the Mahrowaiths would intercept her at the Lonely Valley. She would never reach their brother's stone tomb alive.

The washed-out, opaque light of morning found Cam and his company footsore and weary, peering up from the valley floor of the Braganeth at the enormous walls and towers of the city of Goldereth dominating the cliffs above. The vacant windows of the towers stared down at them, giving Cam the uneasy sense of being watched. And yet, nothing stirred along the cliffs and mountains surrounding them. The castle and all this rugged, broken landscape were as lifeless as the marsh in the reeking valley behind them.

Blood of Your Body

Still, someone was down there. Someone who attacked them with red fire the night before. Someone who did not feel or stink like a Mahrowaith. The only person Cam could think of who could—or would—do something like that was Bardon. But if it were Bardon, why had the stones fallen to bury him before Draig could kill him or Hebron could use his sword? It made no sense.

Cam peered back at the black valley with its cloud of mist in the center. Who had attacked them and why didn't he follow?

"I don't suppose," Spider said, "that we can grab a nap before you make us climb up there."

Cam gazed back up at the towering ramparts, his eyes burning from lack of sleep. He wouldn't mind a nap, though he knew as well as Spider that they couldn't afford the time. It was simply too dangerous to remain in the valley any longer than necessary.

"Nap?" Alaric said. "No, but I'll give you a moment to refresh yourself."

"You're too kind," Spider said and flopped to the ground.

"Who attacked us back there?" Rebecca asked Drakeman before she slipped a piece of salted pilchard into her mouth.

Cam listened carefully, curious what Drakeman might say.

"It happened too suddenly. I didn't see his face," Drakeman answered.

"All the more reason to keep moving," Hebron said.

Cam lay several pilchards on the ground in front of Draig, who sniffed at them before bolting them down. Finding a little divot in the rock, Cam filled it with water for Draig to drink.

"Whoever he was," Slone said, "he went straight for Cam, and he has magic."

Cam shivered at the memory of the horrible agony tearing through him after his confrontation with the Bragamahr. The ache had not yet dissipated. He was far more worried about that than he was about the identity of his assailant. The Bragamahr had done something to him, had stolen something *from* him. Or maybe the Bragamahr was punishing him somehow.

"That's what has me worried," Laird said. "That power didn't feel wholesome."

Spider snorted. "Is power ever wholesome?"

Cam glanced at Spider. Lorna had said power was neither good nor bad, but Spider had accused Cam of seeking attention when they argued back at Abilene. Did he think Cam was tainted because he accepted the Anarwyn?

"When it's used for good it is," Laird said. "But that's not what I meant. There was something wrong with it, like it was broken."

Drakeman nodded. "It felt that way to me, too."

"Well, that clears everything up," Spider said.

"Enough napping," Alaric interjected and kicked Spider's boot. "I want to be through Goldereth before nightfall."

Spider groaned as Hebron hauled him to his feet. "Complain too loudly," Hebron said, "and I'll give you my pack to carry."

"How about I climb into your pack and let you do the walking?"

"You hear this, Cam?" Hebron chuckled. "A mountain boy complaining about climbing a little hill."

"I wasn't complaining," Spider snapped.

"I'm sure we could find a hole for him to crawl into," Cam said. He hefted his pack and grinned at Spider's consternation.

"I'll beat both of you to the top." Spider strode up the old, cobbled road that wound its way up the hillside. Cam watched him go with a knowing smile.

Spider was a tough and hardy Anar. All this bluster was his way of easing the tension and fear. He wasn't really as exhausted as he claimed. He was just deflecting attention away from what bothered him. Cam couldn't decide if Spider was more worried about him or about that vial of water he carried in his pocket and the idea that he might be like his mother.

"Shall I get a stick?" Laird said. "That way, I could beat him all the way."

The others chuckled as they settled into the climb. The road had been eroded in places, leaving washes and gullies filled with debris. Black sand crawled up the hillside, intent on reaching the city. Stone stelae perched at regular intervals inscribed with scenes of warriors and battles. Most were broken and effaced by the desert wind. A few survived to demonstrate the skill of the carvers and the wealth and glory of this once great city. The nearer they drew to the city, the more frequent the skeletons became. Dust blanketed pasty white bones. Whatever clothing they had worn had rotted long ago or had been blasted away by the savage wind. Some had ragged coils of blonde or brown hair tangled in the bones.

Their group clambered over a pile of rubble that had once been some elaborate house, and Rebecca bent to pick up a piece of pottery. It was white with a delicate blue glaze.

"This is even finer than the porcelain of Abilene," she said.

Drakeman stepped over to study it. "Much of the craftsmanship of old was lost in the destruction." He handed it back to Rebecca. She held it out to Cam, who accepted it.

"It's beautiful," he said.

"Are you all right?" Rebecca asked.

"Yes." Cam wasn't certain this statement was true, but he didn't know how to explain to her what was going on inside him. Something had changed. He returned the piece of pottery. "I'm just tired."

Her frown told him that she didn't believe him, but they continued on until they came around a bend and stopped. Before them yawned a deep gorge. On either side, the jagged edges of huge arches were all that remained of the bridge that once spanned the chasm.

"I take it this was our way in," Drakeman said.

"I never came down this way," Alaric said, "but I saw the bridge from a high tower, and it appeared sound."

"Look at this rubble," Hebron said kicking at a stone with his boot.

Cam bent close to inspect it. The breaks were clean with none of the patina of age or the black dust that stained the rest of the rubble.

"This bridge didn't collapse," Hebron said. "It was deliberately destroyed—and not long ago."

"How?" Slone asked.

Hebron simply looked at him. It could only be the Bragamahr and his servants. The thought that there was another person out there wielding the power of the Bragamahr was not comforting.

"There might be another way," Drakeman said. When they all stared at him, he rubbed his jaw. "I spent much of my youth studying Goldereth and the ancient Tathanar heroes. I used to wonder what it would be like to look upon their handiwork with my own eyes. Somehow, I never imagined this sadness."

"I'm not following how this helps us," Slone said.

"There's a small sally port on the west side, but we're going to have to go back down to get around the gorge."

Undead

"Of course, we are," Spider said and started to saunter back down the hill without even waiting for them.

"Maybe you *should* give him a few whacks," Slone said to Laird. "You still could."

"He gets grouchy when he doesn't get enough sleep," Cam said.

"Is that why he's always grumpy?" Laird asked.

They descended back the way they had come until Drakeman found a crumbling flight of stairs that wound its way up through the jagged boulders. Cam didn't relish the climb any more than Spider did. He bit back any complaint and settled into the monotonous ascent. The gaze of the Bragamahr was on them, and there was that piece of himself he had left behind.

An hour of clambering up the broken stairs brought them to a collapsing square tower. A wooden door sagged on its hinges, and they passed beneath the walls into an open corridor.

"I think we want to go up," Alaric said, and they settled into another long ascent through the cobbled streets. The tang of decay permeated the air. Desiccated bodies, including those of children and dogs, lay scattered everywhere. Their flesh had turned to dust, leaving bones and fragments of cloth. But some still had bits of mummified skin clinging to them. It was a ghastly sight. The buildings were grand with curving arches and plastered walls. Some had colored frescoes, now faded with time.

Cam had never seen anything like it. Not even Abilene had been this grand. The city was utterly silent. No potters' wheels whirled. No looms slammed the weft tight. No blacksmith's hammer rang in the silence. The hustle and bustle that must have once echoed in the narrow, curving streets had been forever silenced. It was an eerie place that sent a tendril of dread coiling around Cam's heart. He quickened his pace to catch up with Rebecca. Spider strode ahead.

"I feel like the ghosts of the dead will descend upon us any moment," Cam whispered.

"Don't say that," Rebecca replied. "I'm jumpy enough."

They came to a wide courtyard with hundreds of stalls and rotted wagons that must have been a market area. In the center, lay a pile of bones. Cam came up short when he recognized the skeleton of a Mahrowaith along with a pile of black obsidian with red veins.

"Be careful," he said. "Don't touch that stone."

Blood of Your Body

"Looks like a real battle took place here," Slone said.

Drakeman glanced around. "The *Lamentation of Galad* speaks of a battle in the marketplace. This is where the King fell."

"I don't think we should linger," Laird said.

"The footbridge is this way." Alaric gestured to their right, and he led them up a flight of stairs onto the battlements.

Cam hurried to catch up with Hebron. "I don't like the sound of this footbridge."

Hebron shrugged his pack higher on his back. "You said that before."

Cam shivered at the memory of the horrible vision. "The Life Stone showed me a vision of a footbridge, and...." He paused. The words were hard to say. "...and I saw you die."

Hebron missed a step and scowled at Cam.

"We should go some other way," Cam insisted.

"There *is* no other way, Cam. You heard them."

"But Hebron...." Cam tried to think of something he could say that would convince Hebron they couldn't go this way.

Hebron laid a big hand on Cam's shoulder. "The Life Stone was warning you again, like it did back on the river. Now that we're forewarned, we can be prepared."

Cam frowned. "It didn't help much," he grumbled. "I was still attacked."

"But you survived," Hebron replied. "We cannot avoid danger, so we'll face it when it comes."

The path along the battlements narrowed, and Cam fell in behind Hebron. He'd hoped his warning might be taken more seriously, but Hebron was right. There would be no safety for him until Maelorn and Tara were free—and Bardon was defeated.

They continued following the battlements for several hundred yards. Cam gaped at the majesty of this huge city. How could a place of so much sophistication and beauty be filled with such oppressive silence? What evil would want to destroy such a thing?

Alaric slowed and then stopped altogether. Cam leaned on the battlements to peer around Rebecca and Hebron to find Alaric poised on the edge of a ten-foot gap between the walls and a square tower. All that remained of the small drawbridge that once spanned the gap were its chains dangling on the far side, clotted with rust.

Undead

Even the door was gone.

"Again?" Cam said.

Rebecca peered back at him and raised her eyebrows. "Someone is trying to keep us from getting through Goldereth."

Alaric gave Drakeman a questioning glance. "I thought this was the way to the lower gate."

"It is," Rebecca said. "Master Gari made me memorize a map of Goldereth. He said I needed to understand where my people came from. Anyway, on the other side of this tower, there's another road and a guard post next to a footbridge."

Drakeman chuckled. "You see, it was worthwhile studying old, dead people."

Rebecca brushed a strand of hair from her face but said nothing.

"That must be a drop of at least sixty feet," Slone said.

"What do you say, Spider?" Hebron said. "Ten feet's not much of a jump for a big insect like you."

"Very funny," Spider said.

Alaric's scar pinched as he studied the gap. He shook his head. "We'll have to find another way."

Laird unslung his pack and retrieved a rope. He edged his way past them until he stood beside Alaric. He pointed to a rusted hook twenty feet above the door. "If we can snag that hook, someone might be able to swing over and drop that plank to span the breach." He indicated a slab of wood poking out from the door.

"You had a rope all that time we were scaling cliffs?" Spider said.

Laird smiled at him.

"Or when Rebecca and I were stuck in the pit?" Cam asked.

Laird hefted the rope in one hand. "Didn't need it either time."

"It's too risky," Slone said. "That hook could break."

Laird shrugged. "And we could be stuck in this tomb of a city for days before we find a way out. I, for one, don't like the feel of this place."

"It's worth a try," Alaric said.

Laird tied a slip knot in one end of the rope, created a large loop, and then coiled the rope in his hand. He swung it back and forth a few times before he tossed it. The rope uncoiled as it flew, and the loop caught the hook on the first try.

"Nice toss," Spider said.

Blood of Your Body

Laird gave the rope a good yank to make sure it was secure. Bits of rust cascaded from the hook, but it held. Laird grinned at them, making his mustache quiver. He offered them the rope. "Any takers?"

"It's your idea," Slone growled. "You try it."

"I'll do it," Rebecca said and slipped off her pack. "I'm the least likely to break the hook."

"No, I will," Cam countered. He didn't like the idea of Rebecca risking herself like that.

"You're too heavy."

"Rebecca, I—," Drakeman started, but she cut him off.

"I'm the least important member of this party. It's about time I earned my keep."

"That's not true," Drakeman said.

Slone fingered his axe thoughtfully. "But she *is* the lightest one here."

Cam couldn't let her. "But Spider and I have more experience climbing."

"And you're also fifty pounds heavier," Slone said. "Rebecca can do it."

Rebecca unbuckled her sword and stepped carefully up to the edge and peered down. She accepted the proffered rope from Laird.

"Be careful," he said. "And choke up on the rope so you don't come in too far below the door."

Rebecca obeyed, drew in a deep breath, and jumped. Cam marveled at her reckless courage and watched her sail through the air with his heart in his throat. She slammed into the wall with her feet spread wide about a foot below the door. Though her feet absorbed the impact, she shoved off for a second try.

"Hang on tight," Cam shouted.

She clung to the rope as it swung her back in the direction of the door like a pendulum. Wrapping her legs around the rope, she hauled herself up and grabbed for the opening. She missed. The rope jerked and gave. Cam clenched his jaw, and every muscle readied to spring to her aid, but there was nothing he could do. The rusty hook was bending under her weight.

"Hurry!" Cam shouted.

She glared back at him and climbed higher up the rope. Using her feet to propel her toward the door, she caught the lip and thrust out a foot to hook a leg around the opening. With a sudden surge, she kicked the rope away at the same moment she threw herself into the doorway.

Cam held his breath, listening for her cry of pain. There was nothing but some muffled thumping. Presently, she stuck her head out of the door, grinning from ear to ear. Cam let out his air in relief.

"Well done," Alaric called.

"Now what?" Spider said. "She's over there, and we're over here."

"Hang on," Rebecca said and ducked back into the tower. She returned and shoved a wide plank of wood out the door. "This should reach."

She heaved it up on one end so that it rested on the lip of the doorway. "Here it comes," she shouted and let it drop. The plank descended like a falling tree and landed with a bang and a cloud of dust. It would have bounced off into the chasm had Slone not dropped onto his belly and grabbed it.

Alaric tested the board and smiled. "Rebecca, you just saved us several hours of searching."

After shifting his pack and slinging Rebecca's pack and sword belt over his shoulder, Alaric edged slowly across the plank. It sagged under him but held. Draig followed with his nose bent close to it, and soon, one at a time, they had all crossed. Cam tried not to look down at the dizzying drop below them. Rebecca had risked her life to get inside that door. And what if the plank hadn't reached? She would have been alone, separated from them. It had been a terrible risk.

Once they were inside, Hebron drew the plank back in and leaned it against the wall. "Just in case," he said, and Cam knew he must be thinking about the footbridge. At least Hebron had listened to him.

Alaric led them down some dilapidated wooden stairs littered with stark white bones. Cam glanced at jeweled rings and bracelets encircling boney fingers and wrists, silver and gold belts sagging on wasted hips, necklaces dropping through white ribs. It was a horrible sight, made more terrible by the ever-present musty taste of death. When they reached the bottom of the tower and stepped out into a wide corridor between two stone walls, they paused to rest.

The rush of a churning river sounded over the walls. It reminded Cam of the Falls of Dolroth. The vision of the boiling waterfall the Life Stone had shown him played out before his eyes.

Blood of Your Body

"Hebron," Cam warned, "there was a river in my vision."

Nodding, Hebron rested his hand on his sword.

"Which way now?" Spider said.

No one answered as they took in the scene. Two square towers flanked a yawning doorway a hundred yards down the sloping street. Charred beams of collapsed buildings stabbed into the sky. Between them and the tower, skeletal remains of Mahrowaiths and their black obsidian blood lay strewn about. There had to be more than a hundred of them, and their skeletons had been hacked to pieces—their bones cleanly cut.

"Galad," Drakeman whispered and glanced at Hebron.

A rush of paralyzing terror gripped Cam's throat, and he cast about searching for any sign of a living Mahrowaith. Nothing else could suck the breath away like that.

"They're here," he shouted. "Run!"

They bolted down the corridor toward the yawning gate and freedom, leaping over the ruined bones. Laughter rang out, and a dozen Mahrowaiths came bounding from the shadows. Hebron shoved everyone to his rear and swung the blade of Galad in a deadly arc that sliced three of the Mahrowaiths in half as they flew at him.

Cam fumbled with his pouch and withdrew the Fire Stone. Hebron's assault and the sight of the black blade that glowed in an outline of bloodred light slowed the Mahrowaiths. This gave the others time to retreat to the doorway before more of the monsters encircled Hebron and launched themselves into the fray.

Slone's axe bit into a neck of a Mahrowaith, sending a fountain of blood spurting into the air. The beast bowled him aside. Laird and Spider hacked at another, while Drakeman and Rebecca fought back-to-back, fending off the beasts that came at them, barely managing to keep their claws from their throats. The clash of steel on stone rang in the corridor, echoing off the walls of the long-silent city. Draig dragged down a Mahrowaith by his throat. The gut-wrenching snap of bone proved that Draig had broken its neck.

Cam tried to banish the panic that threatened to paralyze him, and he concentrated on the weight of the Fire Stone in his hands. "Please," he whispered. "Calon est, calon dûr," he repeated the words Lorna had taught him. "Dim ond calon lân all ganu."

Nothing happened, and panic surged into his chest. There was a

Undead

barrier inside him, stopping the flow of the magic. Only now did he realize that *he* was creating the barrier. His fear of the magic would not let it work.

He drew in a deep breath. "It doesn't matter what happens to me," he whispered. "I accept that I must die."

Something snapped inside him, and the yellow fire roared from the stone to engulf a Mahrowaith. It shrieked and fled, lurching about, before it fell to be consumed by the flames. The other Mahrowaiths retreated to scrutinize them warily.

"To the footbridge!" Hebron bellowed.

No, Cam thought, though he knew they had no other choice.

A streak of red fire shot down the corridor and tore into Slone's shoulder. He screamed and fell, knocked backward by the force of the blow. Rolling to his feet, he stumbled toward the gate, dragging his axe behind him. Rebecca grabbed his arm and draped it over her shoulder. They staggered through the gate out onto the footbridge with the others close behind.

The footbridge swayed under Cam's feet as the spray from the waterfall wet his face. "Quickly," he shouted. He didn't want them to be on the footbridge longer than necessary.

Hebron came behind, filling the doorway, keeping the Mahrowaiths at bay with his magnificent sword. Another streak of red lightning shot at Hebron. The sword caught and held it as a man stepped from behind a wall, holding a ball of bloodred light in his hand.

"Zenek?" Cam breathed. How could he have followed them here? And when had he acquired magic?

"It is time to die," Zenek said with a malicious smile.

Chapter Ten
Chasm of Doom

GARETH WINCED AT THE PAIN in his shoulder as he assumed his place beside his father's throne in the Council chamber. The injury from the assassin's arrow was healing, however slowly. He would not sit on his father's throne until he had been proclaimed king. The survival of that kingdom was far more important at the moment than his pride. He surveyed the members of the Privy Council as they assumed their seats. The sweet fragrance of the scented candles burning in the chandelier overhead filled the room.

Sarruge remained standing. "My Lord," he said, "Your Majesty must know how deeply we feel your loss and the loss to this kingdom."

Gareth inclined his head in acknowledgment.

"I would remind Your Grace," Sarruge continued, "of the necessity of your formal assumption of power as soon as possible. And, might I add, with all due respect, your need to marry and secure the line. Your vassals need to have that assurance before their Sire leaves on any campaign."

Gareth sniffed. So that was his approach? He had long disliked and distrusted Sarruge. The man and his pretensions to the throne had been a constant thorn in his father's side. Gareth was determined to blunt that thorn somehow.

"Thank you, Lord Sarruge," he said, trying to hide his annoyance. "But we will not dishonor our father's memory by taking the throne before the month of mourning has been observed." He used the royal "we" to make sure Sarruge remembered to whom he was speaking. "And given the current emergency, there is no time to find a wife and undertake the formalities of a royal wedding. We must begin the immediate preparations for a lengthy campaign. The safety of our kingdom must take precedence over our desire for formal acclamation."

"The safety of this kingdom is precisely our concern, Your Majesty," Sarruge said.

A murmur swept around the table.

Gareth studied Sarruge's smug face and sickly smile. His distaste for the man was rapidly growing to abhorrence.

"Are you implying something, Lord Sarruge?"

Sarruge's thin lips lifted up in a grotesque, patronizing way.

"My only interest is for the welfare of the kingdom, Sire," he said with a bow.

"Good, then you'll be ready to leave with us in a fortnight. We expect your full levy to march with us."

Sarruge's smile faded.

"Your Majesty, so soon? It will be quite difficult—"

Gareth cut him off. "We are aware of the difficulty. But a man of your capacity and skill can surely accomplish the task."

Sarruge glared at him before seating himself without another word.

Gareth swept the rest of the men with his gaze. Several appeared to be sympathetic to Sarruge, and he determined to have them expelled from the Privy Council. How to do it without inciting a general rebellion was not at all clear, and he needed their support—even if it was grudgingly given—until Bardon had been dealt with.

"Gentlemen," he said finally, "in our absence, we will appoint our uncle, the husband of our father's sister, Duke Allred, to act as Regent. Although, as you know, he is not in line for the succession. His son and our cousin, Phillip, is next in line. Should anything happen to us, our uncle will act as Regent for Phillip until he comes of age. That should dispel any concerns about the proper succession."

He scowled at the members of the Council. Most of them appeared satisfied with his compromise. Allred was well-liked, and Phillip was a promising young man.

"One more item," Gareth continued. "We regret that we find

ourselves in this delicate and dangerous position. In two weeks' time, in place of a coronation, we will wait to receive your formal oaths of vassalage before we depart for the campaign."

Surprised exclamations arose from the men.

Sarruge rose with a scratch of his chair legs on the marble floor and the men quieted. "Your Majesty. This is most irregular."

"We are aware of the irregularity," Gareth snapped. "But regicide is also irregular and calls for irregular actions."

The Great Hall fell deathly still. Sarruge's face blanched white, but he stood his ground.

"Your Majesty, do you wish to insinuate something?"

"Not at all." Gareth struggled to keep his contempt for Sarruge from showing on his face. "Our only interest is for the welfare of this kingdom." He waited for Sarruge's reaction to having his own words thrown back in his face before adding, "We intend to discover who plotted the assassination of our father and bring them to justice."

After a tense pause, Gareth deftly brought the Council back to the business at hand, and when it was concluded and the orders for the mobilization had been sealed, he dismissed them.

"Well," he said as he left the room with Roderick at his elbow, "for better or for worse, the lines have been drawn. It didn't go as well as I hoped, but it could have been worse."

"Perhaps," Roderick agreed, "but you may have taken a viper to your bosom."

Gareth grunted. "At least I'll be able to keep an eye on him. It will be more difficult for him to seize the throne if he's a hundred miles away fighting for his life."

They strolled on until they reached the balcony overlooking the courtyard in front of the palace. Messengers in royal blue surcoats were already galloping away with the orders for every vassal to appear at Najera to swear their oaths and mobilize their armies.

"Any word from Connac and the home guard?" Gareth asked.

"Nothing, Your Majesty."

"What has gone wrong?" Gareth wondered aloud as he studied the plains beyond the city walls. Had they waited too long? Did they have the two weeks they would need to gather their army?

Undead

The roar of the river tumbling over a ragged shelf filled Cam's ears. The walls and towers of Goldereth had been built at the edge of the precipice where the waterfall boiled into the chasm below the footbridge. Gentle mist moistened the narrow walkway, making the stones slippery under his boots and soaking his clothing and hair. The gorge was at least sixty paces across and two hundred feet deep. A guard tower protected the other side of the footbridge and beyond that, the rolling hill country swept away to a vague blur.

"Get going!" Hebron shouted from where he held the tower gate against the clot of Mahrowaiths forming in the gatehouse, a menacing pack of black obsidian, bloodred eyes, and salivating jaws. They let off that disturbing grinding rattle that came from the scaly hairs on the back of their necks. But they had learned to be wary of Hebron's sword.

Hebron braced his feet wide as red lightning crashed into his sword. It was like the light Cam had seen in the Life Stone that the Sameel character had unleashed on Galad in Afon Darodel. Cam cringed at the crackle of power. He should have insisted they find a different path. His vision was becoming very real.

Hebron's sword absorbed the attack as though it attracted the lightning to it and hurled it back at Zenek. The light exploded into the tower which erupted in a shower of stone that sent the Mahrowaiths scrambling to avoid a collapsing wall. Zenek vanished in a cloud of dust.

"Now!" Alaric shouted, and Hebron bounded through the door. He and Alaric shouldered the door closed and secured it as best they could with scraps of wood, iron, and stone before joining the others in their flight across the footbridge.

Laird grabbed Slone's other arm and helped Rebecca drag him across the slippery stones. A diffuse, greenish light surrounded them, and Cam thought it might be some strange effect of the mist from the waterfall. Spider had his sling out and kept casting furtive glances behind them. Draig padded behind Cam with his hackles raised and a low growl rumbling in his throat.

The footbridge swayed under Cam's feet as he advanced. The

bridge swung from giant cables spanning the gorge for an easy one hundred paces. Cam glanced down into the dizzying chasm of churning water flowing over the black pitted stone. No one could survive a fall into that maelstrom.

Drakeman reached the other side first and grabbed up a huge stone. "We have to destroy the bridge," he shouted. "That door won't hold them."

Laird helped Rebecca ease Slone down beside a crumbling stone wall once they reached the other side. Drakeman, Hebron, and Alaric scrambled down under the bridge, and using heavy stones, pounded on the four massive, rusted bolts that secured the four iron rails holding the bridge in place. Rebecca, Spider, and Cam took up positions at the footbridge, peering back across the still swaying bridge in case any of the Mahrowaiths broke through the door on the other side.

"Keep that stone out," Spider said, gesturing with his chin toward the Fire Stone in Cam's grip.

"We've got to get off this bridge." Cam had been here before in that horrible vision the Life Stone had shown him. "We should never have come this way."

He glanced at Rebecca. The side of her face was bathed in blood from some wound on her head, but she had her sword drawn, bravely facing the danger.

"You all right?" Cam asked.

She nodded, but glanced at Slone. His tunic was soaked with blood, and the hole in his shoulder smoked. "We'll have to help him down the stairs."

The door shivered and groaned.

"They're coming," Spider shouted.

"Let's go," Cam cried as the panic reached up to throttle him. He wouldn't let anyone die here. He didn't care what the Life Stone showed him. He would change it.

A snap echoed in the chasm over the growling of the waterfall, and the bridge creaked as it sagged heavily to one side. The gatehouse door exploded. Rock and iron spun through the air burning red, hissing, trailing tendrils of crimson smoke. A Mahrowaith jumped out onto the footbridge.

Cam's knuckles itched, and the pull of the Bragamahr clutched at his heart. It would be so easy to accept it. He wanted to. Maybe he should. Cam flung the errant thought aside, raised the Fire Stone, and sent a jet of flame at the Mahrowaith. It dodged aside, causing the footbridge to sway dangerously.

The flame slammed into the wall, sending it crumbling down in a shower of broken rubble and yellow fire. The Mahrowaith paused, raising its arms against the hail of stone. In that moment, Hebron leaped out onto the footbridge facing back the way they had come, the sword of Galad glowing a dull red in his hands.

"Run, all of you," he commanded.

"No, Hebron! No!" Cam cried. "I can do it." The big, redheaded man continued to advance carefully along the twisting, swaying bridge, holding the great sword in front of him, balancing as the footbridge teetered under him.

"Get out of here!" Hebron bellowed, his voice harsh with the command.

This time Alaric grabbed Cam by the arm and shoved him along the battlements. "We have no choice. Hebron has given us the only chance we have to escape. We must take it!"

"No!" Cam cried, the hot tears burning his eyes. The image of the vision flashed through his mind.

Accept us, the harsh voice of the Bragamahr growled into Cam's mind. The desire to give in made him queasy.

The Mahrowaith advanced. It was joined by another and then another, until six of them crept along the swaying footbridge toward Hebron. Cam jerked away from Alaric and sent a jet of flame that cut into two of the Mahrowaiths. They screamed in agony and lunged forward as the fire licked at them.

Alaric grabbed Cam and dragged him, stumbling, down the steps. Cam couldn't peel his gaze away from Hebron, who fought like the heroes of old, his red hair flying, his sword flashing. The sword sang as it sliced through the first Mahrowaith. The two halves of the beast tumbled off either side of the footbridge. The second and third dropped before another jet of red lightning crackled toward Hebron. His sword cut down another Mahrowaith, but Hebron was too late to intercept the bolt of lightning. It caught him in the shoulder, spinning him around. The little group paused in their flight, watching in frozen horror.

The last two Mahrowaiths bounded toward Hebron. Cam let

out a yell and sent a ball of yellow fire into the beasts, knocking them back. The bridge swayed violently, and the two beasts toppled over the side, engulfed in flames, shrieking as they fell.

Hebron grabbed at the railings. His feet slipped, and he tumbled over the side.

"No!" Cam screamed. Had he killed Hebron while trying to save him?

We can save him, the Bragamahr's voice scoured through him.

Cam yanked himself free of Alaric's grasp, and he and Draig bounded up the stairs and out onto the footbridge. He found Hebron dangling from the railing with one arm wrapped around an iron bar. A cry of relief burst from Cam's throat. The rusted metal tore loose, and Hebron jerked and dangled helplessly above the immense gorge with jagged rocks and hungry water far below. He clutched the railing with one hand while the other grasped the smoking sword.

A maniacal cackle echoed in the chasm, and Cam spun to face Zenek, who scrambled on top of the ruined tower beside the yawning gate. Red light danced in his hand. Drakeman and Alaric loosed arrows at Zenek, but the light flared and the arrows hissed as they burned to ash.

Draig jumped past Cam, bounding back toward the gate.

"Come back!" Cam shouted.

The earth shook, and the footbridge rocked wildly. Cam grabbed the railing and dropped to his knees, bracing himself.

"Zenek," he called, "don't do this." The continuing betrayal of the man he thought was his friend cut him to the core.

"You will refer to me as 'Zenek, Prince of the Tamil,'" Zenek shouted back. "You are nothing but usurpers. Murderers."

"Seems like you have that backward," Cam shouted.

The footbridge groaned and lurched. He and Hebron were going to fall.

Zenek raised his hand. "This time you will die as you should have done back at the great bend."

Draig's snarl echoed in the chasm, and his huge black body flew through the air, his teeth flashing. He slammed into Zenek, and they toppled off the wall.

Cam scrambled to grab at Hebron. Drakeman and Alaric joined him, and together, they heaved Hebron onto the footbridge.

Undead

"Draig," Cam yelled, "time to go!"

There was a moment's silence in which Cam experienced the sudden terror that Draig had sacrificed himself for them. But Draig limped through the ruined door and worked his way along the swaying footbridge.

They scrambled off the bridge and started racing for the stairs, where Rebecca and Spider supported Slone. Hebron didn't follow them. He gave Cam one searching glance and bounded down to the iron bolts that secured the footbridge. He raised the sword and hewed at the iron bar. Had he lost his mind?

Any normal sword would have broken, and Cam expected to see the sword shatter on impact. Instead, it cut cleanly through the iron bar as if it were no more than a branch or a twig. Hebron hewed at the two remaining bars, and the footbridge wavered and fell with a horrible crash that rang and echoed through the gorge.

They all stared in dumb silence as the footbridge slammed into the wall on the other side, twisted, groaned, and broke free, tumbling into the abyss where it was swallowed by the raging torrent.

Then Alaric was shouting at them. "We're exposed here. Move."

Cam checked that everyone was there and joined them in their headlong flight down the winding stairs away from Goldereth and the rushing river into the gathering darkness. He risked a glance back. A head rose silhouetted above the broken stone. Zenek's face was bathed in blood, and he grasped at his throat where blood seeped through his fingers. Draig hadn't managed to kill him. Zenek was still alive.

Cam's chest and throat constricted, and tears burned in his eyes. How could he succeed against such odds? The Bragamahr was sending more than Mahrowaiths against him. At this rate, he wouldn't survive long enough to reach the Lonely Valley. Who did he think he was? A poor mountain boy who was going to save the world? The idea was ridiculous. He had demonstrated yet again he wasn't strong enough. It was only dumb luck that saved them this time. Maybe he should go back to Braganeth Valley and let the Bragamahr have him. It would be much easier. If he died, neither magic could use him.

Rebecca stumbled on their descent down the stairs. He caught her elbow, and she gave him a weary smile despite the blood on her cheek. Her gray eyes were alight with the fire of defiance, and in them, Cam found the courage to shove his own despair aside. Rebecca needed him. They all did. They were going to keep fighting, and he would struggle on—for them. When his time came, at least he would know he had died for a good cause—that he had died for his friends.

Lorna let the horse canter at a mile-eating pace as she swayed with the animal's movement. She had been trained to ride from a young age. Careful to keep her shoulders over her hips, she maintained the back and forth swishing motion in her seat that would make the canter more comfortable for the horse. Her second horse trailed along behind.

She had ridden for nearly two days and a night with only a few stops to feed the horses. The mountains surrounding Mawsil grew closer by the hour, silhouetted against the pewter sky as daylight faded. She would cut through the pass, ride around the lake, and head straight for the Lonely Valley. It was the shortest route open to her.

It had been many years since she rode the Crimson Plain and even longer since she had returned to the land of her birth. The memories had been too painful, and she had been needed elsewhere. Now, the final days were coming. Bardon was near, and she had to reach the Lonely Valley before Cam did. Everything now rested on that boy and his courage. It was a slender thread upon which to hang the hopes and future of so many people.

If Cam did succeed, Lorna would have to explain how she had condemned her brother to a living death by her desperate attempt to save him. The thought of Maelorn and Tara sent her mind back to the days of their childhood. Maelorn and Bardon had been so different and not just in stature and temperament. There had always been something petty and small about Bardon's character, though she had refused to see it in the little brother she adored.

One spring day, Bardon and Maelorn had been in the practice yard of the palace at Torwyn, sparring with the servants. Maelorn's wooden sword cracked the wrist of his partner, who yelped and dropped his sword to the sandy floor.

Maelorn strode to his partner with a scowl of concern on his face. "Are you all right?" he asked. "I didn't mean to strike you so hard."

Undead

The servant massaged his injured wrist. "I am well, My Lord." Maelorn escorted him to the healers to make sure his injury was tended. On the other side of the paddock, Bardon sneered at such attention and intentionally whacked his partner on the head and lunged in to seize advantage of his momentary disorientation. His wooden sword cracked and slapped until the man fell curled around a broken arm.

"Bardon!" their father shouted as Bardon raised the sword for another strike. "Come here."

Bardon faced King Gwennan. He glowered and stomped off the pitch, tossing his wooden sword to the sand at the feet of the man who had extended his hand to take it from him.

Father and son glared at each other in a battle of wills Lorna had seen far too often. "You will compensate Erin from your own allowance, and you will serve in the stables for one week."

"I will not," Bardon shouted.

King Gwennan rose to his full height, and his voice become very soft. "You will or else you will spend a few months in the dungeons."

Bardon opened his mouth to argue and then closed it. He could see as well as Lorna that their father meant it. Bardon whirled away and stormed off.

Her father gestured to his seneschal, who eyed him expectantly. "Tend young Erin's injuries and see that he receives triple wages from Bardon's allowance until he is healed. Then King Gwennan grabbed Lorna's hand. "You can judge the character of a man by how he treats those he does not need."

She studied her father's wizened face. He was scowling as his youngest son strode into the shadow of the corridor.

Lorna wiped a strand of hair from her eyes as the memory played through her mind. Her father had known what kind of man Bardon would become and had taken measures to restrain him. And yet, he had failed.

She whistled to the horse behind her, and it sped up to canter beside them. It was time to give this horse a rest. Kicking her feet from the stirrups, she drew them under her until she was standing on the saddle. She waited for the right moment in the horse's stride before leaping into the other saddle and settling into her seat. It was a trick her father taught her long ago. Every minute was precious as she raced to find Cam, and this way, she didn't have to pause or slow the horses.

As she fixed her feet in the stirrups and settled into this horse's stride, Lorna scanned the area. She spied a black dot for a moment on a distant hill to her right. Sighing against the exhaustion, she forced herself to use the opal to reach out in search of whatever might be there. Expecting to find nothing, she was surprised to discover that she was surrounded by riders who were closing in on her. Some were very close. Only the way before her was clear. Was she being herded into a trap? These men all bore the taint of the Bragamahr, and she surmised that they must be wearing one of those obsidian and pyrite stones.

Lorna hissed to the horse and kicked it in the belly, urging it into a gallop. If she could reach the cover of the foothills, she might be able to elude them or find a less exposed place to stand and fight.

The wind whipped her hair behind her as she rose in the saddle and extended her arms to let the horse stretch its neck as it lunged forward. She focused on the opal, trying to keep track of the riders who were approaching fast. Shifting her focus to the jasper, she set the earth of the plain behind her to rolling and buckling. She glanced back. Several of the riders and horses toppled over in the churning earth. A dust cloud billowed up into the sky to screen them from view.

She whipped around to face forward again when something buzzed past her head. She snapped her head around. A rider galloped up on her left, his bow bent for another shot. He released, and Lorna tried to call up a shield. It was too late. The arrow plunged into the horse's side behind its shoulder right next to her knee, burying itself all the way up to the feathers. The horse stumbled and fell. Lorna tried to kick herself free of the stirrups. Her foot caught, and she was slammed to the ground. Her head bounced off the hard-packed earth as she sprawled onto her back.

She was barely aware of the horse kicking in its death throes. Her vision blurred, and a wave of nausea swept through her. She yanked her foot free of the stirrup and crawled to her hands and knees. Her stomach clenched, and she retched. Lights flashed before her eyes, and she wavered, clinging desperately to consciousness.

A rope dropped over her head and burned as it cinched tight against her throat. She reached for the Fire Stone and burned the rope away. Then something slammed into her head, and she groaned and slumped sideways. Someone tore the pendant from her neck. Panic

Undead

gripped her stomach. She would be defenseless without the stones.

An Inverni bent close to peer into her face. The little obsidian and pyrite jewel dangled before her eyes. The man dropped something over her head, and agony such as she had never known sent her mind reeling. Rivers of fire coursed through her veins. Her mind exploded, and every muscle contracted. Her mind and body were being stretched, stretched in every direction by the evil power of the Bragamahr. The taint of it burned within her. Scorching. Tearing. She tried to scream, but no sound came out. The Anarwyn was lost to her. She was aware of morganite and quartz and what might be a topaz gem. Morganite and topaz were not stones of the Anarwyn. They must respond to the Bragamahr, and Bardon was using them to paralyze her.

Rough hands forced her arms behind her back and bound them at the wrists. She was heaved over the back of a horse and was only dimly aware of the pounding trot as her mind drifted, eventually sinking into black oblivion.

Chapter Eleven
Uninvited Guests

"LET'S SEE TO THAT SHOULDER," Laird said, glancing at Slone. "It needs to be treated."

Spider knelt beside Slone where he slumped with his back to a boulder. Maybe he shouldn't admit it to anyone, but he was interested in seeing how Laird would heal Slone's wound. His mother had been a healer, and Spider was growing ever more certain that he would like to follow in her footsteps—even if he didn't drink the Dûr Crishal.

Laird gently unwound the hastily applied bandage from Slone's shoulder before rushing on. Even in the dim light of the fire, Spider could see the oozing wound was serious. Zenek's beam of red light had perforated Slone's shoulder from back to front, and a clear liquid mingled with blood dribbled from it.

They had left Goldereth and Braganeth Valley behind as they descended the long, winding stairway to a narrow cleft in the hills where a spring burst from the mountainside. Following the stream well after darkness overtook them, they camped in a grove of aspen. The gurgle of the stream and a cool night breeze blowing from the valley far below was a welcome relief from the stifling heat and haunting silence of the desert and Braganeth Valley. Laird had already inspected Hebron and found that he was uninjured. Hebron only shrugged. It was clear the sword of Galad was more than a mighty weapon. Not even the blood of the Mahrowaiths injured Hebron.

Rebecca hauled over a pot of steaming water and knelt beside Spider and Laird. She had a bandage on her head that was soaked red, but she wouldn't let Laird treat her until he'd administered to Slone. Drakeman had gone to search their back trail, while Hebron, Alaric, and Cam cooked a meal and repaired their damaged equipment. Draig lay on his belly by the fire, observing Cam's every move.

Spider shifted aside to give Rebecca room to work. Flickering shadows wavered on Rebecca's face as she tenderly washed the grime from Slone's brow. His face was haggard and sunken, his breathing shallow. The front of his tunic was soaked with blood. Firelight danced in his dark eyes, and he stared with a feverish light at Laird.

Rebecca patted his hand. "It'll be all right. Laird is a healer."

"Slone is an Anar," Spider said. "We're pretty hard to kill."

Slone smiled. "No men in all of Anwyn are as tough as the Anar."

Laird snorted as he poured the boiling water into a cup and added some crushed leaves to steep. "Hebron's right. The Anar have an oversized opinion of themselves. Give me a hand Spider."

The two of them tugged Slone's tunic over his head to expose the wound. Slone's burly muscles rippled under his hairy chest. Laird soaked a rag in the pot of hot water and gently cleaned the area around the wound. Then he gestured for Spider to assist him in rolling Slone onto his side so he could clean the exit wound on his back.

"You see here where the fire punched through?" Laird asked, pointing to the exit wound. "It's like an arrow wound, only the fire burned through instead of cutting the flesh. That's what saved him from bleeding to death."

Spider looked on with interest. Slone merely scowled.

Laird stirred the tea and handed it to Rebecca. "Help him drink this—all of it."

Slone wrinkled his nose as she raised his head onto her lap and brought the cup to his lips.

"What is it?" he demanded.

"A mixture of henbane, lettuce leaf, and valerian root," Laird explained. "It will help you relax and dull the pain."

Slone sipped it and shoved the cup away with his good arm. "That's awful," he sputtered.

Uninvited Guests

Laird smiled. "Grown men will drink the most vile liquor, but if you try to give them medicine that will actually help them, they pout and blubber like babies."

Slone sneered at him, seized the cup from Rebecca, and drank it down in one gulp.

"And wounded pride is a great motivator," Laird chuckled.

Spider enjoyed the joke. He'd seen his mother do that a million times. She also seasoned her remedies with honey and cloves to make them taste better. The memory sent a pang of regret through him. How he missed her. Why couldn't he have been there to save her that day the Mahrowaith came looking for Cam?

Laird extracted a small wooden box from his bag and popped off the lid. A rich, garlicky fragrance filled the air. He dipped his finger in the salve and rubbed it into both sides of the wound. Slone sucked in his breath but didn't cry out.

"This is a mixture of curcumin, garlic, and marshmallow, combined with lavender oil. It eases the pain and helps prevent infection."

"How do you know this?" Rebecca asked.

"Experience," Laird replied. When he finished, he returned the box to his pouch.

Slone closed his eyes. "That does feel better."

Laird glanced at Spider and Rebecca and held a finger to his lips. He withdrew the agate from his pouch, closed his fist around it, and shifted his body so the others couldn't see. Bowing his head, he placed his hand on Slone's shoulder and closed his eyes. His breathing slowed. A deep golden light burst from between his fingers. Slone sighed and sagged against Rebecca in sleep. Spider stared in amazement as the burned flesh on Slone's shoulder turned pink, and the wound closed. Laird kept his head bowed long after the skin was healed. When the light in his hand died away, he raised his gaze to theirs. Sweat beaded on his brow. Slone groaned and shifted in his sleep.

"You're using the Anarwyn," Rebecca whispered.

Laird gave them a sideways glance that could only be read as an acknowledgment.

"Then why bother cleaning the wound?" Spider asked.

"Because I want to soothe the injured, and cleaning and salves assist in the healing and help prevent infections. Good medicine is good medicine, whether you use the Anarwyn to heal or not."

Undead

"Why don't you want the others to know?" Rebecca asked.

"You saw how they responded to Zenek," Laird said. "Besides, I've been running from Bardon most of my life, and I don't want him to find out what I am until I have no other choice."

"I won't say anything," Rebecca said. "But we owe you once again."

"Friends don't owe each other," Laird said. "We help because we care."

Rebecca's eyes glistened, and Spider thought she might cry. She held it in and patted Slone's hand. "Thank you," she whispered.

"Now, let me close that wound for you," Laird said.

Spider watched as Laird tended Rebecca. What Laird did fascinated him. He slipped his own hand to the little pouch he wore around his neck, which contained his mother's broken agate and the tiny vial of water. If he drank the water, maybe he could do what Laird did. He could do what his mother had done. Maybe, he could do more than run from the Mahrowaiths. Perhaps he should try.

"We should have had Peylog lead us back to the river," Cam said.

Hebron and Alaric lounged around the fire repairing their equipment or oiling their swords and knives while Laird, Rebecca, and Spider tended to Slone's injuries.

"What makes you say that?" Alaric asked as he peered down the shaft of one of his arrows, turning it slowly.

"Twice now, the Life Stone showed me that footbridge and Hebron falling over the side."

"But you saved my life," Hebron responded. He tugged a thread tight on the hole in his tunic that he was stitching closed, knotted it, and cut it with his teeth.

"Yes, but the Life Stone warned us not to come here."

"Are you sure?" Alaric said. "Maybe it was telling you what to expect." He selected an arrow from his quiver and sighted down the shaft before extending it toward the fire to warm the wood for straightening. "Like it did at Afon Darodel."

Cam wasn't convinced. The Life Stone hadn't shown him anything about Zenek or the Bragamahr attacking him.

Uninvited Guests

"And how did Zenek get the power of the Bragamahr?" Cam asked. "I thought he was Tathanar."

Drakeman stepped out of the shadows. "The back trail is clear." He eased himself down beside the fire and glanced at Cam. "I think I can explain Zenek."

"Okay," Cam said, not trying to hide his curiosity.

"The Tathanar and the Anar are distantly related to the Tamil, who were the first to acquire the power of the Bragamahr. Remember that Ilsie was Tamil. Therefore, her descendants are also related to those first Tamil."

"You mean any Tathanar or Anar could use the power of the Bragamahr?"

"It seems logical. Otherwise, why would my ancestors try so desperately to keep anyone from entering Braganeth Valley?"

Cam rubbed his knuckles as he pondered, and he sensed the Bragamahr. It was there. Lurking. Waiting. He shuddered at the memory of its voice and the horrible wrenching pain that had ripped through him as they escaped the valley. The Bragamahr had stolen a memory from him. Had it taken something else?

Hebron set his tunic aside and lifted the broadsword into his lap. He took out his oil and wiped it along the black blade.

"Drakeman," Hebron said, "what else do you know about this sword?"

"Not much." Drakeman stretched and chugged a swig from his waterskin. "Why?"

"Look at it." Hebron gestured to the sword. "I hacked at three iron bars, and there isn't a single chip in the blade. It's as sharp as if it were new. I know metals, and no metal is capable of doing that."

"That sword's famous for a reason," Alaric said.

"It saved you," Cam said. "Why didn't Zenek's lightning injure you like it did Slone? And why doesn't the blood of the Mahrowaith hurt you? It has to be the sword."

Hebron shifted. "There's more. Several times now, I've felt a presence within the sword. It's aware, almost gleeful when I kill Mahrowaiths."

"Like the Life Stone," Cam said. "It also feels aware."

"Curious," Drakeman said.

"And," Hebron continued, lowering his volume, "a voice whispered to me that I should use the sword to cut the iron bars holding up the footbridge."

"A voice?" Cam said. "Are you saying the sword is alive? Or was it allowing the Anarwyn to speak through it somehow?"

Hebron shook his head and sheathed the sword. "I don't know."

Drakeman leaned back, placing his hands behind his head. "We lost so much knowledge in the fall of Goldereth and the other Tathanar cities. Maybe Lorna knows something about it. I've always wondered why Galad didn't go back to die beside Alys's grave."

"Maybe she wasn't there," Alaric said.

Cam thought that an odd statement. Was Hebron more sensitive to the Anarwyn than Lorna had thought? Or had the sword worked some magic on him, changing him? It had saved them several times now, but Cam wondered what the cost might be. What might the Anarwyn demand of Hebron? He would need to watch closely to see how the Anarwyn affected him.

Sighing, Cam rose to check on Slone and Rebecca.

"How is he?" Cam asked as he dropped down beside Rebecca and crossed his legs. The shadows were deeper here and hid her expression. A blonde hair trailed down her cheek.

Laird rose. "He'll live, but it might take a while for his shoulder to heal completely."

"Did you use the—"

A sharp gesture from Laird cut his words short.

"Quiet," Rebecca whispered. "He doesn't want the others to know."

"Okay," Cam said, though he couldn't see how it mattered anymore since Spider and Rebecca already knew. The others had surely guessed after how quickly Cam and Rebecca had recovered from the rough handling they endured while being dragged across the desert by the Inverni. If they hadn't, it was only a matter of time before they caught on. "But you also caused that light on the footbridge, didn't you?"

Laird glanced at the fire where the other three men lounged, conversing.

"So, you can control more than the agate?"

"No," Laird whispered. "It's just a trick."

"A trick that keeps the Mahrowaiths from seeing you," Spider whispered. "I saw you do it at the great bend."

"The agate can also provide courage and peace," Laird explained. "I use it to enhance those feelings, and it deflects the attention of the Mahrowaiths. It isn't really a shield."

"Interesting," Spider said.

"Yes, well," Laird turned back to Slone, "he may still catch a fever. We'll know by morning."

Laird strode away, and Cam noticed the bloody bandage on Rebecca's lap. He shifted to examine her head where a stone had struck her. Blood matted her hair, but the wound was closed.

"He's useful to have around," Cam said. "Does it hurt?"

"Not anymore."

Cam wanted to tell her that he had been afraid for her. That he was relieved she wasn't seriously injured. That he was sorry he hadn't done a better job of protecting her. But he couldn't do it with Spider sitting next to them.

"I think this is what my mother did," Spider said. "That broken agate I found in her hand is like the one Laird uses. All those times her remedies healed people who should have died—she was using the Anarwyn."

"Probably," Cam said, reluctantly shifting away from Rebecca.

"I would like to do that," Spider said, and his hand drifted to his pouch. Cam knew what he was thinking. That's where he kept the crystal vial of water called the Dûr Crishal. It was the water Cam drank, which allowed him to use the power of the Anarwyn. Cam considered telling Spider to drink it. But he remained silent. It was Spider's decision, and he had interfered enough already. He didn't trust either magic, and he had been shaken by the battle with the Bragamahr. Still, the Anarwyn had saved him twice now.

A low singing reached them, and they all turned toward the fire where Hebron and Drakeman cared for their equipment. Alaric had gone to take the first watch. Drakeman faced Goldereth and sang quietly in a baritone voice. The tune was slow and haunting. It was so sad that it drew tears to Cam's eyes.

"What is he singing?" Spider asked.

"*The Lamentation of Galad,*" Rebecca said. "It's in the old speech. It tells how Galad and Alys were driven from the city and pursued by the beasts. When Alys died, Galad took the sword that had once belonged to the Tathanar king and spent the rest of his life hunting the Mahrowaiths. It speaks of his sadness over the destruction of such a beautiful city and the loss of his only love."

"I'm not sure I need a sad song at the moment," Spider said.

Rebecca glanced at him, the light of the moon shining in her eyes. "Drakeman has lived his life with this sadness. The Tathanar have never forgotten how they were driven from their most beautiful city over twelve hundred years ago, nor how much was lost. Remember that his ancestor, Taniel, founded Goldereth at the end of the Second Age. To him, he is coming home to a land that has lived in his imagination since before he could ride a horse or shoot a bow."

The song ended, and they reclined in companionable silence for a long while as the creek gurgled past and the moon poked its head above the trees to the east. It was sometimes easy to forget that strong men, like Drakeman, Hebron, Alaric, and Laird, might have experienced sadness and despair in their lives.

Spider yawned and shifted. "Well, I'm not taking the next watch." He stretched and strode to his bedroll where he laid down and let out a long, exaggerated sigh.

Cam reached over and squeezed Rebecca's hand. "Slone will be all right," he said and trudged over to his own bedroll. He couldn't remember feeling so exhausted. Using the Anarwyn drained him like nothing else could. Still, it took him a long while to fall asleep. The ever-present sensation of the Bragamahr dwelling just over the mountains disturbed him, as did the fact that Zenek, someone he had called a friend, had tried to kill him. Maybe they hadn't escaped yet.

Zenek crawled from the pile of rubble to prop himself up against the remaining wall. He tore a piece of cloth from his tunic and wrapped it around the wound in his throat where the wolf's teeth had torn a jagged gash. Fortunately, the wolf hadn't punctured the artery, or Zenek would have bled out long ago. The only reason he was alive was that the fall from the wall had broken the wolf's hold and separated them. He had tumbled into a narrow space between blocks of stone where the wolf couldn't reach him.

Still, the wound was serious, painful, and rapidly growing stiff.

Uninvited Guests

The loss of blood left him lightheaded. He was bruised from head to toe from the collapsing wall, and at least one finger was broken. Steeling himself against the pain, Zenek yanked the broken bone into place. Cursing at the flash of agony, he laid his head against the wall to let the pain subside back to the throbbing ache.

He surveyed the battle site. The bodies of his Mahrowaiths lay smoking, cut in two or buried in the rubble. Their blood had congealed into beautiful lumps of red-veined obsidian. He remembered what Spider and Cam had said about the blood of the Mahrowaiths. It was a potent killer that could be absorbed into the body of an enemy where it would consume them from within—turning healthy, living flesh into a muck of black, oozing disorder. No power of the Anarwyn could heal such an injury.

Gingerly, Zenek reached out to touch a chunk of dried Mahrowaith blood. It warmed to his touch but didn't harm him. He permitted himself a sad smile. These Mahrowaiths had been created from his own blood. They would not hurt him. He gathered up several chunks of obsidian and slipped them into his pocket. Perhaps he could find some use for them.

Resting against the stone wall, he surveyed the damage. He toyed with the idea of returning to the Braganeth to create more Mahrowaiths to do his bidding, but the memory of the agony of their creation gave him pause. He had nearly died, and in his weakened condition, the effort would probably finish him for good. No. It was too risky.

The guard tower was destroyed, and the iron footbridge collapsed into the gorge. Nothing had gone the way he planned. He had become so confident of victory with his newfound powers and his beautiful servants. But Hebron's sword ruined everything.

The stories his mother whispered to him on cold winter nights had been true. The sword, Dorandel, was a powerful talisman of the Anarwyn. Too powerful for him. He might have been able to kill Cam if he had been unaided. Hebron would need to be neutralized. To do this, Zenek needed to control more of the stones of power, and he needed aid.

He groaned as he rose to his feet and stumbled down the remaining stairs. He would search for the bodies of the members of the Black Council whom Galad slaughtered at this very gate. Perhaps

159

he could take their stones and learn to use them. Then he would find Bardon and offer to join him. Together, they would be unstoppable. Or perhaps Zenek would find a way to teach Bardon his proper place.

By morning, Slone was tossing with fever, and Rebecca refused to leave his side. Cam left Spider, Rebecca, and Laird to care for Slone while he, Alaric, and Drakeman set out scouting the area for any danger and for a better place to camp.

They didn't return until early afternoon had settled over their encampment. Cam found Slone still feverish, but he was awake and sipping some broth. They fashioned a stretcher from two stout poles and a spare cloak and carried him a few miles farther down the mountain to a place Cam had found. It was a wooded vale near the stream enclosed on three sides by a high rock outcrop. The stone foundation of a rotted hut showed that someone had once lived here.

Draig trotted away to hunt, and they settled in to rest and prepare for the next leg of their journey. By nightfall, Slone's fever broke, and he awoke long enough to sip some broth.

They loitered around the fire while Alaric and Drakeman nibbled on penemel, reliving moments of their trip and wondering where Frederick, Ewan, and the rest of the company they left on an island in the Afon Fathwe were. Surely they had reached Seabrook by now. Messengers must also have carried word to King Chullain of the battle at the great bend of the river.

Cam took the first watch while the others retired. He climbed the leaf-covered slope on the edge of the rock outcrop and found a spot near the crest that gave him a wide view of the little vale. Brilliant stars splashed through the blackness of space, providing a silver light that lent a sense of enchantment to the scene. Draig joined him, and Cam ran a hand through the wolf's soft fur.

"How are you doing, old boy?" he said.

Draig rested his chin on his paws and studied Cam with his intelligent green eyes.

"Thanks for saving us back there," Cam whispered. "If you hadn't dragged Zenek down, I don't think any of us would have escaped."

Frogs and crickets filled the night air with their cadence, and

Uninvited Guests

Cam found himself relaxing for the first time in weeks. It was good to be in the mountains again—even if these weren't the ones he had called home. There was something vigorous and renewing about mountains. They were solid and dependable in a way few things were.

He leaned his head back against the cool stone, wondering how long it would take them to reach the Lonely Valley now that they had passed Goldereth. His eyelids drooped, and he shook himself. He rose to stretch and stay awake. The faint orange glow of the embers from the fire colored the darkness, revealing the lumps where his friends slept. Cam was rubbing his face when Draig started and lunged to his feet.

Cam jumped in surprise and crouched beside Draig, wishing he enjoyed the wolf's sense of smell and hearing. He waited for the crippling terror that preceded the Mahrowaiths. It never came.

"What is it?" Cam whispered.

Draig trotted away heading uphill away from the camp. Cam hesitated and considered waking his companions, but he decided to check it out first. It might just be a deer grazing nearby or some rabbit that had attracted Draig's attention. Cam followed him, using all his hunting craft to keep from making any noise.

They climbed the hill to a pile of boulders at the top and into a stand of aspen gleaming white in the darkness, like bones protruding from the earth. Not far from the outcrop, a pale light glimmered amid the aspen. Cam scowled and skulked through the shadows, every nerve tense until he crouched behind a wide aspen and peered into a small clearing.

What he found confused him. An old man sat cross-legged in a pool of delicate light. He held a glittering quartz crystal in his hand.

"Come sit, my boy." The voice was pleasant with a hint of age and weariness.

Remaining silent, Cam wondered if he should give the alarm.

"They can't hear you, and I won't harm you." The old man raised his head to stare directly at him.

Cam glanced at Draig to see how he reacted. The wolf perched on his haunches, apparently unconcerned.

"Trust the wolf, then," the man said. "He can tell the difference between the power of the Bragamahr and the power of the Anarwyn."

Cam crouched in silence. What did the man mean when he said

his friends couldn't hear him?

"Since you wouldn't come to me, I have come to you."

Understanding crept into Cam's conscious thought. This was no mountain hermit like those who wandered the Haradd Mountains. This could only be Bardon or Jathneel. Yet, surely Draig would know, and Bardon's presence would feel more evil.

The man smiled, showing rotted teeth. "I am Jathneel, as you guessed." He said this as if it was of little importance.

Cam knew better. This was the man who had trained Bardon. But how had he come to be here? And why didn't Draig sense the power of the Bragamahr in him?

"You are as suspicious as Lorna," Jathneel said. "I have already said I mean you no harm."

"What do you want? I know who you are."

"Then you should also know that only *I* have the power to release Maelorn and Tara from their stone prison."

Straightening, Cam stepped to the edge of the circle of light. There was no point hiding anymore. Draig followed him.

"What do you mean?"

"Sit." Jathneel gestured to the ground in front of him.

Cam remained standing. He wanted to be able to fight or flee, should the need arise. He reached into the pouch he wore around his neck to grip the Fire Stone.

Jathneel sighed. "When Lorna tried to stop the curse cast by the power of the Bragamahr using the power of the Anarwyn, she unwittingly created something new. The magics merged in a dyad that can only be broken with the combined power of the Anarwyn and the Bragamahr. This is why neither Lorna nor Bardon can break the curse. Lorna, because she will not accept the Bragamahr, and Bardon, because the Anarwyn rejected him. Do you follow?"

Cam raised his hand self-consciously to the dyad he carried in the same pouch containing the Fire Stone and the Life Stone. He *did* follow.

"That won't work," Jathneel said. "It is made only of the stones of Anarwyn."

Cam snatched his hand away. How had this man known?

Jathneel withdrew an object from the folds of his robes. He raised it, and it floated toward Cam before settling onto the leaves at his feet. Cam stepped back.

"This is the weapon you seek."

Cam knelt and peered at the glittering object but refused to touch it. It was similar to the dyad Lorna had given him, but this had three stones set in gold. A perfect, smoky quartz crystal occupied the center, flanked by a red agate with gold streaks on one side and a milky-white moonstone on the other.

"This dyad is the only way to restore the balance that was disrupted when Lorna combined the two magics."

"There are three stones," Cam pointed out.

"Master of the obvious, I see," Jathneel chuckled. "The quartz crystal is the Union Stone. It acts as a catalyst between two incompatible stones. It is not part of the dyad."

"So, why would you give this to me?" Cam demanded. The man was betraying his own pupil.

"Because..." Jathneel's voice was no longer pleasant. It had a hard edge to it. "...Bardon is a fool who desires only power without knowledge. Without the wisdom to understand how power should be used, a man will simply destroy himself and others with him. Power without knowledge is the most dangerous kind."

"You're afraid of him," Cam said. This thought had never occurred to him.

Jathneel snorted. "Of course, I'm afraid of him, as you should be. Bardon has lost all perspective. He delves too deeply. You see, the Bragamahr is like a parasite. It eats away at memories and feelings of security and happiness until it so perverts and twists reality for its users that they destroy themselves and those they love. This is why Ilsie and her mother fled north. Her father had tried to kill them when the Black Council splintered. You must understand why it is imperative that you succeed. If you fail, the Anarwyn may abandon humankind once and for all. You have felt this, have you not? This is what stirs that vague fear that makes you wish to hide your heritage."

Cam stared in open shock. How did this man know so much? Was he here working for Bardon, trying to confuse Cam so he wouldn't be able to break the curse?

"Why should I trust you?" Cam demanded.

"I can't give you any reason to trust me," Jathneel said. "Were I in your shoes, I would have fled long ago. Your courage does you credit. Now, I ask you to trust where no trust has been earned or deserved. I ask you to trust because, in the deepest corners of your soul, you know that you must."

Cam stared at Jathneel, uncertain, disoriented. Could Lorna have gotten so much wrong?

"I have set the trigger to the same words Lorna has given you. You need only hold the dyad in your hand and utter those words."

"If it's so simple, why don't you do it?"

"Ahh. I wondered when we would come to that. The answer is simple. The Anarwyn will not allow me. It keeps me far away from the Lonely Valley for fear that I might attempt to mingle the two magics further."

"Further? Meaning that you already have?"

Jathneel gestured toward the stone. "Lorna unwittingly combined them. I am trying to restore the balance."

That was an evasive answer. Cam glanced at the dyad. Did Jathneel mean that this dyad combined the powers of both magics?

"I will not serve the Bragamahr," Cam said.

He had already decided this. He *had* to keep the sand under his skin so he could free Maelorn and Tara. After that, he was going to scrape it out.

"I expected nothing less," Jathneel replied. "If I thought you might, I would not surrender this dyad to you. I waited to see how you would fare in the valley of the Braganeth. You surpassed even my expectations. Though I doubt you have any idea what the magics will require of you."

"This is why you paid the Inverni to kidnap me?"

"Yes, but also to save you from Bardon."

"Why take Rebecca?"

Jathneel shrugged. "Lorna valued her so highly, I was curious to see why."

Cam wanted to ask what he knew about Rebecca's background, but he didn't want this man to focus on her. He wanted to keep her safe.

"You think Maelorn and Tara are really alive?"

Jathneel bobbed his head noncommittally from side to side. "Alive? I should think not. But they are certainly not dead."

"That makes no sense."

"Perhaps not."

Uninvited Guests

Cam glanced at the dyad. "This will really work?"

"Most certainly."

"And I have to be the one to do it?"

"I know no one else who can."

Cam studied him. His gut told him there was something not right about this. Something this man was not telling him. And yet, the desire to lift the golden dyad and utter the words Lorna had taught him was strong. If Lorna's dyad failed, he could try this one. It would be a safeguard against something going wrong.

"What will this do to me?" he asked.

Jathneel grunted. "Nothing more than what Lorna's would do. You trust her, do you not?"

Cam scowled.

"If she was willing to send you off on this quest, she must have believed it was safe."

"But you don't think it is?"

"No power is safe to handle." Jathneel raised his hands in surrender. "If Lorna's dyad will not harm you, this one will not. I cannot say more."

Cannot or will not? Cam thought. He glanced at Draig. "What do you think?" he whispered.

Draig blinked at him and bobbed his head.

Jathneel laughed. "The wisdom of the great Maured of Taniel is famous."

Cam rubbed his chin. Why did he feel so conflicted? He should send this man on his way, or even better, separate his head from his shoulders and be done with it. And yet, there was something deep inside that troubled him. Jathneel would know more than Lorna about the Bragamahr and the curse that locked Maelorn and Tara in the stone. Lorna herself had not been confident about her dyad. It was her last desperate effort.

A breeze shuddered through the aspen leaves, and Cam noted that neither Jathneel's hair nor his clothes stirred. He stiffened. "Why doesn't the breeze affect you?"

"My boy," Jathneel chuckled again, "I am not here. I am on my ship anchored on the Brunen River to the south."

Cam glanced at the dyad resting on the leaves at his feet. "Then how…"

Undead

"It's a simple working of the Anarwyn, but it can only be used over a short distance." Jathneel's image wavered. "And it requires great strength to hold the illusion as long as I have done."

"But didn't you betray the Anarwyn? Why can you still use it?"

"My dear boy," Jathneel said, "once it is granted, the power cannot be taken away. Your ability to use the power depends upon your own strength and confidence in it. Besides, I know my limits, unlike some." His image flickered and faded.

"Wait," Cam said. He had so many questions.

"Remember what I have told you, and do not share this information with anyone. They will not understand and will take the dyad from you. Maybe even try to destroy it. The destiny of all Anwyn rests upon your shoulders. Do not fail us."

The light grew dim, and the image of Jathneel became smaller and smaller until the light blinked out with a quiet pop.

Cam sank to his knees on the damp leaves. What should he do? What if this was all a ruse to destroy him? Though it was obvious Jathneel hadn't told him everything, so much of what he said rang true.

Cam stretched forth a finger to touch the dyad. The stones were cold. Nothing happened. There was no sense of danger. No fear. He picked it up. The dyad felt heavy, though it was nothing more than a few stones set in some gold.

He let Draig sniff it. His nose touched it and, he sat back on his haunches, supremely disinterested. Cam slipped the dyad into this pouch next to the Life Stone, the Fire Stone, and Lorna's dyad.

No matter what happened, he would not serve the Bragamahr. He had made that decision already, and he had confirmed it in Braganeth Valley.

Cam crept back to his post in the crags above their camp and surveyed the area to make sure nothing had happened in his absence. All was quiet, and his friends were sleeping. Cam wrestled with his decision. Both Lorna and Jathneel had said the responsibility was his. If that were true, he would make sure he carried it out with as little injury to his friends as possible. And if that meant using a dyad that mixed the two magics, then so be it.

Alaric relieved Cam from the watch, and Cam retreated to his blankets to grapple with this new dilemma. How could he keep such a thing from his friends? Was he endangering them by doing so?

Uninvited Guests

Cam was drifting off to sleep, his mind a fog of confusion, when a low growl from Draig brought him upright. He opened his eyes wide as he reached for the hilt of his sword.

Chapter Twelve
Millstones of the Past

"WHAT IS IT, BOY?" Cam whispered.

Draig's hackles were raised, but Cam couldn't detect anything odd. He peered up to where Alaric leaned with his back to a tree on the rocky ledge above them. Cam could barely make out his form in the shadows. Taking several moments to scan the clearing and the dark bundles that represented the rest of the company, he patted Draig.

"What is it?" he asked again.

Draig stared off toward the undergrowth by the creek that lay dappled with shadows. Something stirred. Cam's muscles tensed. A branch swayed.

Master. A rough voice crackled through Cam's mind, and he sucked in his breath. The presence lurked in the shadows near the creek.

"A Mahrowaith," he breathed. Why wasn't his heart constricting in terror as it always did when the beasts approached? And why had it called him *master?*

Cam jumped to his feet and yanked his sword from its sheath. His movement startled the others, and soon they had all risen— except for Slone—and were staring around at the darkness. Alaric clattered down to them from his watch.

"What is it?" Hebron whispered as Drakeman built up the fire.

The faint stink of rotten eggs and horse musk drifted on the rising air from the creek.

Millstones of the Past

"There's a Mahrowaith down by the creek," Cam said.

Hebron stepped protectively in front of the small group with Dorandel drawn, its blade gleaming bloodred in the darkness.

Master, the horrible voice said again.

A tremor swept through Cam. He could feel the beast meant him no harm. But how could he know such a thing? Was this some trick Jathneel sent to confuse them? Was Zenek behind it?

"Why doesn't it attack?" Spider said.

"It doesn't intend to," Cam said.

"What?" Rebecca stepped up beside him. "How do you know that? And why don't I feel that horrible dread?"

Hebron lowered his sword and studied Cam. "Care to explain?"

"I can't," Cam said. "I don't know myself. Can they just decide who to like?"

"They are creatures of the Bragamahr," Drakeman said. "They exist only to destroy."

"We should kill it," Spider said. "I don't want that thing drinking my blood in the night."

"No, wait," Cam whispered. "Don't kill it—at least, not yet."

The bushes by the creek rustled, and Hebron snapped his sword up, assuming a fighting stance. Draig relaxed and sat on his haunches. Cam scowled at him. This was an odd reaction for a Maured who was supposed to be the most ferocious enemy of the Mahrowaiths. What could it mean?

Rebecca picked up a rock and chucked it into the bushes. A horrible shriek split the air and crashing exploded into the quiet of the night. The sounds soon faded into the distance.

Spider stared at him. "I feel like I should have a grasp on what just happened, but somehow, I'm lost."

"Cam?" Hebron asked as he sheathed his sword.

Cam shook his head and sank to the ground. "I don't know."

He considered telling them about Jathneel, but he figured the strange Mahrowaith was enough for them to worry about tonight. Besides, he didn't know what to say about it. Far off, he could sense the presence of the beast, the way a man could know a predator was watching him. And yet, he felt no terror. What could it possibly mean?

"I don't know," he said again.

Undead

Rebecca started to wakefulness with the splash of a warm tongue across her face. She sat bolt upright to find Draig panting over her. His coat sparkled with droplets of dew. Her blankets were soaked through, and she shivered before patting his muzzle. "All right. I'll get up. Where's Cam?"

"Relaxing," Cam said, "while Slone begins to pull his weight around here."

Rebecca tossed the blankets aside. She should have been up first, tending to Slone and collecting firewood. Sleeping late wasn't the way to show them all she was determined not to be a burden ever again.

Cam leaned against the outcrop with his hands clasped behind his head and his feet propped up on a small boulder. Slone bent over the fire where a rabbit was roasting on a spit. The aroma of cooking meat made Rebecca's stomach growl.

"You're up?" Rebecca asked Slone as she clambered to her feet.

"I'm up, and I've washed and hunted all while you were lazing about."

"Nice," she said. "We tend you back from the brink of death, and this is the thanks we get?"

Slone chuckled and worked his shoulder. "It's a bit stiff, but I haven't felt this good in a long while."

"Excellent," Drakeman said. "It's a long day's hike to the Afon Fathwe from here."

"I'm ready," Slone said, "thanks to Laird."

Drakeman cast Laird a knowing glance, and the rest of the company rolled from their blankets to join them.

"You slept through all the fun," Spider told Slone.

When Slone scowled, Spider and Laird told him about the Mahrowaith that had appeared at the edge of the encampment during the night.

"I'd've parted its head from its shoulders," Slone said, fingering the handle of his axe.

"It didn't stick around long enough," Spider said, though he glanced at Cam, who shifted and averted his gaze.

Rebecca studied him wondering what was bothering him and

why he had been so certain that this Mahrowaith meant them no harm. If he chose to keep his own counsel, then she would respect it. He had taken enough risks for her to earn her trust.

They set out after breakfast, following the creek past the ruins of villages and stone walls that had once marked the boundaries of fields, trending ever southeast. Rebecca sensed a growing anticipation that something was going to happen. Or was it that something had already happened here long ago? She couldn't tell. Still, it was a strange feeling. Ever since they passed the gates of Goldereth, she had been experiencing these moments of awareness.

By late afternoon, the cluster of rotting buildings grew thicker and the herds of wild cattle more numerous. Alaric called a halt behind a tumbled old barn.

"We're near the Afon Fathwe," he whispered. "Travelers sometimes stop here on their way up or down the river. There used to be an old tavern and a little settlement. I'm going to take a look around. We might be able to find news of what has been happening and maybe a boat or two to carry us down the river."

"I'll come with you," Slone said.

Drakeman grinned. "I think I should come along too since Slone and boats aren't exactly friends."

The three of them slipped away while the rest threw off their packs and grabbed a much-needed break.

Rebecca dropped to the ground between Cam and Spider, grateful for the rest. The fishy scent of the river clung to the air. And there was something else just at the edge of her perception, something troubling. After refreshing herself with a few mouthfuls of water from her waterskin, she glanced at Cam.

"Do you feel anything different about this place?" She didn't know how else to explain her strange sensations.

"I feel death," Spider said, stretching out on the ground using his pack for a pillow.

"That's a happy thought," Cam said.

"I'm not kidding," Spider said with a scowl. "People have died here—a lot of them."

Rebecca studied him, trying to make out what he meant.

"There is something strange about this place," Cam said. "It's

Undead

like something has been waiting for us."

"Exactly," Rebecca said. "I'm not sure we should stay here."

Cam lay back and closed his eyes. Rebecca was right, but he was so exhausted. The events of the last two nights meant that he hadn't managed to get much rest.

"Let's give Alaric and the others a chance to see what's about," he mumbled. "I'm going to steal a few winks if I can."

As he relaxed, he became aware of that presence he sensed on the other side of Goldereth and again when the Mahrowaith wandered into their camp. Was that what he was feeling? How had he become connected to a Mahrowaith?

"What's wrong, Hebron?" Spider's voice cut through Cam's thoughts, and he opened his eyes.

Hebron was pacing with his sword in hand. Cam glanced at Rebecca and Laird. They were both watching Hebron's agitated movements. He paused to scowl at them.

"I have to go," Hebron said.

"Go where?" Spider said. "Alaric said to wait here."

"She's calling to me," Hebron explained.

"Who is?" Spider looked over at Cam as though Hebron had gone mad.

"*She* is," Hebron whispered, holding up his sword.

Draig rose to his feet and padded over to Hebron. He nuzzled his hand and trotted a few paces.

"Looks like Draig wants to go, too," Cam said. He grabbed his pack and crawled to his feet. "I'm not letting you go anywhere alone." Maybe this feeling was what Rebecca had been talking about.

The rest joined him, shouldering their packs, and shifting about expectantly as Hebron vacillated. Rebecca gave Cam an I-told-you-so look.

"All right," Hebron said, "but let's hurry."

Draig wagged his tail and trotted away. They followed at a quick pace to keep up, weaving in and out of the ruined village, overgrown fields, and empty corrals. Wild cattle started from their wallows, and a few dogs turned tail and bolted as soon as they caught wind of

172

Millstones of the Past

Draig's scent. Draig led them downhill through a thick rush marsh to the crumbling remains of a little cottage. Its roof had long since collapsed, and the skeleton of a dock clung to the shoreline. The place smelled fresh and clean with the breeze blowing in off the river that gurgled past.

Hebron and Draig stopped as one in front of a monument constructed of smooth river stones stacked in a mound about five feet high. Colorful bits of cloth and half-burned candles had been wedged into the crevices. All around, broken pottery, flowers, and even bones of animals lay strewn about.

"Is this Alys's grave?" Rebecca breathed.

"Apparently," Laird said. "She is still the object of veneration."

Hebron fell to his knees and drew his sword. He held it up before laying it across the base of the monument. Its blade flashed crimson red, and a whispering sounded through the trees.

"I return Galad's blade to you," Hebron said with a bow.

The whispering grew louder, and Cam glanced up at the trees, thinking it was the wind in the branches.

"The spirit of Galad is reborn," a woman's voice said, gentle and sweet. It had to be Alys.

"No, My Lady," Hebron said. "But I am your humble servant."

Rebecca edged closer to Cam, and Spider knelt behind Hebron and bowed his head.

The branches of the tree shuddered. "Do not bow to me," Alys said. "My body is dead, but so long as the sword endures, I remain to fight the servants of the Bragamahr who slew my people."

"I am not worthy," Hebron mumbled.

Tears burned in Cam's eyes. The strongest and bravest man he had ever known was admitting that he doubted himself. Somehow the idea had never occurred to him.

"I have accepted you," Alys said. "You have proven yourself worthy. Now, take Galad's blade, and use it to restore balance to the lands of Anwyn. Only then will Dorandel be sheathed once and for all."

Hebron bowed low. "Yes, My Lady."

He reached out to grasp the hilt of the sword. As he did, a bright red light flashed, and for an instant, the face of a beautiful young woman materialized in the air above the pile of stones. Rebecca gasped, and Laird uttered a low curse of surprise.

Undead

Hebron raised the sword as the bloodred light raced along the blade. "I will be with you," Alys said. "I will guide you."

The rustling in the branches of the trees ceased, and Hebron rose. He sheathed the sword and faced them. A single tear trickled down his cheek into his beard. Rebecca stepped up and hugged him.

When she drew back and wiped at her eyes, Hebron took a deep breath. "Finally, I understand."

"So," Spider said, "she has been in that sword all along?"

"At least a part of her."

Draig's ears perked up, and he tested the breeze with a raised snout.

Cam spun around as Slone, Drakeman, and Alaric parted the rushes and headed toward them.

"I thought I might find you here," Drakeman said. He stopped beside Rebecca and draped an arm around her shoulder. "It's a sad place, isn't it?"

Rebecca glanced up at him. "You've been here before?"

"Once, years ago."

"Did you find any boats?" Laird asked.

Slone grinned. "Nope, but I'm not going to complain. We'll just have to travel the way nature intended."

"On foot?" Spider asked.

"That's what you've got 'em for," Slone said.

Alaric stepped over to bow before the monument the way Hebron had done. Drakeman joined him.

While they waited, Cam interrogated Slone. "Did you find anyone with news?"

"We did," Slone said. "Frederick, Ewan, and the others passed by here several days ago."

Cam smiled in relief. "Well, that's something." He had been worried that he was responsible for the death of all those men.

"Please tell me," Spider said, "that there's a tavern where we can get a proper night's sleep."

"No taverns for you," Alaric said as he rose. "We don't want to attract any attention."

Laird drew his sword. "You've already done that," he said as he peered back the way they had come.

A lone man carrying a long lance stepped out of the rushes. He wore a leather brigandine and steel cap. A shaggy hound padded up

Millstones of the Past

beside him, showing no fear of Draig.

"What do you think you're doing?" the man demanded.

Rebecca flinched at the sight of the stranger. She drew her sword at the same time Hebron drew his and noted that Alaric already had an arrow nocked on his bowstring. The man didn't advance on them. Instead, he examined the monument as if he expected them to have damaged it somehow.

Drakeman sheathed his sword and raised his hands. "We came only to honor the Lady Alys."

The man studied them and set the butt of his spear on the ground. His hound sat on its haunches, its tongue lolling out as it panted.

Three more men stepped out of the rushes, each holding a longbow with arrows nocked on the strings. Rebecca tensed and surveyed the area for cover.

"I see you meant no harm," the man said. "I am Erol, descendant of Elis. We are keepers of the tomb."

Drakeman gave the man a respectful bow. "I salute you. I am Lord Drakeman, son of Chullain, Crown Prince of the Tathanar." He swept his hands in an encompassing gesture. "These are my friends."

The men glanced at each other before lowering their weapons and stepping over to greet them. When they saw the sword in Hebron's hands, they stopped. Hebron sheathed it, but the men gaped.

"You bear Dorandel, the sword of Galad?" The leader's voice was filled with awe.

He and his companions fell to their knees before Hebron and bowed their heads. Rebecca glanced at Cam in surprise.

"How may we serve you?" the leader asked.

Hebron shuffled his feet and looked to Drakeman for assistance.

"We need to travel in secret to the Brunen," Drakeman said.

The men rose. "There are no boats in the village at the moment."

"Can you show us the safest path to remain unseen?"

"Yes, My Lord. Follow me."

The men rose and jogged off toward the rushes without waiting to see if they would be followed.

"I guess it's time to go," Slone said, and they all fell in behind the men.

Rebecca stole one last look at Alys's monument. The wonder at what she had seen and heard would never leave her. That Alys had been fighting this battle for over a thousand years gave Rebecca courage that she could keep fighting as well.

Erol and his men led them in a roundabout way through the ruined village to the rolling hills south and east. They encountered no one, but the dancing light of flames peeked through the trees from the direction of the river.

Night overtook them before they halted to camp in a clearing beside a gurgling creek.

"Thank you," Drakeman said. "How far to the Brunen from here?"

Erol leaned on his spear. "If you head due south, you should strike it before dark tomorrow." He straightened and bowed. "We must be getting back, My Lord."

"Thank you again," Drakeman said.

Erol glanced at Hebron. "May the Anarwyn guide your feet and protect you on your journey."

He and the other three men ducked into the shadow of the trees.

"I'm ready to hit the sack," Spider said. He shrugged off his pack and kicked branches and pine cones out of a flat spot on the ground.

"Good," Alaric said. "You've got first watch."

Rebecca chuckled with the rest of them as Spider sputtered and complained. She found a comfortable spot between the roots of a huge pine tree and settled in to sleep. She was too tired to worry about eating.

Morning arrived damp and chill, and Alaric led them due south. The foothills soon gave way to forests of maple, oak, and beech. By late afternoon, the quiet rush of the Brunen reached their ears, along with the rich fragrance of wet earth and fish. Wild cattle roamed about. Their muddy wallows scoured the earth, and their trails cut through the verdant landscape, tending toward the river.

Alaric brought them to a halt in the shadow of a great oak with its roots buried in the waters of the Brunen. Rebecca stepped up beside Cam to gaze at it in wonder.

Millstones of the Past

"Isn't it beautiful?" she sighed. The magic of the moving water inspired a sense of wonder in her, and she longed to dive in for a good wash.

"Yes," Cam agreed. "Much bigger than I expected."

The river flowed slow and deep. Its waters coiled and churned in a ceaseless, relentless flood. It must have been half a mile wide with a maze of islands below them. Willows bent their branches toward the water, like young maidens letting the river flow through their fingers.

"That's a lot of water," Spider said. "Are we supposed to swim it?"

"Not me," Slone said.

Hebron guffawed and slapped Slone on the back. "Still haven't found those sea legs, have you?"

"I keep telling you, my legs have nothing to do with it. I don't have fins. That's the problem."

"We'll float," Alaric said.

"Uh, how?" Spider asked.

"You'll see. Let's find a place to camp before it gets dark."

They made their camp in a small glade among the willow trees several yards back from the river.

"No fire tonight," Drakeman said. "We don't want to attract any unwanted guests."

Cam slapped at a sting on his neck. "We already have guests." Swarms of blood-sucking mosquitoes and biting flies descended upon them.

Spider wolfed down a quick meal and retreated to the relative safety of his blankets. "I'm not coming out," he announced, "until you do something about those bugs."

Rebecca chuckled at his antics as he burrowed into his blankets and attempted to keep every bit of flesh concealed. She regretted using him the way she had, especially now that she had grown to understand how devoted he was to Cam and Cam to him. Separating them had been cruel.

"You're pathetic," Cam said to Spider and swatted at a black fly that landed on his arm. Despite his words, he drew out his cloak and tugged it close about him.

"No point giving them an invitation," Spider said.

Laird strode to the edge of their encampment where a huge willow had fallen, leaving a hole in the canopy. He withdrew his knife and cut several large clumps of a tall grass with long thin leaves.

A powerful lemony-floral fragrance wafted through the encampment. Laird handed a bunch of grass to each of them.

"Crush this between your hands and rub it over any exposed skin." He demonstrated by rolling the grass into a ball, crushing it, and rubbing the leaves all over his face, neck, and hands.

Spider peeked out from his blankets. "I'm waiting to see if they swarm all over you and carry you away to suck you dry."

Laird chuckled. "Suit yourself. I'll be the one relaxing while you're all swatting yourselves silly."

"I'll try it," Rebecca said, and she crushed the leaves between her hands, rubbing them hard until her palms grew hot. The powerful fragrance made her eyes water and drove away every other scent. She rubbed the leaves all over her bare skin and waited. The cloud of mosquitoes drifted away from her, and she grinned. "It doesn't smell bad," she said. "Reminds me of lemons."

"What's a lemon?" Cam asked.

"A sour fruit that is sold in Abilene in the wintertime. With a bit of honey and water, its juice makes a refreshing drink."

The others followed her example, and Spider eventually crawled out from his blankets to join them.

"What is this plant called?" Drakeman asked.

"I'm surprised to find it here," Laird said. "It's prolific along the southern banks of the Willow River. I've rarely found it north of the Elbrus Mountains. My mother called it Imlid."

"Now Spider can sleep like a baby," Hebron said.

"I plan on it," Spider replied, "after all the abuse you've been heaping on us."

"Who's got the first watch?" Alaric said as he tossed his clump of grass from him.

"It's my turn," Rebecca said. They weren't going to pass her over again. She wouldn't let them. Drakeman studied her and then nodded.

"Ships come up and down the Brunen," he said, "so make sure you stay back from the bank, well-hidden."

"I will." Rebecca strode to the edge of the clearing away from the river where the mosquitoes and flies were less bothersome, grateful for Laird's strange plant.

Millstones of the Past

She leaned her back to a tree, listening to the music of the night as the others rolled up in their blankets. The river lapped quietly at the shores, creating a low cadence that rose and fell with rhythmic regularity. Insects chirped and called to each other. Huge blue and green dragonflies floated through the air before alighting on a branch or blade of grass only to rise and hover somewhere else before fluttering away.

As evening fell, bits of yellow light pulsed and twinkled amid the trees. Rebecca sat erect. She had never witnessed anything like this. Soon, hundreds of little lights floated about the clearing and among the trees, blinking and winking in a silent cadence that added a deep feeling of magical otherworldliness to the night. A sense of peace like she had not experienced since they left Abilene washed over her.

The horror of Braganeth and Goldereth was behind them. Once they crossed the river, it would only be a matter of days before they reached the Lonely Valley. Then what would she do? Cam would go off to the West Mark, and Drakeman would want to carry her back to Abilene. But she wasn't sure she wanted to return to the life of the pampered favorite of King Chullain. For the first time in her life, she felt really alive and free.

The quiet crunch of a boot on leaves brought her around to find Cam strolling toward her, swatting away the mosquitoes.

"Don't bring them over here," she said. "That Imlid plant is working."

Cam jogged around in a circle, swatting at the mosquitoes before he ducked and crawled over to plop down beside her. He raised another handful of the grass and crushed it between his hands.

"I'm gonna sleep in this stuff," Cam said.

Despite his little dance, he seemed so much older now than he had when she first saw him marching into Abilene. But he was also stronger, more confident. He rubbed the grass over his skin and handed it to her. "Better top it off before it's too dark to find the grass." He drew his knees up and wrapped his arms around them.

Rebecca rubbed the grass on her skin again and held it in her lap, enjoying the rich, citrus smell.

"How are you holding up?" Cam asked.

"I'm all right. They sure are beautiful," she said, gesturing toward the shifting cloud of blinking lights scattered amid the trees.

179

"Yep," Cam agreed. "Alaric says they're little bugs."

"Aah, that's right," Rebecca replied. "I forgot. I heard about them once in Abilene. It's like they possess their own magic."

"Do you mind if I ask you a question?" Cam said.

"Hmm?"

"Am I being stupid?"

She grinned at him. "Well, I've known quite a few stupid young men, but I wouldn't count you as one of them."

"I'm serious. What if Lorna and the rest of them have this all wrong?"

Now Rebecca scowled. "What do you mean?"

Cam shifted, and a scared look came into his eyes. "I don't know if I should tell you."

"I think you can trust everyone here," she said, a bit offended at his reluctance.

"I know, it's just that…well…I'm…what if Lorna's dyad doesn't work?"

"Why wouldn't it?"

Cam averted his gaze. "Because it was only created with the power of the Anarwyn."

Rebecca opened her mouth to answer but closed it. Everything was becoming clear. "Lorna told you that she created something different when she tried to stop the spell?"

"Yes."

"So, both magics might be needed to break it?"

Cam rubbed his knuckles where the black scars were and nodded. "I can feel him, you know. The Bragamahr. When we were on the bridge, I was tempted to accept him so I could save Hebron."

A knot clutched at Rebecca's stomach. "You didn't, did you?"

Cam clicked his tongue in annoyance. "Of course not. But I wanted to. Don't you see? I could become worse than Bardon."

"You won't," Rebecca said. She grabbed his hand and squeezed. "I believe in you."

Light from the newly risen moon flickered through the canopy of leaves. Cam blinked at her, and his eyes glistened with moonlight. "I meant what I said," he went on. "If I try to harm any of you, I want you to kill me before I can."

Rebecca leaned in close. "You would never hurt me," she whispered, and their lips touched.

Fire ignited in her stomach, and she longed for his strong arms to enfold her. She shifted so she was facing him more fully. He straightened and drew her close. Their lips met again in a soft, gentle kiss that lingered and lingered. When they parted, Rebecca's stomach tingled. She smiled shyly and leaned back against the tree.

Cam grasped her hand. "You probably shouldn't tell Drakeman about that."

Rebecca chuckled. "He can be protective."

"It felt nice." Cam squeezed her hand.

The heat rose in Rebecca's cheeks. "For me, too."

They sat quietly under the pallid light of the moon, listening to the chirping of the crickets and frogs and the quiet murmur of the river.

"Can I see the Life Stone?" Rebecca asked.

Cam gave her a startled glance.

Rebecca hastened to explain. "Lorna let me help her once with the magic when she was trying to reach you, but she didn't let me touch any of the stones."

"Okay," Cam said. He fished around in his pouch and withdrew the aqua blue opal. It was a beautiful gem that glowed with an internal light.

She lifted it gently from his hand and was surprised when the light didn't fade. Cam straightened and stared at her in amazement.

A warmth expanded from her hand up her arm. "Why is it still shining?"

"It hasn't shone like that for anyone else but Lorna," Cam said.

Rebecca scowled. "What are you suggesting?"

"Where were your mother and father from?"

"I don't know."

Cam withdrew the lump of amber from his pouch. "Try this."

She took it, and the light in the stone died as soon as it touched her fingers.

Cam furrowed his brow. "Hmm. I don't understand."

"Does it shine for Spider or Hebron?"

"No, nor Alaric."

"I wonder if it would work for Laird," Rebecca said.

"Perhaps. Lorna told me the Life Stone was tied to the throne of the West Mark. It would only work for someone descended from that line."

Rebecca stared at him. "No. That's not possible."

"Do you have a better explanation?"

"Lorna told me she wanted my help with something before she left and that she was going to start training me. I think she meant to teach me the magic, but she couldn't until I turned seventeen because Chullain wouldn't let her."

"You think you're an heir?"

"That would explain a lot," Rebecca said. Though she had never thought it through until now, it made sense. It would explain why Lorna took such an interest in her, why Chullain was so anxious to keep her safe and in the palace, and why she had been feeling such a strange connection to this land.

Cam laid his head back against the willow. "I can't believe it. Hebron and Lorna made it sound like I was unique somehow. But heirs keep popping up all over the place. What do they need me for?"

Rebecca handed the Life Stone back to Cam, and he put it away. "We're going to have to ask the others."

"If you are an heir," Cam said, "you should think hard before you accept the Anarwyn."

"Why?"

Cam shifted. "It changes you. You have to surrender control of your life to some force you can't see. I've known since Hebron first gave me that water to drink that it was going to kill me in the end."

Rebecca scowled. "Do you really believe that?"

"I *know* it," Cam said. He rose. "I better go before Drakeman comes to relieve you."

"Okay," Rebecca squeezed his hand again and smiled. "Thanks," she whispered. But their conversation had unnerved her. Wouldn't she know if she could use the Anarwyn? And why would the magic kill Cam? He was trying to save it, wasn't he?

Lorna was dimly aware of the passage of time as she struggled in the gray haze of agony that engulfed her. Someone had dropped her to the ground and left her there through long hours of darkness before flinging her onto the back of a horse again. Her pulse thumped painfully at her temples. The agony of the dyad diminished as her mind and body became mercifully numb to the torture.

The pounding of the horses' hooves changed from the hollow thumping of prairie earth to the clip of a shod hoof on stone. Voices and clamor knocked against the wall of her suffering. Someone called out their wares. A child cried. Hammers beat against metal. Smells penetrated her consciousness. Horse sweat, woodsmoke, human waste. She was in a city or a camp.

She struggled to open her eyes. When she did, she found a flapping black standard with a twelve-pointed star and a six-sided prism with pointed ends stitched in red thread. Rough hands heaved her from the back of the horse and threw her over a shoulder. Something swished, and the air became cooler. She was jostled about until she dropped onto a wooden pallet and her world fell silent again. Her mind drifted. Memories rushed in.

A mischievous grin split Bardon's face as he dashed into her rooms, snatched up her hairbrush, and bolted away giggling.

"You little scamp," she shouted and dashed after him, zig-zagging amid the startled servants, following the sound of his childish snicker....

The memory blurred and rematerialized. She sat beside her mother's deathbed with her head bowed, her hands clamped over her face, shaking with sobs. When she peered up through the haze of tears, she found Bardon peering into their mother's pale face, stroking her hand with his....

A moment of darkness merged into a scene with Lorna cradling little Bardon in her arms, rocking him to sleep. "Hush, little one," she whispered, though her voice caught in her throat. "It'll be okay. I'll always care for you...."

Images blurred past to settle on her holding up the glass vial, her chest swelling with pride. She had swallowed the Dúr Crishal. Her father and Maelorn looked on with broad smiles.

"We never doubted," her father said.

Bardon crouched in a corner with a scowl on his face. She gathered him in her arms.

"You're going away," he said.

She caressed his cheek. "I have to."

"You said you wouldn't leave me." The pout and glare brought a lump into her throat, and all the joy at being granted the power of the Anarwyn evaporated. She had promised him, but there was nothing she could do now. She had a

Undead

responsibility to her father, to the Anarwyn, and even to herself.

"I'm sorry," she said and squeezed him tight. He swatted her hands away.

"I don't believe you anymore," he said and jumped down to scamper from the room.

She turned a pleading gaze on her father, who raised his eyebrows.

"He'll get used to it," he said and gave her a big hug. "I'm so proud of you...."

A confusing rush of memory about her days at Brynach followed. The Master of the Order took her under his wing when it was discovered that she could channel all twelve stones of power. It was a rare gift. Only three or four Varaná had ever achieved it....

The chain of letters and visits to Torwyn swirled together, where she oversaw Bardon's upbringing while her father and Maelorn were busy building alliances and carrying out campaigns to unite the marks once and for all. Bardon was always forgotten. Left behind by their father with tutors and nurses whom he taunted and abused....

The image of the young, handsome Shardana prince, named Zubir, shimmered before her, with his dark skin and bright eyes. The hidden moments of tenderness and his professions of love and offer of marriage.

"I can't," Lorna had whispered, though her heart raced within her. "I can't leave my brother alone. And I have the Order to think about."

"I thought you loved me." Zubir's voice was filled with pain, and he grimaced as if she had slapped him. His cheeks burned red.

She grabbed his hands, willing him to understand. "I do, but we can't be together. My family needs me."

"You would choose your spoiled brat of a brother over me?" His words punched into her like a fist.

"How dare you," she snapped.

Zubir rose to his full height so that he towered over her. "Oh, I dare because the truth must be told. If you do not restrain Bardon, he will drag you and your family down with him."

She slapped him then and whirled away with her hand smarting and her heart broken....

Weeks later, she returned to Torwyn for the winter solstice celebration. Fires crackled in the hearths. Greenery festooned the Great Hall. Feasting and singing commenced before the long dance where the King and his court danced through the night in honor of the Anarwyn's victory over darkness. Lorna had gone to fetch another flagon of wine from the kitchen, when she found a scullery maid curled up in a dark corner sobbing.

Lorna knelt beside her. The girl smelled of smoke and sweat and some fishy odor. "What has happened?" Lorna asked. "Are you hurt?"

The girl started and peered up at her with swollen, red eyes. She was a dainty, pretty thing. The girl shook her head. As the light from the Great Hall washed her face, Lorna saw the rising bruise and realized the girl was clutching at her groin. Understanding dawned on Lorna.

"Who did this to you?" she demanded.

The girl sniffled and shook her head. "I cannot say, My Lady."

"Come," Lorna rose and led the girl to her own apartments and sent for the physician. Then she strode away in search of Bardon.

She found him reclining in a chair in the Great Hall, nursing a goblet of wine. He wore a smug expression. Lorna marched through the crowd and loomed over him with her hands on her hips. Bardon had grown to be a stocky boy with a noble bearing and a handsome face. She noted the fresh red scratch welling up on his neck just below the jaw.

"Decided to come home, did you?" he said.

"What have you done?" she demanded.

A few of the people nearby paused in their conversation.

Bardon sneered. "Have the maids been gossiping again?"

"You forced her," Lorna scolded. "She's barely more than a child."

Bardon straightened in his seat, and he gave her a hard, calculating stare. "Are you going to use your magic on me?" He sniffed in disgust. "Don't blame me for the society our father created. I didn't choose to be born a king's son any more than she chose to be born a servant. I only did what I'm expected to do. Besides, she enjoyed it."

Lorna slapped his face. "You disgust me. You're nothing but a churlish parasite."

Zubir had been right, and she had sacrificed him for this selfish, arrogant boy.

Bardon rose with a growl. "Be careful, sister. When I drink the Dûr Crishal, you won't be able to treat me like a child any longer…."

The memories continued to flow—Bardon's deepening resentment, his insistence on humiliating her or Maelorn at every opportunity, and his rebellion against their father….

She watched as he drank the Dûr Crishal and saw the astonished horror on his face when he confessed that the Anarwyn had rejected him. He raged and cursed before fleeing Torwyn. Lorna let him go, let him have time to work through his anger and disappointment. She should have known he would seek vengeance.

185

Undead

But in her heart, she still loved him, still remembered the smiling boy who cuddled in her lap and caressed her cheek.

Lorna groaned as she became conscious of the hard, wooden pallet beneath her and the taste of vinegar on her tongue. She opened her eyes to stare into the gloom and struggled to ease the burning agony in her limbs. Movement only made it worse, and she sucked in her breath to keep from crying out. She was truly in her brother's clutches, bound by some work of magic she could not understand.

What was she to do? She could lie here and wait for death to come—because Bardon would not let her live. Or she could find some way to free herself from the power of the unnatural dyad draped around her neck. She closed her eyes and tried to settle her mind, tried to find some peace in the desperate agony of being cut off from the Anarwyn. If she could not escape this disorienting anguish, she would fail for the last time.

Chapter Thirteen
Bull Boats

ZENEK STAGGERED INTO the entrance of the royal palace of Goldereth and eased himself down on the wide marble steps. His throat ached, and his broken finger throbbed. His whole body was a chorus of exquisite misery. Even his lungs burned from breathing in the bitter dust of the corpses he had scavenged.

He unballed the fist that held the half dozen bits of jewelry he had clawed from the bones of Galad's victims of all those years ago. The gems sparkled bewitchingly in the late afternoon light, and Zenek shivered at the sight. If only his mother could have seen this treasure. How many times had she lamented that no one ever located Sameel's final resting place so that his gemstones of power could be recovered? For the Tamil in exile, gaining access to the gems of power had been impossible, and Zenek had collected five in one day.

Having them and knowing how to use them were two totally different matters. There was no one to teach him. The Bragamahr had granted the power and given him Mahrowaiths to serve him, but otherwise offered no instruction. He could go back to Braganeth and seek his master's aid, but the agony he experienced during the creation of the Mahrowaiths gave him pause. Each of them had torn away a piece of him, and he wasn't sure he could survive another experience like that. Besides, he now possessed these stones. Surely a man of his intelligence and heritage could figure out how to use them. It couldn't be much different than using the garnet.

Zenek arranged the jewelry with the precious gems on the stair. He studied them as he drank deeply from his waterskin, wincing at the spike of pain in his throat where the wolf had bitten him. Though he consumed most of the water, it did little to assuage his terrible thirst.

The gemstones drew him with an insatiable curiosity. He had an emerald ring surrounded by tiny amethysts, a pyrite cube set in a broach, a tiger eye bracelet, and a blue apatite necklace shaped like a teardrop with a golden chain. What did these stones do?

Taking care not to jar his broken finger, Zenek slipped the emerald and amethyst ring onto a finger on his uninjured hand. A gentle energy swept through him, and a musical tone sounded in his ear. There was power in this stone, but it was beyond his reach.

Use the words of power, the Bragamahr whispered to him.

Zenek closed his eyes and opened his mind to the energy pulsing in the tiny amethysts the way his mother had taught him. Then he whispered the words the Bragamahr had given him in the Braganeth. "Dewder ereem. Ewllys edominud." He repeated them in the common tongue. "Courage to power. Will to dominate."

A cold wave coursed through him, and the pain and fatigue diminished, filling him with a calming ease. He sucked in a deep shuddering breath and grinned. The grinding agony abated, though his wounds hadn't healed. And he enjoyed a peace of mind like he had never known.

Excitement swelled in his chest. His mother had explained the stones of power and given him some idea of their uses. Now was his chance to test the fragments of knowledge his family had preserved from the ancient days. He tried to connect his mind to the emerald stone in the ring. His mother had told him that it was the great healing stone of the Bragamahr. He whispered the words of power again. "Dewder ereem. Ewllys edominud."

The stone responded instantly, and he directed the energy to the punctured wounds in his throat. A strange tingling rippled through the injuries as his flesh stretched to repair the holes in his neck. He experienced a creeping, prickly feeling, as if a thousand tiny ants were scurrying over his flesh. He ripped the bandage away to feel the new scars as they formed.

Bull Boats

"By the fires of creation," he cursed in amazement.

He focused and sent the healing energy to his hand. The cut on his palm closed, and the broken bones in his finger welded together.

"Ahh!" His cry of agony echoed in the hall. The pain dissipated, and he was left with a dull ache.

Staring in amazement, he flexed his hand with the newly healed finger. It was whole. Bursting with excitement, he experimented with each of the other gemstones. The tiger eye didn't respond well to him. Maybe it wasn't good for anything. Or perhaps he simply couldn't use it. His mother said few people could use all the stones of power.

The pyrite and apatite, however, responded readily to him. He experimented with the pyrite, testing its potential. It allowed him to create whatever image he desired. With a wry smile, he used it to craft an image of Cam lying dead with a gaping wound in his throat. The illusion gave him a wicked satisfaction. He used the stone to call up an image of his mother, but the apparition wavered, and her face was blurred. Somehow the Bragamahr had stolen that source of joy and comfort from him. It had been the price he paid for the power.

The apatite granted him a deep sense of self-awareness, and he became conscious of every scratch or bruise and of the horrible ache in his stomach. He imagined how refreshing it would be to sink his teeth into a tender rabbit or grouse.

On a whim, he decided to try linking the stones in what his mother had called a dyad. It took several tries to succeed. Once he learned to listen for the faint tone each stone emitted, he managed to harmonize the two stones to himself and then to each other.

The effect was disorienting, causing him to clutch at the stairs for stability as his perception expanded. He became deeply aware of his craving for revenge and his need to control it and of the thousands of other creatures alive on the mountain, hiding in holes, perched on branches, or roving the barren hillsides or wooded slopes. At the same time, he realized that he could create a false reality for them the same way he had created the illusion of Cam.

Zenek selected a fat grouse roosting in a pine tree near the base of the walls and sent it the image of a shrub bursting with fresh buds at the foot of the stairs. The grouse lifted from the pine branch and fluttered toward him. When it flapped through the doorway, he grabbed it by the head and wrung its neck. As the bird died, he perceived the sense of betrayal coming from the animal. He shrugged off the sensation. What did it matter? Tonight, he would have a good hot meal.

While he gutted and plucked the grouse, he contemplated the strange sensations sweeping through him. Exhaustion overcame him, as did the heady sense of control the power gave him. Still, there was something wrong. He tried to remember his mother's features but could only recall a blurred space framed by her auburn hair. The memory of her gently stroking his cheek when he was small faded. The Bragamahr was taking something out of him each time he used the power—depriving him of the things he most valued. His mother had warned there would be a cost. Was he willing to pay it?

Zenek stared into the flames of his little fire while the grouse roasted on a flat rock. He had plans to make. His Mahrowaiths had been destroyed, and he had felt the death of each one. Now that he was armed with several stones of power, he was no longer a mere soldier. Bardon would have to reckon with him now. The Bragamahr intended Zenek to be its champion—not some Tathanar upstart.

Someone slapped Spider's head.

"Time to crawl out of your nest," Hebron said.

Spider peeked from under his blankets. The buttery glow of morning light stung his eyes, and he blinked. "Did you get rid of those blood-sucking insects?" he grumbled.

"We've been saving them for you. Come on, *Ludo*. We've got work to do."

"Don't call me that," Spider growled and threw his blankets aside. He hated his real name. What had his mother been thinking?

Hebron chuckled. "That's the only sure way to get Spider out of bed."

"One of these days," Spider mumbled and stopped to stare at Alaric, Laird, and Drakeman. They each held a strange-looking frame bent in the shape of a large dish. A pile of bone-white willow branches stripped of their bark lay beside them. They wove the contraption together, using the willow bark to tie the branches in place.

Bull Boats

"What are you doing?" Spider asked. "Building some oversized fish trap?"

Hebron chuckled. "No, it's a spider cage."

Spider smirked at him. "Very funny. What's it for?"

"It's your passage across the river," Alaric said.

Now Spider laughed. He was about to explain that even he knew such a boat wasn't going to make it five feet without sinking, when Drakeman set his basket aside and picked up his longbow.

"Let's go you two," he said to Cam and Spider.

"I want to come," Rebecca said.

"Where exactly are we going?" Spider asked.

"Hunting," Cam said.

Drakeman studied Rebecca for a moment before saying, "If you wish. Cam, bring Hebron's bow." He strode into the trees.

Rebecca grinned, and Spider gestured for her to join them. They followed Drakeman upriver until they encountered a well-worn game trail. He stopped where it entered the trees and motioned for Spider to take the lead.

"You're the tracker," Drakeman said. "Find me some nice big bulls."

Spider jumped at the chance. It had been a while since he tracked anything, and he'd missed the challenge. Tracking wasn't for the simpleminded. It required energy and knowledge to unravel and interpret the tiny messages animals or humans left in their passing. He bent to the trail and was surprised when Rebecca crouched beside him. He squinted at her curiously.

"Show me what you're doing," she said.

"Okay." Spider glanced at Drakeman, who shrugged.

"I don't want to be pampered like I was in Abilene," Rebecca explained. "Teach me everything."

There was something magnetic about her. Spider found his cheeks flushing hot as he pointed to a fresh track. "See how the floor of the track is flat and the edges are sharp?"

"Yes."

"No dirt has fallen in or blown in, and the inside is dark and damp," Spider said. "That tells you it's fresh."

"I understand."

"There's a small herd of cattle that headed for the river, sometime before dawn."

191

"How do you know that?"

"The tracks are different sizes," Cam said as he squatted beside them, "and one has a chip out of it that is distinctive. Cows like to feed in the early morning and head to water before lying down for the day."

"And you can smell them," Spider said not wanting to let Cam outdo him. "They stink like a barnyard."

"Right. *That* I smell."

"Let's find them then," Drakeman said.

Spider rose and ghosted into the trees with Drakeman, Cam, and Rebecca following. They hadn't gone far when he raised his hand to stop them. He pointed to a large bull and several cows waddling up the trail, their tails flicking at the biting flies. After checking the wind, he adjusted so they would be downwind before he signaled for them to conceal themselves.

Drakeman handed Spider the bow. "You and Cam can take the first shots."

Spider wasn't sure he could draw the heavy war bow. He hefted it and fitted an arrow to the string. The bow was light for its size of six feet, and it balanced perfectly in his hand. He tugged the string, testing its draw weight.

"I'll never get this thing to full draw," he said.

"Shot placement is what matters," Drakeman said. "Aim for right behind the shoulder."

Spider glanced at Cam, who also had an arrow on the string of Hebron's bow. "I'll take the cow behind the bull," Spider said.

"I've got the bull," Cam replied.

They waited in silence. The huge, shaggy bull trundled up the trail. Its tail swished from side to side. Spider waited until the cow was right in front of them and only twenty yards away. He drew the string back, straining against the weight, and let the arrow fly with a quiet thwang.

The arrow flew true, burying itself deep behind the cow's shoulder all the way up to the fletchings. Cam's arrow struck the bull at the same time.

Drakeman snatched the bow from Spider and sent two more arrows in rapid succession into the third and fourth cows. The panicked animals bolted, charging up the trail for fifty yards before the

Bull Boats

four wounded ones stopped and milled about, spewing bloody foam from their nostrils. The bull wagged his head and swung back toward the river. They lumbered past the hunters, leaving splashes of bright blood on the grass.

Rebecca tried to rise, but Spider dragged her back down.

"Wait," he whispered.

Spider made them wait for half an hour before signaling for them to follow as he rose and edged his way down the trail. The quiet rush of the river greeted them and mingled with the labored breathing of the wounded bull. Three cows bobbed in a wide eddy, their blood streaking the clear water. The bull faced them defiantly, but he was too weak from loss of blood and sank to his knees, submerging his head. He struggled up again, peering at them with his big, dark eyes. Then he fell, and this time he didn't get up.

"I don't understand," Rebecca said.

"An injured animal will run until he dies if he's being chased," Cam said.

"And," Spider added, "one that is losing blood will often go to water. We saved ourselves the trouble of tracking them by not racing after them."

"You two can compete for Rebecca's admiration later," Drakeman said.

"I'm not—" Spider began as his face grew hot.

Drakeman waved his protestations away. "Let's float these down to the camp. I don't fancy trying to haul a two-thousand-pound bull over land."

Rebecca flushed as well, and she shared a little smile with Cam that Spider found deeply suspicious.

"Slit each cow's throat," Drakeman continued, "but don't poke any holes in the hide, or you'll have to ride in the leaky boat."

"What are you talking about?" Spider asked, glad to deflect attention away from his burning face.

"Bull boats," Drakeman said as he waded out into the river and deftly slit the bull's throat. Blood boiled out into the silvery water. A metallic tang mingled with the musky stink of the cows.

Spider glanced at Cam, who just smiled. Obviously, they had explained everything to him and Rebecca while Spider was sleeping.

He cracked his knuckles and joined Cam as they bled the other animals before tying them in a line.

"Anyone want to tell me," Spider said, "how we're supposed to ride a bull across the river?"

Drakeman chuckled. "A bull boat is a hide boat stretched around a wooden frame while the hide is still green." Dragging the carcasses behind him, he started wading downriver. "They're easy to make and for a short trip that doesn't require any precision, they're quite useful." He grinned over his shoulder at them. "Although it's a bit like riding an old ornery donkey. They never go where you want them to, and sometimes they buck you off. It's a far cry from a good canoe, but under the circumstances, it's the best we can do."

Spider brought up the rear, struggling to keep his footing on the rocky bottom.

"Doesn't sound like a—" He stopped when he spied a figure entangled in the branches of a downed tree. "Drakeman," he called.

Drakeman, Cam, and Rebecca paused and glanced back over their shoulders. Spider pointed, and Drakeman gestured for them to stay back while he waded over to investigate. He rolled the body over to reveal a ghastly face.

Tufts of black hair clung in patches to the raw, rippled flesh that once had been a scalp. The eyelids, eyebrows, and nose were melted away and what remained of the lips curled up in a grisly smile, exposing yellowed teeth.

Rebecca gave a startled gasp and covered her mouth.

"Blood and ashes," Spider swore.

"An Inverni," Cam said.

Drakeman bent over the man and then straightened, wrinkling his nose. "He's dead, all right."

"What about that one?" Spider said and pointed to a second figure wrapped in a water-logged cloak that was draped over a log. Drakeman checked him and shook his head.

"They're burned," Rebecca said. "Their skin is all melted."

"Let's get across this river as soon as possible," Drakeman said, tugging at the string of cattle.

As they sloshed through the water, they came across bits of charred wood and even the lower hull of a rowboat with a rotting body inside it. Spider picked up an arrow from the brush along the bank.

Bull Boats

"These corpses aren't fresh," Drakeman said, "maybe a week old."

"Could they be from Brynach?" Rebecca asked.

Drakeman scowled. "That's what I'm afraid of."

"That's so disgusting," Rebecca said as Cam showed her how to use her fingers to peel the hide away from the underlying fat.

"Makes your hands soft," Cam said. He liked being close to her, touching her hands as they peeled the hide away.

The buoyancy of the water made skinning the cattle much easier. They rolled the big cow as they worked. Laird and Hebron had already finished theirs and dragged the hide and carcass onto the pebbly shore where they carved off the best pieces of meat. Draig was happily gnawing on a huge liver.

Slone, who was letting his shoulder rest, built a smokeless cooking fire and set the meat to roasting, while Laird, Alaric, and Spider heaved the heavy skins over the willow frames, stretching and tugging them into shape.

"Hurry up, you two," Drakeman called to Cam and Rebecca.

"Almost done," Cam said.

He gave a mighty heave as Rebecca worked with her fingers until the skin pulled free. Cam stumbled and fell, plunging beneath the water, pushed down by the weight of the skin. He came up spluttering, and Rebecca splashed water in his face.

He splashed her back, and the two of them dragged the wet hide from the water. The aroma of roasting meat made Cam's stomach rumble. "I'm ready for a break from penemel and pilchard."

"Not until that hide is stretched," Hebron said.

"The meat's still raw anyway," Slone added.

It took the better part of the day to stretch the hides and adjust the frames to fit them. When they finished, they stepped back to survey their handiwork.

Slone rested his hands on his hips. "You've made four death traps."

"I was thinking they looked like furry washbasins," Spider said.

"So long as they float, I don't care," Cam said. "Now, can we have some of that meat?"

After a leisurely evening, they retired with full bellies and awakened early to attempt the river crossing. A gentle mist rose from the whispering waters like fingers reaching for the sky. The air was so chill that the water felt warm to Cam's feet. The first rays of sun slanted through the trees. Birds called in the branches, and squirrels chided them for disturbing their slumber. It was a beautiful sight, marred only by the memory of the corpses bobbing among the branches and the prospect of crossing this wide river in nothing but a hide-covered frame of willow.

They paired off two per boat, each with a single makeshift paddle carved from a willow branch. Drakeman took Spider with him, while Rebecca paddled for Cam and Draig. Alaric and Hebron occupied another, and Slone and Laird climbed into the last.

"Is it too late to change my mind?" Slone said as he eyed the frail little craft.

"You'd rather swim?" Drakeman asked.

"I'd rather ford it or cross on an easy bridge."

"No ford until Torwyn," Alaric said.

"Oh, what does it matter?" Slone grumbled. "If I'm gonna die, let's get it over with." He climbed aboard, gripping the sides so tightly his knuckles turned white. His face paled.

They pushed off into the river and the bull boats spun in the current like a child's top.

"Sweet waters of Anarwyn preserve us," Slone groaned.

Spider clutched at the willow frame, staring at the water with wide eyes. "Blood and ashes," he cursed.

Cam would have laughed if he hadn't experienced the same rush of terror as the current snagged his craft and spun it down river.

"Hang on," Drakeman shouted as he stroked for the opposite shore.

"The frame is jabbing into my knees," Spider moaned.

Cam chuckled. Spider was going to give Drakeman reason to regret riding with him.

"My life is in your hands," Cam said to Rebecca.

She gave him a pretty smile and spun the boat around.

"Whoa," Cam said. "You're gonna make me sick."

Draig rested his front paws on the frame and lifted his nose to the wind.

"Draig likes it," Rebecca said.

"He likes everything."

Bull Boats

The bull boats strung out in a line and swept downriver as they made their way to the center of the channel where a cluster of islands collected debris in huge piles. More charred wood had been caught in the jams, including a nearly complete boat. There must have been a terrible battle for Brynach. Cam hadn't felt anything from Lorna since that night when she had warned him that Bardon knew he was heading to the Lonely Valley. What would they do if Lorna and Brynach had been lost?

Master. The pleading voice burst into Cam's mind. It possessed the forlorn tones of a bleating lamb. Cam snapped his head around. A dark figure paced along the shore they had just left.

"Look," he shouted.

Rebecca paused as they all spun back to peer at the retreating shoreline. "The Mahrowaiths found us again."

"It's the same one," Cam said.

"How do you know?"

He shivered at the odd sensation. "I just do, and I don't feel that paralyzing terror, either."

"It can't cross the river," Rebecca said with an obvious sigh of relief.

The beast loped east along the banks of the river with a sense of purpose. Did that Mahrowaith think he had accepted the Bragamahr? "Is there a ferry across the Brunen?" Cam shouted to the others.

Drakeman looked around at him. "There used to be one at the confluence of the Afon Fathwe and the Brunen, and there's a ford above Torwyn."

"It's going to find some way to cross," Cam whispered. The fact that he knew this disturbed him. How was it possible? What had the Bragamahr done to him?

"We've got other company," Alaric shouted and pointed upriver to where a white billowing sail poked above the trees.

"To the islands!" Drakeman bellowed.

Rebecca paddled furiously until they caught an eddy on the downstream side of one of the islands, and they dragged the bull boats out of the water and into the bushes.

A strange feeling came over Cam as the ship approached. There was a presence on that ship he recognized. "Jathneel?" he whispered.

Undead

Crouching in the shadows, he withdrew the Life Stone from his pouch. A blue light came from it, and he cupped his hands to hide it.

"What are you doing?" Rebecca whispered.

"Checking something," Cam said. He sucked in a long, slow breath and focused on the stone, trying to remember what Lorna had taught him.

His perception expanded, and his hearing became acute. The rush of the river, the call of gulls, the chirping of the insects, and the creaking of the ship's rigging filled his ears. He closed his eyes, and a vision burst upon him.

A swirling cloud spiraled into the sky over a twisted juniper. A line of soldiers marched in single file up a rocky pass. They had Hebron and the other male members of the party bound and gagged. Rebecca was nowhere to be seen.

A voice scoured his mind. The same voice he had heard in the aspen grove.

"You begin to perceive the extent of your powers," Jathneel said. "Good, but do not forget what I have told you. Power is nothing without knowledge. Use both well."

Cam jerked away from the contact. He was trembling and sweating. Draig blinked at him with his penetrating green eyes.

"What's wrong?" Rebecca whispered.

"Nothing," Cam panted.

"Don't lie to me," Rebecca said, and she grabbed his hand.

"Jathneel was on that ship," Cam whispered.

Rebecca stared at him. "Does he know you're here?"

"Yes."

"We should tell the others."

"He's not coming for us," Cam said.

"What?"

"He told me that I was beginning to learn how to use the Anarwyn and that I should use it well."

"That makes no sense."

"It does if he's working against Bardon."

"He wouldn't."

"He might." Cam wrestled with the idea of telling her about his meeting with Jathneel. He hadn't forgotten Jathneel's warning that the others wouldn't understand. And he experienced a deep sense of shame that he was being tempted to use Jathneel's dyad rather than

Bull Boats

Lorna's. It felt like such a betrayal of the people who trusted him.

The ship slipped around the bend, and Drakeman signaled for them to set out again. Within fifteen minutes their bull boats were bouncing and spinning off the undergrowth on the south side of the river. Drakeman found a cattle wallow that gave them room to pull out.

"That was the strangest thing I've ever done," Slone said after he'd scrambled out of the wallow and glared down at the boats. "We paddled across a river in a shallow dish made of a few sticks and a cowhide."

"Let's hope it's the most dangerous thing we have to face for a while," Drakeman said.

Alaric hefted his pack and longbow. "It's time to put some miles behind us. Who else feels like a good jog?"

Spider groaned.

"One complaint out of you," Hebron said, "and I'm giving you my pack to carry."

Spider scowled and adjusted the shoulder straps on his pack. "I can outrun an old man like you."

Cam chuckled. "I said that once and only once."

"I take it we're heading for that mountain," Spider said pointing to a snowcapped peak to the south.

"Yep," Alaric said. "Then we skirt the foothills through the woods and come out west of the Lonely Valley."

Spider grinned at Hebron. "Let's go, old man," and he took off at a run.

"One of these days I'm gonna whip that kid senseless," Hebron growled and jogged after him.

Cam struggled to still the sweeping shiver that ran through him. Only a few more days and he would have to put Jathneel's words to the test. They would soon find out if he was really worth all this trouble.

Chapter Fourteen
Ambush

WEARY MILES POUNDED beneath Rebecca's feet. The ground became a blur of browns and greens as her legs churned, swishing through the prairie grass and past the bunches of buttonbush and dogwood. Though her lungs burned, and her legs ached, she kept running. She was determined to be as hard as the men. She had pulled her own weight while they were in the canoes, but this was a different experience.

Alaric ran them in shifts. Several miles of jogging were followed by a mile of walking, and then they were running again. The pace was grueling as it ate up the miles. The snowcapped peak grew closer as the sun rose like a smudge in the overcast sky. Rain started falling, and soon they were slogging through puddles and leaping over newly formed streams.

They crossed several trails of fresh horse tracks, and once, Laird spied a rider on a distant hill. He was moving away from them, but Alaric kept them off the ridges after that, and he hurried them on into the evening. By nightfall, the rain had ceased, and they were winding their way into the foothills.

"Does he ever get tired?" Rebecca gasped.

Cam shook his head. Sweat and rainwater sprayed from his hair. "Never."

They found a wide trail leading up into the hills between two great outcrops of rock. Alaric angled to the south until he pulled them into a rocky cutaway where a little creek gurgled past and a slab of rock protected them from the rain.

Spider fell to the ground without a sound, and Rebecca and Cam joined him. They slipped out of their rucksacks and lay on their backs, panting.

"I take back what I said about canoeing," Spider said. "I'd rather paddle fifty miles than run it."

"Is that how far we traveled?" Rebecca asked.

"Closer to sixty, I should think," Laird said. He squatted beside them. "How's the shoulder, Slone?"

"I forgot all about it," Slone said. "But if you want to know about my feet, that's a different story."

"We'll camp here," Alaric said. "We can't risk a fire."

"I'm too tired to build one anyway," Spider said.

Rebecca agreed, though she wouldn't have minded a warm stew to fend off the chill.

"I would like to point out," Hebron added, "that I reached the campsite before Ludo did."

Spider grunted. "Only because I took pity on you."

Hebron chuckled. "You're so kind."

Draig padded over from drinking in the creek and nuzzled his wet nose against Rebecca's cheek. She patted him. "Enjoyed that, didn't you?"

He blinked at her and trotted over to lick Cam's face.

"He's barely panting," Spider grumbled.

They shook out their bedrolls and divided up the watch. Cam lay between Rebecca and Hebron as Slone took the first watch. Rebecca stared up into the sliver of starless sky at the edge of the overhang, wondering what was going to happen when they reached the Lonely Valley.

"Hebron," Cam said.

"Hmm?"

"Do you have a family?"

Rebecca stiffened. She knew how much Cam wished he had known his parents, but he had always had Hebron. She had had Chullain, but no real mother figure. What she wouldn't have given to have someone to ask about the parents she had never known.

Undead

"Why do you ask?" Hebron said.

"Just curious."

Hebron was silent for several moments, and Rebecca decided he wasn't going to answer.

Then he sighed deeply and said, "I had a wife."

"What happened to her?" Cam prompted.

Again, there was a long pause.

"She died in childbirth a couple of months after I was chosen to be your mother's guardian."

A pang of sadness swept through Rebecca. Her mother had survived childbirth. Rebecca had been a few months old when they found her in her mother's arms. A fleeting thought, like a memory on butterfly wings, fluttered through her mind, and she almost remembered something about her mother. As soon as it appeared it was gone, slippery and ephemeral like everything about her life before Abilene. Why couldn't she remember?

"What happened to the child?" Cam asked.

"He was born dead," Hebron said.

"I am sorry. I didn't know."

Hebron rolled to his side. Rebecca rose to her elbow so she could see them.

"It was long ago," Hebron said. "Sometimes I wish it had been different."

Cam nodded but didn't say anything.

Hebron reached over and good-naturedly ruffled Cam's hair. "I haven't had much time to feel sorry for myself. You and Spider have kept me pretty busy."

Rebecca settled back down to her uncomfortable bed. Hebron had lost his family, too. Did anyone get through this life without pain?

The day dawned gray and dreary with a gentle downpour. The sun gnawed at the clouds on the eastern horizon but couldn't break through. Drakeman and Alaric didn't string their bows. Instead, they tucked the strings in waxed linen pouches to keep them dry. Shouldering their packs, the company continued up the rocky, broken trail, made treacherous with rain.

Ambush

Cam fell back to the rear as he struggled to shake a sense of dread that had been coiling around his heart ever since his meeting with Jathneel. The sight of the bodies and the wreckage floating in the Brunen River also made him worry about Lorna. So much was at stake, and everything kept going wrong. There had to be a way to improve their odds of success.

Distracted by his thought, he slipped and fell to his hands and knees on a slab of limestone slick with rain. As he crawled to his feet, he noted a lump of something blue half-buried in an eroded little wash that skirted the edge of the limestone slab. He snatched it up and jogged to catch up with the others. The stone was a lump of turquoise with an irregular coloring. Most of it was blue, though there were also streaks of green and yellow. He sensed a latent energy in the beautiful stone and studied it more carefully. Could this gemstone channel the power of the Anarwyn?

The trail came to a cleft in the gray limestone with a steep rocky incline. He gripped the turquoise in his hand, determined to show the others what he had found as soon as they were past the gap. When they clambered through the cleft and came out into a canyon, Spider called them to a stop. They gathered around as he pointed to a scuff mark on a bit of moss. It was fresh. A little farther on, there was the distinct impression of the heel of a boot.

"Someone's been on the trail before us," Spider said.

"The city of Hannoch is not far from here," Hebron said. "Could be scouts from the city."

"Or it could be Bardon's men searching the foothills," Laird said.

Alaric rose to scan the sides of the canyon. They were covered in tumbled stone and juniper with a few large pines.

"It's the perfect place for an ambush," he whispered, scanning the rocks above them.

"Should we go back?" Hebron asked.

"I was going to leave this canyon there." Alaric pointed to a gap in the rock on the south side no more than half a mile away. "There's a narrow pass up that way that will bring us down into the woodland. It's not far."

"Let's get going before we're spotted," Slone said.

They set out again, and Cam nudged Spider. "Look what I found." He handed the turquoise to Spider.

"So?" Spider said.

"So, this is one of the stones of power," Cam said.

"Really?" Spider held it closer to examine it. "Did it do anything when you picked it up?"

"Well, no, but…"

"Then how do you know it's one of the magical stones?" Spider handed it back to him.

"Well, I don't know. I felt something…" Cam trailed off. Maybe he was being stupid. The turquoise set in the wall at Bear Cave had kept the Bragamahr from entering. Maybe if he could get it to work for him now, it would keep the Bragamahr far from him or the Mahrowaiths from finding them.

There was one way to find out, though he didn't know if he could do it. Lorna said she could attune stones to herself. What if Cam could do it, too?

He focused his gaze on the stone and willed it to work for him. To his surprise, the stone responded, and a rush of warmth tingled up his arm.

"It worked," he gasped. Rebecca paused to glance back at him. At that precise moment, a shout rang out, and an arrow buzzed overhead. The company ducked and scrambled for cover. Rebecca and Cam crawled behind a crumbling limestone boulder. Draig remained on the trail, his hackles raised.

"Draig," Cam whispered. "Come here." The wolf padded over to him, and Cam gestured for him to sit.

"Where are the others?" Rebecca breathed.

The top of Spider's head was barely visible on the other side of the trail. Slone lay prostrate behind a fallen juniper with his axe in hand. Drakeman crouched behind a rock, trying to string his longbow without exposing himself to danger. Cam couldn't see Laird, Hebron, or Alaric.

"This is not good," Cam said.

"Surrender and you will not be harmed." The voice echoed off the canyon walls. Cam tried to pinpoint its location without success.

"What do you want?" Alaric shouted, and Cam caught sight of him kneeling on one knee with his bow strung and an arrow nocked.

"You are trespassing on the lands of the Earl of Hannoch," the man said.

Ambush

"Does he claim all the lands to the Brunen now?" It was Hebron's voice, but Cam couldn't see him.

Spider unwound the sling from his wrist and pointed to the rocks above them. Cam scanned them, trying to see what Spider saw.

"There," Rebecca whispered and pointed.

A man with a crossbow rose from behind a fallen juniper.

"This is bad," Cam said again. There had to be something he could do.

"I'll say it again," the man called. "Surrender peacefully and no harm will come to you."

"Does the Regency Council know the Earl is unlawfully detaining innocent travelers on the king's land?" Hebron shouted back.

"The West Mark has no king."

Rebecca glanced at Cam.

"Let us pass," Drakeman called. "We are emissaries from the Tathanar of Abilene."

"You have lost your road then, stranger," the man said. "If you are emissaries, the Earl will be happy to have you as guests."

Rebecca elbowed Cam, and he glanced back the way she pointed. Five more men with longbows or crossbows were now showing themselves. One held the trail behind them. They were surrounded.

"I count twenty at least," Cam whispered. "It would be suicide to try fighting them."

The men advanced, closing the circle. Drakeman shot a nervous glance at Cam and Rebecca and gestured for them to hide. He stepped out from behind his rock and raised the war bow over his head.

"I am Lord Drakeman, Prince of Abilene," he said. "I will accompany you to Hannoch, but I must ask that you let my companions go."

"No," Rebecca breathed.

Cam cast about, trying to find someplace to hide Rebecca. He didn't know what Drakeman intended, but a beautiful young woman in the hands of bandits was not a pleasant thing to contemplate.

The turquoise he gripped in his hand grew warm, and he glanced down at it. The stone must have responded to his sense of urgency. A gentle tone filled his mind. The stone had attuned itself to him, but what did it do? Lorna had said the turquoise could protect.

On an impulse, he held it up and whispered the words of power,

Undead

"Calon est. Calon Dûr." Energy flowed up his arm. "Protect us," he said.

A translucent blue field expanded from the stone until it encased him, Rebecca, and Draig.

Rebecca gasped. "How are you doing that?"

"I don't know."

He glanced at Drakeman, who was staring his way with wide eyes. Spider's face had frozen in an expression of astonishment. The men advanced up the trail and leveled their crossbows at Spider and Slone, who both straightened with their hands in the air. Cam waved at Rebecca to keep hidden and eased around the boulder for a better look. The crunch of gravel sounded, and he spun to find one of the men advancing on him. He crouched and placed his hand on the pommel of his sword. The man kept walking, his gaze trained on Spider.

What was happening? Cam edged out a little farther. No one noticed him, so he rose to his full height. Still, nothing happened. Had the turquoise made them invisible to their attackers?

The men disarmed Drakeman, and soon Hebron, Laird, and Alaric were likewise surrendering their weapons. Cam considered charging the men. He was certain he could kill two or three of them before they stopped him. But what good would that do? His only hope was the Fire Stone.

Cam withdrew the Fire Stone from his pouch and extended it toward the men. If he could aim the thing and get a jet of light like he did the first time he used it, he might be able to attack from his hiding place.

"Be careful," Rebecca whispered.

Cam concentrated on the Fire Stone. "A beam of light," he whispered. "I need a beam of light."

He pointed the stone at one of the men with a crossbow, whispered the words of power, and willed it to attack. A ball of yellow fire slammed into the man with the roar of a hurricane wind. He erupted into flames as did the two men standing next to him. Cam lost control of the fire, and it flared, scorching Spider and Slone before he could stop it. They both dropped to the ground, struggling to extinguish the flames as Cam stared at them in horror. He was not master of the Fire Stone. He could not control it.

Rebecca grabbed his hand. "Come on," she said and dragged him away as crossbow bolts and arrows rushed toward them. Most clicked into the stone or flew overhead. One cut through the little blue bubble of light and grazed the sleeve of Cam's tunic. Clearly, whatever this light was doing didn't protect them from arrows.

Rebecca dodged behind a nearby pine. Ducking low, they raced back down the canyon the way they had come. The turquoise nudged at Cam's mind, and he shrugged it away, trying to concentrate on keeping his feet in the rugged landscape. It nudged again using a gentle pressure behind his eyes, and he paused to glance at the turquoise stone. It was trying to direct them and shield them from sight.

"Come on," Cam said, and obeying the stone's prompting, angled off the trail toward the high ground.

"What are you doing?" Rebecca whispered.

"Following the stone."

"What?"

"I don't know. It told me to go this way."

"Can a rock do that?"

"It just did."

Rebecca followed without further questions until they dropped to their bellies on a wide flat rock commanding a view of the canyon floor. The turquoise bubble enclosed them.

"Look," Cam pointed to a cluster of men hunkered down behind a pile of boulders. The trail Rebecca had been following would have led them right into the trap.

"Useful little rock," Rebecca said.

The rest of their company stood in a line with their arms tied behind their backs. More than one hundred men surrounded them. This hadn't been a simple ambush. Something else was going on here. Spider was scanning the slopes, searching for them.

Cam gave the quiet hunting call Hebron had taught them to use, and both Spider and Hebron slowly turned their heads to stare in their direction. He knew they were trying not to give him away, but at least they knew he was alive.

"What now?" Rebecca asked.

Cam shook his head, panting hard. "I don't know."

"We can still try to make it to the Lonely Valley," Rebecca said.

Cam scrubbed his face with his hands. "I hurt them." He struggled to subdue his growing panic and sense of shame and loss. "The Anarwyn didn't work the way I told it to."

Undead

"It worked," Rebecca said. "You just don't know how to control it yet."

She was right, though it didn't make it any easier to accept.

"I knew something like this would happen." Cam watched as Spider, Hebron, and the rest were kicked and shoved up the trail.

"We can worry about that later," Rebecca insisted. "What do we do now?"

Cam clenched his jaw. "I won't leave them. Maelorn and Tara aren't even alive. They're just not dead."

Scowling, Rebecca glanced at the blue bubble and swung her legs to dangle over the edge. "That makes absolutely no sense."

"I know," Cam joined her. The rough surface of the rock scraped his hands. He pointed to where the soldiers were leading his friends away. "But *they* are alive, and they're our friends."

Rebecca beamed. "Let's follow them. We'll get a chance to free them eventually."

"There's too many men to fight," Cam said.

Rebecca gave him that mischievous and disarming grin she had first given him in the palace gardens of Abilene. "Leave that to me."

"What do you mean?"

A gust of wind flung Rebecca's hair about her face. It brought with it the pleasing fragrance of cedar from the forest.

She brushed the hair away and winked at him. "You've forgotten who you're dealing with. If there's anything I know, it's how to cause trouble in a city and get away with it. If they get them to Hannoch before we can rescue them, I'll figure something out."

Chapter Fifteen
Bardon's Guest

BARDON TWISTED THE RING with the tiger's eye stone around his finger. Lorna lay unconscious on the pallet in the center of the tent, which stank of urine and filth. Her clothes were torn and grimy. Her thick, brown hair was matted with blood and dirt. She appeared so small and vulnerable that it was hard to believe she was the most powerful practitioner of the Anarwyn in centuries. And he had crippled her with a simple dyad of morganite and topaz mediated through the quartz crystal.

The Varaná had always been so arrogant and yet so ignorant. Even though the Anarwyn rejected him, it was possible with tremendous effort to bend the gemstones of the Anarwyn to his will. The quartz crystal, or Union Stone, was the secret, though he hadn't needed to use it here. By combining the Bragamahr's Opening Stone with the Concentration Stone, he created a powerful weapon that crippled Lorna's ability to access the power of the Anarwyn. He had cut her off—leaving her helpless. It was time for her to awaken. He wanted her to know what was happening. He needed her to feel the betrayal he had endured for so long.

Bending over her, he touched the dyad and let the connection collapse. A sudden rush of long-forgotten affection flooded into him, and he caressed her cheek with a trembling finger. A vague memory of a boy cuddling in her lap and touching her face washed over him. He jerked his hand away in confusion, and the feeling dissipated. When he looked on her again, he saw only his hated enemy, the one who *should* have been faithful but had betrayed him.

He nudged Lorna's shoulder with the toe of his boot.

"Wake up, sister mine," he purred.

Lorna groaned, and her eyelids fluttered open. She bore a lost, confused expression. Her gaze rose from his boots to his face.

He sneered. "Feeling well?"

Recognition blossomed on her face, and she tried to scramble away from him, but she was too weak. Instead, she curled into a ball and studied him like a frightened, cornered rat.

"It's been many years," Bardon said. "I believe the last time we met you were trying very hard to kill me."

"No. Just to stop you."

"And you've been keeping yourself young and beautiful," he sneered. "You couldn't even age with dignity."

"Stop what you're doing," she mumbled. Her voice was weak. "Before it's too late."

"Oh, it's already too late," Bardon scoffed. "Too late for you—and for the Anarwyn."

"Don't. You're better than this."

Bardon snorted. "I *am* better. Stronger. Wiser. I, alone, understand what must be done. I, alone, have the courage and strength to do it. You Varaná skulked around in your castle, afraid of the power and unable to admit your own feebleness."

"It isn't too late," Lorna said. "You can still stop this. No one else needs to die."

"*You* need to die," Bardon snapped. "Then anyone else who stands in my way. Have you figured out where you are?"

Lorna's gaze took in the tent walls and the trampled grass. She shook her head.

"We're going to Mawsil," Bardon said, "and I'm going to kill you where the people of the North Mark can witness the death of their precious princess. Your life will end." He let the reality of her situation sink in. "And so will this useless hope that Maelorn can return from the prison to which you condemned him. I would have been kinder. I would have let him die."

"Please," Lorna whispered.

Bardon's Guest

"Now you beg," Bardon scoffed. "Where were you when the Anarwyn rejected me? Where were you when our father humiliated me? Where was your sense of honor and justice when you let our mother die and our father neglect me?"

Lorna gave him a feeble shake of her head. "Your memories are twisted by your hatred and by the influence of the Bragamahr. It is evil and can only destroy."

Bardon chortled. "You know nothing of the Bragamahr." He whirled away from her, afraid he might succumb to the temptation to kill her now and lose the value of her public execution. Why did she always blunt his efforts to make her feel the pain and shame he had felt? Why couldn't he penetrate that infuriating calmness? He pointed to a tray of food and water. "Eat and drink while you can. I don't want you dying before I can make a public spectacle of you."

Cam, Rebecca, and Draig crouched behind a thicket of mountain laurel several bow shots from the walls of the city of Hannoch. Glossy, green leaves and clusters of purple flowers that smelled like grapes concealed them from view. The city wasn't large compared to Abilene and Goldereth, but it was big enough. Its walls rose at least fifty feet, and two square towers protected the gates. Plaster flaked off the walls in great clumps, showing cut stone underneath. No attempt had been made to repair it.

Hannoch was situated on a hill so the inner walls surrounding the palace, with its round keep, soared above the rest of the city. It sagged on the landscape, slouching beneath steely gray skies and the bright smudge that was the sun. A steady stream of peasants dressed in simple linen shirts and trousers passed under the gate and before the watchful eye of the guards.

"Have you ever seen so many redheads?" Rebecca whispered.

Cam glanced at her and tried to rub the burning sleep from his eyes. The men of Hannoch had marched through the night without rest, giving Cam and Rebecca no chance to rescue their friends. Cam had struggled to deploy the turquoise again, hoping he could use it to create an opportunity.

However, once he let the blue bubble that protected them from view fade away, he hadn't been able to get it to work again. Nothing worked for him—not even the Life Stone. The old barrier had returned with a vengeance.

"They might let us stroll right in," Cam said, "but once inside, what do we do? How are we going to find the others?"

"This is where *I* take over," Rebecca said with a sly grin. "Wait here. I'll be back in a while."

Cam grabbed her arm and dragged her down. "I'm not letting you go in there alone."

Rebecca gently withdrew her arm from his grasp and kissed him. Her lips were soft and so inviting.

"You don't have a choice," she said. "Draig will draw too much attention, and you'd fall afoul of the first peddler hawking his wares."

"I would not."

She tilted her head and raised an eyebrow. "You don't know your way around cities like I do."

Cam started to protest. "What if—"

Rebecca placed a hand over his mouth. "I'll scout the situation, and I'll be back in a couple of hours."

Cam scowled. "What am I supposed to do while you're gone?"

"Get some sleep and figure out how to use those stones. I have a feeling we're going to need the Anarwyn's help to get out of here." After kissing him one more time, she jumped to her feet, yanking up her hood. She scurried back into the thicket of pines, where she could reach the rutted road leading to the city gate without being seen from the walls.

Cam considered following her, though he knew she was right. Still, it worried him that he wouldn't be there if anything went wrong.

A wagon trundled into view from around the bend, and Cam crouched lower. Rebecca fell in behind the wagon along with several other figures shuffling along in its wake. One of them glanced at her briefly. No one seemed to take any particular interest. The wagon paused at the city gates, and the guards lifted the covering to peer inside before waving them in. Rebecca's slender form slipped through the massive gates and disappeared.

Cam settled back to wait, but he couldn't sleep. His mind kept racing over all his mistakes of the last few days and the danger they were now in. If the Earl of Hannoch was anything like the lords and nobles Hebron had described, this could go sour quickly.

He withdrew the items from his pouch one at a time—the blue turquoise, the opal Life Stone, the two dyads, and the yellow lump of amber. The dyad Lorna had given him had a green malachite and an agate set in silver. The other from Jathneel held a smoky quartz crystal flanked on either side by a red agate with gold streaks and a milky-white moonstone set into gold. Which dyad would work? Or would neither of them? If he chose wrong, could he ruin everything?

Cam slipped the dyads back into the pouch and studied the opal Life Stone. He closed his eyes, trying to relax, straining to forget the sight of Spider and Slone writhing on the ground in an attempt to extinguish the flames he had caused. That experience reignited all the trauma from his mother's death and the deep unwavering certainty the Anarwyn would betray him in the end. The barrier snapped into place, and he could not activate the stone.

He let himself drift into the exhaustion as he focused on the Life Stone. Maybe if he didn't try so hard…. His mind wandered, and his breathing slowed. Calmness swept into him, and he dozed. With the tranquility of sleep came the sensation of the hillside evaporating.

He was gazing down on a dimly lit dungeon from a bird's vantage point. A man slouched against the wall with his head bowed. Something clanged, and he lifted his head to watch the door as it slowly opened. It was Ewan—the big redheaded Lakari from Yarwick who had traveled with them down the Afon Fathwe. He was supposed to have gone with Frederick, the Shardana, to carry the wounded Tathanar from the battle at the great bend to safety in the south. Why was he alone in a dungeon? A guard dropped a tin plate with some food at Ewan's feet and closed the door. The vision shifted, and Hebron and Spider curled up on a similar stone floor….

The vision changed, and two figures raced desperately through the tall prairie grass with a snarling Mahrowaith at their heels. The smaller figure whirled around to stare at the monster. Cam cried out as he recognized Rebecca's frightened face and wide, gray eyes. The fear surged up inside him, and with it came the barrier.

The vision dissipated, and he was staring up at the pale blue sky with streaks of white clouds. His pulse raced, and his head ached. He glanced around. Draig studied him, his head cocked to one side.

"I'm all right," Cam whispered.

Stuffing the Life Stone and the Fire Stone back into his pouch, he straightened. He and Rebecca had been fleeing from a Mahrowaith. Cam fidgeted before peering through the laurel leaves at the gate. Rebecca had set out in the early afternoon. Why wasn't she back yet? He had just resolved to go into the city in search of her when her familiar form passed between the two towers. And she wasn't alone.

The blackness resolved into a gray haze of pain and confusion. Lorna groaned and blinked at the shadows. She tried to swallow, but her throat wouldn't work. The sour stink of old sweat and urine filled her nostrils. It took her long minutes to remember what had happened. Bardon had been there. He had made sure she choked down some food and water before he activated the dyad again, sending her into another agony of confusion.

Now, she was awake, and the image of Bardon's standard kept intruding into her pain. It contained a twelve-pointed star like the one that symbolized the twelve stones of the Anarwyn. It also contained a six-sided prism, the shape of a quartz crystal. Why? Had Bardon simply stolen the idea from Jathneel, or did it have some significance? Why would he combine a symbol of the Anarwyn with the sign of the Unity Stone?

Muffled voices penetrated the buzz in her ears and the fog in her mind.

"A full detachment set out for the Lonely Valley this morning," a gruff male voice said. "The master is through playing games."

Someone snorted. "He's afraid of a rock. We should go home before he stirs up a hornet's nest. These Dinera don't want us here."

"Keep your fool mouth shut," the first voice said. "The master will lead us right. This war will be over before the autumn harvest."

"If you say so."

Bardon's dyad lay icy cold against Lorna's skin, and she shifted, trying to push it away. It burned her fingers. She needed to get out of here. There had to be some way to escape this debilitating torment. Yet, Bardon was not one to make mistakes. He had probably tested this dyad on other heirs of Anarwyn over the years. If only she had her pendant with its stones of power, she might have been able to protect herself.

Bardon's Guest

Scuffling sounded behind her, and Lorna started. Had a rat scurried into the tent? They had been known to chew on helpless men left injured on battlefields. A child's face peered up at her from under the tent's wall. It was a little brown-haired girl no more than six or seven years old. No smile formed on her long face. Instead, a frown furrowed her brow as she wrestled with the tightly stretched canvas until she could wriggle underneath. After dragging a bulging satchel through, she knelt before Lorna, pressing a finger to her lips.

The child wore a linen shirt, dyed yellow, and a long skirt. Her eyes were a deep brown, and though young, she possessed a presence of maturity beyond her years. The girl lifted the dyad's golden chain from around Lorna's neck with a grimace of distaste, taking care not to touch the dyad itself.

The instant the chain slipped off over Lorna's head, her mental haze lifted, and the pain subsided to a dull ache. The child dropped the dyad in the trampled grass and withdrew a water skin and a lump of old cheese and bread from her satchel.

"Thank you," Lorna whispered. She gulped down the water, desperate to assuage her horrible thirst, and nibbled at the bread while the child watched. Feeling a bit stronger, Lorna patted the girl on the arm. "Who sent you?"

"The woman," the child whispered, "the one who talks in my mind."

Lorna scowled. "The Anarwyn?"

The girl nodded and withdrew Lorna's golden pendant from the satchel. Before she could think better of it, Lorna snatched it from the girl, who scowled.

"I'm sorry," Lorna hastened to explain. "It's just that…" She trailed off. The child wouldn't understand. "How did you get this?"

The child pointed to Bardon's dyad and said, "Kill it."

"You mean destroy it?"

"Kill it." She said again and reached for the pendant.

Lorna studied her. Could the child be an heir? What did she mean the Anarwyn had sent her? She let the child's little fingers close around the pendant, but she didn't relinquish control of it. She couldn't. She was naked without the power of the Anarwyn. Weak. Vulnerable. She couldn't endure the terror of that defenselessness again.

The ruby on the pendant flared, as did the sapphire, and the dyad snapped into place. The child had formed the dyad on her own. It was incredible. Lorna had never seen anything like it. Most children who were sensitive to the Anarwyn might show that inclination as toddlers, but it usually receded and didn't manifest itself again until they entered puberty or even adulthood. Had the child been trained? If so, by whom? Why had she never found her while searching for heirs?

Bardon's dyad glistened as the girl picked it up by the chain and dropped it between them in the muddy grass. "Kill it," she repeated.

A gentle fluttering rippled through Lorna's mind as the child fumbled for a mental connection. Allowing the bond to form, Lorna marveled at this child's understanding and control. Together, they sent the enhanced power of the ruby surging into the morganite and topaz dyad. At first, nothing happened. Then the quartz crystal glowed, and the dyad exploded in a blast of energy that sent them tumbling away from each other.

Lorna scrambled to her knees, desperate for the girl's safety. She shook the ringing from her ears and crawled to the child's side. The little girl was on her hands and knees. Blood dripped from her nose. Who was this child?

The tent flaps flew open, and guards rushed in. Lorna reacted instinctively. A bolt of white light shot from her fingers as she activated the pearl in her pendant, ripping the two men apart. Lorna scooped up the child and fled as fast as she could in her weakened condition. Sunlight scorched her eyes after the shadows of the tent. Yet, she staggered on, blindly seeking escape from the camp.

Shouts followed her, and confused Inverni soldiers attempted to bar her way. Few survived the fury of her flight. She needed to get this child away from here. This girl was more competent and powerful at age six or seven than most Varaná had been at thirty. Perhaps she was the answer to defeating Bardon once and for all.

A trumpet blared, and Lorna ducked behind a tent. The camp was coming to life. They would be searching for her. She considered casting up a shield, but in her weakened condition, she wouldn't be able to hold it and flee.

The child clung to Lorna's neck and whispered, "He's coming."

Lorna leaped over stacks of supplies and dodged between tents. There was no real direction to her flight, just the desperate need to get away. She hoped the confusion in the camp would give them enough time. Stumbling and then righting herself, she staggered on. A man leaped in front of her, and she used the pearl to blast him out of the way. Her mind was still vapid, her vision hazy. Her trembling legs burned with exhaustion, and her breathing came in ragged painful gasps. She used the agate to ease her discomfort but was too weak to do more.

Bardon's voice boomed over the tumult, and dark energy slammed into her back, sending her sprawling. The child tumbled from her arms but came up running, her long skirt clinging to her churning legs. Lorna scrambled after her, trying to concentrate on casting a shield with the malachite, when a flash of white light seared the side of Lorna's face and cut into the child. A black hole punched through the child's back, and she fell, soundless and limp.

The strangled cry died in Lorna's throat, caught on the sob of dismay. A child. He had killed a child! What kind of monster was he?

Rage surged through her as she spun, sending a spray of fire from the Fire Stone to ignite the camp. Flames roared into the tents and supplies. Men screamed and burst into flames. The heat of the inferno drove her back a step. She reached for the jasper and set the earth to heaving. A roar of stone grinding on stone split the chaos, and a wall of earth and rock soared forty feet into the air, stretching a mile. It would take Bardon and his minions time to get around that.

"She died because of you," Bardon shouted. His voice must have been magically magnified because it burst through the roar of surging earth.

Tears poured down Lorna's cheeks. She snatched up the child's body and fled into the foothills, fighting the despair and exhaustion. What had she done?

The air scorched her throat, and her chest burned. The girl hung limp in her arms, and her face was pale. A black hole burned through her little body that produced a curl of rancid-smelling smoke. Lorna dove behind a rock outcrop and lay the child down, calling up the power of the agate. Healing energy rushed from her fingers, seeking out the injury, but there was no life to save. The child was dead. Lorna let the power withdraw into the agate and bowed her head. Tears dripped onto her lap. How could she prevail against such reckless disregard for human life and goodness? How could she overcome such evil?

Undead

Cam parted the branches of the laurel tree to get a better view. Who was with Rebecca? His pulse quickened, and he reached for his sword. Had she been discovered? Was this a trap?

The two figures strolled down the dirt road, kicking up dust as they came. Rebecca no longer wore her hood drawn up. Her blonde hair was tied back with a string. The other figure was about her size but kept their hood raised, so Cam couldn't tell whether it was a man or a woman.

They ambled past the place where Cam and Draig were hidden until they disappeared around the bend. Cam gestured to Draig, and together, they slipped into the trees to crouch out of sight. The rich tang of pine filled his nostrils. Boots crunched through the dry pine needles and twigs, and Rebecca came to an abrupt halt. She frowned and tossed her head back and forth, searching for them. Cam waited. He wanted to know who the stranger was before he revealed himself.

The stranger knelt to examine the ground and then rose. They exchanged a few hushed words, and the stranger pointed to the ground and strode toward where Cam and Draig hid. Rebecca followed.

Cam slipped his sword from its sheath. Draig sat on his haunches, at ease. It annoyed Cam that he wasn't taking things seriously. As the pair approached their hiding place, Cam jumped out with his sword extended at the stranger's chest. The stranger stumbled backward, and Cam leaped after him, intent on pressing his advantage. He slammed the stranger to the ground, stomping his boot on his chest, and leveled his sword at his throat.

The stranger's cowl fell back, revealing the pink features of a boy with blonde hair. Cam paused in astonishment as Rebecca grabbed his sword arm.

"Cam, no," she gasped.

Cam scowled in confusion. Rebecca had gone into the city to find help, and she brought back a boy who couldn't be more than fourteen years old.

"It's okay," Rebecca soothed. "This is our way into the prison." She gestured toward the boy.

Cam hesitated. "A boy?"

Bardon's Guest

"You're not much more than a boy yourself," the stranger said.

Cam scanned the boy from head to toe. This kid was either an overconfident fool or someone to be reckoned with.

Rebecca squeezed Cam's arm. "It's all right. Let him up."

He lifted his foot from the boy's chest and sheathed his sword. "I assume there's an explanation for this," he said.

Rebecca bent to help the boy to his feet and dusted off his cloak.

"Cam," she said with a sweep of her arm, "meet Tad. He's going to help us liberate our friends."

Cam scanned the boy from head to foot. He was handsome in a boyish way with his short-cropped hair, blonde eyelashes, and twinkling blue eyes.

"You're a boy," Cam said.

"You keep saying that." Tad raised his eyebrows as if he didn't much like being called a boy. He had a thick Lakari accent. "I'll wager I am as good as you with a sword, and I know every hiding place in Hannoch."

Rebecca laughed at Cam's surprised expression. "Sit, Cam," she said. "Let me explain."

After studying them for another moment, Cam dropped to the ground with a grunt. The other two sat cross-legged on the soft woodland carpet of leaves and pine needles, and Rebecca began.

"I told you that I knew how cities work." She grinned. "I found this villain harassing a patrol of soldiers, and I followed him after they chased him off. More than once, he tried to lose me. I kept after him until he vanished down a side street. I searched for over an hour. I finally gave up and returned to the street where he had disappeared. Three men surprised me and dragged me into a dark room. When they lit a candle, I found this little imp staring at me."

Tad chuckled. "I had to know who was following me."

Rebecca continued. "Tad is the leader of those resisting the tyranny of the Earl of Hannoch."

Cam raised his eyebrows, reassessing his original impression. "The leader?"

"My father started it," Tad said. "He led us until he was killed in an ambush. The resistance kept growing, and the men followed me. I've been trying to extend the resistance outside the city."

Rebecca cut in. "I simply explained our plight, and luckily one of the members of the band recognized me from a trip he'd taken to Abilene a couple of years ago. So Tad decided to fall in with us and give us what aid he could."

When she finished, Cam studied the boy again. "How old are you?"

"Almost fourteen," Tad grinned. "And of all people, you shouldn't question my youth."

"What's that supposed to mean?"

"Aren't you too young to bear the Life Stone and the sword of the King of the West Mark?"

Cam snorted. "You *told* him?"

Rebecca shrugged.

"I think you'll agree," Tad continued, "leadership is not a matter of size or age. Cunning, skill, and wit can be far more valuable than brawn. What I lack in age, I make up for in experience and training."

Cam pondered all that the boy had said. He *did* seem more mature than he appeared. Rebecca trusted him. And despite his misgivings, Cam couldn't help but like the boy. "All right," he said. "I apologize for my rough handling."

"That's behind us now." The boy grinned and stuck out his hand.

Cam shook it and was surprised at the boy's strength. "You're taking it remarkably well."

"I know when to fight," Tad said. He shot Rebecca a grin. "Now, let's see if we can't get your friends out of that dungeon."

"You know where they are?" Cam asked.

"Of course. What kind of rebel leader would I be if I didn't? Anyway, if we're going to do it, we better go in tonight. The Earl held court this evening. Your friends will likely be dancing at the end of a rope before noon tomorrow."

Cam gasped. "What have they done?"

Tad sniffed. "Nowadays it doesn't matter what they've done. If the Earl thinks they were up to mischief—and he thinks that of most everyone these days—he'll simply get rid of them. The Regency Council at Yarwick tries to exercise authority over these lords. They seldom listen." He studied Cam with narrowed eyes. "Maybe you need to witness this if you plan to reign over this land."

Cam was taken aback. "I have no desire to reign anywhere."

"Pity," Tad said with a frown.

Cam shifted uncomfortably, but Rebecca came to his rescue.

Bardon's Guest

"What about tonight?"

Tad studied Cam for another moment before answering. "I've already set plans into motion. We only need to smooth over a few details, and we'll need your help."

"Of course," Cam said.

By the time Tad finished outlining the plans for them, the sun had slipped behind the mountains, casting up a brilliant crimson fire that ignited the clouds with a ruddy glow.

"You two rest," Tad said. "I'll wake you when it's time."

Cam was reluctant to sleep while a stranger watched over him. Rebecca, however, curled up without a word and slept as if she hadn't a care in the world. Cam lay down beside her but kept his hand on the pommel of his sword.

It seemed like mere moments later when Tad was shaking Cam's shoulder.

"It's time," he whispered.

They rose and followed Tad as he set off through the woods where the trees became mere blobs in the darkness. How did Tad keep his sense of direction? Then again, he probably knew this area as well as Cam knew the trails and terrain around Stony Vale. Unfortunately, Tad's knowledge didn't stop Cam from stubbing his toe against unseen stones or the stumps of fallen trees.

After trudging for half an hour, Tad whispered, "Hold up a minute." They crouched beside a gurgling stream among the dense underbrush. The stark white walls of the city gleamed in the darkness as though they were emitting all the light they had absorbed during the day. Occasional torches cast dancing shadows on the walls as guards paced back and forth along the ramparts. Cam, Tad, and Rebecca were so close that the jangle of the guards' armor and the tread of their booted feet on the stone seemed loud.

Tad bent to whisper to them. "The wolf cannot follow where we need to go. If all goes well, we'll be back here with your friends in a few hours. If not, at least he'll be free to seek aid."

Cam scratched Draig's ears. "You'll have to wait here, old boy. We'll be back."

Draig settled onto his belly with his head toward the city wall and his tail curled around his feet. He cut a noble figure there in the darkness, and Cam admired his ability to accept the inevitable.

"That's some animal," Tad said.

They tripped through a dry creek bed and scrambled up through a tangle of roots before Tad paused again. "No more speaking from here on out. We'll enter a tunnel that is nearby. I'm sorry. I'll have to ask you to permit me to blindfold you before we approach."

"It's already dark as pitch," Cam protested, but Rebecca squeezed his arm.

"I apologize," Tad said, "but if either of you get caught, what you do not know you cannot tell."

"It'll be all right," Rebecca said.

"Okay," Cam relented, "but I don't want any more stubbed toes."

Tad chuckled. "I'll do my best."

Rebecca grasped Cam's hand and intertwined her fingers with his as Tad tied dark cloths over their eyes. Rebecca hauled him after her, and Cam realized that Tad must be holding her other hand. An unreasonable flame of jealousy surged through his chest, and he struggled to keep from ripping off the blindfold and confronting Tad right there. But he was being silly. He tried to focus on keeping his feet under him and the thrill of Rebecca's strong, cool hand in his.

They didn't go far before the air changed from the open, vibrant fragrance of the forest to the close, moldy aroma of an enclosed chamber. Tad untied the blindfolds and motioned for them to follow. The flickering yellow light of a single lamp struggled to push back the oppressive blackness of the cavern, like the tunnel under Donmor. A little shudder rippled through him. He wasn't anxious to repeat that experience.

"How are the toes?" Tad asked.

"Good," Cam said. "Thanks."

"Don't thank me yet. We still have a long way to go." He picked up the lantern and continued down the damp corridor.

Rebecca clasped Cam's hand again and interlaced her fingers with his. They followed Tad to the top of a twisting flight of stairs and started down. Rebecca let go of his hand and climbed down after Tad. Cam brought up the rear. They descended several hundred steps before the tunnel flattened out.

The reprieve didn't last long. Soon they were climbing another flight of roughly hewn stairs that curled in a constant spiral. Cam's thighs were burning by the time they reached a landing, and he stared at a row of iron rungs set in the stone that led up into a black hole.

"That's the way out," Tad whispered.

"After you." Cam gestured for him to lead the way.

Tad started the climb, and Cam let Rebecca go next as they clambered up the ladder. Tad paused at the top and pressed his ear against a board. Apparently satisfied, he motioned for them to follow and blew out the light. Darkness swallowed them, and Cam experienced sudden disorientation. Rebecca gasped as her foot slipped and kicked Cam in the head. He reached up to steady her, but she had already recovered. Wood grated on stone, and pale light diffused the tunnel as Tad ascended and disappeared. A moment later, his face smiled down at them.

"Keep low," he whispered.

They wriggled through into a narrow space barely high enough for Cam to slip through on his belly. Tad motioned for them to scoot out, and they found they had climbed through a trapdoor hidden under a bed.

Cam opened his mouth to say something, but remembering they were supposed to keep quiet, he snapped it shut. Tad led them to the back of the house until they encountered a small, wooden door. He bent to peer through a tiny hole as footsteps thudded past.

After the sound faded away, he turned to them. "We're near the green by the castle walls," he whispered. "We have to cross the green to the well. It's not far. The area is frequently patrolled. If we are accosted, do not stop, whatever you do. Follow me."

Cam didn't bother to tell Tad that if he was captured they couldn't possibly follow him. He simply nodded his understanding. Tad peeked out the spy hole once more before unbolting the door and slipping it open. The outside air blew in cool and refreshing after the damp mugginess of the tunnel, carrying with it a myriad of scents from the city. They slipped into the street and melted into the shadows. The idea of venturing into a place he didn't know filled Cam with unease. If things went wrong—as they usually did—he would be lost.

Tad crept catlike from shadow to shadow. The moonless night helped to conceal them. Several troops of guards marched past on their rounds, and Cam, Rebecca, and Tad had to dive into the shadows to wait breathlessly as they passed. When they reached the green,

Undead

they drifted from tree to tree, three dark specters moving swiftly and silently through the inky night.

They came to a halt in the shadow of a conical outbuilding to catch their breath. Tad pointed to a stone well not thirty paces from them on the other side of a large oak. The well had a triangular roof, and a wooden bucket balanced on the stones. The music of the crickets and tree frogs filled the air, along with the occasional barking of a dog or yowl of a cat.

Tad raced toward the well when a man stepped out from behind the old oak right in Tad's path. Tad crashed headlong into the man, and they fell in a tangle of arms and legs.

Chapter Sixteen
Dungeons of Hannoch

"SHE HAS GROWN POWERFUL." Bardon sent the message over the tenuous link he maintained with Jathneel. He kept his breathing low, and his gaze focused on the pink morganite gem set in the golden band encircling his finger. The Opening Stone pulsed as he reached across the expanse to where Jathneel, his former master, awaited his instructions. Bardon reclined on a cushioned couch in his command tent on the plains before Mawsil. Fragrant herbs smoldered in the brass incense burner, helping him maintain the trance. The light of several dozen candles danced on the walls of the tent.

"She has not been idle," Jathneel said. "Your sister is perhaps the greatest of the Varaná since Lindian, who received the Water Stone from the jaws of the great serpent. You underestimate her to your cost."

Bardon ground his teeth in annoyance. "You promised me when we awakened the Mahrowaiths that they would eliminate all the heirs, and yet, this child escaped them."

"The Mahrowaiths are mere beasts," Jathneel said. "You have been hasty. Your too frequent use of the Bragamahr is warping your judgment."

"Don't lecture me, old man," Bardon spat. He adjusted his seat to ease the strain on his back. "I have the courage to do what you were too weak to even contemplate."

Undead

A long silence ensued.

"Perhaps," Jathneel said, "but you will never defeat your sister with blustering complaints. What is your plan?"

Bardon began to respond but paused. Jathneel had never been comfortable with his extended probing of the powers of the Bragamahr. He was still too much of a Varaná to recognize the superior control and mastery of men the Bragamahr could provide. Perhaps it was better to keep him guessing.

"I will heal what never should have been broken," he said.

"I see," Jathneel replied.

But Bardon knew that he did not see, not really.

Jathneel continued, "And you think you know how to do this?"

"I do know. A simple dyad—" He broke off. He had said too much. "Have you accomplished what I sent you to do?"

Jathneel snorted. "I am not your servant."

"You will be if you want to survive."

Bardon enjoyed Jathneel's surge of anger that pulsed through their connection. It served him right after all the years of arrogance. Bardon had fled to him a frightened boy, and Jathneel treated him like a spoiled child. He had been stingy with his knowledge of the Bragamahr, but once Bardon had taken the sacred black sand into his body, he set out to probe its depths on his own. He traveled alone to the Braganeth to greet his true master and no longer needed Jathneel to teach him. He traced the raised black scar on his hand, enjoying the warm rush of power.

"I have done my part," Jathneel said. "The boy will die."

"You are certain?"

"I do not dabble in half-baked plans," Jathneel growled. "When I set out to do a thing, it is done."

"Good," Bardon said. "Should your plans unravel, I expect you to meet me at Torwyn. If Maelorn escapes, he will flee to the city of his childhood, thinking I cannot breach those walls." He gave a sardonic laugh. "He always was a fool."

"So be it," Jathneel said, and the link collapsed.

Bardon snarled and wiped the sweat from his brow, breathing in the fragrant air. The candles danced at his movement. How dare Jathneel break the link without Bardon's permission. He would have to teach Jathneel once and for all who the master was now. Still, he had planned for every contingency. Lorna may have escaped him for now—but only for now.

Word had reached him of the existence of a large quartz crystal that might suit his purposes. Once he obtained it, Lorna would be powerless to stop him.

Cam and Rebecca rushed to Tad's aid, where he struggled with the guard beside the oak tree in the center of Hannoch. In the few heartbeats it took to reach him, Tad had extricated himself from the predicament. He rolled to his feet, leaving the guard twitching, and grasping at his throat. A dark stain gushed from between his fingers.

Tad sheathed a knife up his sleeve.

Cam glared at Tad in disbelief. "Was that necessary?"

"This is the unfortunate consequence of warfare," Tad whispered. "The sooner it ends, the better off we all will be."

With that, he dragged the guard's body into the bushes before sprinting to the well and climbing inside. Rebecca followed. What could Cam do but race after them? He glanced once more at the dying man and jogged after Rebecca.

A set of iron rungs had been cemented into the side of the well, and they scrabbled down as fast as they could. Before they reached the bottom where the dark water glittered, Tad led them into another tunnel. This opening was small, and they had to crawl on their hands and knees through a layer of slime for fifty yards before they came to another landing where the tunnel ended.

This time, Tad knelt and tapped a soft, rhythmic combination. He waited until another tapping sounded on the other side. He tapped again. Metal grated on stone, and Tad heaved the slab up. They jumped down into a storage room filled with barrels and piles of weapons. Two dozen armed men formed in a wide circle, watching them.

A tall man with a square face stepped up to Tad, and they shook hands.

"Is everything ready?" Tad asked.

"Yes, sir," the man replied.

"Have you already recovered their weapons?"

Undead

The man nodded.

"How far to their cells?" Tad spoke with an air of authority that shocked Cam. He was even more surprised by the unquestioning confidence these men placed in him.

"Three of them are on this level," the man said. "And the other three are up one."

"So, we split up then," Tad said. "What of the guards?"

"There are six on each level and twenty in the guardroom. They've been drinking the wine we gave them and shouldn't be a problem."

Cam shuffled his feet.

Tad gestured to him. "Rebecca will go with me, and you will go with Clydeff," he said, motioning to the man with whom he had been speaking.

"I don't think—"

"Cam," Tad interrupted, "your friends will come with us more readily if one of you reassures them. A dozen men will accompany us in case there is trouble."

"How will you open the doors?" Rebecca asked.

Tad grinned. "We have acquired a set of keys." He took a deep breath. "We meet back here within half an hour. If one troop is caught, the others must escape the way we came. My men know what to do."

"Be careful," Cam said to Rebecca.

Excitement danced in Rebecca's eyes. This kind of thing thrilled her. He wished he felt half so confident.

She disappeared with Tad, and Cam followed Clydeff through the doors and jogged down the corridor. Torches set at intervals to light the passage gave off an acrid reek. They wound around, passing a dozen rusted iron doors before Clydeff stopped in front of one near the end of the corridor.

He tried several keys until one finally resulted in a metallic click that echoed in the enclosed space. The door creaked as he pushed it ajar. The fetid stench of a dungeon slapped Cam in the face, and he covered his nose with his sleeve. Something shuffled within, and the troop slipped through the door and closed it, keeping it open a crack. One man guarded the door, peering through the gap to keep watch. A slit high above let in enough dim light for Cam to make out the three forms huddled in the corner. Their heads were raised, watching him.

"Spider?" Cam whispered. "Is that you?"

All three men scrambled to their feet, their chains jangling loudly in the silence.

"Cam," they all whispered at once. Surprise, excitement, and not a little fear sounded in their voices as Spider, Hebron, and Laird jumped to greet him.

"It's all right," Cam reassured them. "We've come to get you out. I'll explain later."

In a few minutes, Tad's men had unlocked their manacles, and the friends embraced each other.

Clydeff didn't give them time for explanations. "We must go," he insisted, moving toward the door.

Two of the men handed Spider, Hebron, and Laird their weapons.

"How did they know these were ours?" Spider asked.

Cam shrugged. "They know a sight more than they're supposed to."

They dashed into the corridor and soon found themselves back in the storage room. Their mission had gone off without a hitch. Cam's elation at recovering his friends was snuffed out by the delay of the other group's arrival.

"How long should we wait before we go after them?" he whispered to Clydeff.

"We don't go after them," Clydeff said.

Cam glowered. He would not leave them behind. Not for anything.

They paced the storage room for an eternity, listening for even the slightest noise. During the silent waiting, Cam remembered what the Life Stone had shown him only hours before, and he jumped to his feet.

"What is it?" Clydeff demanded.

"Another of our friends is in this dungeon," Cam said. "He's a big, redheaded Lakari."

"Ewan is here?" Hebron said. "How?"

"I don't know," Cam said. "The Life Stone showed me."

Clydeff spun to one of the men, and they conversed in low tones for a moment.

"Pavon says he knows where he is. On the first level. Why didn't you tell us this sooner?"

Undead

"Things were happening so fast it slipped my mind."

Clydeff sighed. "This time, only us three will go. The rest of you make sure these three are safely out of here before morning. Rennen, take charge."

"Wait," Spider said, "we'll come with you."

"No. We were sent to liberate you, and that is what we will do."

Spider stepped after them, and Clydeff spun on him, his face red with fury. "Do not make me order these men to restrain you. We already have enough trouble."

A hardheaded, rebellious glower came into Spider's face.

"Do as he says," Cam said.

Hebron grabbed Spider and yanked him down onto a barrel as Cam followed Clydeff out the door.

Clydeff glided into the passageway, climbed a flight of stairs, and skirted a group of sleeping guards before turning down another corridor. Pavon led them straight to the door, and they found Ewan inside, chained to the floor. He had lost weight, and his eyes were sunken, but his face split into a wide grin when he recognized Cam.

"I thought you were dead, lad," Ewan said as Pavon and Clydeff unlocked his chains.

"Not yet," Cam said. "We must hurry."

"I'm injured," Ewan said. "I'll only slow you down. Leave me."

Cam grabbed his arms. "I'll carry you if need be."

Ewan snorted. "That would be a sight to see."

Clydeff peeked out the door into the hall. "Go now," he whispered.

Ewan winced as he limped along, favoring his right leg. Cam and Clydeff each draped an arm over a shoulder and helped him along as fast as they could. Pavon led them back the way they had come. When they reached the stairs, sounds of fighting echoed from below.

"Quickly," Clydeff breathed as they struggled down the stairs with the limping Ewan. "This is the only way out."

The sounds of fighting grew louder, and the slap of racing feet echoed behind them.

"Hurry," Clydeff snapped, "before we're trapped in the stairwell."

A shout rang behind them and booted feet pounded on the stairs above. They reached the lower level, half-dragging Ewan, only to find their way blocked by several men dressed in the greenish-blue of the Hannoch guard engaged in a heated battle with Tad and his men. Pavon leaped into the guards without hesitation, and Cam followed, leaving Clydeff to help Ewan along.

Cam's sword hissed from its sheath and sliced into the back of a guard. The man fell and two more were down before the rest realized what was happening. They fought desperately, but there were too few guards. Soon, Tad was racing past their writhing bodies, shouting for them to follow.

Cam glanced at Rebecca. Her hair was in disarray, and her sword was stained red. She nodded that she was okay, and Cam greeted Alaric, Drakeman, and Slone briefly before they joined the flight down the corridor. One of Tad's men heaved Ewan onto his back and jogged along behind them.

More men from the guard poured into the hallway and rushed after them. A handful of Tad's men fell back to act as a rear guard while the rest fled. Cam and the others crashed into the storage room and barred the door.

"Go!" Tad shoved them toward the trapdoor in the ceiling. The others had already left with Hebron, Spider, and Laird.

"What about the men we left behind?" Cam panted.

Tad stared at him with hard, solemn eyes. "The guards will not get past while one of them lives."

Shock and dismay punched into Cam's gut. He glanced at the door trying to decide if he should go back and help them.

"You mean you're leaving them to die?" he demanded. The bitterness and disbelief must have echoed in his voice because Tad scowled at him.

"They chose their own time to die. And I will honor their sacrifice."

Lorna cradled the child in her arms, fighting the sob that struggled to burst free. The insipid wash of dawn colored the world in depressing browns and grays. Her every step had been a failure. For fifty years she had failed, and now, the final confrontation threatened to overwhelm her.

She lay the child on the stone slab she had called from the earth with the jasper before kissing the girl's cold cheek. She stepped back and raised her arms. The earth groaned and solid rock curled up over the child's body into a cairn with a wide, flat stone on top. In the center of the slab of rock, Lorna etched the shape of a twelve-sided star and carved the runes for the sapphire and the ruby—the Water Stone and the Strength Stone. These were the stones the child had commanded with such skill and power.

Standing back to survey her work, she wondered from where the child had come. What her name had been. Lorna had spent the better part of fifty years trying to find and protect anyone with the capacity to wield the gemstones. Here was the most powerful heir she had encountered in decades, and there had been nothing she could do to save her. Would this be the fate of all the heirs of Ilsie?

Her mind returned to the day she condemned Maelorn and Tara to the stone. The guilt burned in her stomach after all these years. *Tara had been a doe-eyed princess who observed everything and spoke little. When she did speak, she proved herself wiser than her years. She and Maelorn had fallen in love as children when King Gwennan had taken Maelorn to Yarwick. They would sometimes meet at the Trysting Tree in the Lonely Valley when Maelorn was in the area.*

Bardon used to fawn over Tara, inserting himself into any activity or conversation where she took part. When Maelorn and Tara became betrothed, Bardon sulked for weeks. They were supposed to wed the same summer Bardon had returned with an army and murdered his father. Only then did Lorna learn that Bardon had cast some working of the Bragamahr that would ensure that if Maelorn and Tara ever touched, they would both die. It was the kind of vicious, vindictive tactic Bardon liked to employ. How he had done it Lorna didn't know, but her attempt to save them had gone terribly wrong.

Lorna stirred, shoving these bitter memories aside. She used the agate to tend the wound Bardon's white fire had burned on her cheek. Two choices remained. She could return and seek death at Bardon's hands, hoping she might destroy him at the same time. Or she could race for the Lonely Valley in the hope that somehow Cam would succeed, that Maelorn could rally the people of the marks to finally face Bardon and his armies. Weariness seeped into the marrow of her bones. It would be so easy to let Bardon kill her now. She had given her life to resisting him. Who would blame her if she died in battle trying to subdue him? No. She couldn't—not while there was a chance to save Cam.

Heaving a deep sigh, Lorna set out over the rolling hills to the wide lake that filled the eastern end of the valley. Her father would expect her to fight on. She had to continue. Bardon was hunting her, and he would be hunting Cam, as well. Everything now relied upon that boy. If Maelorn could not be released, the East Mark would not come to their aid, the North Mark would not unite, and all would be lost.

She waded into the lake to wash the grime and filth of her captivity from her body and her clothing before trudging west toward the Lonely Valley. The weary miles passed beneath her feet as the dawn gave way to an overcast day. She skirted the edge of the lake until she found an isolated farmhouse with an old man who fed her and lent her the use of his pony. She used the agate to calm the animal and dragged herself onto its back. Clinging to its mane, she hissed a command and kicked it to a canter. If she had to ride a hundred horses to death to reach Cam in time, she would.

"May I see it?" Tad asked Cam.

They had struggled through the tunnels, up through the well, and back into the long cavern that led them outside the city walls. The pearling glow of dawn sifted through the leaves, casting dappled shadows on the forest floor where the cluster of men gathered beside the little pool.

"See what?" Cam replied without looking at him.

He hadn't forgotten Tad's callous disregard for his men's lives. The guard Tad had slain hadn't meant them any harm. But the worst were his own men. He had left them behind. Locked them in the dungeon where there would be no escape. Cam found his blood racing at the betrayal. Hebron never would have done such a thing.

"You are angry with me," Tad said.

"We should have tried to get those men out." Cam finished cleaning his sword and sheathed it.

Tad glowered. "You don't think it hurt me to leave them behind?" He stepped closer to Cam. His face burned red. "They were *my* friends. Unlike you, I know their names, their families. And I'm the one who has to tell their kin what they died for."

Cam scowled. He hadn't considered things from that perspective. He'd been so angered and guilt-ridden that good men had died. Still, Tad had sacrificed their lives without a second thought. He wasn't sure he could forgive him. "You're right," he said. "I'm sorry."

"I'm sorry, too," Tad said and stepped back. "I'm sorry for all the fatherless children. All the wives who will weep. I'm sorry for the injustice that crushes this city and this kingdom. I am also willing to die to set it right. Are you?"

Cam was taken aback by the intensity of Tad's declaration. Was he willing to die to bring justice and stability to the West Mark? He didn't know. He had accepted the mission to free Maelorn and Tara with the knowledge that he would most likely die in the attempt. He hadn't seriously considered what it might mean to accept the lordship over lands and people he didn't know. Should he tell Tad that he planned to refuse the kingship and go off with Spider and Rebecca to some secluded place where the world would not intrude? Or should he give Tad hope that he would consider the idea that left him trembling with self-doubt? He was no king, after all.

"I'm sorry," he said again and looked away from Tad's burning gaze.

Spider was carrying on an animated conversation with Rebecca, while Laird had just finished healing Ewan's leg. Hebron, Alaric, Drakeman, and Ewan had their heads together planning something. Slone lay back with his eyes closed, while Draig studied them all with his keen eyes.

"May I see it then?" Tad asked again.

Cam glanced back at him. "What?"

"The Life Stone." Tad said this like it should have been obvious.

Cam hesitated. It was difficult for him to relinquish the stone to anyone. Still, he owed his life and the lives of his friends to Tad. He slipped the stone from the pouch. It glowed an iridescent blue as he handed it to Tad, who accepted it reverently. The glow faded as soon as it left Cam's hand.

"It's beautiful," Tad whispered. "I've never seen anything like it."

"It's called a Vision Stone by the Varaná," Cam explained.

Tad handed the Life Stone back to Cam and the opal glowed again. "Use it well."

"I'm sorry your men had to die for so little," Cam said.

Tad studied him with a little scowl. "What would you have men die for?"

Cam shuffled his feet. "Not for me, I guess."

"Don't let their lives be wasted. Free Maelorn and secure the throne. Restore justice to the West Mark. That's all I ask."

"That's all, huh?" Cam sniffed. Did Tad understand what he was asking?

"It is enough," Tad replied. He grinned a boyish smile. "Do you think your friend will forgive us?" He gestured toward Spider. "He apparently refused to go into the tunnel, and my men had to gag him and truss him like a pig. They weren't too pleased with having to carry him through. They tell me he fought like a bear as soon as he saw our mode of escape. It's curious behavior for one of your champions."

Cam pressed his lips together for a moment. "He had a bad experience a while back, and he's not yet over it."

"We should be going," Hebron said as he ambled up to them. He already wore his pack, and the sword, Dorandel, swung at his hip.

Yet again, Cam thought how much more Hebron and Alaric looked like the warriors of legend than he did. Why couldn't one of them become king?

Cam shouldered his pack. "Thank you," he said to Tad and extended his hand.

Tad grasped it in a powerful grip. "My sword and my men are at your service. Call, and we will come."

"I appreciate that," Cam said. "Good luck and stay out of trouble."

Tad chuckled. "There's no fun in that." He handed Cam a tiny gold ring with a red jewel cut in the shape of a small rosebud. "Should you need me, send this to the baker on Earl Street. He'll know where to find me."

Connac knelt beside the wounded Inverni his men had dragged in and peered at the little black and gold stone around the man's neck. He tore it free and reeled as some dark energy burst into his mind. He released the stone and caught himself on his hands and knees, staring down at the odd gem.

The home guard had spent more than a week pursuing the bands of Inverni raiders who ransacked the towns and villages, carrying away food, killing the men and boys, and carting off the women. Connac had adopted a policy of executing every Inverni swine who fell into his hands, but something had been nagging at him since their first battle.

These Inverni did not fight like the ones they had battled on their southern border for years. These were reckless of their lives and, consequently, had done great damage to the home guard, whose numbers had thinned. If Gareth was going to march out to meet Bardon's army in open battle, Connac needed to make sure Gareth knew what he might face.

He righted himself but didn't touch the trinket. "What is that thing?" he demanded of the wounded Inverni. The man's face was scarred, and blood bubbled on his lips.

He shook his head. "I don't know. We all have one."

"What is Bardon planning? Where will he strike first?"

"I'm just a soldier," the man gasped.

Connac resisted the urge to slap the man senseless. "Is he going to invade the East Mark?"

The man shook his head. "We're foraging parties. He's after some boy."

"Who? Where?"

"To the west." The man coughed up a blood clot, and his eyes widened.

"Where have they taken the women and children?" Connac asked.

"To Mawsil. Bardon holds the city."

Connac considered the situation for a moment. Should he wait for Gareth and the rest of the army? Or should he race after the captives and rescue those he could? His orders were to repel the raids, and the home guard was not supposed to leave Rahil lands. They were the last line of defense. If he rode for Mawsil, he would be disobeying direct orders. The home guard might not follow him.

Muttering a curse, Connac rose. This is what came of having an old king who refused to see sense and hid in his mountain fortress. Maybe Gareth would do better. Connac lifted the stone from the mud by its leather string. The jewel glinted in the waning light. He stepped to his horse and slipped it into his saddlebag. Perhaps this would be of some use later. If Bardon was making his men wear it, it must have some purpose. Perhaps Connac could turn it to his own designs.

"Kill him," he said to the guard, "and gather all those stones you can find, but only touch their leather straps. No one in the army is to keep one."

Chapter Seventeen
Homecoming

"I GUESS WE'RE GOING through Yarwick first," Slone said as Cam and his company followed Ewan in their descent through the rugged mountain passes, avoiding all roads and trails.

"It's not ideal," Alaric replied. "I'd hoped to have Maelorn with us when we confronted the Regency Council."

Cam glanced back at Spider and Rebecca. Rebecca gave him a resigned smile, and Spider simply shrugged. Aside from hiding in the mountains, there wasn't much he could do to avoid what was coming.

"Bardon will be waiting for us in the Lonely Valley," Drakeman said. "If he knew enough to send men to the great bend in the Afon Fathwe, he'll suspect our ultimate destination."

"He does," Cam said. "I told you that Lorna contacted me."

"I remember."

"There are those in Yarwick who will help us," Alaric said.

Cam shook his head in disbelief. They were risking so much on the hunch that the Lakari would accept a total stranger as their king. And what was he supposed to do as king anyway?

They fell silent as Ewan led them down a steep, rocky slope onto a game trail barely wide enough for them to pass. The trail slipped into a thick stand of mixed oak, pine, maple, and birch and through patches of briars, forcing them to crawl under or over fallen logs. Draig experienced no difficulty navigating the path. His human companions had to duck and scramble.

"Does he think we're rabbits?" Spider said to Cam and Rebecca after a particularly narrow bit of trail left them wriggling through on their bellies.

"He thinks," Hebron said, "that you'd rather arrive at Yarwick without being captured and tossed into prison again."

Spider harrumphed and kept crawling. "I was ready to give that earl a piece of my mind."

"You mean when you were so scared you were shaking in your boots?" Hebron taunted. "You should have seen his face when the earl said we were all going to dangle from the gallows."

Cam couldn't laugh. They had come very close to being hanged, and if it hadn't been for Tad, he and Rebecca would have strolled into the city to find them all swinging from the end of a rope. The thought made him sick.

"I wasn't ready to die," Spider said. "I mean, I haven't even kissed a girl."

Hebron gave a gruff laugh and craned his head around to look back at Spider as they crawled through the undergrowth. "Are you sure about that? Old Hetty used to say you were a fabulous kisser."

"Enough of that," Spider snapped.

"Who's Hetty?" Rebecca called from behind Cam, but Cam was laughing too hard to answer.

"Who's Hetty?" Rebecca insisted.

"No one," Spider grumbled.

"She was an old crone that liked to flirt with Spider," Cam said. "I think Spider actually liked the attention."

"I see," Rebecca said.

They passed through the brambles and were able to rise to their feet again. Spider's face burned a bright red.

"The first thing you should do when you become king," he said as he brushed himself off, "is get rid of the Earl of Hannoch and demote Hebron to slopping the pigs."

"He's so sensitive," Alaric said.

"They say," Slone added, "that women like the sensitive ones. Is that true, Rebecca?"

"Of course. They especially like the ones who aren't afraid of older women."

Undead

Cam chuckled with them, but Spider was getting annoyed. "All right," he said, "Spider's been a good sport." He laid a hand on his friend's shoulder. "Everyone here knows how brave you've been. We wouldn't trade you for anyone."

"I'd trade him for my wife," Ewan said.

This time even Spider joined in the laughter.

They settled into the long descent through the wooded hillsides of the West Mark. Spider's comment had disturbed Cam. He didn't want the authority that would allow him to dispossess a man from his family's lands and position. Even if he survived the attempt to free Maelorn and Tara, would anyone actually want him as their king? And what about Rebecca? She had refused Briallen when he offered to make her a queen because she didn't want to be trapped in a palace. If he ever asked her to marry him, would she throw the idea back in his face, as well? Would he even have a choice whom he married?

After two days of scrambling, they dropped out of the passes and into the rolling hill country. The birches fell away behind them, and the oak and pine forest spread out. They found a well-traveled path that led past little cottages with square patches of forest cut away where green shoots poked from the neat rows of well-tended fields.

In the early afternoon of the third day, they broke through the trees, and the yellow walls of Yarwick loomed up on a rise in the distance. The company stopped as one.

Cam gazed around him. The forest had been cleared, and plowed and planted fields dotted the landscape in a patchwork, divided by dry stone fences with wooden gates. The rich fragrance of plowed earth and cut grass wafted on the breeze.

Yarwick perched on an elevated knoll in a large bend of a blue river, which curled around the base of the hill. Boats plied the waters of the river, shuffling to and from a series of docks. The city commanded a view of the countryside. A wooden drawbridge spanned the river, and the gates yawned open, allowing a constant flow of people to stroll in and out of the city. Some rode in carts drawn by donkeys or horses, while others trudged in on sandaled feet. A strange sensation stirred in the pit of Cam's stomach. His father and mother had lived in this city. They had been killed somewhere in this valley.

Rebecca stepped up beside him and grasped his hand. "What an interesting city."

Cam glanced at her. The slanting afternoon light was behind her, giving her hair an angelic glow. "I don't belong here," he whispered.

"You were born here," she said. "This is your true home."

Cam didn't reply. A home wasn't simply where you were born. It was where you were loved and accepted. Where you made your life. These things he could never hope to find here. He already had enemies who had never even met him.

Spider joined them. "I don't know about you, but I'm ready for a soft, straw mattress and a home-cooked meal."

"And who are you going to get to cook it for you?" Rebecca asked.

Spider pursed his lips. "I'm sure the ladies will oblige."

"I keep telling you," Hebron said, "the Anar have far too high an opinion of themselves."

"Hang on," Slone said in mocking offense.

Everyone laughed, and with the release of tension, they started forward again, passing a mixture of flaxen and copper-haired people. A palanquin passed them with a guard in front moving the common folk aside. A richly clad woman wearing a tunic with long, pointed sleeves dangled her arm out of its window. Her hair was pulled up in an elegant bun with jade pins holding it in place. The more common people wore long linen shirts secured at the waist with belts of leather or woven reeds. The men wore trousers while the women seemed to prefer green skirts.

Folks on the road gave them a wide berth when they saw the black wolf padding along beside Cam. Ewan hobbled up to the guard beside the gate, who glared at him until recognition brightened his face.

He snapped to attention. "Lord High Marshall," he said, "we weren't expecting you."

"Clearly," Ewan said. "Send for Derek and have him meet me at my house."

The soldier cast a shifty-eyed glance at the other soldier. "Yes, My Lord." And he darted away.

"Follow me," Ewan said and led them through the bustling streets away from the curtain wall toward the higher section of the city.

Yarwick was very different from Abilene. One got a sense of order and pride in Abilene that was lacking in Yarwick. Here, the streets were befouled with waste, the buildings were in ill-repair, and people cast nervous, distrustful glances at any who passed too close. The unkempt nature of the city contrasted with the ordered fields they had seen earlier.

"Friendly place," Spider whispered to Cam.

Cam grunted. He hadn't felt this much out of place since they had staggered into Abilene. He kept having a tingly, nervous feeling that someone was watching him, waiting for him to make a mistake.

They passed shops filled with wares. The rich aroma of cooking barley bread competed with a cinnamon smell that seemed to come from the men who lounged in doorways or in front of taverns smoking long tubes with bowls on the ends. Cam had never seen such a thing and pointed it out to Spider.

"What do you think they're doing?" he whispered.

"Trying to kill themselves, I would guess," Spider said.

"It's a weed that grows near forest ponds," Rebecca said from behind them. "I heard about it in Abilene. They trade it to the Shardana who mix it with resin and sniff it up their noses."

Cam glanced around at her to see if she was joking.

She laughed. "I'm serious."

"What for?" Spider asked.

"It's supposed to make them more alert and able to withstand the rigors of long voyages."

"No thanks," Spider said.

Cam didn't bother telling him that no one had offered him any.

Ewan quickened his pace until Cam had to jog to keep up. The speed of Ewan's limp surprised him. As they ascended the winding streets, Cam noted that the carvings on dark teak wood lintels above the doors became more intricate. They depicted mountain scenes, and some had images of a woman with flowing hair holding out one arm. They reminded him of the statue of the woman they had seen in the valley before Mendefra when Peylog was still with them. It could only be Ilsie. He elbowed Spider and pointed to the images.

"I noticed," Spider said out of the side of his mouth.

A short, stocky man with a golden oak leaf badge on his breast jogged to meet Ewan from an intricately carved doorway, and the two embraced.

"My Lord," he said. "We had given up hope."

Homecoming

Ewan released the man with a pat on the back. "Good to see you, Derek. How is my family?"

Derek frowned. "They're fine, at the moment. I have much to tell you, but surely you are tired from your long journey."

Ewan gave him a distracted wave and strode to the fine arched doorway, lifted the latch, and entered. A cry burst from within, and Cam reached for his sword until he realized it was a woman's cry of surprise. Derek waved the company in, and they entered the dark interior where candles burned in sconces along rich, tapestried walls. Apparently, Ewan was a man of consequence.

Three redheaded children scampered in crying "Papa," and Ewan released a sobbing woman and knelt to enfold the children in his burly arms. Cam glanced at Rebecca and found her studying him. Could she be sharing his thought that it would be nice to have a family like that—someone waiting for you when you returned home?

Ewan rose with tears glistening on his cheeks and faced his companions.

"This is my wife Elatha."

She curtsied to each of them as she wiped the tears from her cheeks. Elatha was a round, full-faced woman with auburn hair and a fair, lovely face.

"Welcome to our home," she said. She gave Laird and his bullhorn mustache a curious look, but she paused when her gaze rested on Hebron. "Do I know you?"

"Yes, My Lady," Hebron said.

Elatha's eyes widened. "You left with *her*," she breathed. She glanced at Cam and Spider and back to Cam. "Is this…" She paused.

"Yes," Hebron said again.

Elatha's face flushed, and she bowed low to Cam, who squirmed under her gaze.

Ewan came to his rescue. "Let me introduce everyone." He went around telling Derek and Elatha each of their names and where they were from. When he finished, he said. "Now, let's get cleaned up and give Spider his home-cooked meal before he starts gnawing on the furniture."

The meal was the noisiest Cam had experienced since Abilene. The children scampered about, getting underfoot, as the servants brought in the food and cleared it away after each course.

Undead

The first course consisted of a thick, barley soup with a side of barley bread drizzled with a dark, oily sauce Ewan called carnis. The sauce had a delicate nutty flavor that Cam quite liked. Scrambled eggs, with a mixture of a dark fungus Ewan called truffles soaked in the carnis oil, came next alongside a helping of sautéed greens.

"You grow this?" Spider asked as he picked at the dark fungus.

"No," Ewan chuckled. "You can't grow it. Truffles only grow in the wild. We have dogs and pigs specially trained to find them in the forest. The woods around Yarwick are especially rich in the stuff."

Cam sampled it and was pleased by the earthy flavor. "It's good," he said.

"And quite expensive," Alaric said. "So don't get used to it."

"I'm glad you like it," Elatha said. "It's best fresh, but when soaked in carnis oil, it will last several months."

The warm meal was so satisfying that, by the time they finished, Cam was ready for a long nap.

"Thank you," he said to Elatha. "It was delicious."

"I'll tell the cook," Elatha said as she ushered the children off to bed with the help of a female servant. The flames in the stone fireplace burned low and cast mournful shadows on the walls. Their party relaxed around the table, while Draig lounged sleepily by the fire.

"Things are bad," Derek said without any preamble.

"All right," Ewan said with a glance at his wife. "Let's hear the worst of it."

Derek glanced at Elatha, as well. "To start," he said, "your position on the Regency Council has been challenged. Amón has motioned that you be declared dead. He is actively seeking not only your lands and position, but also your wife."

Ewan's eyes narrowed, and his ruddy complexion deepened to match the fire-red of his beard. He set his goblet down, and his hand slipped idly to finger the hilt of his sword.

"Elatha has informed me of his attentions," Ewan said. "Doubtless, he will have some explaining to do."

Derek continued. "He is also seeking to have the Regency Council disbanded. The Earl of Hannoch has drawn away the north wood and is gaining a following here in the east wood. He claims the right to the throne."

"We've experienced his hospitality," Hebron said.

Homecoming

Derek studied their reaction and clasped his hands in front of him.

"Bardon's army has already marched north."

"We know," Ewan said.

"He was repulsed at Brynach, which no longer stands," Derek said.

"What?" Alaric scanned their faces in open disbelief. "It's impossible."

"Brynach is gone," Derek said, "vanished. Our scouts reported a violent storm with red flashing lights, and when it was over, the castle truly was gone."

"Lorna," Drakeman breathed. "She did something."

"That would explain the bodies and wreckage we found in the Brunen," Laird said.

"Did Lorna and the Tathanar escape?" Drakeman asked.

Derek shook his head. "We have no word. Bardon's armies have withdrawn to the City of Mawsil. We received word last night that his foraging parties are harassing the borders of the East Mark, and he has sent riders scouring the land from the Lonely Valley to the Brunen in search of something—or someone."

"That would be us," Alaric said.

"But why?" Derek asked. His eyes shone in the firelight.

"We've grown rather popular in recent weeks," Slone said.

Alaric gesture to Cam. "Show him."

Cam's insides squirmed as he withdrew the Life Stone from the pouch around his neck. The opal caught the light of the fire and glittered in his hand. A delicate blue glow rose from the stone to fill the room. He sensed the gentle connection of the stone with the sword.

Elatha sucked in her breath and covered her mouth with her hand.

Derek stared, his mouth working. "Where did you get that?" he finally managed.

Cam glanced at Hebron, who straightened in his chair.

"King Hewel delivered it into my keeping," Hebron said, "along with his sword, before he died. I have given them both to Cam so that he may claim the throne."

Derek's gaze shifted from Alaric to Hebron and then to Cam. "You're serious?"

"I am," Hebron said.

"Then Hewel chose you to succeed him."

Undead

"No. He never intended for me to become king. He knew I could not. I was simply the bearer of the stone and the sword."

Derek fixed his gaze on Cam. "I mean no disrespect, but why Cam?"

"Exactly my question," Cam mumbled.

Rebecca reached under the table and squeezed his hand.

Hebron scowled. "It was Queen Elisedel's wish that Cam be made King of the West Mark."

Cam stared at him. Hebron had never told him this.

"After the assassins killed Sora and Jarlath and Hewel fell to the poisoned arrow," Hebron said, "Elisedel took Cam and the Twenty and fled toward Abilene. We were caught at the Brunen, and the Queen was badly injured in the battle. I escaped with her in a skiff. She died weeks later from her wounds. Her last words to me were that she had adopted Cam as her heir and wished me to give him the Life Stone and the sword when he came of age."

Cam passed a hand over his face. Hebron glanced at him with a glower of regret. "I'm sorry I didn't tell you the whole story," he said. "I wanted you to accept it for yourself."

Derek rose and fell to one knee before Cam and bowed his head.

"Sire," he said. "Forgive me. I did not know."

Cam stiffened, and his insides squirmed. What was he supposed to do? He gave Hebron a wide-eyed plea for help, and Hebron came to his rescue.

"Derek, you do us all honor to have such confidence in us, but Cam is not yet prepared to assume his throne. He must complete his mission first."

Derek looked up with tears glistening on his cheeks. "Can it be true?"

Alaric answered. "I assure you it is."

"This changes everything," Derek said as he rose and retook his seat at the table.

"Can you call a meeting of the Regency Council?" Ewan asked.

"I've already done so. When I received word of your return, I sent messengers immediately. We meet tomorrow midmorning."

"Good." Turning to Ewan, Alaric added, "Did you send the messages I gave you?"

"Yes."

Homecoming

"Then we have an hour to plan our approach before I ask you all to accompany me to an important gathering."

An hour and a half later, Cam found himself in a large cavern somewhere under the city. Torches sputtered in black iron brackets on the walls, filling the air with their pungent oily odor. The room had a large stone table on a raised platform directly in the center of the chamber. The tabletop was cut from a single slab of dark granite. In a semicircle on one side of the stone table were many rows of stone benches—enough to seat several hundred men.

Cam picked the hem in his tunic, wishing he could crawl under the table. Alaric and Hebron were seated with him behind the big slab of stone. Draig sat at his side. The other members of the company congregated on the first row of stone benches. Already the chamber was half-full, and men kept arriving. They wore the same long, red tunic of fine linen emblazoned with a silver teardrop shield split in half by a diagonal line. In the upper portion was a good imitation of the Life Stone. In the lower portion, a black-gloved hand gripped a longsword and held it upright. The men's tunics belted around the waist with a white leather belt. In addition, they wore the royal oak leaf of the West Mark pinned to their tunics.

Alaric and Hebron were dressed in the same fashion as the other men, except they wore black belts instead of white. Cam surmised that this was a mark of rank. They were both attired in glimmering mail from head to foot, and Alaric had a green wolf's head broach over his right breast. Hebron had insisted that Cam also slip into a mail coat, though he wore no outer tunic over the mail.

When three-fourths of the seats were filled, Alaric signaled the guards to close the doors. He raised his arms, calling the assembly to order.

"My brothers of the Order of the Sword and the Stone," he said as the men fell silent. "Thank you for responding to my summons. As you know, Bardon is on the move, and it is only a matter of time before the West Mark will once again fall under his foul gaze. We must be ready. I have returned not only to prepare for that eventuality but also to present to you the heir to the throne of the West Mark."

Undead

After a moment of absolute silence, the gathering erupted into a pandemonium of shouts and questions. "Who is he? Where has he been? Why now?" It was some time before Alaric could calm them down again.

"I understand your apprehension," he said. He gestured to Hebron, who rose. "You will all recognize Hebron. He and I are all that is left of the Twenty who fled with Queen Elisedel. Hebron was with the Queen when she died."

Hebron began his tale without preamble. He spoke of fleeing to the Brunen, the terrible battle, his flight with the Queen in the skiff, and their rescue by the fisherman, who kept them alive. He told of Elisedel's death from her injuries and his escape to the Haradd Mountains, where he raised Cam until the Mahrowaiths came hunting for them.

The men gaped in stunned silence as he related his story. When he finished, Hebron gestured for Cam to step forward. Cam's insides churned as if he'd swallowed a hornet's nest.

He rose and raised the sword in one hand, gripping it by the blade as Alaric had instructed. Then he raised the Life Stone in the other. The brilliant aqua-blue opal sparkled in the darkness of the cavern, casting a pleasing light over the men's astonished faces.

A somber hush settled over the gathering, and Cam feared these men might reject him. If they did, all he could do was go to the Lonely Valley and hope for the best. He wouldn't be able to return to Yarwick.

His palms grew sweaty. He felt utterly alone and vulnerable standing in front of several hundred armed men he did not know and whose loyalty he so desperately needed.

Just when the silence became deafening, a lone knight from the back of the room banged his shield with his sword. One by one, the assembly followed his example, and soon, the cavern echoed with a din as ear-splitting as their silence had been.

Cam realized that he'd been holding his breath, and he let it out with a loud sigh. Once again, Alaric raised his arms to quiet the assembly.

"Brethren," he began again, "our oaths bind us to protect the King and the kingdom with our lives. Will you keep that covenant sworn so long ago?"

Homecoming

Again, the din of swords banging on shields erupted. Cam wished he could slink off into a corner to hide. These people had expectations of him that he was sure he could not fulfill. He glanced at Rebecca, wondering if she would consent to be his queen. Did he dare ask her? Would Hebron and Alaric let him? Or did they already have a woman selected for him? Without Spider to help him keep his sanity and the others to give him guidance, there was no way he would survive a single week as a king.

Alaric raised his hands.

"Then our task is before us," he said. "Tomorrow, we escort our young king to the Valley of the Undead King and help him complete his quest. We must ride by his side as he assumes his rightful place as the sovereign King of the West Mark."

Again, the din ensued.

Cam tensed at Hebron's side. More than once, he'd hoped that it was simply a bad dream or a vision of the Life Stone from which he would soon awake.

He glanced again at Rebecca who stared up at him with shining eyes. Spider gaped in shock. Laird was as nonchalant as ever, though he fingered his mustache thoughtfully. Slone, Derek, and Ewan appeared deeply moved.

Orders were issued for the departure the next afternoon, and, one by one, the men came forward and knelt before Cam in a spontaneous act of fealty. Cam didn't know what to do, so he simply grasped their hands in his and squeezed them tightly, looking each man in the eyes. Each knight searched his face intently as they rose, and in many eyes tears glittered. He was surprised at how old they seemed. These were not young men anymore. They were all at least Hebron's age, and some even had white hair showing at their temples.

How could they trust an unknown boy so completely on nothing more than the word of Alaric and Hebron? The magnitude of their selflessness made Cam's eyes burn. He blinked to keep his tears at bay. A nagging doubt surged behind his rush of emotion, along with the fear that he might fail them.

When only the members of his company remained, Alaric grunted. "That went much better than I feared."

"I had no idea the old Order still existed," Ewan said.

"This improves our situation considerably," Derek said. "No

one will dare stand against us."

"Perhaps not," Hebron sniffed. "But few on the Council will readily surrender power. We must delay any open conflict until we return from the Lonely Valley."

Cam frowned at Rebecca. He would not survive the valley. He knew it. Ever since the Life Stone had come to his aid beside the Afon Fathwe and told him that it was his doom to die for his friends, he had been convinced that that doom would fall in the Lonely Valley. The Life Stone hinted as much with the vision of him and Rebecca racing across a valley pursued by Mahrowaiths. His fate was fast approaching, and he could not turn aside. Not now.

Chapter Eighteen
The Undead King

THE NEXT MORNING, Cam tugged at the uncomfortable, close-fitting breeches and red tunic that Hebron forced him to wear. The short-sleeved mail shirt underneath the tunic rested heavily on his hips where a bejeweled belt held his dagger and sword. The padded jerkin was hot and a bit too tight. The outfit included a black leather pouch where Cam stored the Life Stone he knew he would be forced to produce at the meeting. He kept his other gemstones and dyads safely hidden in the pouch at his neck.

"I feel like an imposter," Cam said.

Hebron adjusted the sword at Cam's hip. "You need to wear the mail, just in case."

"That makes me feel even more welcome."

"You will be welcomed by most," Derek assured him, "but it's best to be cautious."

Ewan led the company into the Council room before the other members arrived. The chamber was crafted with teak wood that gave off a rich, leathery smell. Natural brown streaks of the wood had been artfully managed to create a wavy pattern on the walls. Columns supporting the ceiling beams were carved like twisted ropes.

The beams themselves had florid patterns with stags and bears intermingled. In the center of the room hulked a long oval cedar table, strangely reminiscent of the opal Life Stone. Carved, leather-backed chairs displayed scenes of the forest. Cam found the room much more alluring and comfortable than the marbled halls of Abilene.

Alaric and Hebron wore the livery of the Order of the Sword and the Stone and positioned themselves in the far corner of the room with their hoods drawn up. Cam, Rebecca, Spider, Drakeman, Slone, and Laird sat on a teak bench against the wall beside Alaric and Hebron. Draig perched on his haunches beside Cam.

Derek and Ewan assumed their seats at the cedar table and waited. The other nine members of the Council arrived singly or in pairs. Some hurried to Ewan and greeted him warmly, shaking his hand and embracing him. A few of the new arrivals eyed the other members of the group with suspicion and only nodded to Derek and Ewan before assuming their seats. Their gazes lingered on the large, black wolf.

As they entered, Cam knew immediately who Amón was. The man wore brilliant red leather breeches and a dark blue linen shirt. His hair was combed back and tied with a leather strap, exposing his tanned, wrinkled brow. A gold chain hung around his neck, and his fingers were studded with rings of gold and silver that glistened with jewels. The gemstones reminded Cam of Lorna's pendant.

The man clearly thought much of himself. His hawk-like nose was overly large, and his dark eyes glimmered with treachery from under black eyebrows. The lean face was partially hidden by the clipped beard. He was not handsome. If it had not been for those penetrating eyes and his elaborate attire, there wouldn't have been much to draw attention to him.

Finally, a bent old man with white hair shuffled in leaning heavily on a cane and dropped into a chair at the other end of the table. After exchanging a few words with some of the other members of the Council, he pounded the table with a wooden mallet and called the meeting to order. Cam liked the man with his gentle eyes and wizened face. When he spoke, his strong voice did not betray his obvious age.

"Lord Ewan," he said, "it is truly a pleasure to have you back amongst us."

Ewan nodded his acknowledgment.

"We are most anxious to hear your report. But Lord Derek has called this meeting and so may speak first."

Derek arose.

"Thank you, Chancellor Barlothian. I have called the Council precisely to hear Ewan's report."

Ewan arose. "My friends, I will get straight to the point. The Tathanar are preparing an army to come against Bardon. The Shardana and the Anar will do so, as well. An embassy has been sent to the East Mark. The Tathanar have already repelled an attack on the Varaná's Keep at Brynach."

A few of the men shouted questions until Ewan raised his hands. "Please allow me to finish. Then I will take questions. As to the monsters that have been terrifying our people, they are called Mahrowaiths of the ancient world—the same that once destroyed Goldereth and Donmor, as is told in the olden tales."

"Fairy tales, you mean," Amón sneered.

"Please, hear me out," Ewan said. He cast his gaze over the other eleven men. "I return with King Hewel Cystenian's heir."

The men gaped in stunned silence for a moment before several men leaped to their feet while the rest shouted. Barlothian had to pound the table several times with the big mallet to bring them to order. Through it all, Amón leaned back in his chair with a little smirk playing across his face.

Ewan motioned for Cam to rise. Cam willed the wriggling sickness in his stomach to stop and joined Ewan.

"My lords," Ewan said, "I present to you Cam, son of Sora and Jarlath, the child Queen Elisedel took as her own and adopted into the house of Cystenian after she fled to Abilene."

The men murmured amongst themselves. Barlothian motioned for Cam to come to the head of the table. He did so, striding deliberately, intensely conscious of their gazes upon him and the weight of the sword at his hip.

"Lord Chancellor," Amón interrupted, "you cannot seriously be entertaining this nonsense. All the honor guard are dead. The Queen disappeared. Are we really supposed to accept any young whelp Ewan drags in here?"

Barlothian shifted his gaze to Ewan. "Do you bring proof that Elisedel adopted this boy as her heir?"

"Of course, Lord Chancellor. Allow me to present Alaric, son of Faelorn, and Hebron, son of Howard the Gray. The last two remaining members of the honor guard."

As he spoke, Hebron and Alaric arose and shrugged off their cloaks. Their crimson livery with the stone and the sword stood out bold and bright.

An audible gasp exploded from the assembled men.

Barlothian struggled to his feet, leaning with his hands on the table.

"Alaric, Hebron?" he gasped. "You are yet alive?" His wrinkled face twisted into a grin, and his eyes swam with brimming tears. Both Alaric and Hebron approached the head of the table and knelt before him.

"Lord Chancellor," Alaric said, "we have returned. We regret to inform you that her Ladyship Queen Elisedel did not survive the flight to Abilene. But we have kept our charge and returned Cam to this city to claim the throne she intended for him."

"His name was not Cam," Barlothian said.

Hebron glanced at Cam and gave him a little shrug of apology. "I called him Cam to hide his identity. His mother called him Crisanto."

Spider smirked, and Cam glared at him, his face growing hot.

"I like it," Spider mouthed to him.

Cam promised himself he would give Spider a good kick later.

"A stable boy's son?" Amón sneered. "You must be joking."

"He possesses both the sword and the Life Stone," Alaric said.

"Let us see them then," Barlothian said.

Hebron nodded to Cam, who slipped the Life Stone from the black leather pouch where he had placed it that morning. It's light flared at Cam's touch. He drew the sword and displayed the hilt.

Amón sniffed. "So what? King Hewel died before he bestowed that stone."

"No," Hebron said, "he gave it to me, and I have delivered it freely to Cam, as Queen Elisedel commanded."

Silence followed his words while Amón studied Cam with renewed interest.

"Then the boy will not object to a simple test." Amón rose to his feet. "Let him injure someone with the sword and heal the injury with the Life Stone."

A gasp came from where Rebecca sat, and Cam glanced at her pale face.

The Undead King

"I volunteer," Alaric said, but Cam was already shaking his head. If he was going to injure anyone it would be himself.

He held the blade over the meaty part of his palm and drew it sharply back. Pain lanced up his arm, and the blood gushed from the wound to drip on the floor.

Cam sheathed his sword and grasped the Life Stone in his right hand. He pressed it to the bleeding gash, willing it to heal the wound. The stone flared an iridescent blue light, and energy flowed out of it. A beautiful opalescent glow filled the room. It felt similar to the way the Anarwyn worked, but its source was more distant. It was a power that did not come from him. It was latent in the stone itself.

When the pain in his hand ceased, he lifted the stone away to find the wound completely healed with only a little white scar to show where the cut had been. He held it up for them to see.

No one spoke for a long moment.

"That is ample proof that he rightfully controls the stone and the sword," Barlothian said.

"But he is untried and untested," Amón scoffed. "We cannot place our trust in a child we do not know."

Clearly, Amón hadn't expected the stone to work. Cam couldn't keep the little smile from his face.

"What do you suggest? Barlothian asked.

"A trial," Amón said. "Let him prove himself on the field of battle as a warrior and a leader of men."

Barlothian frowned.

"We can accept a trial," Alaric said. "This afternoon we leave with a guard of the Order of the Sword and the Stone to the Lonely Valley where Cam will release Maelorn and Tara from their stone prison."

"What?" Barlothian fell heavily into his chair.

Cam wondered if the old man might have a heart seizure.

"He has been so charged by her Ladyship Lorna Carnawyth of the Varaná and King Chullain of the Tathanar," Hebron said. "Once that task is completed, Cam can return and lead our armies against Bardon."

"I believe we need to hear this tale," Barlothian said.

Both Alaric and Hebron recounted their stories from the time they fled with Queen Elisedel until the attack of the Mahrowaith in Stony Vale. Then they told what had happened at the Council at Abilene and of their flight down the Afon Fathwe, even until they had reached Yarwick. They left out certain details about going through Goldereth and the manner in which the spell was to be broken because, like the rest of their company, they had sworn an oath of secrecy to Chullain.

When they finished, the sun was considerably higher in the sky and was slanting through the windows, casting long rays across the table. The Council chamber had grown so silent that the breathing of the men sounded like winded horses. Amón listened to the story with a sour grimace on his face.

"Well," Barlothian said, "I call a vote to accept Cam of Stony Vale as the legitimate heir of King Hewel. And that he be acclaimed King of the West Mark after a trial period of one month in which his skills and aptitude for rule shall be proven on the field of battle."

Eight hands rose into the air.

Barlothian pounded the table with his mallet. "The motion carries. Eight to four."

Cam allowed himself to breathe. Alaric and Hebron patted him on the back with broad smiles while Amón exited the room without a word to anyone. Five men of the Council, including old Barlothian, bowed to Cam and kissed his hand. He resisted the desire to wipe his hand on his trousers. No one had ever kissed his hand before. It was kind of disgusting. The sick knot that had been growing in his belly lodged there, like a lump of undigested cheese. His stomach gurgled, and he thought he might be sick.

Ewan and Derek led them from the Council chambers into the crowded streets. Alaric and Hebron followed behind, and Rebecca and Spider ambled on either side of Cam. Draig padded along in front of them.

"That was interesting," Spider said. "Am I supposed to bow to you now, Crisanto?"

"You do, and I'll whack you upside the head," Cam said. "And don't call me that."

"Ahh," Spider mocked, "now that the boot is on the other foot, you don't seem to think it's so funny." He chuckled. "Crisanto. I like the sound of it."

"I would be careful if—" Rebecca said, but she never finished her thought. A drunken sot, reeking of liquor, stumbled past her, and bumped heavily into Cam. "Hey," she said, "watch where you're going."

The Undead King

Cam caught the man and tried to help him stand when he saw the flash of a steel blade.

Zenek crouched behind a boulder as the Tathanar rider wearing his forest green clothing swept around the base of the outcrop. He had followed Cam as best he could, though crossing the Brunen had delayed him. He was tired of walking, and the lone rider offered a tempting target.

If Bardon was hunting Cam, then the quickest way to find Bardon was to follow the boy. Zenek had lost Cam in the foothills of the mountains around Hannoch and decided to head straight for the Lonely Valley, avoiding the more populated areas. He was on foot and could use a mount. Perhaps this Tathanar could provide him one.

He had not expected to find Tathanar scouts so far south. They couldn't be members of the original party that floated down the Afon Fathwe. They hadn't had horses for one thing. Wherever they came from, they were clearly guarding the pass south to the Lonely Valley. He witnessed a skirmish the day before between the Tathanar and a small band of Inverni, who apparently had the same idea.

The gemstones he gleaned from the dead in Goldereth lay close to his heart in a slender pouch. His experiments with them had gone well enough that he dared use one now. The Tathanar warrior paused and stood in the stirrups, casting his gaze down the narrow cleft that dropped from the rocky outcrop into the tall pines below. He leaned low to study the ground, probably searching for a sign of Cam and his party.

Zenek focused his mind on the golden cube of pyrite and cast an illusion of a deer bounding from the trees. The Tathanar jerked upright in the saddle, and Zenek's beam of bloodred light from the garnet punched through his chest with an ominous hiss. The Tathanar made no sound but merely toppled from the saddle and hit the stony earth with a hollow thump.

Grinning with satisfaction, Zenek strode up to him and searched his pockets as the man tried feebly to resist. The stink of charred flesh filled Zenek's nostrils, and he swept a blade across the man's throat to make sure he couldn't survive and tell anyone what he had seen. Then he stuffed his own gear into the saddlebags and mounted the horse.

The illusion worked better than he could have wished. If he found Cam first, he would deprive Bardon of the pleasure of killing the boy. Bardon might even reward him for it. Either way, Cam's death would mean one less foe to worry about.

"Die impostor," the drunk man growled and stabbed for Cam's heart. Cam twisted sideways. The blade scraped on his mail shirt. Adjusting with lightning speed, the man thrust the blade at Cam's unprotected throat. Cam caught the hand that held the knife, but the man was powerful. The blade edged closer to Cam's throat as they stumbled backward.

The man's eyes were large and glowed a strange aqua blue. He landed on top of Cam and tried to use his body weight to drive the blade home. His rancid breath washed over Cam, and the muscles in his jaw twitched. His lip lifted in a snarl, and he let out a wild growl. The blade inched closer, the sharp point hungry for Cam's blood. Cam was going to die. The man was stronger than he was. A rushing sound filled Cam's ears, blotting out the distant cries of dismay. His gaze focused on the trembling point of the knife as it edged closer. He strained with all his might to keep it from plunging into his throat.

The man grunted, and surprise wrinkled his brow. He wavered, and Cam renewed his efforts to shove the blade away from his throat. Sunlight flashed on steel, and a fountain of blood erupted from the man's head. His face twisted in pain as he slumped over.

Cam kicked him off and scrambled to his hands and knees, wiping at the warm blood on his face. The assassin lay in the dust of the street, his lifeblood flowing onto the cobblestones. The knife fell from his fingers with a clang.

Derek knelt by the assassin's head and grabbed the front of his tunic. "Who put you up to this, man?" he shouted, shaking him viscously.

The man blinked. A lost, confused expression slipped across his face, and he raised a hand to grab Derek's tunic. He exhaled and went limp.

The Undead King

Alaric and Hebron jumped to Cam's side.

"Are you all right?" Alaric asked.

Cam waved them off. "I'm fine. Let's get out of the street."

He crawled to his feet and dusted himself off. Spider's sword was stained red. So was Rebecca's. How long had he wrestled the assassin? Could it only have been a few seconds?

"Thanks," Cam mumbled and wiped the blood from his hands.

What had he expected? He had jumped into this seething cauldron of ambition and intrigue with both feet. At his rate, he would be lucky to survive long enough to reach the Lonely Valley.

"It sure is nice to have my backside in a saddle again," Spider said.

Cam glanced over at him. Only a few hours had passed since the Council meeting, and they were preparing to set out for the Lonely Valley.

Spider rode astride a big mare, holding the reins in his gloved hands, waiting for the column to set out. Like Cam, he was dressed in a mail hauberk with a mail coif. His sword was newly oiled and sharpened, and the leather scabbard cleaned and oiled. He wore an overtunic of black with the golden oak leaf of the West Mark stitched into the shoulder. Even dressed like a lord, Cam struggled to see Spider as anything other than his childhood friend.

"Your horse doesn't seem to like it much," Cam said as the mare pranced sideways. "Maybe she's scared of spiders." But Cam knew it was because Draig was there, and the horses could smell him.

"Yep, you and Hebron are always so funny," Spider said. "I'm just saying we've been run off our feet and pinched and battered by those canoes. It's nice to have some solid horse flesh to do the work for once."

"I never noticed you working much," Laird cut in. "I'm sure I did most of the paddling."

"Oh, so now they've corrupted you, too." Spider grimaced at Rebecca, where she sat astride her own horse, dressed like Cam and Spider. "I believe it's your turn to take a jab at me."

Rebecca beamed. "I would never poke fun at a man named Ludo. It wouldn't seem fair." She winked at Cam. "Nor would I tease a man for being named after a flower, like Crisanto."

Laird laughed, and Cam couldn't help but chuckle at the way Spider spluttered. "Who told you my name?"

"Cam did the first day we met, and Hebron keeps teasing you about it. You forget I was you for more than a week. It was a real education."

Spider glared at Cam. "Big mouth."

"Give it up, lad," Slone said. "You'll never match wits with her."

A horn sounded, and Hebron, Alaric, and Drakeman galloped up from where they had been conversing with the general who would lead them to the Lonely Valley. Hebron wore the crimson tunic of the Order of the Sword and the Stone, while Alaric had changed to a silver tunic with an emerald wolf's head displayed prominently in the center.

"It is time, Your Majesty," Alaric said.

Cam nodded his assent, and Alaric whirled away to give the orders. A mist rolled in from the forest encircling Yarwick. Three hundred and fifty members of the Order of the Sword and the Stone surrounded them, all smartly dressed in their crimson tunics. The knights rode lightly armored horses to allow them to travel more quickly.

They all wore mail shirts and conical helmets. Each man carried either a lance or a short bow with arrows and had a sword and knife at his belt. Lancers bore a teardrop shield bearing the arms of the Order. A crimson standard of the Sword and the Stone and a black banner of the West Mark bearing a golden oak leaf fluttered overhead in the breeze that kicked up to scatter the tendrils of mist.

Cam was positioned in the center of a triangular formation of three dozen royal guards wearing the same black that he, Spider, and Rebecca wore. Inside this guard, Alaric, Hebron, and Drakeman took up places in front of Cam. Rebecca and Spider occupied a place on either side of him, and Slone and Laird followed behind.

This way, Cam was protected on all sides by people he could trust. After the assassination attempt that morning, they weren't taking any chances. Ewan and Derek assumed their places among the other men. Draig sat quietly on his haunches, oblivious to the fact the horses didn't much like his presence.

It was an impressive array of military power. Though Cam was grateful for them and the knowledge that at least now they had a fighting chance to reach the valley, he couldn't shake the sense that he didn't belong here, that he didn't deserve all this attention.

A messenger galloped up to Alaric who then reined his horse around to approach Cam. He saluted, and Cam nodded at the gesture. Alaric was saluting for the benefit of the men.

"All is in order," Alaric said. "The scouts report the way is clear. Shall we proceed?"

Cam gave another curt nod. He might as well start acting like a king. "Yes, thank you." He tried to project more calm than he felt. This was the day he had been dreading for weeks. Alaric saluted again and rode away to give the orders.

"Today's the day, lad," Slone said. "We should arrive before dark so long as we don't run into any trouble."

"When haven't we run into trouble?" Cam asked—then regretted the words for how negative they made him sound. How was one supposed to stroll composedly—even cheerfully—into the arms of death?

Spider edged his horse close to Cam's. "We're protecting your back."

"I know," Cam said, "that's what has me worried."

Spider snorted. "You're in high form today."

Cam chuckled. "Sorry, picking at you helps relieve the tension."

"Pick away then," Spider said. "What do I live for but to amuse my friends?" Horns blared, and the company set out with much creaking of leather and stomping of horses' hooves. Cam had been fighting the growing knot in the pit of his stomach since he awoke. Today he would fail or be victorious. Either way, he would probably die.

He surveyed the glittering sea of armed men with their forest of lances. Up on the city walls, throngs of people cheered the departing men. Would they cheer if they understood how much was at stake? His mare pranced sideways, and he realized he was transmitting his own nervousness to the horse. He patted her neck. "I'll try to relax."

It was a strange thing to be riding willingly toward his own death. He had so much more to lose now than he did when their journey began—friends who stood by him, an entire people looking to him for relief after decades of unstable rule—and Rebecca. He dared to imagine a life with her and before the sun set, he would find out if it would be permitted or if he would be dead.

Terror washed over him. He shuddered. His horse pranced sideways, and he patted her again. It wasn't the terror of death itself that he feared. It was the lost opportunities, the end to all he loved and valued.

Maybe it would have been better if the Mahrowaith had caught him in Stony Vale and ended his life before he had even joined this quest. It would have been easier to drown at Afon Darodel with a Mahrowaith clinging to his throat. Death would have come suddenly without this long, deliberate journey to face it. Always before, the task had been somewhere in a future time, but now, that time had come.

Lorna had transferred to him the task she could not complete. Had she known that he would sacrifice anything—everything—to keep his friends alive? To save them from Bardon and his plans to destroy the world as they knew it? Perhaps she had. Or maybe it was the Anarwyn that had chosen him to be the sacrificial lamb. It had been seeking him even while he lived up in Stony Vale. Cam took a deep breath and straightened in the saddle. It would do no good to keep dwelling on what he could not change. He would do what he must, and if it cost him his life, so be it. He would die like his mother, fighting to protect the ones he loved.

The city fell behind him and was soon devoured by the dense, green forest. They advanced at a steady canter, causing travelers to scurry off the road to avoid the column of grim men. By mid-afternoon, they had passed through the woods and were well out onto the plains. Cam posted outriders to shadow their advance and bring word of anything unusual. He began to hope that, by some miracle, they might make it to the valley without trouble, when one of the scouts came galloping up from the south. He reined in and saluted Cam smartly.

"Sire," the man panted.

Cam balked at the title, but nodded to the soldier as Alaric, Hebron, and Drakeman galloped over to hear what the man had to say.

"A large band of riders is approaching fast from the southeast."

"How many?" Cam asked, nudging his horse closer to the man.

"Hard to say, My Lord. I would guess about three hundred."

"How far?" Cam asked.

"They cannot be more than twenty to thirty minutes behind me."

Alaric cursed. "We're still several hours from the valley."

The Undead King

"Can we outrun them?" Cam asked. "Or should we stand and fight?"

"If we fight," Hebron said, "we'll not reach the valley tonight. Our forces are more or less evenly matched."

Cam struggled with indecision. He was no commander of men. "All right," he said, "let's ride to the valley with a guard of fifty while the rest stay and fight a delaying action. This may only be the vanguard of a much larger army."

Hebron and Alaric exchanged glances, apparently pleased with his willingness to take charge.

"Wise precaution," Alaric said.

"Would you please give the orders, then, Alaric?"

A smile of approval touched Alaric's lips as he turned to Rindorf, the next in command of the Order of the Sword and the Stone. Rindorf's brown eyes shone out from under graying eyebrows as he faced Alaric.

"General, we are leaving you with the bulk of the men to fight a delaying action. Handpick your fifty fastest riders to accompany us. We must be away—and soon."

Rindorf sent out the appropriate orders, and before five minutes had passed, Cam and the company with their fifty-man escort were racing across the prairie heading due east. Draig loped along beside them. They rode for hours, only periodically resting the horses as they ate up the miles of rolling prairie. The horses' flanks were lathered. Froth flecked from their mouths, spattering their chests and the legs of their riders with white, slippery foam. Cam wondered how much Spider was enjoying his ride now. His own backside was complaining from the abuse.

They slowed to pick their way up a narrow draw before climbing the last rise into the valley. The sun had dropped below the western horizon, and diffuse gray light settled over the world. Cam's insides twisted into a knot. This was it. He glanced at Rebecca, wondering what he should say to her in case the worst happened. How could he tell her how much she meant to him?

"Sire," one of the men shouted, and Cam twisted in the saddle. Riders in mottled cloaks crested a rise to the south of them. He didn't see more than twenty-five, but they were coming fast.

"Protect," Cam called.

The fifty soldiers swung their mounts around in a coordinated

Undead

maneuver. The lancers lowered their spears and the archers nocked arrows. They formed up, two-ranks deep, and charged to confront the new threat. Bardon's riders carried short bows and loosed a volley before they clashed with the guard. Men fell. Horses reared and screamed. A stray arrow sailed over them and buried itself into the back leg of Rebecca's horse.

The horse reared, throwing Rebecca from the saddle. She sprawled headlong onto the rocky ground, before scrambling out of the way of her stomping horse. The strap on her helmet snapped and the helmet bounced away.

Cam reined his horse around. Rebecca jumped to her feet, blood streaming from a gash on her forehead. Cam grabbed her arm and swung her up behind him. Together, they raced on toward the crest of the hill with Draig beside them as the crash and clamor of battle filled the air.

Chapter Nineteen
Fire and Blood

REBECCA CLUNG TO CAM as his horse lunged up the rise. The rest of their company spread out around them, seeking their own paths up the rocky hillside. Her forehead stung, and she wiped the blood from her eyes. Thoughts flew fast and furious as they approached the end of their quest. She had never really belonged anywhere. They hadn't invited her to come. And she had never fit in at Abilene.

Even though King Chullain loved her, she wanted so much more out of life. She had grown close to Cam, but if he became King of the West Mark, there would be no place for her in Yarwick, either. The nobles would insist that he take one of their daughters to wife. She would be alone again and have no choice but to return to Abilene. The horse stumbled, and she clutched at Cam to keep from sliding off the horse's rump. She was being selfish. She should be more worried about what would happen to Cam.

The horse labored over the rise. On the plain before them three hundred paces away, a dried creek bed split the earth under a single twisted tree rising from its banks. A statue stood rigid beneath its branches, letting off a gentle glow. It was strangely beautiful and lifelike, marbled with transparent crystal and shiny black obsidian.

Ever since childhood, Rebecca had heard the story of Maelorn and Tara, and now she was in the valley where it happened—where

Undead

all those years before, Lorna had accidentally sealed her brother and his betrothed in a tomb of stone. The statue proved more lovely than she could have imagined. In moments, they would discover if Cam could accomplish what Lorna had sent him to do.

A wail ripped through the air that sent a chill surging into Rebecca's body. With it came a haunting terror that caught the breath in her throat.

"They're here," she shouted into Cam's ear.

He didn't answer. She didn't need him to. She could feel the tension in his body. Cam knew what was about to happen, and he told her that he had been dreading it ever since Abilene.

Dark, loping figures of several Mahrowaiths scattered across the wide valley encircling the tree and the statue—dozens of them. The valley reeked with their putrid sulfuric stink. Rebecca ground her teeth as new resolve coursed through her. She would find a way to save Cam or die with him. There could be no other outcome.

"Hang on," Cam shouted as the horse plunged down the hillside. The Mahrowaiths materialized from out of the waving grass, their images shimmering and flickering. There were so many of them—black, armored beasts, bred solely for the purpose of killing. And they had come to kill him. The creeping dread pinched his stomach tight. He fought against the desire to whirl around and flee. Everything now depended on him reaching the statue before it was too late.

The horse's ears laid flat, and it raced through the swaying grass. Alaric and Spider rode close on either flank, and Slone, Hebron, Laird, and Drakeman trailed behind. A horn blast sounded, and Cam glanced up to see more horsemen crest the hill to the north. His heart sank. They were surrounded. The horsemen paused and plunged down the hill toward them.

Hebron shouted, and Cam glanced back to see his horse crash to the ground with a Mahrowaith clinging to its back. Hebron kicked free of the stirrups and rolled to his feet. He came up with his sword drawn. Two Mahrowaiths rushed him. His sword flashed. Both beasts tumbled to the earth in a shower of blood.

Fire and Blood

"Cam," Rebecca cried in his ear, and he swung around. A Mahrowaith leaped toward them. Their horse shied, but Draig met the attack. His great jaws locked on the monster's throat, and he dragged it to the ground. The Mahrowaith shrieked and tore at Draig. He refused to release his hold.

Cam and Rebecca galloped past him. White lightning flashed over the hill directly to the east, casting a ghoulish light over the valley. Everything was chaos. The riders that appeared on the northern hill swept into the Mahrowaiths, and Cam thought they were wearing forest green like the Tathanar. It wasn't possible.

More white lightning flashed, and a single figure galloping on horseback emerged on the eastern hillside behind the statue. It was a slender woman with long, flowing hair.

"Lorna," Cam breathed.

He didn't have time to feel grateful for her presence. A Mahrowaith materialized in mid-leap out of thin air. It crashed into Spider, dragging him from his horse. They vanished into the undulating grass. Desperate horror gripped Cam's throat. Not Spider. Cam was supposed to die to save his friends, not the other way around. That was the deal he had struck with the Anarwyn when he accepted its power.

He tried to check the horse, but Alaric bellowed at him, "No! Run! Run!"

Tears burned his eyes. Cam ground his teeth in frustration and leaned forward, letting the horse gallop as fast as it could. The horrible cries of the Mahrowaiths and the shrieks of dying men and horses filled the air.

The statue grew closer, no more than seventy yards away, when his horse reared, slipped, and fell. Cam and Rebecca tumbled into the long grass. Two more horses fell, whinnying in pain and terror. Drakeman rolled to one knee and sent shaft after shaft into the monsters. His arrows pierced eyes and throats, sending the beasts reeling and careening about, mad with pain.

Cam fumbled with the pouch and brought out the Fire Stone. Two Mahrowaiths rushed him, and he cast up a wall of fire that disintegrated them in a ball of flame. He whirled and blasted two more away. The grass caught fire and roared with a sudden intensity.

Drakeman fell under two Mahrowaiths and sprawled unmoving

Undead

in the trampled grass. The Mahrowaiths threw back their heads and emitted their bloodcurdling cry before bending over Drakeman's body. They reached for him, only to be bowled aside by another Mahrowaith that came barreling through the grass.

Laird slashed and stabbed at the Mahrowaiths. A bubble of greenish light surrounded him, confusing the beasts.

Slone leaped from his horse's back with a battle cry, swinging the great axe in a deadly arc, hacking at Mahrowaith necks. Hebron charged into the massive pack of monsters gathering around them. His sword gleamed bright red as it slashed. The Mahrowaiths fell away before him like chaff on a stiff fall breeze.

"Run!" Hebron shouted. "Run!"

For a moment, Cam wondered what had happened to Lorna, before Rebecca grabbed his hand and dragged him down the gentle slope toward the statue under the old, gnarled tree.

The ghastly crunch of steel on bone and the screeches of the Mahrowaiths chased them as he and Rebecca raced hand in hand, the long grass whipping at their legs. Lorna's lightning flashed. Tathanar warriors engaged the Inverni who had somehow managed to evade Cam's rearguard. Steel rang off stone. Men died with gruesome gurgling noises. Mahrowaiths screamed their hideous cries. Terror clutched Cam's throat. He wasn't going to make it, and everyone he cared about in the world was about to die.

Draig bounded past him to engage another Mahrowaith. Cam held up the Fire Stone and sent a beam of yellow fire to cut through the beast's head. The scream died in its throat as it toppled.

Cam and Rebecca reached the dry brook, scrambling over stones and boulders and up the other side. Cam gazed up at the glittering statue, his blood throbbing in his temples.

"The dyad!" Rebecca shouted. "Try the dyad!" She drew her sword and spun to protect Cam's back. "Hurry!"

Cam fumbled for the dyads in his pouch. Which one should he use? Deciding to trust Lorna, he drew hers out. He owed her that much.

Lorna's dyad was set in silver with an orange-brown agate on one end and a green malachite on the other. She had assured him it would work and that he was the only one who could do it. The power of the Bragamahr inside him intensified, and he was aware that all the Mahrowaiths in the area were focused on him. His time was running out.

Rebecca shouted a warning, and Cam spun with the Fire Stone already up. A salivating Mahrowaith with its bloodred irises glowing in the gathering darkness bounded toward them. Cam sent a ball of flame that engulfed the Mahrowaith, incinerating it to ash.

"Hurry!" Rebecca screamed again. "What are you waiting for?"

Cam grasped Lorna's dyad in his hand and extended it toward the statue. Cold rippled through him. His heart pounded so loudly against his eardrums that he could hear nothing else. It labored, preparing for the final shock as if it knew that this was his moment to die. His hand trembled, and he glanced once more at Spider fighting to reach them and then at Rebecca. They could not take this final journey with him. Spider would never understand.

"I love you," he shouted to Rebecca. Their gazes met, and her face paled as she realized what he meant. He wanted time to cease its forward rush, but it was no use. He had to act before everyone he loved perished.

Cam shouted the words, "Calon est, Calon dûr." He cringed in expectation of the explosion of pain. Energy flowed out of him, but nothing happened.

"They're coming." Rebecca crouched, ready for battle.

Cam concentrated, focusing all his attention on the dyad. He tried to slow his breathing the way Lorna had taught him. Tried to forget his longing for life. Tried to ignore the sweet breeze that cooled his brow. There was no barrier inside him this time. The power of the Anarwyn seemed to be working, but it had no effect on the statues. Something was wrong with the dyad. He shouted the words more loudly but to no effect. A sick knot clutched at his throat. Lorna had been wrong. They had all come here to die.

Cam dropped the dyad and spun at a howl of pain near him. Hebron waded through the throng of Mahrowaiths and took up a position on the other side of the creek. His sword flashed red, dealing death to any Mahrowaith who attempted to reach Cam. Draig was by his side. Together, they kept the little rise clear of Mahrowaiths, giving Cam precious time. It was all in vain.

"Why isn't it working?" Rebecca yelled.

A Mahrowaith broke free of Hebron and Draig bounded up the hill after it. It was coming fast. Draig would never catch it. Panic gripped Cam's throat. He raised the yellow amber, hoping against hope that it would work even though the dyad had failed. He tried to slow his breathing. He would only get one chance. The Mahrowaith loomed large, and Cam reached for the latent power in the stone, when a black flash slammed into the Mahrowaith, sending it tumbling into the stones of the dried creek bed. It was another Mahrowaith. Cam couldn't believe it until he recognized the feel of the new creature. It was familiar. They had met before. The new Mahrowaith ripped the head off of the one that had been racing toward Cam and turned to face him, straightening to its full height of seven feet.

Master, it said in his mind and bounded away to attack another Mahrowaith. Draig raced after it.

Rebecca gasped, and Cam's mind reeled as he fumbled in the pouch for the dyad Jathneel had given him. The old man had predicted Lorna's dyad wouldn't work, and he had been right. Had he told the truth about *his* dyad, as well? It was a beautiful thing, made of a smoky quartz crystal flanked by a red agate with gold streaks and a milky-white moonstone.

Did Cam dare use something that possessed the power of the Bragamahr? For all he knew, Jathneel created it to corrupt the Anarwyn and unleash the Bragamahr. It would be the perfect solution to Bardon's problem—to use the one who was supposed to undo his curse to enhance his own power. Ever since the confrontation with the Bragamahr in the valley of the Braganeth, Cam had sensed it growing more powerful, reaching for him.

His connection to it had deepened. If he used the power of the Bragamahr to release Maelorn and Tara, he might succumb to it himself. His vision on the banks of the Afon Fathwe River would become a reality. He would destroy the very people he struggled to protect. He shuddered at the thought. There were no good options left.

Hesitating, he cast a glance at Rebecca's wide, terrified eyes and the battle raging around him. Men were dying, sacrificing everything to give him the chance to right a wrong done decades before. Could he admit defeat and simply walk away? If he didn't try, everything would have been a waste—all the sacrifices, the suffering, and the death would have been for naught, and he would guarantee that Bardon would win. If he did use it, he and his friends might live to see another day, but at what cost?

Fire and Blood

The memory of the peddler and the doll, of Dara's blank staring eyes, and his mother's blackened hand washed over him.

"Cam!"

Rebecca's voice cut through his fears, and he stared at her. She believed in him.

"What can I do to help?" she asked.

Cam's chest tightened. He had to make one more attempt. The Life Stone had said his doom was to die to save his friends. That time was now.

Cam stretched forth his hand and mumbled the words Jathneel said would activate the dyad. "Calon est. Calon dûr."

Agony burst into his brain. A new barrier, different than the one that had troubled him since he first encountered the Anarwyn slammed into place like a hammer striking hot steel. A fleeting whisper pierced the torment rippling through his brain.

I will not let you. It was a woman's voice. The Anarwyn's.

Cam collapsed to the stony ground, the dyad falling from his trembling fingers. He curled into a ball, fighting the splitting pain. The Anarwyn was going to kill him because he dared to use a dyad that combined the powers of the Anarwyn with the Bragamahr. He had failed to save those he loved. His death would mean nothing.

Rebecca fell to her knees beside Cam. His groans of agony cut her to the heart. What was wrong with him? How could she help? As she grabbed his hand, her fingers brushed the dyad in the grass. A rush of icy cold flooded into her, and she yanked her hand away before gingerly picking it up. The chill pierced her to the bone. This thing was filled with latent energy struggling to be released. Something had stopped it. She glanced at Cam where he writhed in anguish, clutching his head. Tears blurred her vision. She couldn't let it torture him. She couldn't lose him. Not now.

She focused on the dyad again, struggling to understand what she should do. It was dazzling with its quartz crystal. Cam had repeated the same words Lorna used to create the dyad back at Abilene all those weeks ago. Why hadn't it worked?

A discordant note hummed in the air around her. It took her a moment to realize the sound was coming from the dyad. Lorna said the stones each had their own resonance, but if she didn't possess the Anarwyn, how could she hear it?

Just to see what happened, Rebecca raised the dyad, touching it to the statue, and mumbled the words, "Calon est. Calon dûr."

A great silence settled around her, cutting off the noise of the battle like a thick blanket. An image of her mother anointing her tongue with water and telling her to swallow flashed through her mind. "Trust the Anarwyn, child of my heart," her mother had whispered. She drew something on Rebecca's forehead, and energy flowed through her.

The image shifted and events she was too young to remember came back, vivid and painful. Her father had been a Tathanar peasant and a warrior. Her mother had been a dyer. They lived on the northern edge of the Silver Wood when a mob dragged her mother from the house to stone her. Rebecca's father fought valiantly but was overwhelmed. Her mother set the house ablaze and escaped into the foothills through the concealing smoke, carrying her baby girl with her. Badly injured, her mother wandered deep into the forest, seeking shelter in a dark hollow. She had placed the water on Rebecca's tongue, and a young woman surrounded by silver light had appeared to her.

The memories explained everything—why she was so drawn to the Anarwyn, why she took to fighting so naturally. She was a survivor, saved for this final moment.

Something tugged at her insides that sent a spasm of nausea sweeping through her. The energy from the dyad permeated some unseen barrier, desperate to be released.

No, the female voice whispered to her mind. It was filled with despair. The Anarwyn wanted her to stop. A desperate terror joined the nausea. Rebecca tried to draw back, but the dyad had set things into motion. The barrier thinned, and the power surged against it.

You were too young to accept me, the Anarwyn said with a note of panic. *I can't stop you.*

Rebecca recalled a conversation with Cam in which he told her he didn't have to accept the Anarwyn to use the dyad—that it was already triggered to work once the words had been spoken. This explained what happened to Cam. Because he had accepted the Anarwyn, it was able to stop him. She had been too young when the Anarwyn appeared to her. The Anarwyn had no control over her. And yet, why hadn't the Anarwyn come to her earlier?

Please, the Anarwyn begged. *Don't do this.*

The barrier collapsed, and the energy of the Bragamahr burned through Rebecca, scouring her soul, tearing at her precious memories, joining with the power of the Anarwyn.

A flash of understanding rippled through her pain. Her mother's face smiled down at her, then another woman and another until generations uncounted danced before her mind all the way back to a tall woman with black tattoos covering her face in a haunting pattern of geometric designs. The woman opened her arms to embrace Rebecca. "Child of the Tamil," she said in a deep, husky voice. "Servant of the Bragamahr."

Rebecca recoiled against the revelation. It couldn't be true. Her mother had given her the water of the Anarwyn. The last words her mother spoke entered her mind. "To protect you," she whispered with her last dying breath, "from your heritage."

"No!" Rebecca screamed.

To be a descendant of the enemy—to be tied to the Bragamahr—was a nightmare. This explained why the Anarwyn had never appeared to her as it had Cam. A fountain of misery doused her mind. She screamed as a thunderclap pealed through the air and a brilliant pillar of white light stabbed into the sky to swirl and churn above the statue. Wind rushed into the valley, bending the grass to the ground.

Rebecca staggered and fell to her hands and knees, the dyad still clutched in her hand. She tried to let go, but her muscles wouldn't obey her. Something tore loose inside. She screamed and screamed. She had never known pain like this before. It was as if her soul was tearing away and flowing out of her. A man's harsh laughter and a woman's cry of pain rang in her ears, and she instinctively knew the sounds came from the Bragamahr and the Anarwyn. She blinked and peered up at the statue. The gaze of the woman fixed upon her, and she understood that this woman was her distant kindred. Rebecca collapsed onto her belly, too weak to do anything but stare wide-eyed at a blade of grass that danced before her vision.

Chapter Twenty
The Price

CAM JERKED AS THE AGONY released him, like the snap of a branch. Someone was shrieking. He crawled to his feet, grasping the Fire Stone, expecting a Mahrowaith to be upon them, but the battle in the valley had ceased. Those still able to stand were facing the statue. Wind whipped across his face, stinging it with bits of broken stone and twigs. He peered up at the twisting column of light in shock. Had *he* done that? The screaming quieted to a sob, and Cam spun to find Rebecca sprawled on her belly in the grass, thrashing about.

Cam snatched her up and hugged her to him, shielding her from the wind. What was happening? Horror gripped his throat in an iron fist. Had he inadvertently shifted the pain from himself to Rebecca?

Hebron rushed to his side. His clothes had almost completely burned off. He was covered in black blood that smoked and hissed but didn't otherwise harm him. Bending close he rested a hand on Cam's back.

"Are you all right?" Hebron panted. "What's happened to her?"

"I don't know." Panic gripped Cam's chest. "Something went wrong. It didn't work, but…" He trailed off and glanced back up through the dust and debris at the gyrating column swirling around the statue. What could he do?

The Life Stone had healed his wound back in Yarwick. Maybe…. He snatched at the pouch, fumbled with the Life Stone, and pressed it to Rebecca's forehead. The opal flared an iridescent blue that reflected off the sweat dripping from her face. Cam's breath caught in his throat with the sudden hope. Nothing happened. Rebecca continued to writhe in pain. Despair choked Cam.

Laird staggered up to them, his face bathed in blood.

"Help her," Cam pleaded.

Laird dropped to his knees without a word and drew the agate from his pocket. Cupping it in one hand, he rested the other on Rebecca's brow. He bowed his head and mumbled a few words. Cam waited, breathless, as Laird swayed where he knelt. His eyes popped open, and he yanked his hand away from Rebecca. A tear slid down his cheek. He shook his head. His lip trembled.

"What is it?" Cam said.

"She's dying," Laird said. "I can't save her."

A rock landed in Cam's stomach. His chest heaved. This couldn't be happening. He was the one who was supposed to die. Not Rebecca.

Laird lifted her hand and studied the object she clutched.

"A dyad?" Laird said.

Cam recognized it immediately. It was Jathneel's dyad. He grabbed her hand, trying to pry her fingers away, but her grip was like iron. He cast a glance at the statue. The pillar of white light swirled above them. Color returned to the figures, starting at their feet, and working its way upward.

In that horrible moment, he understood. They had all been wrong. Lorna. Jathneel. Chullain. All of them. Rebecca was sensitive to the Anarwyn, which meant she was also sensitive to the Bragamahr. She must have seen him fail and tried to save them by activating the dyad. It had worked because she was also related to Lorna in some way. The Anarwyn had been able to stop him because he drank the Dûr Crishal and had accepted the Anarwyn. Rebecca hadn't. So the Anarwyn could not stop her.

A sob escaped his throat, and he lifted Rebecca into his lap and tried to calm her. He didn't care about anything anymore. Not if it meant he couldn't save Rebecca.

"Please," he sobbed, "please, take me instead."

The swirling column continued as the wind whipped the prairie grass, casting up dust and debris. Color and texture filled the statue, which burned with an unearthly, blinding light. Energy pulsed in the air like a gigantic heartbeat. The statue was stealing Rebecca's life away.

"Cam!" Someone laid a hand on his shoulder. It was a familiar voice. He peered up through his tears to find Lorna bending over him. Blood and grime streaked her face. Hope leaped into his chest, and he bounded to his feet. "Do something for her," he gasped.

"What is she even doing here?" Lorna asked as she knelt beside Rebecca and lay a hand on her arm. She glanced at Laird. "Are you a healer?"

"Yes."

"Help me, then."

Laird lay his hand on Rebecca's brow again and closed his eyes. The two of them remained motionless for a long moment. Rebecca shuddered and lay still. Her chest barely rose and fell.

Lorna gazed up at Cam. A tear slid down her cheek, leaving a muddy trail. "All we can do is ease her suffering."

Cam fell to his knees again, brushing a strand of hair from Rebecca's eyes. The color reached the waists of the statue. It was working its way up. As it did, Rebecca grew weaker.

"Make it stop," Cam begged. "Please make it stop. It was supposed to be me."

Lorna shook her head. "It cannot be done. No one can stop it now."

Cam spun on Lorna. "You knew we were coming to die, and you let us come anyway?"

"I didn't know." Lorna's voice was soft and her eyes sad, brimming with tears. "I only guessed at Brynach."

Spider limped up to them and knelt beside Cam.

"What's happening?" he asked.

Cam couldn't speak. He shook his head. Spider frowned as he glanced between the column of light and Rebecca. He draped an arm around Cam's shoulder and drew him close. "I'm sorry," he whispered.

Drakeman stumbled to them, blood bathing his face and soaking his tunic. He had a terrible wound on his neck, and his face was deathly pale. The Mahrowaiths had mauled him savagely, but somehow he was still alive. He fell to his knees on the other side of Rebecca's body.

"What's wrong with her?" he said, scanning her body, searching for some sign of injury.

Cam didn't know what to say. The dyad was sucking her life away. Desperation burned in his throat, and tears spilled from his eyes.

Rebecca coughed and opened her eyes. "Cam," she murmured.

Cam lifted her hand and held it to his cheek. "I'm here."

"Did it work? Are they free?"

Cam choked back a sob. His tears stained her dusty hands. "It worked."

A faint smile slipped across her lips. "I finally made up for all the trouble I've caused." She coughed again and reached to Drakeman with her other hand. He grasped it in a bloody fist.

"I'm sorry I was so much trouble."

"You were never any trouble," he mumbled. "You've been my sister."

Her smile was cut off with a grimace of pain.

"Tell Chullain, I'm sorry I disobeyed him. I meant no harm."

"He knows." Drakeman choked and blinked rapidly. A tear dripped from his long eyelashes, and he bent to kiss Rebecca's hand, leaving a bloody stain on her knuckles.

"Everything is so dark," Rebecca said. "I'm drifting away. Hold me, Cam. I don't want to go."

Cam raised her slender body and hugged her close, burying his face in her hair. "I love you," he whispered into her ear. "Please don't leave me."

"I can't stop the darkness."

She coughed once again. "There's a light," she mumbled, her words barely audible. "Mother?"

She let out a long sigh as a clap of thunder tore through the air, sending Cam's ears ringing. A wave of energy bowled them over. Cam sprawled to the earth, which heaved and rolled. He protected Rebecca as best he could as the wind rushed in and out again. The wave of energy knocked him back before another immense explosion shook the heavens.

Cam struggled to lift Rebecca into his arms. She lay still. Her golden hair shrouded her face, and her lips parted. The gray eyes stared blankly into the sky.

Cam broke inside. He had prepared himself for his own death. Not Rebecca's. He couldn't accept it. It wasn't right. Part of him had

Undead

died with her. He bent over her and wept, losing all sense of time as he clung to her limp body, rocking back and forth. "It should have been me," he sobbed. "It should have been me."

Another thunderclap rolled over the hills.

Zenek reined the horse he had seized from the Tathanar soldier to a stop, staring at the flashing lights and the spiraling column that twisted through the gathering darkness. Wind rushed over the valley, bending the grass to the ground, and kicked up an immense cloud of dust. It was an impressive display. The power of the Bragamahr swelled within him, sending a sick feeling swimming through his gut. The cries of the Mahrowaiths rang over the prairie. Some battle was taking place—one the Bragamahr was not winning. Zenek was too late.

He galloped the last mile and dismounted behind the crest of the hill. Crawling on his belly through the sharp prairie grass, he reached the summit and peered down into the valley. Fires burned, and clouds of black smoke coiled upward. Flames illuminated the dark shapes of bodies sprawled in death. A ring of soldiers in red uniforms circled a cluster of people bending over someone lying in the grass. It was too dark to discern faces clearly, but he recognized Drakeman's tall form kneeling beside two figures, and the big red-headed man called Hebron fighting off the last of the Mahrowaiths.

A column of brilliant light emanated from the stone statue that was slowly changing from the glistening crystal and obsidian to true human forms. It could only mean the boy had succeeded and that it had cost him his life. Well, that was something at least. Zenek had not been able to kill Cam, but the Bragamahr found a way. It always did.

Zenek gasped at a sudden burst of rage surging through the Bragamahr. He reached for the jewels he'd found in Goldereth and one by one attempted to use them to see what was happening in the valley. When he tried the morganite stone, his perception expanded like the rush of a great wind, and he saw her.

Rebecca, King Chullain's favorite from Abilene, groveled in the trodden grass, her life being sucked out of her. With that connection came a vision through the Bragamahr of who she was. Not only was she of Tamil descent, but she was also one of the royal line. Her mother was the woman who had betrayed

The Price

her people and her heritage to marry a simple Tathanar farmer. Zenek had been young, but he remembered the attempted stoning of the woman and the farmer rushing in with a threshing flail to drive the crowd back. The Tathanar man had been dragged down and beaten to death. When the mob finished, the woman was gone, never to be seen again, and her house was in flames.

The vision faded, and Zenek drew back, breathing hard. He half-rose, intending to save Rebecca. She was Tamil, after all. One of *his* people. He should save her. But he stopped himself. It would be foolish to gallop in there with no idea what was happening. And Lorna Carnawyth was down there. He couldn't hope to stand against her. Not yet. He needed more understanding and more control of the stones.

Without warning, a tremendous explosion shook the hills, followed by a wave of energy that tumbled him from the crest. One last roar echoed over the hills, and the earth became deathly quiet. Zenek scrambled to his feet and leaped to calm his panicking horse.

He snatched the bridle. "It's okay," he soothed. He patted the horse's muzzle. "It's okay." The horse yanked its head up, its eyes rolling. "Calm down."

The horse eventually settled, and Zenek kept stroking it while he pondered on what he had seen and experienced. Since the time he fled the northern Silver Wood for Abilene, he had thought he was the last Tamil. Maybe he really was—if Rebecca was dying.

Still, this release of Maelorn and Tara changed everything. Bardon would be seeking allies, and maybe Zenek could earn his trust, just as he had the Tathanar among whom he had lived for so many years. Surely Bardon would welcome him, especially since he descended from the princes of the Tamil. Even if he didn't, he did possess an army and perhaps Zenek could find a way to use Bardon's army to defeat Cam and Maelorn and then turn it against Bardon himself.

Lorna picked herself up after the blast of energy and dusted off her tunic. She was afraid to look where the statue had been for fear that she might have finally killed her brother and Tara. The air stank of burning grass and the foul reek of the Mahrowaiths. After glancing at Cam and Rebecca, she revolved slowly, her pulse pounding in her ears and her blood racing.

Maelorn and Tara released their hold on each other, and Tara collapsed to her knees with a groan of pain. Maelorn clutched at his chest and grimaced. A sinking feeling swept through Lorna's stomach. Had she failed again? Would Bardon's curse kill them despite everything she had done?

Maelorn crouched beside Tara, and together they rose unsteadily to their feet to examine the valley before them. Maelorn hadn't changed. He stood tall and commanding in his early thirties with shoulder-length hair. He held himself in a way that indicated he was accustomed to being in charge. Confusion swept across his face as his hand drifted to the hilt of his sword.

Tara moved with an elegant grace born of long training that the Varaná had schooled out of Lorna. Her long brown hair and intelligent face gave her enchanting beauty that took one's breath away. Her gaze rested on Cam, and her brow furrowed. She raised a hand to her head and grimaced.

"Maelorn," she said. "What is happening?"

Lorna followed her gaze to where Cam had ceased rocking and knelt, sobbing quietly, hugging Rebecca to his chest. Drakeman knelt beside him with his head bowed, blood and tears staining his face. He rested a hand on Rebecca's pale arm. Slone dropped his axe to the churned earth and wiped at the tears in his eyes with a bloody hand. Spider knelt beside Cam, his arm draped around Cam's shoulder, while Hebron gently brushed the hair from Rebecca's damp cheek. It was a horrible, melancholy sight. Lorna had sensed the Anarwyn's panic when Rebecca had activated the dyad. It had tried to stop her and failed.

Alaric rose to face the royal couple, and Lorna followed his example.

"Lorna?" Maelorn said. "Who are these—"

His words cut off as she flung herself into his arms with a cry of relief and sorrow. All the years of pent-up guilt and shame burst from her in a torrent. Not only had she trapped Maelorn and Tara in the stone for nearly sixty years, now she had cost Rebecca her life. The poor child. It was too much.

"Easy," Maelorn said as he held her, stroking her snarled hair. "Tell me what has happened."

The Price

Lorna clung to him with a desperation she hadn't allowed herself to feel in many years. Maybe now they could fix her errors of so long ago, though the price had been heavy indeed.

The sound of galloping horses punctured the silence, and Maelorn eased his hold on her. She pulled away and wiped her eyes. Armored Knights of the Order of the Sword and the Stone swept into the valley, joined by a couple hundred Tathanar riders in forest green. They pounded up to the little cluster and formed a protective circle around them.

The still-smoking remains of dozens of Mahrowaiths littered the hillside. Hebron rose at the approach of the riders, standing with his tattered clothes smoking, grasping Galad's sword in his hand. He resembled some creature of magic himself, with his body covered in black blood and his red beard almost as bright as the crimson light that flashed along the blade of his sword. Tendrils of smoke lifted from his body where the Mahrowaith blood burned away his clothing, yet had not harmed his skin.

"Lorna," Maelorn whispered, glancing around with unease. "What is happening?"

Lorna embraced Tara. "I don't know how to tell you." She sniffled.

Alaric bowed the knee and soon all the men dismounted and knelt on one knee to Maelorn.

"You are free at last," Lorna said in a voice so low she didn't know if Maelorn could hear her.

Maelorn scowled. "I think you had better explain—in detail."

"Later," Lorna said. "We need to leave the valley as quickly as possible. Bardon might be approaching with the army he gathered at Mawsil."

When Maelorn didn't move, Lorna added, "Bardon tried to kill you, but I stopped him. You've been locked in a statue of stone for nearly sixty years."

A smile played at the side of Maelorn's mouth. "You jest."

Lorna motioned toward Cam and Rebecca. She tried to speak, but her voice caught in her throat, and she had to clear it before she could try again. "That young woman sacrificed her life to restore yours."

Tara gasped. "What has Bardon done?"

"It wasn't just Bardon," Lorna said. "I...." She paused, unable to admit that *she* had sealed them in the stone.

The bitterness of Rebecca's death also choked her. If only she had known. But if she had, would she have stopped Rebecca? She was afraid to answer that question, even in the privacy of her own mind.

Alaric rose and strode across the dry creek bed—his silver tunic so torn that Lorna could barely make out the wolf insignia.

"My Liege," Alaric said with a bow. "Please, your situation is perilous. We must away. Bardon's riders will return in greater strength, and the ancient beasts of the Bragamahr are abroad in the land." He pointed toward the smoking corpses of the Mahrowaiths. "Explanations must wait until your safety is secured."

Maelorn studied Alaric. "What is your name and office?"

"My Lord, I am Alaric, son of Faelorn, Knight General of the Order of the Sword and the Stone and Commander of the Order of the Wolf."

"Eric is my Commander. Where is he?"

Lorna grabbed Maelorn's arm. "You will find that much has changed. You must trust me for now. We can explain everything later."

"Where is Eric?" Maelorn insisted.

"Long dead," Lorna said. "It has been fifty-odd years. Please."

"What?" Tara gasped, her hand clutching her throat.

Maelorn scowled as he studied Lorna's face. "What is this?" He insisted again.

"Please," Lorna begged, "we must go."

Reluctantly, Maelorn allowed her to draw him and Tara away from the tree.

The soldiers rose and climbed into their saddles. Several horses, deprived of their riders, were brought forward.

Maelorn and Tara paused to frown down at Cam. He had stopped weeping and only held Rebecca close to him in silence. Draig curled at his feet with his tail draped around them protectively, his nose dripping blood. Lorna's heart ached for them both.

"Cam?" Lorna whispered.

Cam lifted his head slowly as if bowed down by a great weight, blinking his red, swollen eyes.

"This is King Maelorn and Lady Tara."

Cam tenderly lay Rebecca on the ground and rose to face them. Scrubbing the tears from his eyes, he bowed.

The Price

"My Lady. My Lord," he said in a shaky voice. "This is…was Rebecca. She freed you." Tears rolled down his cheeks, and his voice quivered. Spider stepped over to drape a comforting arm around Cam's shoulders.

Tara knelt beside Rebecca and brushed a strand of blonde hair from her face. "One so young and so fair." She gazed up at Cam. "I am sorry. I see that you loved her."

Cam's lips trembled.

Maelorn stretched forth his hand to grasp Cam's.

"Thank you, lad," he said. "How may we repay you?"

Cam lifted his head to look Maelorn straight in the eyes. "Don't let her life be sacrificed in vain."

Drakeman bent to lift Rebecca, but Cam jumped to stop him.

"May I carry her?" he asked.

Drakeman pinched his lips tight and nodded.

Cam lifted Rebecca and stumbled to a waiting horse. Drakeman met him there and took Rebecca's body from him while he climbed into the saddle. Drakeman kissed her cheek and lifted her limp form onto Cam's lap. He quietly stroked her hair for a long moment before he met Cam's gaze briefly and looked away. Lorna swallowed the knot in her throat. What could she say? What could anyone say?

She bent and picked up the dyad that had fallen from Rebecca's grasp. The little quartz crystal between the two stones had blackened and cracked. The red agate of the Healing Stone of the Anarwyn was also cracked but the milky-white moonstone was whole. A moonstone had never been a stone of power. It wasn't even a precious gemstone. This must be a stone of the Bragamahr, and the quartz had been used to fuse the two together. In the process, the agate had broken, while the moonstone remained apparently unharmed. A dread like she had never known seeped into her soul. What could it mean?

Chapter Twenty-One
Lament

SPIDER WRESTLED WITH a feeling of utter helplessness that threatened to drive him mad. He could do nothing to comfort his friend as Cam rode away with Rebecca clutched in his arms.

The battle in the Lonely Valley had been bloody and sharp, but it ended quickly. Once the rear guard arrived and the Tathanar came galloping over the hills, the outnumbered Inverni broke and scampered into the tall prairie grass. Those who remained were slaughtered. The Mahrowaiths were another matter. A trail of their corpses showed where Cam, Lorna, and Hebron had fought. There were dozens of them. Most had perished on the end of Hebron's sword and lay in a tumbled, grisly pile.

The leader of the Tathanar approached Lorna and Drakeman with a salute. They carried on a hurried conversation before Lorna and the others mounted and prepared to follow Cam. Spider found a horse and mounted. A sudden movement on the crest of the hill caught his attention, and he swiveled in the saddle to get a better view. A single Mahrowaith rose on its hind legs to peer down at them before dropping to all fours and bounding over the ridge. Spider watched it go and kicked his horse to join the line of soldiers bringing up the rear.

What had that meant? Why hadn't he sensed the paralyzing fear the presence of the Mahrowaiths usually brought? He thought he'd

Lament

seen a Mahrowaith battling others of its kind, but he had discounted that as impossible. Still, maybe he *had* seen it.

Soon, columns of Lakari and Tathanar soldiers were cantering through the valley and over the rise, past the bodies of dead men, horses, and Mahrowaiths. A bright full moon lit their way. The serenity of its silver light washing the gently swaying prairie grass could not penetrate the deep gloom that pierced Spider's heart.

He galloped up to ride beside Cam, glancing at his friend now and then, wishing he knew what words of comfort to say. But there were no words. For some reason, Rebecca had done what Cam was supposed to do. Cam would blame himself.

Rebecca's blonde hair draped over Cam's arm, and Spider struggled to ignore the awful fist that gripped his throat. She had been so vibrant and witty. He remembered the day he first met her in the garden at Abilene. She proved as masterful at the sword as she was with her tongue. Maybe she *had* clubbed him from behind and nearly gotten him killed, but she had also become his friend. She had meant so much to Cam that Spider had experienced a twinge of jealousy on that front, for which he now burned with guilt. He accepted that there would be danger, though he never imagined that the very thing they had come to do might kill them.

They camped in a wooded valley with a wide pool of clear water. Spider waited until the camp was quiet and slipped off into the trees. He didn't know when he had made the decision. Somewhere on the ride from the Lonely Valley, he realized that it was time to drink the Dûr Crishal. Maybe if he hadn't let Cam convince him to wait, he could have saved Rebecca or at least been there to help Cam when he most needed him. He never wanted to feel this helpless again, not if he could do something to prevent it.

Finding a secluded spot well out of sight and earshot of the camp, he slipped the crystal vial from the pouch at his neck. His mother had sacrificed her life to save this tiny bit of water. If it didn't work, Lorna would be furious that he had wasted it, but he didn't care. The water belonged to him—not her.

Spider unstopped the bottle, breathing in the gentle aroma of the aromatic resin that had sealed it. He peered at the vial and sniffed it. It was odorless. Whispering fluttered through the air, muttered words in a language he couldn't understand.

Undead

When he held the vial up in a gesture of salute, his hand trembled. "To you, Mother." He upended the vial, swallowing the water in one gulp.

A gentle warmth filled him, completing him, forging a link with his past, present, and future. The heady rush sent his head spinning, and he reeled, staggering to a nearby tree. His head split open in a burst of agony, and he collapsed with a groan.

The whispering became a young woman's voice, urgent and taunting. *I wondered when you would have the courage.*

Spider blinked, and the image of a young woman dressed in white with long, flowing hair swam in the air before him.

You think you have a right to wield the Anarwyn because your mother did?

There was a note of sarcasm and anger in her voice that he didn't understand.

"No," he gasped, clutching at his chest. "I just want to help. I don't want to be defenseless anymore."

She studied him, her gaze boring into him. *Then face reality. Face the truth of what you are.*

Spider's mind whirled as memories flooded in. *Cam was gracefully working through the sword form Hebron was teaching them, looking like he'd known it all his life. Jealousy pinched at Spider's throat, and he wanted to chuck a stone at Cam for being so much better than he was.... The insults he shouted at the old woman who liked to pinch his backside floated into his ears. "Hag. Crone," he chanted.... Why did Rebecca find Cam attractive and not him? He was the one who had hunted the Mahrowaith alone. He had tracked Cam and rescued him.... Why did Hebron favor Cam over him? Every act of unkindness, every selfish thought or deed flowed through his mind.*

"I'm sorry," he said as he wept in shame. "I was—"

Weak, the young woman finished for him. *All humans are feeble. Few rise to self-mastery. Instead, they are content with their foibles. Their prejudices. Their vanity. Always they are tempted by power. Always they fear what they cannot control.*

More memories flooded into him again. *This time, he remembered caring for his mother while she was sick, sponging her forehead and arms to bring down her fever.... Commiserating with the grieving father after his son died.... Taking extra game to the widow woman who lived on the edge of the village.... Feeling pride in Cam's successes. Desiring to keep Cam and Hebron safe.*

You are a composite, the young woman said, *of all the good and bad*

Lament

you have done. You may only serve me if you accept this fact and choose the path of courage and truth.

"I will," Spider whispered, and he meant it.

You are different, the young woman said, her tone softening. *I cannot see your road. Your fate is not clear to me.*

"Can I save my friends?" Spider asked.

The young woman frowned. *That may not be up to me.*

"What do you mean?"

Her brow wrinkled, and Spider noted a calculated rage coming off her like heat from flames. The Anarwyn had made a decision. She was planning something.

She studied Spider. *I will accept you because I see you are earnest and may resist the influence of the Bragamahr better than the others. Be warned, I cannot allow the joining of the magics. What Rebecca has done this night, may change the destiny of all Anwyn. You must not let it happen again.*

"What has she done?" he asked. "I don't understand."

The young woman glared at him. *She defiled me. She forced a perversion of my power. I will not permit it again.*

"But what exactly—"

Enough. I will not give you more knowledge than you can bear. You must promise me that you will never succumb to the enticing of the Bragamahr.

"I'll try," Spider said, though he wasn't certain he understood what she meant.

Will you accept me, then? the young woman asked.

"I will," Spider said.

Her eyes narrowed. *Your friend Cam is walking on dangerous ground.*

"What do you mean?" he repeated. This woman spoke in riddles.

Her image wavered and faded.

"Wait!" Spider cried. "Can you give me some weapon to use?"

The young woman smiled. *What weapon is more powerful than the ability to mend that which is damaged and broken?*

The vision grew more and more faint until it faded altogether, and Spider found himself flat on his back, staring up at the leafy canopy with a few stars blinking through the gaps in the leaves.

He crawled to his knees and rubbed a hand over his chest. He had been scoured clean on the inside at some deep spiritual level. His head ached, and his knees trembled. He hardly knew what to think. The excitement was tempered by the terror of what he had done.

Undead

Would the Anarwyn kill him, like Cam expected? She was not happy with Cam and had even seemed to threaten him.

Spider grasped a nearby tree to clamber to his feet, fighting the rushing nausea. Only then did he realize he hadn't asked her how his mother had died. That had been his one chance, and he had failed to do so.

He started back toward camp, stumbling at the sudden weariness. He would have to tell Lorna and Cam eventually what he had done—but not tonight.

"Now, tell me everything—from the start," Maelorn insisted after he dismissed everyone but Lorna and Tara.

Darkness enfolded them while the red coals from the fire burned and sputtered. Starlight twinkled in the pond as the breeze rippled the waters. They had left the stench and the horror of the battlefield far behind. Guards paced around their encampment.

Cam and the others retired after Lorna and Laird had healed their injuries. She would have to find out his story. Yet another heir of Ilsie had been found. Had the Anarwyn been hiding them from her?

Lorna drew her knees up to her chest, struggling to decide where to begin. Her muscles ached from her long ride to the Lonely Valley. She hadn't slept properly in days. Pushing through the exhaustion, she took a deep breath. She had so longed for this day and despaired that it would never come. Even so, she didn't know where to start.

Tara shifted and scowled at Lorna. "Is what you said true? Has it really been sixty years?"

"Almost," Lorna said.

"And what of our families? Our kingdoms?"

Lorna shook her head. "Gone."

Tara gasped and reached over to grab Maelorn's hand. He sat rigid, glaring. "Bardon—that traitorous wretch," he said.

"After you were locked in the stone," Lorna explained, "the marks descended into civil war, and Bardon used the chaos to hunt the heirs of Anarwyn almost to extinction. He also tracked down anyone with the royal line in their veins and slaughtered them. I sought the protection of the Tathanar in Abilene."

Lament

Tara raised a hand to cover her mouth. Her eyes brimmed with tears. "Then what is left for us?" she whispered.

"To rebuild," Lorna said. "To destroy our brother's hold over the land once and for all."

Maelorn narrowed his eyes at her. "You don't appear a day older."

He had a way of making her feel like a child again, bringing her troubles to her elder brother, seeking his acceptance and approval. "I had to survive until I could find a way to free you."

"So, you used the Anarwyn to prolong your life?"

"Of course."

"And Bardon?"

"He used the Bragamahr."

"Has he come to full power?"

"Yes. He is terribly strong."

Maelorn studied her. "What aren't you telling me, Lorna? I can tell when you're hiding something."

Lorna bit her lip and clasped her hands to keep from wringing them. "It was my fault," she whispered.

Maelorn stared at her, waiting for her to explain.

"I discovered that Bardon had worked some evil of the Bragamahr that would kill you and Tara when you touched," she confessed, "and I raced to save you. By the time I arrived, it was too late." She wiped away a tear.

"*You* were the rider," Tara said, "who crested the hill."

"I tried to stop the spell," Lorna explained. "In doing so, I created something new. Some combination of the powers of the Bragamahr and the Anarwyn."

"Is that possible?" Maelorn asked, kneading his forehead as if to force this new information into his brain.

"Clearly, but I couldn't undo it unless I surrendered myself to the Bragamahr."

"The girl could?" Tara asked.

Lorna shrugged. She would never be free of the image of Rebecca's beautiful, youthful face so twisted in pain. "I don't know how. I'll have to speak with Cam to know for sure, but I don't want to disturb his grief just yet."

"What do you plan then?" Maelorn asked.

What *did* she have planned? One would think after nearly six decades, she would have every detail mapped out. She had guessed wrong so often in the last few weeks.

She sighed. "Alaric will gather the remnants of the North Mark to your standard. The boy, Cam, may yet claim the throne of the West Mark, and he will support you. I have been to the East Mark, and Gareth, son of the late Trahern, is bringing an army. We must defeat Bardon's armies and destroy him."

Maelorn stared at her. "He is our brother."

Lorna shook her head. "Not anymore," her voice caught, and she had to swallow. "The Bragamahr has corrupted him completely." She picked at the bloodstain on her tunic—the one left from the little girl Bardon murdered. "He tried very hard to kill me." Her lips trembled at the memory of the child who had saved her. "I looked into his eyes, and he is not there."

A breeze fanned the coals, causing them to burn brighter.

Maelorn rose and paced before them. "So be it. I would have it differently, but the little tyrant has grown to manhood and must now be destroyed."

The three of them sank into subdued silence. How did one get their brain and feelings around such a horrible idea? Lorna stirred. Perhaps now was the time to ask the question that had haunted her for nearly sixty years.

"What was it like?" Lorna whispered.

Both Maelorn and Tara exchanged a confused glance.

"I mean," Lorna said, "what was it like being trapped in stone?"

Tara scowled. "All I remember is the sudden shock of cold and pain and then a long, terrifying silence."

A knot rose in Lorna's throat. She had caused this.

Maelorn rested his hand on Tara's. "I thought I heard a horse galloping, and then it was like being frozen in thought. I don't know how else to describe it. When I came to, it felt like plunging frozen hands into a pot of boiling water. It hurt, and yet, it felt so good." He paused as he saw the tears trickling down Lorna's cheeks.

"You mustn't blame yourself," he said.

"Then who do I blame for my folly?"

"The one who caused it." The muscles worked in Maelorn's jaw. "Blame the one who caused all of this."

Lament

Spider gripped the empty vial that had held the Dûr Crishal as he approached Cam the next morning. A cool mist had descended over the little wooded vale and lifted in silent tendrils from the placid surface of the pond. Horses stomped their feet, and injured men limped about packing their gear. Cam slouched on a rock with his head bowed and his hands clasped in front of him.

"I have to tell you something," Spider said. He tugged on Cam's sleeve to urge him away from where Drakeman watched over Rebecca's body.

Cam's eyes were rimmed with red as if he hadn't slept at all. He allowed Spider to lead him away. They stopped beside the pond where the mist was so thick it wet their clothes and beaded on their faces and hair.

"I did it," Spider said. He extended his fist and opened it so the empty glass vial that had once held the Dûr Crishal rolled on his palm.

"I thought you might."

"I want to help," Spider said. "I can't stand being helpless. The Anarwyn said I would be able to heal."

Cam didn't seem surprised at all. Just weary. "I hope you don't live to regret it like I do."

"I'm sorry, Cam. Really, I am."

"I guess she won't be knocking you over the head anymore. Or calling you Ludo." Cam gave Spider a sad smile as his eyes brimmed with tears. "It hurts worse than I could have imagined."

"I know. I don't think the pain ever goes away."

"Well, that makes me feel better." Cam kicked at a stone sticking out of the mud. "It was supposed to be me, you know."

"Yes, but I'm glad it wasn't."

Cam snapped his head up, his eyes blazing.

Spider reached out to grab his arm. "Hang on. I wish it hadn't been Rebecca either, but you can't expect me to regret that you're still alive."

Cam drew his arm from Spider's grasp. "You might not, but I do."

"Cam, you can't—"

"Blame myself," Cam finished for him. "Yes, I can. And I can blame the Anarwyn because she stopped me."

Spider stared at Cam. Was that even possible?

"You can't trust the magic," Cam said. "No matter how much you might want to. I hope it does you some good in the end."

He whirled and stalked back to his gear where he heaved his saddle up onto his horse, which was picketed nearby.

Spider sensed a sudden prickling in his mind, and he glanced down at the stone Cam had been kicking. It was about the size of a chicken egg. Bold red and brown lines cut through the stone in a delicate lacy pattern, and it had a waxy luminescent look to it. Spider bent and tugged it from the mud. Immediately it let off a gentle crimson glow and warmth rushed up Spider's arm. He almost dropped it in surprise. Then a grin spread over his face. This stone was meant for him.

Cam rode in silence as the party, escorted by the Tathanar warriors and the remaining members of the Order of the Sword and the Stone crossed the plains to the green woodland. Rebecca's body had been wrapped in a blanket, and he insisted on carrying her back to Yarwick rather than having her flung over the back of some horse. It wasn't much, but it was the last act of respect and affection he could give her.

No more tears would flow, yet the ache consumed him. He'd never experienced such pangs of loneliness and sorrow. He stoically accepted the words of comfort offered by the men, though no words could assuage the self-condemnation and rising fury at the betrayal of the Anarwyn. If he ever got his hands on Jathneel, he'd throttle him. And then there was Lorna. How could she have been so wrong? If her dyad had worked, he wouldn't be feeling this agony. He'd be the one wrapped in a blanket.

By late afternoon, they broke from the cover of the trees into the broad plain before Yarwick. Word had gone before them, and people lined the roads, waving flags and banners, cheering them on. The entire population of the city came out to greet them. Women threw flowers and sprinkled scented water on the advancing column. Red and black banners draped from windows. Men embraced one another, and some wept openly. Carpets were spread on the road before them as singing broke out to echo down the streets. Cam found himself studying the jubilant crowd.

These are my people, he thought. Could he come to care for them, as he had for the people of Stony Vale? Would he ever be able to feel anything ever again? Right now, his heart, though it still beat against his ribs, was broken, leaving him incapable of emotion.

An official delegation from the Regency Council met them at the gates with the blare of trumpets. They formally welcomed Maelorn and Tara to the city with rich gifts and much fanfare. Cam silently endured the useless ceremony and was surprised to see Tara appearing impatient with it, as well. She kept glancing at Maelorn and fiddling with the reins in her hands.

He could only imagine what Tara might be feeling as she approached the city of her childhood, knowing that her father and mother would not be there to greet her. In fact, no one she knew would be there. How cruel the bitter irony of Bardon's treachery was. It must cut her to the quick. Cam knew he'd guessed right when he caught the twinkle of tears glistening on her cheeks.

Maelorn sat straight-backed and proud, being gracious to all who approached him. He looked and acted like a king, whereas Cam felt like a lump of wood, awkward and incompetent.

When they paused near Ewan's home not far from the palace gates, Drakeman lifted Rebecca from Cam's lap. He searched Cam's face for a moment and turned away to carry Rebecca's body to the healers to prepare her for burial. Slone held the door for him. He caught a strand of Rebecca's blonde hair dangling from the cover and let it sift through his fingers as Drakeman passed under the lintel.

Spider rested a hand on Cam's leg. "I'm sorry."

Cam nodded, wrestling with the emptiness and desolation. Had he made the wrong decision in accepting the Anarwyn rather than the Bragamahr? If he had chosen differently, would Rebecca still live? And what role did Jathneel play in all of this? Was this some trickery on his part?

He dismounted and brushed past all the well-wishers to duck inside Ewan's home. Lorna followed him in. He flopped onto the ground by the fire to stare into the flames.

"Cam?" Lorna eased down beside him. "I think we should talk."

Undead

Cam said nothing. He picked at the bits of charcoal on the hearthstones.

"I'm sorry," Lorna said. "I wish it could have been different."

Cam spun to gaze up at her. "Different? How? Do you wish that *I* was dead instead of Rebecca? Is that what you planned all along?"

Lorna scowled. "Of course not."

"Jathneel told me his dyad wouldn't do any more damage than the one you gave me."

Lorna was taken aback, her mouth opened in shock. "Jathneel? Where? When?"

"On the hillside after we passed through Goldereth. He appeared to me and said you were wrong and that only *his* dyad would work." Cam ran a hand over his head. "Looks like he was right."

"I need to know everything he said." Lorna's eyes glittered in the firelight, and her face grew solemn.

"I don't feel like talking," Cam said as he turned back to the fire. He considered refusing to tell her anything—ever again—but what good would it do?

"Please," she said. "You think you are the only one hurting? I've known and cared for Rebecca since she was a baby."

Cam rubbed his face, attempting to scrub away his shame. A long silence ensued. His words came haltingly at first. But the more he talked, the more he found he had to say. He told her how he and Rebecca had been captured by men employed by Jathneel, how they had escaped and been forced to follow the path through Goldereth, how they crossed the river, escaped Hannoch, and finally rode to the Lonely Valley. He considered telling her about the Mahrowaith who kept calling him *Master*, but he didn't know what to say about it and she didn't give him a chance.

"But the dyad," she asked. "Did you try *my* dyad?"

Cam nodded. "It didn't work. I felt the dyad activate, but nothing happened. So, I tried to use Jathneel's, but the Anarwyn stopped me. I thought it was going to kill me. When I came to, Rebecca was screaming in agony and that column of light was churning over the statue while they came back to life." He glowered at Lorna. "It sucked her life away." Somehow, speaking about it made the pain simultaneously sharper, yet more bearable.

Lorna frowned. "I'm sorry," she said again.

Lament

"When I accepted the Anarwyn at the great bend, the Life Stone told me I would die to save my friends. It was supposed to be me. Not Rebecca. But the Anarwyn wouldn't let me. Why?"

"I've never heard of the Anarwyn doing anything like that," Lorna said. She folded her hands in her lap. "Once the power has been granted, it cannot be taken away. That's why the Anarwyn is so careful about whom it will accept."

Cam pulled out the lump of amber. He called up the light, and a beam of it crashed into the fireplace, sending up a shower of sparks and ash about the room.

"What are you doing?" Lorna demanded, shielding her face.

"It didn't take the power away. It just wouldn't let me activate that dyad."

"I can't explain it," Lorna said.

"Then explain why your dyad didn't work."

"I can only guess. I believe it was only channeling the Anarwyn. That dyad Jathneel gave you is a combination of the power of the Anarwyn and the Bragamahr. That must be why the Anarwyn stopped you."

"That's what Jathneel said. But if it's true, why could Rebecca activate it? Why didn't the Anarwyn stop *her*?"

"Cam," Lorna's voice was tired, "I have suspected since she was a child that Rebecca was an heir with some power. King Chullain wanted to let her have a normal childhood and forced me to agree to wait until she came of age. I had to leave the night before her birthday and so never had the chance to test her. I know she had some potential. Perhaps it was enough."

Sudden understanding blossomed in Cam's mind, but it was an understanding tainted by the knowledge that it came too late.

"That explains everything," he said. "It explains why Jathneel's men captured her along with me. It explains why the Life Stone responded to her. She was an heir. She was related to you, too."

"Perhaps," Lorna said.

Cam grunted and turned back to the flames, afraid he might say something he would regret. His chest burned with helpless fury.

"Cam, you must understand there is a price to every decision we make. We cannot control the consequences. I never intended for you or Rebecca to die."

Undead

Cam didn't look at her. He smeared a bit of black ash over the hearth stones with his finger.

Lorna leaned toward him, studying his expression. "Do you remember when I told you about Alys and Galad?"

"Yes. We actually visited Alys's grave."

"You did?"

"Hebron said he could hear a voice from the sword. We even heard her and saw her for a second."

Lorna stared. "That makes sense."

"It does?"

"At Brynach, I found an old version of the Alys and Galad story. That's when I first guessed the dyad I made for you might be dangerous." Lorna hesitated and fiddled with the hem of her tunic. "Alys used the same dyad I created for you to heal Galad by transferring her life force to him. When he created the sword Dorandel, he must have transferred some portion of her life force into the sword."

Cam studied Lorna as the implications of what she said hit him.

"You mean Rebecca could be alive somewhere?"

"What?" Lorna shook her head. "No."

Cam jumped to his feet bursting with excitement. "Couldn't we take some of her life force back from Maelorn and Tara and still save Rebecca or…or…" He paused, realizing how far-fetched that sounded. "…or maybe put her life force into something like a gemstone?"

"Cam," Lorna began.

He spun on her. "Why can't we do it?" he shouted.

"I don't know how Galad attached Alys to his sword. Nothing like this has ever been done before or since."

"But it is possible. I saw it."

Lorna bit her bottom lip. "I understand what you're feeling."

"No, you don't." Cam sank back down into a chair and buried his face in his hands. He was grasping at straws.

"Don't suppose you're the only one who has lost a loved one," Lorna snapped. "Drakeman has loved her far longer and just as deeply as you, although certainly in a different way. *I* loved her. How many mothers, fathers, brothers, sisters, wives, and children are mourning their own dead at this moment—many of whom fell to protect your life?"

A chill swept through him. "I never wanted anyone to die."

Lament

"It's normal to mourn, Cam," Lorna said. "Mourn for Rebecca. She deserves to be mourned and to be remembered. Don't shut out the friends who would share your grief. Let the pain you feel strengthen your empathy for the pain of others. Few qualities are more important in a leader of men than empathy."

Cam licked his lips and rubbed at his burning eyes. Rebecca would want him to fight on, and Lorna was just trying to help. She was as confused as he was.

"You're right," he muttered. "I am sorry. I just…what if some part of her is still out there somewhere?" He shook his head. "How did she know?"

"I don't think she did," Lorna said.

"Then why did she do it?" Cam asked.

Lorna shook her head. "Only she could answer that question."

"I don't want to be king," Cam said. "I want to go home and forget all of this ever happened."

Lorna gave a short laugh. "I hid away for fifty years in Abilene, and what good did it do? I told myself I was studying and preparing, but I was frightened. Afraid of what I had to do. Afraid I couldn't do it." She paused and continued in a quieter voice. "You understand that I must kill my own brother."

Cam *did* understand, and he did not envy her. He would never be able to kill Spider or Hebron, no matter what happened. He and Lorna sat silently for a long while listening to the gentle crackling and popping of the fire until Cam broke the stillness.

"What other prices must be paid before this is over?"

"I don't know," Lorna said. "I only hope the price we pay will be enough."

Lorna left Cam to his sorrow and stepped out into the cool evening. There was much celebration in the city streets. Torches flared and bonfires cast dancing shadows off the stone buildings. The aroma of roasting meat and woodsmoke saturated the air. Someone strummed a lute, and a chorus of voices sang about the glory days of Goldereth and the majesty of the high kings of Torwyn. If only these people understood the real battle hadn't yet begun, they

Undead

wouldn't be so joyous. She would let them have their merriment. They would not enjoy it for long.

She peered up at the twinkle of stars. Something had shifted in the Lonely Valley under that ominous, twisting column of light that returned her brother and Tara to her. The Anarwyn had changed. A chill swept through her, and she hugged herself. Something terrible was coming. Something that had never happened before. Something for which she was utterly unprepared.

Chapter Twenty-Two
Haunted

THE EVENING AIR STIRRED, carrying with it something that made Spider shiver. He paused while brushing the horses and scanned the area. Men were working at the same task of preparing their horses for the night. No one noticed him.

Spider returned to his work of ensuring that his and Cam's horses were brushed and fed a supply of grain in their nosebags before leaving the picket lines. Riotous singing and dancing spilled out of the city gates. The walls were alight with dozens of bonfires and torches, casting the city in a haunting, yellow glow. He paused to study the light dancing on the waters of the river where boats were moored against the docks and wondered how many peaceful nights he would see before the war came.

The power of the Anarwyn stirred, and he shifted his feet, still uncomfortable with this new feeling. He didn't dare try to use it until he could speak to Lorna, Cam, or Laird. He might transform himself into a stink bug or burn his life away because he didn't know what he was doing. He hadn't forgotten the sight of his mother's blackened fingers. Spider straightened to go in search of Cam, when a shiver swept through him, making the hairs on the back of his neck stand on end. His hand drifted to the hilt of his sword. Something was out there.

Spider listened with the skill of an experienced hunter. He could hear nothing out of the ordinary, but a scent reached him. It was the pungent, musky smell of a fox. Spider crouched and peered into the darkness. The fox was upwind of him and might not know he was there. If it was just a fox, why did his skin crawl?

Unnaturally blue eyes peered at him from a deep shadow beside a stone wall. Spider waited, curious. There was something odd about this fox. Every fox he had ever seen or heard fled at the first sight or scent of man. Yet, this one crept deliberately toward him and eyed him like he was a piece of meat. His first thought was hydrophobia. But rabid animals didn't watch and wait like this. They stumbled about in their madness, foaming at the mouth. This fox was not mad. It was intent and focused, like any predator about to spring upon its prey.

Spider straightened and waved his arms. "Get out of here!"

The fox trotted forward until Spider could see it clearly. It was large and red with a bushy tail. Its lips curled into a snarl, exposing sharp fangs. It wasn't a bit afraid of him.

He drew his sword and backed away toward the city. He didn't want to tangle with a sick fox. The animal's eyes glowed brighter, and it lunged for him.

"What the…?" Spider gasped and jumped aside. The fox skidded to a stop and whirled to face him.

"You crazy beast," Spider shouted. "Get out of here."

The fox crouched, and Spider had the sudden sensation that it knew him and saw him as a competitor. Spider scowled as he tried to work out what was going on. The fox sprang again.

This time, Spider swung his blade and delivered a glancing blow to the fox's head. It didn't yelp or give any other sign that it had been injured. It skidded to a stop and whirled about to stare at him with glowing blue eyes. It growled, and it bounded toward him.

A buzz sounded, followed by the hollow thump of an arrow striking flesh. The fox faltered and fell. It struggled to its belly and crawled toward him when another arrow pinned it to the ground. A single emotion slipped through Spider's mind. "Pain."

Drakeman strode up to him, with his great war bow in his hand. "I thought it was Draig at first," he said as he peered down on the fox's quivering body.

"It was mad," Spider said.

"How many foxes have you seen with blue eyes?" Drakeman stooped to study the animal. "Alaric shot a deer that attacked him. It had blue eyes, too."

He retrieved his two arrows, wiped them in the grass beside the road, and they strode toward the glowing city.

"Is the Bragamahr using animals now?" Spider asked.

"Don't know," Drakeman said, "but Cam has called a meeting, and he wants you there."

Cam glanced up as Spider and Drakeman strode into Ewan's house. Spider's scowl told him something had happened. He would have to wait to find out what. A fire crackled in the fireplace, and candles flickered in sconces along the wall. The stink of men and horse sweat filled the air. All who remained of their company as well as all the leaders of the Order of the Sword and the Stone packed into the room. Maelorn sat erect in a chair, looking regal even in that humble setting. He more resembled a king than Cam ever could.

Hebron, now clothed, lurked in the shadows miraculously unharmed from the Mahrowaith blood that had covered his body after the battle. The sword, Dorandel, dangled at his hip. Lorna had explained that Galad had also been unaffected by the blood, and she assumed the protection extended to whomever the sword permitted to wield it.

Slone rested his hands on his battle axe but kept his head downcast, reminding Cam of how much Slone had cared for Rebecca. Cam wished he could simply go off and be alone with his pain and guilt. But he couldn't.

The singing and revelry rang through the streets outside. Like people everywhere, the Lakari would seize any opportunity to throw a party. If only they understood what was coming.

"That's everyone," Cam said, and he gestured for Ewan to close the door.

He would rather be anywhere else than here, but he would not be permitted to mourn. Rebecca would expect him to go on fighting, and he would—for her. There was nothing else left for him to do.

"Bardon is coming," Cam said. "I have sent messengers to all the lords of the West Mark to gather at Yarwick with their armies." He glanced at Maelorn. "Messengers are also riding to the Dinera and the East Mark. It will take time to assemble our forces. In the meantime, we need a plan. How do we survive until our men can be gathered?"

Cam nearly wilted under the gaze of all these men so much wiser and more experienced than himself. No one sneered at his youth.

"A defensive posture from behind solid walls is the safest course, Your Majesty," Rindorf said.

Cam flinched at the title but forced himself to consider the wizened soldier wearing the coat of arms of the Sword and the Stone.

"That would leave the land open to the ravages of Bardon's army," another man said, "and we don't have the time to lay up enough supplies for a prolonged siege. He would trap us in Yarwick and starve us out while he destroyed the North Mark and then the East Mark."

Both men were right. How was he supposed to choose? He glanced at Hebron, who grimaced. There were no good choices.

Someone pounded on the door, and Ewan yanked it open to find a soldier wearing the oak leaf livery of the kings of the West Mark.

"I must speak with the King," he panted.

Cam glanced at Maelorn, thinking he was the only real king present. Maelorn shook his head. "You are king here."

That's what he was afraid Maelorn would say. Cam rose and strode to the door. The soldier bowed and gestured to two children sitting astride a lathered horse, which sucked in air while its body trembled. A girl of about than eleven or twelve held the reins while holding a boy no more than five or six.

"Get them down before the horse collapses," Cam ordered.

As soon as the soldier touched the girl, she shrieked in pain and nearly dropped the boy, who started crying. Cam jumped to catch him, cradling him close as he inspected the young girl.

"She's injured," he said. "Laird, Lorna, I need you."

He handed the sobbing boy off to Ewan's wife, Elatha, and hefted the injured girl in his arms.

"It's all right," he soothed. "You're safe now."

Her face was ashen white, and she blinked up at him as if trying to see his face. Her tunic was sticky with blood.

"Ewan," he called, "we need hot water."

Lorna met him at the door and laid a hand on the girl as he carried her to the fire. The company within backed away to give them room.

"Her back," Lorna said. "Her back is injured."

Tara and Elatha descended on the children, washing away the grime and caring for their needs.

"See this?" Lorna said and pointed to a long slice across the girl's back. A sword wound.

Cam cursed softly. What would possess a man to do that to a child? "Can you heal her?"

Lorna scowled. "I have never been good at healing."

Cam didn't bother trying the Life Stone. He had learned that it only worked on wounds caused by *his* sword. Searching the gathering, he saw Laird working his way toward him and gestured for him to hurry.

"Can you do anything?" he whispered.

Laird nodded. "I want Spider to help."

Cam had almost forgotten that Spider had accepted the Anarwyn. He glanced at Spider, who shifted his feet. Cam would have to get used to this new reality.

"Do what you can," Cam said.

He turned to Elatha. "Is the boy injured?"

She pinched her lips tight and shook her head.

Cam flinched as icy cold fingers grasped his hand. He glanced down to see the girl's fingers clutching his. He knelt beside her.

"It's okay," he said. "This man will make you feel better."

"They're all dead," she said, and a tear spilled down her cheek. "The monsters killed them."

Cam patted her hand. "I know."

"Where are you from?" Lorna asked.

"Anabá."

"By the black sands," Ewan swore. "This child has ridden over fifty miles."

Laird and Spider knelt on each side of the girl, and Laird laid his hand on the girl's head. "It'll be all right, little one," he said. "Close your eyes and go to sleep."

The girl's eyelids fluttered and closed. Her breathing deepened.

Undead

"Get the packet of herbs from my pack," Laird said to Spider. "Crush them and mix them with warm wine."

Spider shouldered through the crowd in search of Laird's pack. Laird lifted the girl in his arms. "I think we should treat her in private."

"Of course," Cam said.

Maelorn rose as Laird left the room. "My brother will expect us to hide behind walls, while he spreads this terror. He's done it before."

Lorna straightened to gaze at him. "We should ride out to meet him, or you will see more of this."

Cam studied the young boy's face. A cold hatred for Bardon and his Inverni dogs grew inside him. Bardon had robbed both him and Spider of their mothers. He had taken Rebecca, and now he was murdering more innocent people. Cam would not stand by and let him go unpunished.

"Alaric," he said, "how soon can we have an army ready to ride?"

"No sooner than a week, Your Majesty."

Cam shook his head in annoyance. He was going to have to get used to this "Your Majesty" nonsense.

"Unless there's any more discussion," he said, "I propose to ride out to meet Bardon."

The men glanced around with grim faces, but no one spoke.

"All right," Cam said. "Alaric, please send out whatever orders you need. I want the army ready as soon as possible."

Turning to gaze into the fire, he wondered when his own doom would come. How much suffering would he have to witness before this was over? He straightened to his full height and strode to the window to peer out at the inhabitants of Yarwick reveling in happy ignorance. Rebecca had died so they could have a chance to defeat Bardon. He would not squander her sacrifice.

Off in the distance, far beyond the walls of Yarwick and the glittering waters of the river, he sensed the presence of the Mahrowaith that had followed them ever since Goldereth. It had saved Drakeman and himself in the Lonely Valley. It was out there now, searching for him, and he was tired of running.

From now on, he was going to carry the fight to Bardon and the Bragamahr. Let them see how they liked being chased and hounded like a fox on the run. They were not yet so powerful that they couldn't feel fear. Cam would make them afraid. Very afraid.

After all, both the Anarwyn and the Bragamahr dealt in fear of one kind or another. Why not turn it against those who deserved to be afraid? Fear would be his weapon. It would be his solace.

"I'm coming for you, Bardon," he breathed.

I hope you've enjoyed *Undead* Book 2 in the Heirs of Anarwyn Series. Please leave an honest review for me on Amazon.

Continue the adventure with Book 3 Shattered.

Please accept a free story by signing up for my email list at www.jwelliot.com

Lithomancy of Anwyn

EONS BEFORE LIFE EMERGED in Anwyn, two sentient magics—the Anarwyn and the Bragamahr—formed in the fires of creation. They became self-aware and sought out human hosts with whom they constructed symbiotic relationships. Both magics remained bound to the place they first emerged, but they created channels of power that ran beneath the land like arteries and veins. Where those arteries rose to the surface, they created places of incredible power. Locations where the channels crossed became liminal spaces of danger and instability.

The magics of Anwyn could only be used by those descended from the first human to possess them. But that potential couldn't be realized until an heir accepted the burden of the magic and was accepted in turn. The Bragamahr was the first to find a human host. It developed a parasitic relationship in which it fed on and warped the host's memories of love and happiness into hate, jealousy, and distrust and so eventually left the bearer an empty shell. The first to accept the Bragamahr was a man named Dengra, who used the power to defeat his enemies and conquer his neighbors.

Dengra's descendants formed the Black Council, which ruled from a tower in the mountains surrounding Braganeth, the valley where the Bragamahr emerged. After a thousand years, the Black Council collapsed into civil war, and Serena, the high priestess, fled

Lithomancy of Anwyn

from her husband's wrath in search of a magic that did not twist and destroy everything it touched. Together with her daughter, Ilsie, and those who would follow her, Serena fled far into the Haradd Mountains, where she died and Ilsie accepted the power of the Anarwyn. This new magic formed a mutualistic relationship with humans by enhancing the host's abilities while the host's use of the magic reinvigorated and nourished the magic. The people who followed Ilsie took the name "Anar" and settled in the mountains, eventually creating the great Kingdom of Donmor.

Those who could wield the magic were called "heirs of Anarwyn" or "heirs of Ilsie." The ability to use the magic was not uniform among the descendants. Some had only a slight sensitivity to its influence while others had none. Very few could fully utilize the power and control all the lithomantic stones, though many could control the power of one or more individual stones. The ability often skipped generations and could weaken the further the descent. For those of weak descent, the gemstones could enhance certain abilities but could be fully used.

The Bragamahr personified as male in the image of Dengra, the hunter, because he was the first to accept the Bragamahr. The Anarwyn personified as a female in the image of Ilsie because she was the first to drink the crystal water and accept the Anarwyn.

Because these magics spawned in the bowels of the earth, the powers of the Bragamahr and the Anarwyn could only be channeled through specific stones. Each stone possessed certain capabilities and had to be attuned to the bearer before those abilities could fully manifest. An experienced and powerful heir could attune the stones to themselves. Only pure stones with no cracks or weaknesses could channel these powers. Once a gemstone was attuned and had channeled magic, it could only be destroyed through magical means. If a stone was forced to channel too much power, it could crack or break, becoming useless. Such stones were called "tired stones" or "dead stones."

Each gemstone emitted a delicate musical note when activated and was identified by a name and a rune drawn from the ancient Tamil or Anarian languages. Stones were classified as higher and lesser stones, based on the value given their abilities by the different practitioners. Because those who served the Anarwyn valued char-

Undead

acter and the improvement of the human mind and condition, the higher stones fulfilled those objectives. Because those who served the Bragamahr valued power, dominance, and control, the stones that allowed them to accomplish those were considered the higher stones.

The keystone of the Anarwyn system was the clear sapphire, also called the Water Stone, because it resembled solidified water. It restored balance and repaired things that were broken. It also enhanced the power of all the other stones and could form dyads with any stone of the Anarwyn.

The keystone of the Bragamahr was obsidian, also called the Death Stone. It was the stone of fragmentation and death. Like the sapphire, it could enhance the power of the other stones and form a dyad with any stone of the Bragamahr.

In both lithomantic systems, each stone could form combinations, called dyads, with other stones. Dyads were formed only with two stones. Each dyadic structure made a unique musical tone when connected. It was accepted as an unbreakable rule that any attempt to form a triad or a quadrad would end in an uncontrolled expansion of energy that would almost certainly kill the one who attempted it.

The most powerful and stable dyads could only be formed with those to which the stone formed a pyramid of power, as shone in the accompanying illustrations. Stones set opposite each other in the diagram were not compatible and would either refuse to form dyads or do so in extremely unstable and dangerous ways. A quartz crystal, called the Union Stone in both systems, could be used to force incompatible stones to create dyads, but the resulting dyad would remain unstable and potentially dangerous. Silver and gold conducted both magics and could be used to facilitate and enhance dyadic connections—especially for one who was weak or just learning to control the magic.

Lithomantic Gemstones of the Anarwyn:

Sapphire—Water Stone (Carreg Vûr)—The sapphire is the keystone and, hence, the most powerful stone of the Anarwyn. It controls the water in the heavens and on earth. It restores balance and can mend that which is broken. It enhances the power of all other stones and can be used in dyadic connections with all of them.

Lithomancy of Anwyn

Pearl—Lightning Stone (Carreg Tan a Dûr)—Though not a true stone, the pearl's origins in water allow it to channel the Anarwyn. The pearl harnesses the energy in the air that manifests as lightning. It is most compatible with opal and jasper and least compatible with ruby.

Jade—Wind Stone (Carreg Gwynt)—Because it is the product of the interaction of the mountains and water, Jade represents the unified powers of heaven and earth. It harnesses the power of the wind. It is most compatible with malachite and agate and least compatible with turquoise.

Amber—Fire Stone (Carreg Tan Melune)—Though amber is not a true stone, it is fossilized resin and a potent gem. The ancient Varaná believed amber was congealed sunlight because it channels yellow fire that can consume any material. Consequently, it is most often used as a weapon. It is most compatible with lapis lazuli and turquoise and least compatible with opal.

Onyx—Blood Stone (Carreg Rhyfel)—Onyx is the stone of war and bloodshed. It enhances prowess in combat, including skill in strategy and tactics. It is most compatible with sapphire and ruby and least compatible with malachite.

Jasper—Earth Stone (Carreg Dayar)—Red jasper is believed to be the congealed blood of creation. This stone harnesses the power of the earth and allows stone and soil to be moved and shaped. It is most compatible with pearl and opal and least compatible with lapis lazuli.

Agate—Healing Stone (Carreg Yachad)—Agates of all colors and shapes are associated with courage, boldness, vigor, health, longevity, and peace. Any pure agate can grant healing power, but only the blue-banded agate can extend life. No agate can restore life once it is extinguished. Agate is most compatible with jade and malachite but has no incompatible stones because sapphire, its opposite in the lithomantic pyramid of power can form powerful dyadic connections with all stones.

Ruby—Strength Stone (Carreg Wayd)—The ruby is associated with zeal, power, and invulnerability. It grants protection from metal weapons and physical harm. It is most compatible with amber and lapis lazuli and least compatible with pearl.

Turquoise—Wisdom Stone (Carreg Doethineb)—Associated with the harmony of mind, body, and spirit, the turquoise grants wisdom and protection from harmful forces. It is most compatible with onyx and sapphire and least compatible with jade.

Opal—Vision Stone (Carreg Golug)—Opal enhances cosmic consciousness and induces psychic and mystical visions. Opal grants the bearer the ability to perceive the past and the future. It is considered the most dangerous lithomantic stone because it cannot reveal the connection between the past and the future. The present can always modify the future and give different meanings to the past. And yet, the idea of being able to predict the future and correct the past is addictive. For this reason, the opal and its use are carefully guarded by the Varaná. Opal is most compatible with pearl and jasper and least compatible with amber.

Malachite—Protection Stone (Carreg Puer)—Malachite absorbs and dissipates magical and physical attacks. It is most often used as a shield. It is most compatible with jade and agate and least compatible with onyx.

Lapis Lazuli—Magnifying Stone (Carreg Gallu)—Lapis Lazuli is associated with ability and creativity, this stone enhances natural ability—especially those of a creative nature, such as arts and crafts. It is most compatible with amber and ruby and least compatible with jasper.

Quartz Crystal—Union Stone (Carreg Undeb)—Quartz does not fit neatly into the lithomantic systems. It possesses no compatibilities nor incompatibilities and is used to form dyads between otherwise incompatible stones. Yet, it possesses no power of its own and cannot be used by itself but only in combination with two other stones. The Varaná rarely use the quartz crystal to form dyads because when stones are forced to create dyads against their natures they become unstable.

Lithomancy of Anwyn

Lithomantic Stones of the Anarwyn

Sapphire
Water Stone
(Carreg Vŵr)

Lapis Lazuli
Magnifying Stone
(Carreg Gallu)

Pearl
Lightning Stone
(Carreg Tan a Dŵr)

Malachite
Protection Stone
(Carreg Puer)

Jade
Wind Stone
(Carreg Gwynt)

Opal
Vision Stone
(Carreg Golug)

Amber
Fire Stone
(Carreg Tan
Melone)

Higher

Quartz Crystal
Union Stone
(Carreg Undeb)

Lesser

Turquoise
Wisdom Stone
(Carreg Doethineb)

Onyx
Blood Stone
(Carreg Rhyfel)

Ruby
Strength Stone
(Carreg Wayd)

Agate
Healing Stone
(Carreg Yachad)

Jasper
Earth Stone
(Carreg Dayar)

Undead

Lithomantic Gemstones of the Bragamahr:

Obsidian—Death Stone (Carreg Gwaider)—As the keystone of the Bragamahr system of lithomantic stones, obsidian is the stone of fragmentation and death. It can enhance the power of the other stones and form a dyad with any stone of the Bragamahr. That which is created with this stone remains fragmented. This is why the blood of the Mahrowaiths, which turns into a type of red-veined obsidian when it dries, destroys whatever it touches. However, one should not confuse all obsidian with the congealed blood of the Mahrowaiths. Mahrowaiths are created by forging a dyadic link between the blood of a human donor and the obsidian of the Bragamahr. Consequently, the donor retains a psychic connection with the Mahrowaith, and the Mahrowaith takes on some of the characteristics of the donor.

Moonstone—Wind Stone (Carreg Klead)—Moonstone is associated with the movement of the moon and the constant flow of change. It is associated with transformation and restoration. It harnesses the power of the wind and is most potent at night. It is most compatible with red garnet and aquamarine and least compatible with topaz.

Tiger Eye—Seeing Stone (Carreg Gweld)—Tiger Eye is called the eye of the Bragamahr. This stone perceives magical attacks and can both warn of magical danger and protect from such attacks. It is most often used as a shield and is most compatible with emerald and apatite and least compatible with pyrite.

Morganite—Opening Stone (Carreg Agorial)—Morganite is associated with the pale rays of sunrise. This stone grants the bearer a sense of one's place in the vast universe and opens to the overwhelming presence of the Bragamahr. It is used to communicate over distance and to meditate. It can also be used to penetrate the mind of another individual, though this practice is very dangerous and usually kills the person so violated. It is most compatible with diamond and topaz and least compatible with red garnet.

Amethyst—Tranquility Stone (Carreg Tawluch)—Associated with peace of mind and sobriety, the amethyst can remove pain and unease but cannot heal. It is most compatible with obsidian and pyrite and least compatible with apatite.

Aquamarine—Youth Stone (Carreg Tan Glass)—Thought

by the ancient Tamil to be the sweat of the Bragamahr, aquamarine is associated with vigor and health. It can suspend the advance of time and grant youth and vitality. It is most compatible with moonstone and red garnet and least compatible with diamond.

Emerald—Curing Stone (Carreg Deruid)—The Tamil associated the emerald with fertility and rejuvenation. Called the master healer, this stone can heal any injury, save from death or the acid of the Mahrowaith. It is most compatible with tiger eye and apatite but has no incompatible stones because obsidian, its opposite in the lithomantic pyramid of power, can form powerful dyadic connections with all stones.

Topaz—Concentration Stone (Carreg Crynodial)—Associated with focus and deliberation, topaz directs energy to where it is needed. It is frequently used as a weapon, but it can also quicken learning and growth. It is most compatible with morganite and diamond and least compatible with moonstone.

Pyrite—Illusion Stone (Carreg Reith)—Pyrite, called Anar gold, is associated with falsehood because it is often mistaken for true gold. This stone creates illusions that deceive the mind and tantalize the senses. Consequently, it is one of the most valued stones of the Bragamahr. It is most compatible with obsidian and amethyst and least compatible with tiger eye.

Red Garnet—Elemental Stone (Carreg Elfenau)—Thought to have been born of fire in the bowels of the earth, the red garnet controls both earth and fire. It can control neither wind nor water. It is most compatible with moonstone and aquamarine and least compatible with morganite.

Apatite—Manifestation Stone (Carreg Nerth)—Apatite is thought to combine the energies of mind, body, and soul, this stone deepens self-awareness and reveals both strengths and weaknesses. As such, it can be used to enhance physical strength. It is most compatible with tiger eye and emerald and least compatible with amethyst.

Diamond—Purity Stone (Carreg Purdeb)—Though diamonds come in many colors, only the purest can be used in the system of the Bragamahr. Thought to harness the pure white light of the stars and moon, diamonds provide strength and endurance and enhance the power of other crystals. It is most frequently used as a weapon in the form of lightning. It is most compatible with morganite and topaz and least compatible with aquamarine.

Quartz Crystal—Union Stone (Carreg Undeb)—Does not fit neatly into the lithomantic systems. It possesses no compatibilities nor incompatibilities and is used to form dyads between otherwise incompatible stones. Yet, it possesses no power of its own and cannot be used by itself, but only in combination with two other stones. Practitioners of the Bragamahr value quartz crystal for its ability to corrupt a stone's nature and to create unusual manifestations of power.

Lithomantic Stones of the Bragamahr

Obsidian
Death Stone
(Carreg Gwaider)

Diamond
Purity Stone
(Carreg Purdeb)

Moonstone
Wind Stone
(Carred Klead)

Apatite
Manifestation
Stone
(Carreg Nerth)

Tiger Eye
Seeing Stone
(Carreg Gweld)

Red Garnet
Elemental Stone
(Carred Elfenau)

Morganite
Opening Stone
(Carreg Agorial)

Higher
Quartz Crystal
Union Stone
(Carreg Undeb)
Lesser

Pyrite
Illusion Stone
(Carreg Reith)

Amethyst
Tranquility Stone
(Carreg Tawluch)

Topaz
Concentration Stone
(Carreg Crynodia)

Emerald
Curing Stone
(Carreg Deruid)

Aquamarine
Youth Stone
(Carreg Tan Glass)

ABOUT J.W. ELLIOT

J.W. Elliot is a professional historian, martial artist, canoer, bow builder, knife maker, woodturner, and rock climber. He has a Ph.D. in Latin American and World History. He has lived in Idaho, Oklahoma, Brazil, Arizona, Portugal, and Massachusetts. He writes non-fiction works of history about the Inquisition, Columbus, and pirates. J.W. Elliot loves to travel and challenge himself in the outdoors.

Connect with J.W. Elliot online at:
www.JWElliot.com/contact-us

Books by J.W. Elliot
Available on Amazon and Audible

Archer of the Heathland
  Prequel: *Intrigue*
  Book I: *Deliverance*
  Book II: *Betrayal*
  Book III: *Vengeance*
  Book IV: *Chronicles*
  Book V: *Windemere*
  Book VI: *Renegade*
  Book VII: *Rook*

The Ark Project
  Prequel: *The Harvest*
  Book I: *The Clone Paradox*
  Book II: *The Covenant Protocol*

Heirs of Anarwyn
  Book I: *Torn*
  Book II: *Undead*
  Book III: *Shattered*
  Book IV: *Feral*

Worlds of Light
  Book I: *The Cleansing*
  Book II: *The Rending*
  Book III: *The Unmaking*

The Miserable Life of Bernie LeBaron
Somewhere in the Mist
Walls of Glass

If you have enjoyed this book, please consider leaving an honest review on Amazon and sharing on your social media sites.

Please sign up for my newsletter where you can get a free short story and more free content at: www.JWElliot.com

Thanks for your support!

J.W. Elliot

Writing Awards

Winner of the New England Book Festival 2022 for Science Fiction for *The Covenant Protocol (The Ark Project,* Book II*).*

Honorable Mention in the New England Book Festival 2022 for General Fiction for *Torn (Heirs of Anarwyn,* Book I)

Runner Up in the **New York Book Festival 2022** for Young Adult Fiction for *Torn (Heirs of Anarwyn,* Book I).

Runner Up in the **San Francisco Book Festival 2022** for Science Fiction for *The Covenant Protocol (The Ark Project,* Book II).

Honorable Mention in the **San Francisco Book Festival 2022** for Young Adult Fiction for *Torn (Heirs of Anarwyn,* Book I).

Runner Up in the **Los Angeles Book Festival 2022** for Science Fiction for *The Clone Paradox (The Ark Project,* Book I).

Runner Up in the **Los Angeles Book Festival 2022** for Young Adult Fiction for *Torn (Heirs of Anarwyn,* Book I).

Honorable Mention in the **Los Angeles Book Festival 2022** for Science Fiction for *The Covenant Protocol (The Ark Project,* Book II).

Winner of the New England Book Festival 2021 for Science Fiction for *The Clone Paradox (The Ark Project,* Book I*).*

Award Winning Finalist in the Fiction: Young Adult category of the **2021 Best Book Awards** sponsored by American Book Fest for *Windemere (Archer of the Heathland,* Book V*)*.

Award-Winning Finalist in the **American Fiction Awards 2021** for Young Adult Fiction category for *Walls of Glass*.

Award-Winning Finalist in the Science Fiction: General category of the **2021 American Fiction Awards** for *The Clone Paradox (The Ark Project,* Book I).

Chet Kevitt Award for contributions to Weymouth history for the publication of *The World of Credit in Colonial Massachusetts: James Richards and his Daybook, 1692-1711*. Awarded by the Weymouth Historical Commission, 2018.

Writers of the Future Contest
      Honorable Mention for *Recalibration*, 2018.
      Honorable Mention for *Ebony and Ice*, 2019.

Made in the USA
Middletown, DE
19 September 2024

60701030R00194